Swim
DEEP

Swim DEEP

Beth Kery

ISBN-13: 978-0-578-43058-4

Library of Congress Control Number: 2019900787

Chapter One

THIS IS WHAT COMES FROM USING A DAMN DATING SITE.

The miserable thought came at the same time as a dull throb from an oncoming headache. I approached the maître d' of the sleek Financial District restaurant.

"I'm meeting Evan Halifax," I said.

His skeptical gaze dropped over my secondhand wool coat and my cheap flats. In a fit of rebellion, I'd changed at the last second before leaving my rented room located in Central Sunset. Not completely: I still wore the only decent black dress I owned. I'd take off the Cartier earrings Evan had given me, of course.

It was time to stop pretending that this thing between Evan and me was real.

The maître d's stare finally met mine. A knowing, slimy smile spread on his thin face.

"Of course, mademoiselle. Mr. Halifax has been waiting," he said, waving gracefully. I skewered him with my stare. I knew what he was thinking. A guy like Evan Halifax had enough money, looks, and charm to have as many hot, clueless young blondes in his bed as he wanted. *You don't know anything, you smug French snot,* I thought bitterly. *You don't know anything at all.*

His smirk wavered. He turned. I followed him through the crowded but subdued restaurant. True luxury was never boisterous. That was something I'd learned in the past eight weeks, dating Evan.

1

He stood when I approached the table, as he always did. My heart tightened in my chest at the vision of his tall form and his familiar rugged, strong face. He was dressed impeccably, as usual, in a black suit with a muted gold tie. Looking up at him, I tried to avoid his gray eyes. My gaze landed instead on his starched white collar. It made such an appealing contrast to his tanned skin and the crisply trimmed line of his dark hair.

I resisted a wild urge to cry. Or run like hell.

"Is everything all right?" His lips brushed my cheek. "You're cold, Anna."

I felt his warm breath on my skin, and experienced that inevitable draw... that predictable desire. Annoyance bubbled up in me. It wasn't *fair* that an attraction could be so hideously one-sided.

"I'm fine. I'm sorry I'm late. The bus was behind schedule, and I had to walk a ways to get here," I said, pulling my hand away from his.

"Didn't you have any cash for a cab?" he asked, taking his seat across from me.

"I did," I told him, waiting until the waiter poured me a glass of sparkling water and walked away. "I actually have quite a bit of your money. It's been accumulating," I said, holding up my evening bag, a receptacle of my guilt. The sapphire earrings were in there as well. I faltered, thinking of the moment when he'd slipped that leather box into my hand the other night.

"*I thought they'd match your eyes.*"

I'd been flying.

"Anna?"

"I have it all here. I'll give it back to you after dinner. I mean... if you still want to have dinner. Maybe you won't," I mused, distressed I hadn't thought of this detail.

His dark brows scrunched together, but otherwise, his face remained stony. "Why wouldn't I want to have dinner?"

"I don't know," I said, my already thin courage going completely transparent.

"I gave you that money to use for incidentals, like getting to our dates. I know you don't have extra cash for things like that. I didn't mean to offend by giving it to you. But I have, haven't I?" he said slowly, his eyes narrowing on my face.

"There was nothing offensive about you offering it."

"There was nothing offensive about you accepting it, either. Maybe it's selfish on my part, but I don't want to make things harder on you in order for us to see each other."

"Evan—"

My evening bag buzzed. I pulled out my cell and clumsily knocked my bag onto the booth seat. When I saw who was calling, I swiped to ignore it.

"My sister. I'll call her later," I said, leaning over to retrieve the bag from the seat.

"You and your sister look alike?" he asked. I realized he'd seen my sister's photo on the screen when she called—or at least he'd glimpsed a brief, upside-down version of it.

"Some people say we do. I don't see it much," I replied, both frustrated and relieved to be sidetracked from breaking up with him. I slipped my phone back in my purse and set it aside. The waiter arrived with a bottle of chardonnay.

"Jessica's only a year and a half younger than I am," I said after the waiter had poured and left. "We both have blonde hair. I think that's where most of the similarity begins and ends, though. Everybody thinks young blondes look alike, right?" I muttered sarcastically under my breath. I took a healthy swallow of the chilled chardonnay. Evan pinned me in place with his stare, his eyebrows arched slightly. I felt my cheeks go warm and carefully placed the wine glass on the table.

"Go ahead. Get if off your chest. Tell me what's bothering you, Anna."

Unable to repress my anxiety anymore, I leaned toward him. "Evan, what are we doing, exactly?"

He blanched at my intensity. "*Doing*? What do you mean? We're dating, aren't we? Getting to know one another? Appreciating each other?"

"Yes, but... "

"But what?"

"It's not *normal*," I declared heatedly under my breath. I hated the way his features stiffened. Despite his restrained quality, Evan had always been kind to me. I didn't want to hurt him. Still, I stumbled on. "I mean... the sexual part. We've spent *a lot* of time together. You've only kissed me that one time. In eight weeks. And even then, you pulled back, like... " I halted abruptly, instinctively afraid to put that ugly thought into words. I inhaled and commanded myself to continue in a more measured, adult tone. "I

3

know I told you I'd be patient, that day we had the picnic at Half Moon Bay when we... you know. Kissed." I closed my eyes briefly in humiliation, acutely aware that I was failing. I sounded like a heartbroken sixteen-year-old.

"I told you that I understood," I continued in a low voice. "But to be honest, I *don't*. I'm sorry if that makes me needy or naïve, but maybe that's what I am. It doesn't seem healthy. Us. I feel like you're not ready for this. I like you, Evan. I like you so much." *You're such a little liar. You more than like him.* "But I don't want to get hurt, and I feel like I will, if you're constantly thinking about... "

My mouth hesitated in forming her name, but I pushed on, fueled by my rising doubt. "If you're thinking about your wife all the time."

Elizabeth.

A silence stretched between us, strained and nearly unbearable.

"Why now?"

I blinked at his quiet question, confused.

"Why *now*?"

"Yes. What's brought on this sudden rash of nerves? I saw no sign of them the other night when were together."

I made a high-pitched, desperate sound and rolled my eyes. "Sudden? My doubts have always been there. Surely you get that. Why *now*? It's just a basic law of emotional physics, I guess." I reached for my wine and took another swallow, aware of his tight attention on me the whole time. "Things build until they reach a boiling point. And once that point is reached—boom. Everything changes."

He said nothing, only watched me with that enigmatic, steady gaze that was either cool or hot. I could never decide which.

"I Googled her. Elizabeth," I admitted impulsively, wild to break the silence, crazy to get past the finish line now that I'd started. Surely mentioning his dead wife would bring things to an abrupt end. "At first I tried Elizabeth Halifax, but then I remembered that Tommy had mentioned her father's name. Noah Madaster. Tommy doesn't seem to like your former father-in-law much."

"A lot of people don't," Evan said evenly enough, but I saw the glint of curiosity in his eyes. "Tommy knows Noah?" We referred to my boss and mutual friend, Tommy Higoshi.

"Only briefly. He met him once at a medical technology conference," I said, watching Evan's reaction to my miniscule knowledge of his deceased wife's family. I realized he wasn't going to say anything else, so I continued on my suicide mission.

"So I Googled her maiden name: Elizabeth Madaster. I just thought you should know," I said lamely. Was he angry at my admitted intrusion in his carefully guarded past? Mildly curious? Politely disinterested? I was flailing for a hold in this conversation. In this whole affair.

"And what did you find out about her?"

"Not much. Most references were to her father and his political career, and a few charities Elizabeth was involved in." I hadn't even been able to locate Elizabeth's obituary or the circumstances of her death. The small amount of information I'd been able to find about Evan's wife had only served to make my curiosity—not to mention Elizabeth's invisible, suffocating presence—grow.

Evan didn't speak. He gave nothing away. I was mad at him for making this so hard, and pissed at myself because I was pushing him. Was I ruining something special because of my own insecurities?

You're taking care of yourself. Who else will?

"I just don't think you're ready. You're still grieving for her." *And I'm not the Band-Aid to your grief.*

"She's been gone for more than seven years."

I found myself studying his face closely, searching for some hint of how he felt about Elizabeth Madaster, right now in this very moment. I found nothing, which is what I really expected to find. The past eight weeks of being with him had taught me that.

"There isn't a time limit on grief, Evan. I understand."

"Do you? Would you mind explaining to me what it is you understand, precisely?"

"I understand you don't want me," I snapped.

His jaw tightened. I was doing this messily, but there was no going back. "Maybe you feel guilty, or maybe you just want some companionship because you're lonely, but you aren't interested in the physical side of things, so whatever the reason—"

"You think I don't want you?"

I went still. His voice was a quiet, ominous rumble. I could tell by the sudden gleam in his gray eyes I'd seriously offended him.

"Don't you have any idea how beautiful you are?" he asked bitterly. "Don't you notice the stares you get when you walk into a room? You told me once that you used that dating site because men don't approach you. Don't you get why? They stay away because you *intimidate* them, Anna."

"No," I said, thrown off balance. "That's not the point—"

I faded off when I noticed his furious expression. He was like a precision blowtorch in those seconds. I cringed under his stare. I'd never seen him like this. I didn't know what to say or do. He abruptly rose from the table, towering over me. My stomach dropped. He was going to leave. I'd never see him again, all because I couldn't go with the flow and keep my stupid mouth shut. He put out his hand.

"Let's dance," he said, tight-lipped.

Through the muted roar in my ears, I realized that a jazz quartet was playing across the room.

"I don't think—"

"Let's dance, Anna," he repeated. He took my hand when I didn't offer it. I rose and followed his tall, formidable form, swimming in confusion.

Through my distraction, I noticed a small dance floor overlooked the Bay Bridge and a magnificent sunset. To this day, I have no idea what song the musicians played. I'd been so anxious about the meeting, so overwhelmed by his presence, I'd never heard music. He turned and took me into his arms. He pulled me close, his hold on me firm and unrelenting. His body felt hard, yet fluid, moving next to mine.

We didn't speak. There wasn't any need to, I realized after a moment. His eyes said it all as he looked down at me. His body shouted it so loudly, the truth roared in my ears and stung in my veins.

Evan Halifax *did* want me. Badly. Here was undeniable proof. Our bodies subtly stroked one another until tears of frustration and wonder welled in my eyes.

"*Why?*" I whispered. I felt so close to him in that moment, I somehow knew he'd understand I asked him why he was holding back, when he felt so much.

He pressed his lips against my temple. He kissed my neck, pausing to inhale my scent. I shivered uncontrollably in his arms.

"Because I didn't plan for this, Anna," he said quietly near my ear. "I didn't plan for *you*. Did you ever consider that I'm just as confused as you are? Because I am. I'm scared of how much I want you."

His confession of uncertainty stunned me. It cast a whole new light on the shadowed, possibly dangerous landscape of Evan Halifax.

When the song had finished, he led me off the dance floor. At our booth, he picked up my evening bag and handed it to me. I could feel the Cartier box beneath the mesh material. As I looked up into his eyes I knew something with a sudden, swift adult certainty that I'd craved for so long.

I'd never return those earrings.

"Let's forget dinner here. Maybe we can go and check out that Vietnamese street vendor you like and take it up to your room?"

"You're sure that you want to? *There*? At my place?" I asked softly.

He nodded. "I'm sure. Except about the street vendor thing. Let's skip dinner."

"Yes," I agreed breathlessly.

I realize that so much of the beginning of Evan's and my story sounds cliché: a young, relatively inexperienced girl swept off her feet by a handsome, worldly, older man.

Well, here's another cliché for you. It turns out the steady handhold I needed, that certainty at the eye of the storm, was sex. The physicality of it. The heat. The liberation of emotion. The feeling of being needed, and needed hard.

It was that solidity I craved, the tangible reality of flesh. Desire binds us, sometimes flimsily and shortly, but the bond is there in the exchange. What Evan and I shared that night was something bigger, though. Passion isn't necessarily the end result of love. But it sure as hell is a great start. A start to what, I couldn't have envisioned at the time.

It wasn't until later that I began to understand that our connection was more than that of intense desire. Ours was the bond of fellow prisoners, a tie that time or choice couldn't dissolve.

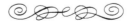

Thankfully, we didn't run into any of my nutjob roommates on the way to my rented room. Somehow, it didn't match up in my mind, the idea of introducing Evan to vegan, pot-smoking performance artist Tarquin or aura-seeing jewelry maker Iris. It'd be like presenting beings from different worlds to each other. I conveniently forgot that I was one of the denizens of that fringe existence as I snuck him up the familiar squeaky wooden staircase. I listened to Evan's solid tread behind me, and thought how impossible it all seemed. It was like sneaking Prince Charming into some kind of alternate, hippie universe.

But Prince Charming wasn't the right descriptor for Evan. Not unless Prince Charming burned.

He caught my hips when we reached the landing. He gently pushed my front against the wall and pressed his body behind me. I gasped in surprise and abrupt lust at the sensation of my cheek and nipples against the cold plaster and his unrelenting male body behind me. He was hard... hot. For a brief second, I had a moment of misgiving. This *thing*, whatever it was, between us: it was the kind of thing that could destroy me.

He brushed back my hair from my neck, and then both of his opened hands charted the shape of my waist and hips for the first time.

"I'm going to drown in you, Anna," he breathed out, his rough, quiet voice and his lips moving on my neck, coaxing goose bumps from my skin. "I've waited, but it's been so hard." He bit gently at the shell of my ear. I shook. I couldn't believe this was happening. At the same time, the truth glowed like an ember between our pressing bodies, growing hotter. One of his hands crept between me and the wall and swept across my belly. It lowered, leaving a trail of awakened flesh in its wake. He turned my chin—not roughly, but boldly, a hint of desperation in his touch. His mouth closed on my mine at the same moment he cupped my sex.

I moaned and pushed back against the wall with my hands, increasing the pressure between our bodies. This need was intimidating, but unstoppable. He stroked me with slow, firm, rhythmic caresses until I struggled in his hold. Not because I wanted to get away, but because I was wild to absorb more of him. He ran both his hands up my arms and pinned my wrists against the wall. He broke our kiss and sank his dark head, his lips and teeth scraping the skin between my neck and shoulder.

Had I guessed this storm raged inside him? Is that why I'd been so confused—so frustrated—by his reserve?

"*Evan*," I whispered. The raw evidence of his desire left me rattled. Exposed.

"Which room is yours?" he grated out.

I only had the wherewithal to nod at the door at the end of the hall. He grabbed my hand and led me down the hallway, his mouth set in a grim, unyielding line.

When the storm finally exploded, it was epic. But I imagined that his need, which grew anguished and even forceful at times, was a tribute to me... to us. I loved it. I craved more.

All through that night, he made love to me under the cover of darkness.

When dawn peeked around the blinds, he pressed his mouth to my temple and rose from my very messed up bed.

"You must be hungry," he said as he found his strewn clothing on the floor. I loved the sound of his low, rough voice washing over me in the muted morning light.

"You too," I murmured amusedly, content to watch him slip naked between the shadows.

"I'll go get us some coffee and something to eat."

"There's a café on the corner. A skinny latte with an extra shot of espresso, please?"

"I thought you were cappuccino with two yellow packets?"

I laughed, and buried my face in my pillow to hide my rush of euphoria. It didn't work.

"*What*?" he asked, pausing in his dressing and looking over his shoulder. I took in the harsh, unexpected angles of the gray and pale gold palette of his face. The artist in me took over. My infatuated hysterics came to a skidding halt.

His face held me completely enthralled for a stretched moment. It was as if his features had been separate once, like they'd belonged to different men, and had somehow come to rest uneasily on this face. The mouth belonged to a sensual, sometimes angry person who had learned control the hard way, the brow to a strong man who had known suffering and loss, the nose to a warrior, the rare smile to a fifteen-year-old small-town dreamer and heartbreaker.

The eyes, which could go hard and also surprisingly soft, belonged to a poet who could see my art. Who could see *me*. I resisted a wild urge to spring up from the bed and grab my sketchpad. *Here* was one of the things that had drawn me to Evan Halifax from the very start. His face, staring back at me steadily from the nine by twelve inch screen of my computer, silently speaking to me.

"Anna?" he asked, his brow creasing in confusion.

"What? Oh, nothing. It's just… I was thinking how nice it was. That you know what kind of coffee I drink in the afternoon." He turned to me slowly, hitching up his pants and swiftly fastening them over his taut abdomen. "But this is our first morning together," I added.

"Ah," he said, his face smoothing into a contained mystery yet again. "And you have a different coffee preference in the mornings."

My flash of artistic vision fled. I was having trouble reading him again. But then he took two long strides to the bed and leaned down. He gave me a hard, swift kiss on the mouth. *Zap.* That electrical conduit between us, that primitive knowledge, sizzled again to life.

"I want to know all your morning preferences," he said against my parted lips a moment later. "I want to know what you'd prefer every minute of every day, Anna Solas. I want you to be happy."

When he returned twenty minutes later, he kicked off his shoes and tossed off his jacket before he climbed back into bed with me. At first, a playful, intimate mood prevailed. I feasted on almond croissants, fruit from a plastic cup, and his rare smiles.

I tried to feed him the last strawberry. But his mood had sobered as the light grew brighter in the room. He turned and caught my wrist, the red fruit hovering just inches from his lips. I felt a sinking sensation. His intense passion in bed and our new intimacy could erase that sad, brooding side of him.

But not forever.

"What have you got planned today?" he asked me, carefully removing the strawberry from my fingers and dropping it in the cup I held.

"I'm at the museum today from noon to six," I said, referring to one of my two jobs. They were definitely jobs, not careers. In my mind, I was a painter, first and always. But according to the IRS, I couldn't list that officially as my occupation. So until I made enough to support myself with my painting, I paid my rent and kept ramen noodles and canned soup in the pantry by working part-time as both a museum docent at the San Francisco Museum of Modern Art, and in sales at a posh, but substantial art gallery called Yume in the Mission Bay area—Tommy Higoshi's gallery.

"So you're not at the gallery this evening?" Evan asked, twisting to set the fruit cup on a nightstand.

He rolled over to face me. His hand snaked beneath the blanket. He spread it on my naked hip. Sexual awareness flickered through me yet again. His hands were large and warm. If I painted those hands, how could I demonstrate how they had started to encompass my world?

"Anna?"

I blinked at his slightly amused tone, willfully jerking my awareness from just beneath his opened hand on my skin and back to our conversation.

"No, I'm not at the gallery today."

"Do you enjoy them? Your jobs?" He ducked his dark head and our mouths met in a brief, warm kiss. I squeezed a curving, dense shoulder muscle in my palm.

"They aren't my ideal jobs or anything. But I get by with them well enough."

"You'd rather be using your days to paint, wouldn't you?"

"God yes. That's the dream."

"Why does it have to be a dream?"

"Because it's the opposite of reality," I said, striving to sound airy despite the nearness of his mouth and his scent and the memories of what we'd done in this bed all night filling my head. He'd dominated my body. My senses. My spirit. It hadn't been an intentional thing on his part, I don't think. He hadn't *thought* to conquer me. His hunger had ruled him during the night. And it ruled me, in turn. He'd made it clear, somehow, that he'd dominated me sexually because *I'd* dominated his thoughts.

"Reality is making rent and paying bills and eating," I told him.

He searched my face. "I believe you deserve more than that."

"Do I?"

"Yes. You deserve the opportunity to make your beautiful paintings. To create in the light. To capture it, like only you can."

His praise took me back to the first time we'd ever met. It'd been at my first showing at Yume. I vividly recalled how I'd stood there next to Evan Halifax, trembling in the expensive heels I'd borrowed from Ellen Higoshi, as he inspected my paintings.

It'd felt like a stranger was studying me while I was naked... and I thrillingly allowed it.

He stared at the painting for what was likely seconds, but felt like an hour.

"It's like it is a nature painting, but it's not... like you're painting a tree, but a tree seen from a different world." My lungs burned upon seeing for the first time that small, sexy smile that occasionally shaped his mouth. He flashed a glance at me. "The view from fairyland," he murmured, his gaze lingering on my face.

"Are you calling my paintings supernatural?" I joked, trying to diminish the effect of his quiet, deep, voice. But his smile had vanished as he'd returned his attention to the painting.

"Maybe. What you did with the light on this one is extraordinary. It's so soft. But your precise technique gives the trees an almost photographic quality."

"Thanks. That's what I was going for. This is part of a series I did in Muir Woods." I waved in the direction of other paintings. Evan's attention was caught by the next piece. I followed him when he moved toward it. We paused, and again I experienced his total focus as he studied my work. He was the most handsome, confident man I'd ever met. There was no way I could capture the attention of a guy like him, but apparently, my paintings could. It felt illicit, somehow. Exciting. I searched for something to say to fill the sucking void of silence.

"Tommy told me once that there are certain words in Japanese that have no equivalent in English. There's this one word: komorebi," I said. He gave me a sideways questioning glance. "It means sunlight filtering through trees. You know, that soft, luminous quality it gets? Almost as if it's alive?" I waved at the canvas. "I wanted to capture that contrast: that intangible glow alongside those hard, enduring trees with roots that go so deep... "

I faded off, realizing too late I'd started to ramble.

"I think maybe you're like that, aren't you?"

I'd blinked in surprise at his quiet question. "Like what? The sequoias?"

"No. Like the paintings. Soft and hard at once. You may look like cotton candy on the outside, but there's steel underneath. Isn't there?"

"You can't paint when you're holed up every day inside the museum or the gallery," Evan was saying, his voice pulling me soundly back to the present.

"I find time to paint."

"You paint at night. In the darkness, Anna. Are you saying that you wouldn't rather paint in the daylight hours, when you can capture your favorite subject?"

"Of course I would, if I had the time."

"Why don't you let me give that to you?"

"What?"

"Time. I'll give you all the time you want. All the light, as well. All the beauty you could ever hope to put on your canvases."

"I'm not used to hearing you talk so poetically," I told him wryly to cover my confusion.

"I'm not being poetic," he stated bluntly. "I've decided to move back to Tahoe. I'm asking you to come there with me. Take some time off. It's the most beautiful place in the world, and the light is extraordinary. You'd be in heaven there. You could paint from dawn to dusk, if you wanted."

My incredulous laugh was cut short when I noticed that his expression remained solemn, his eyes searching.

"Seriously? You're asking me to go to Lake Tahoe with you?"

"Yes. I think I mentioned I had a home there."

You mentioned your wife did.

I pushed aside the poison thought.

"You told me you grew up in that area," I recalled.

He'd been the only child of an investment banker and a world champion ice skater. After she retired from competing, his mom had started an elite training center for skaters at Tahoe that regularly spit out world champions and Olympians. I also remembered that his parents were retired and had moved back to Long Island, where they'd grown up.

Evan had grown up on the shores of Lake Tahoe, though. Elizabeth and her family had lived there, as well. Evan and she had been teenage sweethearts.

"How long would we stay there?" I asked.

"As long as you like. It's amazing there during the summer, the fall... the winters are spectacular."

"Just leave San Francisco? Leave my jobs?" I asked, my voice flat in disbelief. The past twenty-four hours had provided more shocks and surprises then I'd had in a lifetime.

"Yes," he said.

"You can't be serious. What would I do when I got back? Look for jobs all over again?" I started to rise to a sitting position, feeling disoriented lying there staring into his X-ray eyes. He pressed gently with his hand on my hip and I remained in place.

"You just said you're working for money to survive. I have plenty of money, Anna. You can focus on painting. Finally."

"You're asking me to live with you? Live *off* you?"

"I don't see it that way. If you're concerned about it, I have no doubt that if you're given time and opportunity to paint, you'll eventually be able to support yourself, and then some. You're very talented. I know the owner of a very reputable gallery in South Lake. I'm sure she'd consider herself lucky to show you. Look at your last exhibition. You sold three paintings in one night."

"Two of them to you. I'm not sure that counts."

"Of course it does. I have excellent taste, you know," he said, that tiny, distracting smile flickering across his mouth. "You just need the time and the opportunity to create... to do what you're meant to do."

As always, his absolute certainty stole my voice. I can't begin to describe what I was feeling in that moment. Disbelief, of course. A sense of the surreal. I was like a lifetime prisoner, and he'd just casually flung open the door of my cell. The bright light of the outside world stunned me. I didn't know how to just take a step from the world I knew into freedom.

Into joy.

He saw my bewilderment, of course. He exhaled and shut his eyes for a moment.

"I realize this must feel like it's coming out of nowhere for you. You don't know what's been going on in my head. You have no idea, Anna, about the battle I've been fighting on the inside, ever since I first saw you."

"Sometimes I feel like what goes on in your head is the biggest mystery in the world."

"If it is, I'm trying to demystify things now," he countered quietly, but firmly. He leaned down and pressed his forehead next to mine. "I'll admit it. I was hesitant to plunge in, head first. I was hesitant to sleep with you, because—"

"Of Elizabeth," I whispered when he broke off midsentence.

"Yes," he confessed tensely. "I was afraid that if I touched you, if I crossed the line, there'd be no going back. But now that it's happened... Well, it's happened."

"*What's* happened?" I asked, praying to God he'd tell me the answer to that question.

He smiled. It transformed his face when he did. He ruffled my hair in a fond gesture that made me feel about eight years old. "I've fallen for you, Anna. Uncomfortably hard," he added with a gruff, endearing laugh. He swung his long legs off the bed and sat up, his back to me.

"You know, I don't think I can live or rest, knowing you're out there in the world... separate from me," he mused, almost as if to himself. Suddenly he looked over his shoulder at me. "If you don't feel the same way, then—"

"I feel the same way," I said in a rush, anxious I'd miss the moment and be left like a kid with a dollar clutched in her hand, watching forlornly as the ice cream truck pulled away from the curb and down the street.

A crooked half-smile broke over his face. My flash of panic melted at the sight of it. He cradled my jaw and caressed my cheek with his thumb, and there I was...

Flying all over again.

Chapter Two

Seven Weeks Later

*IT WAS LIKE THE FIRST COUPLE MONTHS OF EVAN'S AND MY RELATION-*ship had been filmed in slow motion. Then some unseen hand had flipped the speed button on the camera. Suddenly, we flew down a golden slope, a twisting, exhilarating rollercoaster, all inertia, no effort required.

But then, abruptly and unexpectedly, the ride slowed.

"Everything you've told me so far is a bunch of bullshit, and you know it. You're marrying this guy after knowing him for three months? And all I get is this 'charming, incredible, unbelievable' crap? You make it sound like you fell in love with Prince-Fucking-Charming. It's like you're nine all over again, crushing over Justin Timberlake."

It was my sister's muttered words resounding from next to me in the passenger seat that put the brakes on that golden rollercoaster ride. Strangely, the car I was driving continued to glide forward at a silent, modest sixty miles an hour.

"*You* crushed over Justin Timberlake, not me."

"Liar. You always did have the heart of a romantic beneath all those black, artsy clothes you wore all the time. Seriously, Anna. Tell me what's going on!"

Sunlight streamed in on the right side of the car, illuminating Jessica's face. Despite her ballsy tone, her appearance was that of an angel—albeit an earthy, approachable one, like one of those voluptuous creatures in that painting by Burne-Jones we studied once in History of Art.

"The Golden Stairs," I muttered, recalling the name of the angel painting.

"What?" Jessica demanded, her perfect face screwing up in consternation. "You're acting weird. Mom and Dad are worried about you, you know."

I glanced uneasily to the backseat. My mom was passed out cold, her cheek on my father's chest, her head rising and falling to the cadence of my dad's soft snore. Mom's face was an older, more interesting version of Jessica's.

"Ambien," Jessica said in a clipped tone before she popped two Tic Tacs in her mouth. "Mom got them from her doctor. She's been nervous about flying lately. I guess Dad decided he didn't want to miss out on the party, and took one too. They'll be out until we reach his Highness's castle, at the very least. I doubt the news of your sudden wedding helped Mom's anxiety much."

"Don't be such a bitch, Jess," I said, but there was no heat in my tone. Jessica wasn't being unkind, not really. Knowing her as well as I did, I understood she was in a state of frantic curiosity and concern. I hadn't done much to help soothe her in the past two weeks...

Ever since Evan and I had called all three of them and announced the news of our engagement.

It was just so hard to put what had happened to me—what was still happening—into words. I sensed Jessica next to me as I drove, waiting with increasing impatience and worry. She wanted to understand, but she couldn't. As long as she didn't understand, I was like a stranger to her, and she to me. *That's* what was causing Jessica's sharp tone.

"It's really been more like four months since Evan and I first started talking, you know," I said lamely. I glanced over and saw Jessica's rising irritation: the wrath of an angel.

"What do you want me to tell you? It'd probably be best if you just meet Evan. Then you'll understand. He really is amazing."

"I don't care if he's the Second Coming," Jessica said petulantly, slouching in her seat and distractedly petting the supple leather of the cushion. Despite her uneasiness over this whole situation, my little sister couldn't help but admire the uncustomary trappings of luxury. Evan had given me his Mercedes to pick up my family at the airport, while he and Tommy and Ellen Higoshi had gone ahead to Tiburon to prepare things for guests and the upcoming wedding. My family, Tommy and Ellen would be the entire guest list for the small ceremony.

At first, I'd been taken aback at the idea of so few guests, especially when I understood that Evan's parents wouldn't be there. But Evan had explained that his father was recovering from a surgery. His doctor didn't want him to fly, and his mother didn't want to leave him alone.

In a roundabout way, I'd managed to get the idea that Evan had hated his first wedding: the elaborate details, the hundreds of guests he barely knew, and the artificiality of it all. I knew him well enough by now to understand how much he despised inauthenticity, so I agreed to the small ceremony in the natural setting. I didn't need hundreds of people telling me how happy I was to know I was ecstatic.

Last night had been the first night I'd spent away from Evan in the past six weeks. Did that have something to do with the abrupt halt of the dream-ride, or had it been the appearance of my mom and dad, practical, down-to-earth, Dick and Amanda Solas from Oak Park, Illinois?

"I honestly don't know what more to tell you about him than I have—"

"I don't care about *him*," Jessica growled loudly. She grimaced and glanced into the backseat, clearly worried she'd awakened one or both of our parents. "I care about how he makes you feel. What would make you act this insane, Anna?"

I gripped the wheel tighter, searching for an answer.

"Evan *gets* me," I finally said. "He sees me." I glanced aside and see Jessica's puzzlement. No cheeky remark this time. She was interested, at least.

I inhaled. "Remember that painting I showed you when you guys visited two summers ago, and we went to the SFMOMA?"

Jessica rolled her eyes. She didn't have to reply. I knew she didn't recall. Like my father, who was a corporate lawyer, Jessica was all about numbers and practicalities. She'd graduated from the University of Wisconsin this spring with a business degree, and planned to get her MBA from the University of Illinois starting in the fall.

"All right. So you don't remember. I thought you wanted me to give you an idea of why I'm acting insane, as you so nicely put it."

"I do," Jessica said.

"Well, I'm sorry I can't do that with a pie chart or statistical analysis, Jess."

"You're right," she said quickly, sounding a little contrite. "I'm listening. Go on. But don't just tell me about some boring painting. Tell me how the hell you two matched up, and I'm not just talking about on that dating site."

So I tried to shed some light on what my family obviously considered a case of my early onset madness.

This all happened before: before the night of the Cartier earrings and my guilt burning a hole in my evening bag, before the night of the restaurant and the dance, when everything had changed. Because although I hadn't fully understood the deep connection between Evan and me until that night, even though I had been swamped with doubt, the promise was there. I still sensed the hint of something bigger and brighter than I'd ever even guessed at so far in my relatively small and light-muted world.

I started with the question, because in the beginning, that question was everything. Why would a thirty-seven year old, good-looking, widowed, private fund manager want to date *me*? I didn't even know what a fund manager was. At twenty-three, I had only a vague, hazy idea about what it would be like to be married. I was completely clueless about what it would be like to wake up every morning and have to cope with the painful wound of losing a spouse.

I didn't tell Jessica this part, but in the beginning, I figured Evan Halifax had probably expressed interest in me on the dating site for the same reason a lot of guys had in the past. I had a college degree and a lot of blonde hair. My parents' investment in braces had paid off. I looked okay in a tank top. You know the drill. Like hundreds of thousands of others, I'm swipe-rightable. It means absolutely nothing.

Point being, I figured Evan's motivation was likely as calculated as mine for expressing interest. His claims of being a Stanford graduate and the owner of a private fund might have been false, and maybe he really didn't enjoy hiking, jogging, skiing, hockey, scuba diving, sailing, and art, like he claimed. But photos don't lie, for the most part. Evan Halifax filled out that business suit extremely well.

I didn't tell my little sister that the attraction between Evan and me was off the charts. I knew hearing about our blistering sex life wouldn't reassure her. Or maybe it was *me* who was still in awe, and a little uncomfortable, about the power of our need for each other. A veil of mystery still hung about our shared bed.

"Are you saying everything Evan put on his dating profile was true?" Jessica interrupted skeptically at this point of my explanation. "I tried to look up his profile after you told me about him, but he'd already taken it down."

"That's a *good* thing, Jess," I reminded her. "And yes. Evan was like the polar opposite of most guys on dating sites. Unlike most girls, too, because there was no need to fluff the personal details. Everything he mentioned wasn't only true, it was an understatement."

"I'm hearing Prince Charming's theme again."

"Do you want me to talk about this or not?"

"*Okay.*"

The sound of a chuffing breath and rustling could be heard from the back seat. Both of us glanced over our shoulders. Mom took a heaving breath and sagged again onto my Dad's shoulder. Ambien to the rescue.

"Just get to the part about how he gets you or sees you, or whatever the hell you were talking about," Jessica hissed.

I thought back to three months ago, when Evan and I went to the SFMOMA on a gorgeously gray and rainy afternoon. He had showed me a few of his favorite pieces at the museum. Again, I was impressed by his artistic knowledge, clear insight, and sensitivity to the work. It was a novel quality in such a masculine man, and far too irresistible for a girl like me.

"Now let me guess one of your favorite pieces," Evan said, taking my hand.

I laughed. "You're joking, right?"

He just gave me a bland, knowing glance and began to walk, leading me through the museum.

I was tickled by his playful proposition. What were the chances he would guess correctly? He'd only known me for about three or four weeks at that point. But my amusement quickly faded to amazement as he led me—very accurately—to a small, exquisite portrait from a Nigerian artist of a young village girl. I've loved the piece from the moment I first saw it. There was a dreamy quality on the girl's face, but also a strength that was almost noble, somehow.

"How did you know?" I asked him. My hands and feet tingled with disbelief. I couldn't comprehend that he could understand me so well.

He shrugged. "It reminds me of you," he said simply. "Innocence as power."

The small gallery we were in was empty, except for us. I stared up at him as he studied the portrait for a stretched, silent moment.

"I know that I'm older than you," he said abruptly. "I know that I'm... complicated, Anna."

"I like complicated sometimes."

"I'm not sure that's wise in my case. But what I'm trying to say is, I care about you. I don't want to ruin your life."

"Ruin my life? How would you do that?"

He shook his head. "I don't know. Maybe just by being with you."

"I've never been so happy in my life as I have been spending time with you," I told him in a burst of honesty. He reached and opened his hand at the side of my head, his thumb gently tracing my cheekbone. I waited in anguished anticipation. Was he going to kiss me? Finally? I couldn't imagine a more perfect moment.

"Thank you for that," he said. "I'm glad. Because I want you to be happy. I want that very much. I hope you believe me."

"Of course I do," I whispered, trying to decode the message in his light eyes, unable to breathe because of my craving to feel his mouth on mine.

But then he dropped his hand from my face and led me into the next gallery.

And the message remained a mystery.

Of course, I didn't tell my sister that stuff about how Evan had said he worried about ruining me, or how he'd dropped his hand during such an intimate moment. Why didn't I tell her?

I told myself it was because everything had changed since then. Completely altered.

I was gratified to see that Jessica seemed mollified by my little story. Maybe even impressed?

As we got closer to Evan's home in Tiburon, my parents must have sensed the car's slowing motion as we left the highway. They snuffled, yawned, and roused. I heard the click of my mother's compact and pictured her putting on her lipstick and smoothing her bobbed blonde hair. Jessica didn't ask any more impertinent questions. We all grew silent as we stared at the palatial homes set into the hillside.

Finally, the GPS directed me to turn down Evan's drive.

Evan walked out of the sprawling Italian villa. He wore jeans—something I'd rarely seen him in—and a short-sleeved sports shirt that showed off his athletic build and tan. His saunter toward us was casual and confident. Undeniably sexy. I sensed his stare on me through the window, and felt that familiar charge.

I glanced over at my sister, and saw that she watched me, as well. There was this tinge of wonder on her open, frank face, like I wasn't precisely who she'd thought I was.

It made me feel hollow, to see someone who filled up my very first memories, look at me that way.

Evan was the perfect host and gentleman when it came to my family. I worried when my mom and dad launched into embarrassing stories about my childhood, or retold snippets about their college days at nearby Berkley that Jessica and I had heard hundreds of times. But my concern was short-lived. Evan seemed relaxed and content listening to boring family history and nostalgia. His indulgent smiles at me while those stories were being replayed warmed me to the core.

On Friday evening before dinner, Evan offered everyone a tour of the gardens, where we would be married tomorrow. My parents, Jessica, and Ellen trailed after him onto the terrace, glasses of chardonnay reflecting like liquid golden globes in everyone's hands. I started after them, but Tommy Higoshi snagged my wrist, holding me back.

Tommy was the owner of Yume, but gallery ownership was just a hobby for him. Tommy is one of these guys with the Midas touch who created some kind of blood testing technology that made him a fortune. He'd been only twenty-six years old when he'd become a multimillionaire. Like lots of brilliant people, Tommy was an expert on a mind-blowing number of things, art being one of them. Tommy had introduced himself to me at a Curator's Circle cocktail party at the museum where I work, and he eventually offered me a job at Yume. He'd become like a San Francisco big brother or uncle figure for me.

Since I'd started seeing Evan, I'd learned that Tommy was a client of Evan's private fund. Both men shared a passion for yachting. They'd crewed together competitively off and on over the years. At first, I thought that Tommy and Evan were merely acquaintances. Over the past few months, however, I came to understand how close they really were.

"How are you feeling?" Tommy asked in a low voice.

"Fine," I replied breezily. My gaze narrowed on Tommy's face. I spied a shadow beneath the luminous Northern California evening and his bright smile.

"What's up, Tommy?"

"I just wanted to check in with you before the big day tomorrow. You're still feeling good? Still Cinderella swept off her feet?"

"Please. Don't bring up Cinderella. I'm getting enough of the fairy tale crap from Jessica. That isn't worry I see on your face, is it, Tommy?" I asked, smiling but cautious. "Not from the man who praised Evan to the high heavens ever since I first mentioned matching up with him on the dating site?"

"No. It's not Evan. You know I think Evan's a terrific guy. It's not you, either. I'm just doing my due diligence, asking about the state of things before the wedding."

"I suppose you *are* kind of like the best man and the maid of honor combined. You're certainly the person that's most responsible for bringing Evan and me together. If it hadn't been for you, I wouldn't have ever agreed to meet him in person after we matched up online."

"It wasn't that long ago that you were convinced Evan Halifax was a dog who went after girls fourteen years younger than him as a matter of course."

"I've gotten past all that. I hardly ever think about our age difference anymore."

It was a lie, but only a partial one. Everything was relative. Compared to how I used to think about Evan's and my difference in not only years but also experience, I'd advanced by light-years in the insecurity department.

"I forget the age difference most of the time, too," Tommy mused. "I forget how young you are. You have an old soul, Anna." Something about the way he watched me—like his words meant something entirely different than the context of our conversation—worried me.

"There *is* something wrong," I said, taking a step toward him. "What is it?"

Tommy shook his head and laughed before taking a swallow of his wine. He noticed my determined expression and shrugged.

"I've never been in this situation before—been both the best man and maid of honor, as you put it. It's a little scary." "What do you mean?"

"If something goes wrong between you two—"

"It'll be Evan's and my responsibility, just like it's the responsibility of every couple when they take a vow of marriage and something goes wrong. It would have nothing to do with you. You know that."

"Yeah, of course," Tommy said, but I still sensed his unease. "Okay, there is something I want to get off my chest."

This didn't sound good. A confession on the eve of my wedding?

"Okay, go ahead," I said quickly, even though I was overwhelmed with trepidation.

"I showed Evan some of your work a while back, when he visited the gallery. I want you to understand," he said, noticing my blank expression. "This was *before* you two met through that dating site. He seemed very taken by your painting."

"Oh."

"The thing is, I think that's why he looked you up on that dating site... " Tommy hesitated. "In fact, I think it might have been the reason he *joined* it, Anna. To meet you, exclusively. I mean... you know Evan. I can't really see him needing to use a dating site, can you? I don't want to give you the impression he's some kind of Lothario, but he's never struck me as the type of guy who has trouble getting female companionship."

It wasn't what I expected. Not at all. No room filled with former murdered wives' bones and dripping blood. I was stunned by his admission. Confused.

Pleased?

Wasn't it *good* that Evan had been explicitly interested in *me* versus any generic form of female companionship to help him through a difficult time in his life? Wasn't it *hopeful* that he'd sought out the artist whose work had touched him, versus seeking out just any young blonde during a time when he wanted to rekindle not only his libido but also his optimism about living again?

Still, it was weird. Why wouldn't he want me to know that he'd admired my paintings before he'd met me?

"Why didn't you mention it to me before?" I asked Tommy.

"Evan asked me not to say anything about it."

I rarely saw Tommy look uncomfortable, but he did in that moment.

"I don't understand. Why would Evan not want me to know he'd seen my work? He made it seem like he never had before, like the gallery showing was the first viewing for him."

"I honestly don't know why he asked me not to say anything, Anna."

"But you must have an idea—"

He held up his hand, cutting me off mid-sentence.

"I'm serious, I don't know. I won't claim that I understand the depths of Evan Halifax. He's a dark horse sometimes. But I will say this: it doesn't surprise me that you caught his interest. It doesn't surprise me at all. You're beautiful, you're brilliant, you have your own unique vision and you defend it, despite other people's opinions. You're genuinely kind, which is a characteristic in very short supply in the world nowadays. But I wanted you know about showing him your paintings that time before you two ever hooked up. I wanted you to know... before tomorrow."

Before you marry him and it's too late.

"Anna?"

I started guiltily at the sound of Evan's voice behind me. I turned. He stood at the top of the terrace stairs. His light-infused gray eyes— gold and silver combined—flickered between Tommy and me. His brow creased in polite puzzlement.

"Is everything okay?" Evan asked, walking toward us.

"Yeah," I said brightly. I put out my hand. He took it and bent to place a kiss on my temple. Determined to ignore my anxiety at Tommy's strange confession, I turned my chin up. Our mouths met in a warm, lingering kiss. For a too-brief moment, my world narrowed down to Evan's scent and taste.

"Tommy was just doing his duty, checking in with the bride before the wedding," I told him softly.

"Quieting bridal nerves?" Evan asked.

Tommy looked away at Evan's sliding stare in his direction, so I spoke for him.

"There wasn't a single nerve to quiet," I insisted, taking Evan's hand and urging him toward the stairs and the gardens.

That vague, unsettled feeling I'd acquired on the terrace with Tommy stayed with me through dinner like a sour stomach that wasn't bad enough to send me to bed, but unpleasant enough to taint what should have been a beautiful evening.

Evan had catered a meal from Caprice, which we ate *alfresco*. The conversation was good, the food excellent, the wine sublime, and the view of the bay like something you'd see on the cover of *Condé Nast Traveler*.

As for myself, I couldn't keep my eyes off the Evan-portion of that ideal picture. I caught him a few times watching me with his typical focused, calm stare while he laughed at one of my father's lame jokes, or listened attentively while my mom explained one of the many challenges of teaching art to public high school students. If I'd had to interpret that stare of his, I'd guess I was doing an awful job of acting like I didn't have a care in the universe. I'd told Jessica that I'd fallen in love with him because he *saw* me, after all. So I had no call for complaining when he did so, even when I was trying to hide something.

As it turned out, there was more to Evan's concern for me that evening than I'd ever begun to imagine.

At around eight o'clock, the doorbell rang. Everyone paused in the mellow after-dinner conversation, looking blank at the banal interruption. Evan was the only one who reacted as if he had expected it. He stood and caught my attention with a tilt of his chin, then held out his hand.

"Anna? There's someone I want you to meet. Please everyone, go on without us. There's more cake and coffee," Evan said.

I gave Jessica a big, reassuring smile and followed him inside.

There was a man standing at the front door, a briefcase dangling from his fist.

"Anna, I'd like you to meet Jerome Hathaway. He's an old friend. Jerome, this is Anna Solas."

I shook hands with him. "I'm glad to meet another one of Evan's friends. Will you be able to attend the wedding tomorrow?"

BETH KERY

"I'm not that type of friend," Hathaway said, his tone clipped.

That sour-stomach feeling amplified briefly into full-fledged nausea, but I couldn't have said why, exactly. Bewildered, I followed Evan along with this friend-who-wasn't-a-friend into a large study. Hathaway pulled some documents out of his briefcase and set them on a big desk, all brisk and business-like. Evan sat down next to me and grasped my hand.

"I'm sorry to leave this until the final moment," he said, speaking directly to me in a low voice. "But there hasn't been much opportunity beforehand. I want to make sure certain matters are put into place before we marry. Certain legal things."

"Oh," I said, glancing over at Hathaway uneasily. "Uh... *what* legal things?"

"I want to make it clear what you'll inherit in the event of my death. I know to someone who's so young, it must seem uncomfortable to speak of it. But it's important that things like this are set into place now."

"Not just in the case of Evan's death. In the case of divorce, as well," Hathaway added.

I strained to keep my expression neutral. This was part of the grownup world I was entering. I had to deal with it.

"You mean a prenuptial agreement, don't you?" I asked Evan.

Evan gave Hathaway a sharp glance. Hathaway looked down at Evan's silent reproach. I understood Evan was angry at his lawyer's insensitive introduction of the topic. His tone sounded level enough when he spoke to me, though.

"Yes. Jerome has prepared a will and a prenuptial agreement for us to sign." He sighed and closed his eyes briefly. "I can tell from the look on your face that you think this is cruel of me, Anna. But—"

"I don't think it's cruel," I interrupted. "I realize that you're a very successful man. You have homes and cars and boats. You have investments and savings, and God knows what else." *God knows, because I certainly don't.* But I met his stare squarely. "None of that has anything to do with me. I don't own much of anything of value. If, God forbid, our marriage doesn't work out—"

"This isn't a matter of me being cynical. It's a matter of practicality," Evan interrupted.

"I'd walk away with what I brought into the marriage," I continued, unfazed. "Please don't think that I have a problem with that."

28

"Evan has provided you with much, much more than the clothes on your back, even in the case of divorce. You're a very fortunate young woman, Ms. Solas," Hathaway said with a bitter, sly little smile that I didn't like. I didn't like *him*.

Hathaway handed me a packet of papers. I stared at it without comprehending much until Hathaway flipped a page and pointed at a paragraph. My eyes widened when I saw the number and the amount of zeroes that followed it.

"Is this the will or the prenuptial agreement?" I asked hollowly.

"The prenup," Hathaway said as he walked behind the desk. From the tone of his voice, I understood that Hathaway had drawn up the agreement to Evan's specifications, but didn't agree with the wisdom of it. In fact, I had the impression he'd probably argued heatedly with Evan over the topic.

I was stunned. It was more money than I'd ever imagined in my life.

I looked at Evan, confused. He planned to give me *that* much money, even if I divorced him on a whim? He gave me a small smile.

"Your father has a legal background. We'll have him take a look at these, as well. But they're pretty cut and dried. I don't want you to have to worry, in any circumstance."

I turned my head, so that Hathaway couldn't hear or read my lips, and whispered to Evan.

"It's too much. I don't expect it. Any of it."

His smile struck me as a little bitter and very sad.

"It's for putting up with me. No matter for how long. Who knows, in a few months, you may think that number is way too low," he said. I opened my mouth to protest, but he stood.

"I'll go and get your father. You two can read through the documents thoroughly together. Jerome is going to stay to answer any questions, and of course, you or your father are welcome to call a family attorney if further consultation is needed."

My dad came to the study, and Evan insisted on giving us privacy. After staying for a while, Hathaway eventually left as well, saying he'd pick up the documents in the morning.

Nearly two hours later, my father and I sat together at a round table in Evan's study, the documents sprawled out before us.

"He's a strange man, your fiancé," my dad said, looking up from rereading the prenuptial agreement.

"Strange? You said earlier that the terms were incredibly generous."

"They are. You could divorce him in six months, if you chose, and he'd still be obligated to not only pay off your remaining college debt, but to give you five million dollars."

"I'm not going to divorce him in six months. That's ridiculous."

"I know that, sweetie," he said, squeezing my hand. Despite his reassurance, the creases of concern that remained on his usually smooth forehead bothered me. He noticed my expression and smiled. "What do I know about these things, really? Wealthy people operate very differently than we would, when it comes to marriage. Marriage is a legal contract, after all. I suppose it's better, to get it all arranged beforehand instead of risking having to battle it out in the courts later?" His pale blue eyes sharpened on me. "He must care about you a great deal, to be willing to give so much."

"Do you really think so, Dad?"

I waited anxiously for his response. It was a little long in coming for my comfort.

"Yes. I believe that he cares about you. I see the way he watches you across a room. I see the way you watch *him*. I happened to agree with what your mother said when she noticed the same thing. *That's some powerful stuff, Dick*, she said. Your sister told me that you told her that Evan *sees* you, and if that's true, than he sees something special. Just like I do." He gave one of his practical-Dad shrugs. "But then again, you know what my German grandma used to say. *Liebe ist blind.*"

Love is blind, indeed.

"Thanks, Dad. That's a real helper."

He chuckled. "It all comes down to instinct in the end, doesn't it? The question is, is this what *you* want to do? Whatever you decide, I'm one hundred percent behind you, now and forever."

"Thanks," I murmured, covering his hand with mine and squeezing. "Can I tell you something?"

It happened sometimes, annoyingly, that the small voice of a thirteen-year-old girl would come out of my mouth when I was with my dad and feeling vulnerable.

"Always," he said, just like I knew he would.

"I'm more nervous about Lake Tahoe than I am about the idea of marrying Evan," I admitted shakily.

I'd told my family about our plans to move to Evan's house on the eastern Tahoe shore in some of our early phone conversations. I'd only confessed to my parents when they'd arrived here, at Tiburon, that the Tahoe home used to belong to Elizabeth Madaster, Evan's dead wife. Even when I had told them the truth, however, I'd made a point of making it seem like I was just mentioning an inconsequential detail.

"You're worried you're going to be walking in the shadow of his first wife?"

I nodded, avoiding his stare. Hearing my dad put my fear into words made my throat tight, as if I were sucking in oxygen through a narrow tube.

"I don't think that's anything you need to worry about. Not in the least bit."

I met his gaze, amazed by his blunt certainty.

"How can you be so sure?" I asked.

"Because I saw the way he watches you across a crowded room, like you two were the only people on the planet. Stuff that powerful rarely happens once in a lifetime. But twice? Your man may have been blessed with an unfair allotment of gifts, but no one gets *that* lucky," Dad said wryly. He held up a pen and nodded down at the document. "What do you want to do, honey? I trust your judgment."

"I want to marry him. I love him. So much."

My dad nodded once and pushed the prenup toward me. I signed.

We were married the next afternoon. The sun shone down on us while we faced one another and pledged our love and fidelity. From up on the hillside, we had a clear view of San Francisco, the bay, and the Golden Gate Bridge.

The surroundings were idyllic. Almost *too* perfect. Too civilized. I had this strange thought in the middle of the proceedings that I would have preferred crashing surf on a rocky beach, rugged mountains, and sunlight penetrating fast-moving clouds. The uncompromising, almost harsh beauty of that imagined scene somehow matched better how I felt when I looked into Evan's gray eyes as we took our vows.

I'm complicated, Anna.

Everything went smoothly, despite my random thoughts about marrying Evan in that other, moody landscape.

Too quickly, it was time for my parents and Jessica to leave. Tommy and Ellen left just before the limousine arrived to take my family to the airport. I became unusually emotional saying goodbye to them all.

After the limousine disappeared down the road, Evan took my hand and led me inside the house. He plucked some tissues out of a box in the kitchen and handed them to me.

"Are you all right?"

"Yes," I said, wiping my cheeks. He was examining me with a sort of patient compassion, like an adult regards a sobbing child. I was embarrassed. Saying goodbye to Mom, Dad, and Jessica had brought on a strong upsurge of homesickness, even stronger than I'd ever experienced moving alone to San Francisco for college.

This time, saying goodbye to my parents had been different. I wasn't their little girl anymore. I was a married woman. It had never struck me harder that I was about to enter an exciting dream, but also an alien world.

"I'm fine," I insisted finally, giving my cheeks one last swipe with the tissues and forcing a smile. "I don't know where all that came from."

"Weddings are emotional occasions. You were sad to see your family go," Evan said, grabbing my forearms and pulling me closer to his body. "That's completely natural." He leaned down and brushed his mouth against mine.

"But I can't say that I'm sorry to have you all to myself again," he murmured. His low rumbling voice and warm breath against my lips brought back vivid memories of last night. Our wedding night. It had been decadent and beautiful, what had transpired between us in the darkness.

"Do we really have to leave for Tahoe this afternoon?" I asked, nibbling at his mouth. "Can't we stay here, in Tiburon for a while? Can't we just enjoy each other a little longer?"

He abruptly caught my mouth in a drugging kiss. I felt his body respond. I felt sure I'd convinced him.

"We'll leave as scheduled," he said a moment later, stepping away from me.

"But—"

"You deserve a honeymoon right now, not in a few months. I realize that. This bank acquisition couldn't have come at a worse time. I'm sorry to disappoint you."

"You're not disappointing me," I exclaimed truthfully.

Soon after he'd asked me to marry him, Evan had explained to me that one of the companies in his fund—a major bank—was going to acquire another major bank. I didn't really understand all the details, except to say that it was the type of business transaction that would take months, if not years, and ruin a lot of people's vacation plans. Evan had suggested that we move to Tahoe right after we were married, where we both could work, and yet we'd still have time together in a beautiful, secluded place. He proposed a European tour for our honeymoon a few months down the line, when his work schedule had cleared.

How could I be *disappointed* with those plans?

"You'll love it in Tahoe, Anna. Trust me. Please?"

He'd seen the doubt on my face. "Of *course* I will."

He dropped one last chaste kiss on my mouth before he walked away.

We drove from Tiburon to Tahoe. When I asked Evan why he wanted to go by car versus plane—I knew he often used a private plane service—his answer surprised me.

"I realize you're leaving your entire world behind, marrying me and moving to a place you've never seen," he said, his eyes trained on the road in front of us. "The drive will prove to you that we're not going to be living that far from the familiar. You can hire a driver and escape back to San Francisco in a matter of hours, if you should want to."

"Don't say that," I admonished. He glanced over at me swiftly. "I'm not going to want to escape anything. I'm going to love it as much as I love you."

He gave that small, distracted smile, and turned his attention back to the road.

We talked a good deal on the first few hours of the trip. It seemed to me, however, that Evan grew more and more withdrawn as we began our steep climb into the Sierra Nevada Mountains.

In the silence, I had the opportunity to reflect on my nervousness about going to Tahoe instead of staying at Evan's home in Tiburon. Or maybe the quiet and the unknown road unwinding in front of me caused that charged issue to push up to the surface of my awareness like a splinter being rejected by the body. Evan had told me that he bought his home in Tiburon six years ago, *after* his wife had died.

But he'd lived at Tahoe with her.

With Elizabeth.

Why did he want to take me, his new bride, to a place where he'd lived with, and lost, his first wife? The question started to expand inside me. I was about to explode with it as we left the main highway and took a road that dipped and climbed through a rugged mountain landscape.

"Evan?" I began uneasily after a pause of us not speaking for nearly an hour.

"It's okay," he said. "I know the road is twisty and it may seem like I'm going a little fast. But I've driven this highway since I was sixteen. You're safe. I would rather you had me drive you around here, though, until you get used to the mountain roads."

"No. It's not that." *At least not entirely.* I actually did appreciate the reassurance about the curving, steep road and his deft, swift driving. I placed a hand on my lurching stomach.

"You lived in this house. The one we're going to, I mean. With Elizabeth. Isn't that right?"

I felt him glance at me and wanted to scream out for him to keep his gaze on the road.

"Yes."

"I don't understand. Why do you want to go there? *Now.*"

"You're wondering why I want to return to Les Jumeaux after marrying you?"

"Le jumu... " I attempted to repeat, confused.

"Les Jumeaux. It means *the twins*, because it's two identical homes, separate, but side by side."

"And we're going to live in..."

"The North Twin," he finished for me.

34

"And the other house?"

"Is owned by Elizabeth's father."

Noah Madaster. The name popped into my head, a remnant of me doing all that online research about Elizabeth. Elizabeth's father had been a high-profile figure from a prominent family, I recalled, a former doctor and one-time governor of Nevada.

"But he won't be there, will he?" I asked, finding the idea of being neighbors with Elizabeth's dad awkward.

"No. He and his wife have retired to their ranch in the Carson Valley," Evan said.

At my sigh of relief, he grabbed the hand resting on my thigh and held it firmly.

"And as for your question, I wanted to come back now because I *could*. With you at my side, Anna, I can finally return to the place where I grew up, the place I consider home. You've made me strong again."

I watched him as he pressed the back of my hand to his mouth. I felt his kiss all the way to my core.

At that moment, we rose to the summit of the mountain. I had my first glimpse of the expanse of Lake Tahoe, a sparkling sapphire gem nestled in the rocky, pine-covered cradle of the mountains.

It was like an opening. Not just in the landscape. In my spirit. It was the strangest thing.

It felt as if I'd come home, too.

Chapter Three

WE ARRIVED AT LES JUMEAUX JUST BEFORE SUNSET. THE ANTICIPATION built in me as we coasted down the winding, steep highway surrounding the lake. The only things that stopped me from digging my nails into the leather seat were Evan's calm, skilled driving and the distraction of the jaw-dropping view. I found myself absorbing the unique hues of green and blue present in the water and mentally detailing what paints I'd use to replicate them.

An expectant silence hung in the car when Evan finally turned off the highway onto a shadowed, narrow road that led into the pine forest. We arrived at a small stone house in front of a tall wrought iron gate. It was a gatehouse, a checkpoint that had probably once housed a security guard. It stood empty now. Moss and creeping vines grew on the limestone. I watched as Evan leaned out the window and pressed a card to an electronic reader.

With the evening gloom, the giant, sentinel-like pines towering over us, and the quaint stone gatehouse, I felt a little like I'd just entered the scene from a fairy tale. The security system Evan used seemed highly out of place, a technical anomaly in a Hans Christian Anderson tale. *Attempted* to use, I should say. I saw him press the card to the reader for the fourth time, his jaw tight. The gate didn't budge. He cursed quietly.

"Here," I said.

He glanced over at me as if he'd forgotten I was there. But then he blinked and handed me the card. I rubbed it on my jeans shorts.

"Anna, that's not going to—"

"Try it now," I said, handing it back. He reached out the window again.

"I have a feeling something else is the prob—"

The wrought iron gate slowly swung open. He gave me a surprised glance. I grinned. He shook his head sheepishly.

"I should have known it only required a sprite's touch," he said under his breath as he put the car in Drive.

The road meandered through a ravine, the steepness of which was emphasized by the giant pine trees that surrounded us. After a moment, I realized we followed the path of a creek that ran to the left of us. Sunlight barely penetrated the tunnel-like entrance. I found it beautiful, and a little eerie. At one point, the narrow road forked. Evan veered to the right.

"Where does the other road go?" I asked.

"To the South Twin. The garages are on opposite ends of the property."

"Are the two houses connected somehow?"

"They were once, by a corridor. Not anymore. They're completely separate," he stated. Something grim in his tone made me study his profile closely.

"Your father-in-law... I mean your former one, Elizabeth's father," I said. "You don't like him much, do you?"

"I've never known anyone who does."

That gave me pause for a few seconds. Even *Elizabeth* hadn't liked her own father?

"He was a physician, wasn't he? Before he became the governor of Nevada?"

"Before he was forced to resign as governor because of a scandal of his own making? Yes. That's right. He was a neurologist, actually. Brilliant man. What he did with that genius was the stuff of horror stories, in my opinion."

"What do you mean, the stuff of—"

"Can we not talk about Noah Madaster right now, just when we're arriving at our new home?" Evan interrupted. He glanced sideways and saw my open-mouthed surprise at his sharpness.

"Sorry," he muttered. "Madaster is a topic from my past. Talking about him always sets me on edge."

Obviously.

"We don't have to talk about him if you don't want to."

He gave me a quick, grateful glance and pointed out the window.

"This is one of the only stretches of shore on the eastern side that has sugar pines. That's one there. See how giant the cones are?" he said, pointing at a suspended pair of cones that must have been a foot long each. Warmth had crept into his voice, despite the earlier edge to his tone.

"You really love it here, don't you?"

He gripped the wheel tighter. "It's a wonder. But I suppose part of me does, yes."

He loved the place, despite the fact that he snarled even at the mention of Noah Madaster's name... despite the fact that he'd lived with and lost Elizabeth here.

An invisible hand seemed to squeeze at my heart.

We broke the tree line. Light poured into the car windows, lighting a fuse of excitement inside me. At our elevation, we were above the main part of the mansion, but only just. I stared over four steep gables and two tall turrets of what looked like one sprawling stone house. Because of several giant pines, I couldn't see the gap between the properties. Tahoe glowed like sun-shot turquoise glass on the horizon.

Evan glanced over at me, and I realized I'd gasped. I suppose it only made sense that a fairy-tale castle existed in the magic forest alongside the enchanted lake.

"Welcome to Les Jumeaux," he said.

A moving van would be arriving the next day with select pieces of furniture from Evan's homes in San Francisco and Tiburon, along with some of my completed paintings. But we still were pretty loaded down with what we'd brought in the car as we approached Les Jumeaux that late afternoon. Evan carried our luggage, and I hauled several blank canvases and art supplies. We walked up stone steps to a small porch. Evan unlocked a pair of enormous carved wooden doors.

The silence hung thick as I followed him into a vaulted entryway, and then into a two-story high great room. I stared wide-eyed at what must have been a twenty-foot-tall row of gigantic windows overlooking the incandescent lake. Overflowing bookshelves lined each side of the massive room.

It was decorated in a style I'd never seen firsthand, but associated with grand hunting lodges or mountain retreats for the wealthy. I had the impression of being in a giant stone and wood cave and peering out into a world of light and color. That hushed sense of charged expectation prevailed.

"It's like it was waiting for us," I whispered.

Evan's deep laughter broke the trance. I realized how stupid I'd sounded. I smiled at the soft light in his eyes, so rarely seen. He parked the suitcases and came to me. He methodically unburdened me of my art supplies one by one, setting them on a nearby table.

Then he took me into his arms.

We stared out the floor-to-ceiling windows onto the cerulean blue waters, our fronts pressed together. That fullness in my chest that I associated exclusively with Evan's embraces expanded in me, exponentially bigger this time as we stood together in what was to be our new home.

Our home.

Will I ever wrap my head around all this?

"I want you to be happy here, Anna," he murmured, nuzzling the top of my head with his chin.

"If I were any happier, I'd burst," I said before I pressed my face to his chest and inhaled the subtle scent of wood, spice, and citrus: the singular smell of *him*. I could substitute the scent of him for a meal.

"You belong out there." I felt him tilt his head in the direction of the lake.

"In the water, I suppose."

"No. In the light." He kissed my head and took my hand in his. "Come on. You haven't seen anything yet. I'm going to show you the grounds... and the most perfect place."

"Perfect for *what*?" I asked suggestively, following him down a shadowed hallway.

He arched his brows, catching my playful sexual innuendo. "Almost anyplace is perfect for that, when it comes to you. But I meant your painting."

"But what about the rest of the house?" I asked, craning my head over my shoulder and taking in the beamed ceilings, huge wrought iron chandeliers, and a Y-shaped, dramatic mahogany staircase in the distance.

"There'll be plenty of time to see the house later. Let's go out on the grounds while the light is still good," Evan insisted.

At Les Jumeaux, it was hard to tell where the stony landscape of Tahoe ended and the bridges, folly towers, fountains, and walls of the grounds began. It was like the house itself had sprung up from the craggy mountainside. Even the peaceful waters of the beach enclosure had been fabricated, I realized. A rocky jetty had been built to create a small harbor, protecting the calm blue and green waters of the private beach from rough waves. Evan told me that Cornish stonemasons and miners had been imported by some ancestor of Elizabeth's back in the early 1900s to build the home and handcraft the beach, fanciful gardens, paths, and elaborate fountains.

"There are floats and kayaks in storage over there, if you should ever want them for the beach," Evan said, waving in the direction of a distant boathouse built from the same gray stone as Les Jumeaux. "The enclosure is perfect for swimming. It's shallow, and always stays calm. Come on. I want to show you something you'll like."

We left the house and grounds behind us. Evan led me up a mountain trail surrounded by towering pines. Suddenly, we stood at a rocky promontory about twenty feet wide, the tropical-like, brilliantly blue water shimmering some eighty feet below us.

"Do you like it?" Evan asked, eagerness in his quiet voice. "Do you think it'd be a good spot to paint?"

"Absolutely," I breathed, spellbound by the magic of the place.

"The new easel and chair I got you will come with the other things tomorrow. I also got you a waterproof locker where you can store your supplies, so you don't have to haul things back and forth. I'll bring everything up here as soon as they arrive."

"You spoil me," I murmured, completely distracted. Overwhelmed, I dropped his hand. Slowly, I spun around in a full circle. From here, every landscape was available to me: the lake, the mountains, the highest gables and turrets of Les Jumeaux soaring side by side with the huge pines. Beauty poured into me. I couldn't drink it in fast enough. The quality of light was unlike anything I'd ever seen.

"It's like it's alive, the light," I whispered, my voice sounding hollow with awe.

Evan reached for my hand. He bent his arm, drawing me close. I bumped against him, our bodies pressing tightly together.

"So you really do like it?"

"It's not like anyplace I've ever seen in my life. It's like something out of a fairytale." I peered up at his sunlit face. My throat felt very tight with emotion. "You were right, to want to come. It's amazing."

A small smile flickered across his mouth. His head dipped. I opened my eyelids a dazed moment later, the intense sunlight and his kiss leaving me disoriented.

"*You're* like something out of a fairy tale," he said.

I smiled, squinting more because the light from the setting sun was fierce. He moved me, adjusting where I stood so that his head blocked out the reddish-gold ball descending over the mountains.

"Such a gentleman," I murmured.

He gave a swift glance behind me, toward Les Jumeaux. He pulled me higher in his arms and leaned down to kiss me... to devour me.

"Let's go back," he said a moment later, nuzzling my nose with his and nipping at my parted lips.

"Let's hurry," I agreed breathlessly.

He laughed, seeming pleased by my haste. Hand in hand, we raced down the trail.

The heavy curtains were drawn in the bedroom suite to which he led me. He pulled me into his arms the second after he shut the door. I loved his single-minded intensity, his heat. For a moment, I let it overwhelm me as we clawed at each other's clothes and staggered deeper into the room, neither one of us willing to fully take our mouths or hands off each other. But then I stumbled slightly a few feet from the bed. He caught me. I laughed, startled, panting to catch my breath. He smiled.

I found myself glancing warily around the large, shadowed room.

"What are you looking for, Anna?" he asked after a moment.

I blinked, glancing up at something I'd heard in his tone. His smile was gone. He'd seen something on my face. Or caught my mood.

"Nothing. I was just curious. It's dark in here. Is this... is this *our* bedroom?"

"Yes." He dropped his hands and moved back slightly, beginning to unbutton his shirt.

I shivered at the loss of his heat. The air suddenly felt cool. The sun must have finished its descent behind the mountains. The light peeking from behind the curtains had turned a lurid scarlet. He removed his shirt, a band of red illuminating the otherwise gray shadows of his powerful body.

"But there are nine other bedrooms here. You can choose another one, if you like," he said.

"No," I said breathlessly. "I'm sure it's wonderful." I stepped forward, my hand extended to touch the temptation of his naked chest, eager to cast off the sudden shadows. He caught my wrist.

"This wasn't Elizabeth's and my room, Anna."

I stared up at him, my mouth hanging open. "How—"

"Of course you'd wonder about that. I may be insensitive, but I'm not that dense. I hired a cleaning service to come in a few days ago and get the house ready for us. I asked them to fix this room up. It's nice, and it faces the lake. Turn on the light." I saw him nod in the direction of a lamp. "Go on. Look it over."

"No. I'm sure it's beautiful. It doesn't matter," I whispered, moving into his arms, ashamed of my insecurity. I kissed his chest. He put his hand at the back of my head. I became more feverish, my mouth moving lower on his body, so eager to forget my flash of uncertainty.

A moment later, he groaned gruffly and urged me to straighten. He lifted me into his arms and laid me down on the bed. He removed his remaining clothes. I started to frantically strip, but he spoke tersely.

"I'll undress you."

He sat at the edge of the bed.

He took off my clothes, his manner deliberate, but strained, as if he were unwrapping a present that he was determined to savor instead of devour in a rush. My desire grew so sharp, I broke out in sweat in the ensuing silence.

By the time he entered me minutes later, I was already near the breaking point. I stared up at his shadowed form as he came down over me, gasping when he filled me.

"Any time you find yourself doubting, remember me saying this: I'm only thinking of you when we touch," he said next to my upturned lips. His body tensed and flexed under my anxious fingers. I cried out in pleasure.

"Only you, Anna," he repeated harshly next to my ear before he began to move in earnest.

Evan got up at around eleven that night and went in search of something for us to eat. He left the lamp on when he walked out the door. I lay in the giant bed, the thick, soft comforter pulled up to my chin. I surveyed the suite, moving just my eyes. It was comfortably anonymous. It might have been the bedroom at a luxurious five-star hotel. I was relieved there were no personal photos, no remnants of Evan's former life here.

But maybe it wasn't so impersonal, after all.

"Is that an original Bierstadt?" I murmured when Evan returned carrying a tray. He kicked the door closed with that male grace I loved, never so much as causing a ripple in the wine he carried in two goblets. He glanced over his shoulder to where I pointed at the painting on the wall. But my attention had transferred to the much more interesting natural landscape of his half-nude body.

"Yeah. It used to hang in the great room. I had it moved up here last week."

"For me?"

"For whom else?" he asked me with a small grin as he set the tray on the bedside table. I couldn't unglue my eyes from him as he stood there, wearing a pair of pajama bottoms and nothing else. A feeling of self-consciousness overcame me... an uncommon shyness.

"And that," I whispered, pointing behind me at an exquisite white ceramic, surrealist sculpture of two lovers, their mouths poised to meet in a kiss. "Evan... is that a Tsang?" I asked, referring to the sculptor, Johnson Tsang, whom I admired deeply.

"Yes," he said matter-of-factly. "It's my wedding gift to you. Do you like it?"

"Are you kidding? It's incredible. Tsang is one of my favorite artists."

"I know. You mentioned it once, so I looked him up. You were right. As usual, you have impeccable taste."

"Thank you."

I stared up at him in rising awe. I was surrounded by treasures at every turn: a vast mansion, an idyllic landscape, museum-quality art pieces casually displayed for my pleasure.

But *he* was the biggest wonder of all.

"You're my husband," I murmured, hearing the edge of possession and the tinge of wonder in my own voice.

A strange look settled on his face. He sat on the edge of the bed, peering at me from beneath a lowered brow.

"You say that like you're amazed."

I reached out and touched the gold ring I'd put on his finger yesterday.

"I say it because I *am* amazed," I told him frankly.

"No, Anna. I'm the one who is stunned."

He leaned down, nuzzling my chin until I lifted my face for him. His mouth covered mine. A moment later, he turned out the lamp and joined me beneath the covers.

Our dinner was forgotten.

When I woke in the morning, brilliant sunlight poured around the curtains. I was alone. I felt like a kid who had fallen asleep on the last leg of a vacation trip, and woken up in Disneyland.

"Evan?" I called out as I sprung out of bed. It only took a split second of silence for me to recognize he wasn't there. I flung open first one window's drapes, then another. The room was transformed into a golden cube. I held my breath, staring out at the brilliant water and the smoky-blue mountains on the far side of the lake.

I hurried to get dressed.

A few minutes later, I reached the bottom of the grand staircase, panting from haste and excitement.

"Evan?"

Thick silence was my only reply. Bright sunlight poured in through the giant windows facing the lake, but a good portion of the great room resisted the shining streamers of gold. Stubborn shadows hung on the forest side of the room like heavy drapery. I had the strange impression that my voice hadn't been substantial enough to penetrate there, like Evan might be sitting in one of those wingback leather chairs and blending with the darkness.

But he wasn't, of course, I told myself firmly as I crept into the center of a giant, exquisite Oriental carpet. The forest side of the room wasn't actually as dark as I'd first imagined. My eyes had adjusted. I absorbed the room, scanning the carved mahogany shelves brimming with books. It took me a moment to realize I searched for photos, for any remnant of the past.

To my relief, I saw none.

Evan had never gotten around to showing me much of the house last night. I explored now to my heart's content. At first, I was a little cautious about throwing open doors and wandering down unfamiliar hallways. But when I was delighted again and again with one amazing space after another, I grew bolder.

I found another set of stairs leading downward, not as fancy as the main staircase, but still fashioned from lovely, carved mahogany.

At the bottom of the stairs was a kitchen. Not just any kitchen, a lavish, cozy, enormous affair. It still held the charm of an old school service kitchen, although it'd been given a modern renovation that included two quartz-covered islands, a double oven with warm red brick lining the wall above it, a pressed tin roof, a seating area with deep leather chairs situated in front of a fireplace, and a casual dining table placed next to another bank of windows.

Here was the lake again, in all its glory. Although I'd come downstairs, the house was built into the mountainside. On this level, I was still a floor above the beach. A stone terrace ran outside patio doors and windows, a built-in outdoor cooking space, table and seating area awaiting some golden midmorning brunch or romantic magenta sunset.

I discovered a half full coffee pot on the counter—welcome evidence of Evan's presence here before me.

"Evan?" I called out, but again, the vast spaces of the house swallowed up my voice.

The kitchen cabinet doors were made of paned glass. I hesitated as I looked for a coffee cup, wondering who might have drunk from it before me. Would my cup be chipped from some previous user?

Maybe smudged with old lipstick?

I found myself counting stacked plates of various sizes, teacups and coffee mugs, knowing all along I was being ridiculous. Obsessive, even. But I couldn't stop myself. There were sixteen of each. Only one coffee cup was missing, which surely had been taken by Evan. I took down a mug, loving the heavy, creamy feeling of the everyday china in my hand. The dish looked brand new.

"Any time you find yourself doubting, remember me saying this: I'm only thinking of you when we touch. Only you, Anna."

The memory heartened me. I suspected that Evan had purchased the dishes recently. For me. For us.

A fresh start.

Now carrying a steaming cup of coffee and feeling very happy, I opened door after door on this level, breathless with excitement. I felt like the winner of the best lottery in existence, going through her treasures for the first time.

Here was a well-stocked pantry that was twice the size of my rented room in San Francisco, and here a mahogany wine cellar with a tasting table in the center of it. Down a jog of stone steps, I located a changing room for the beach and exercise room, a wet and dry sauna, and a large laundry room.

I spied another closed door down the passage and headed toward it, positive of another treasure about to be discovered. I opened it and stood on the edge of utter blackness.

Disorientation struck me. I realized later it was because the room was on the beach side, and so I'd expected bright sunlight. Instead, there was an open space in front of me, but it was a black hole. I reached and immediately found a porcelain light switch. Ever so briefly, I thought of the story of Bluebeard's wife opening the forbidden door. Ignoring the stupid, intrusive thought, I flipped on the light.

Color assaulted me. Forget the blue of the beard. This was red. *Everywhere.* There were rows and rows of velvet lounging chairs and couches, smooth monochromatic scarlet intermixed with complex tapestries. Red velvet fabric covered the walls, sometimes in a wallpaper, sometimes swooping in lush U-shaped drapery.

I'd lit a crystal chandelier that hung in the center of the room. The cut glass teardrops absorbed the pervasive scarlet, turning them into bloodshot diamonds. There was an elaborate bar and storage unit to the side of the room, the amber, brown, and green liquor bottles providing the only variance of color.

Dust lay heavily on everything—the crystal decanters, the overhead chandelier, the oceans of velvet.

This was beyond luxury. It was decadence. There was some odor, something I didn't like. Moisture and mold. Sweat? The heavy fabrics held on fast to a stew of cloying scents: the lingering stench of old cigars and women's perfume. Exhaled liquor.

A rich musk.

I didn't want to breathe it in. This room was unlike any other I'd seen in the house so far. It was a sealed-off chamber, no windows, and seemingly no decent ventilation.

I backed out quickly into the hall without thinking, and then paused as I remembered the light. I reached around the doorframe, hesitant this time. My fingers skittered reluctantly along the velvet. It felt slightly moist and rough, warmer than I'd thought it would, like I'd thrust my hand into a living thing, as if my fingers ran along the inner lining of a mouth or something even more illicit...

"Anna?"

My forefinger encountered the switch at the same moment I heard Evan's voice behind me. I flicked it and hurriedly shut the door.

It wasn't until I turned to face his approaching figure that I realized I was behaving guiltily, like I'd been caught doing something bad. Evan slowed as he reached me, his brow creasing as he studied my face. My cheeks felt hot.

"Exploring?" he asked me. His voice sounded level—calm even—but his eyes were searching.

"Yes. I was just—" I pointed lamely at the closed door and laughed.

"Looking at the viewing room?" he finished for me.

"Viewing room?" *For viewing* what, *exactly*?

He nodded, his gaze narrowing on me. He took my hand.

"For viewing movies?" he explained slowly.

"Oh," I gasped, understanding hitting. I gave a bark of relieved laughter. The movie screen must have been hidden behind those dusty, heavy velvet drapes.

"What did you think it was for?" Evan asked, pulling my hand and leading me along the hallway. He looked over his shoulder as he walked, his gaze on me sharp.

"I didn't know what it was for," I admitted, trying to hold back a jag of hysterical laughter. "Caligula's party room, maybe?"

I thought he'd laugh. Instead, he paused. I saw him mouth my answer silently, a strange expression overcoming his face.

"Evan? I was just kidding. It was all the velvet. It seemed a little tacky, that's all, very different from the rest of the house."

He nodded once and resumed walking.

"It needs to be demolished completely and renovated. I asked the cleaning crew to make sure it was locked, but apparently, they forgot. All that fabric is rotting. There's mold. It's not safe to breathe in there."

"It didn't smell very good."

"It's past time it was renovated," he said.

Who had *ever* thought designing a room like that was a good idea? Was it Evan's first wife who had that bordello-taste, or some former owner? Hadn't Evan said Les Jumeaux had been in the Madaster family for over a hundred years? But obviously, a movie viewing room was a more modern addition. Whatever the case, that room certainly hadn't matched the tasteful, warm elegance of everything else I'd seen at the North Twin.

And what kind of movies had been viewed in there, exactly? Had Elizabeth and Evan entertained in the viewing room? I wondered, thinking of that well stocked bar. I winced. I even hated the name: viewing room. It struck me as dirty and furtive somehow, like a peeping Tom.

Was any of that repulsive scent a remnant of Elizabeth and her husband? My husband?

Stop it. Stop thinking about her. About them.

"Best to stay away from that room," Evan was saying briskly as he led me into the magnificent kitchen. He turned toward me and grasped my shoulders, waiting for me to look up at him.

"Best for you to stay in the light, Anna."

So I did.

For the next week or so, I spent a good portion of my mornings and my afternoons painting on the overlook. The pure, saturated light and crystalline atmosphere put me into a kind of creative trance. I lost track of hours at a time. Despite the spell of the place, my focus had never been clearer, my strokes on the canvas never more sure.

I swam in the afternoons when it grew too hot on the overlook. I promised Evan I would swim alone only in the idyllic, manmade sandy enclosure. It'd been designed and engineered for safe, casual swimming, with a maximum depth of only about five feet.

Sometimes, I explored the grounds after I swam, hiking around the many mountain trails or rocky beaches, walking on Les Jumeaux's hewn stone pathways and charming little bridges that led to dozens of small gardens and secret sitting benches, just waiting to be discovered and enjoyed.

One day, the back of my neck prickled as I painted. I had the thought I was being watched. But when I turned around, I saw nothing unusual. The tops of the enormous pines swayed peacefully in the breeze. I searched the tall branches. A bird of prey might have watched me while I painted. Maybe some primal instinct in me had sensed it. My gaze was drawn to the South Twin's turret where it poked through the tree line. The way the light struck the windows made them appear shiny and opaque, like a dark mirror.

I turned back to my work, but that uncomfortable sensation of being watched persisted.

After I'd stored my canvas and painting supplies that day, I headed down the entrance road for my daily walk.

When I reached the fork in the road, I took the left path, toward the South Twin. Perhaps I was influenced by that feeling of being watched while I worked earlier. I could see the South Twin well enough from the front of the property and the beach, and the great south turret loomed to my left when I painted on the overlook every day. But I was curious to see the back entrance to the South Twin.

When I reached the clearing and saw the house, it was like looking at a mirror image of our home. It had the same stone carvings on the house's exterior, the delicate, decorative ironwork on the chimneys and lanterns. I couldn't find one difference.

A mechanical hum resounded into the still summer evening, making me jump. I realized that a door was electronically rising on the South Twin's garage. Much to my amazement, someone was about to drive out of what I'd supposed was an uninhabited home.

Embarrassed at my intrusion on private property, I hurried out of the road into the cover of the pines. A moment later, I watched a silver Toyota sedan go past me. I saw the driver well from my position: a woman of about forty with dark hair pulled back into a thick, tight bun. She was much too young to be Elizabeth Madaster's mother. Who was she?

Evan and I ate dinner on the terrace that night after sunset, our only source of light the candle I'd lit and the midnight dome of stars above us. I described what I'd seen that afternoon to Evan, asking him if Elizabeth had siblings who could have been visiting the South Twin.

"Elizabeth was an only child," Evan said as he buttered a roll. I was relieved he didn't seem irritated by my admission of walking over to the South Twin. If anything, he seemed thoughtful. Reflective. "It was probably the Madaster's agent, or maybe just a friend checking up on the property for them? Probably better to stay away from that house, though. Madaster wasn't exactly thrilled that Elizabeth left me this property. He threw away a lot of money on expensive lawyers, trying to find a loophole to keep me from inheriting. He might get unpleasant if he found out we were trespassing over on his property," Evan said.

I agreed with him completely. I didn't want to do anything that would worsen what appeared to be a bitter relationship between the two men.

"Are you going far when you take your hikes?" he asked in a neutral tone.

"No. Just along the trail above the beach and on the nearby forest paths." He didn't reply. He seemed distracted.

"Evan? There's not a problem with me hiking around here, is there?"

"No, it's just that I'd prefer you weren't alone. Some of the trails are steep. Isolated. What if something happened to you while you were out?"

"I'd call you. I always have my cell phone," I reminded him wryly. "I used to hike alone at Land's End and the Presidio all the time. I'll be fine, Evan."

"This isn't the Presidio. If you haven't noticed, we're in the wilderness here. We're very isolated. I'll get you a bell you can tie to your shoestring to help warn animals of your presence, and some bear spray at the very least," he said after a pause. His gray eyes met mine. "And I'd like you to tell me which direction you're hiking before you go out. Okay?"

I laughed. "Why are you so worried? I'm just walking."

His hand snaked out, grasping my wrist. I started.

"Just promise me," he said. I stared at him, my mouth hanging open in surprise. "It can be dangerous here, Anna. It's important that you understand that."

"At Les Jumeaux?" I asked disbelievingly.

He seemed to come to himself, releasing my wrist. He picked up his knife and cut his steak.

"Not just at Les Jumeaux. In the forest. In the water. This isn't a place to let down your guard, that's all I meant." He reached and took my hand, this time gently. "Just promise me that you'll be careful. Please? You're very precious to me. I'd feel very... "

"Evan?" I asked when he trailed off.

"Bad if something happened to you," he continued as if he hadn't heard me. "Because I'd brought you to this place."

My dropped fork rattled loudly on the china. I sandwiched his hand between mine and squeezed.

"*Nothing* bad is going to happen to me," I insisted. I smiled brightly, trying to coax away his dark mood. When his expression remained unchanged, I stood and went to him. I removed his steak knife from his hand, setting it on his plate. I calmly straddled his lap and opened my hands on his shoulders. He remained very still and watchful, but I felt the familiar tension leap into his flesh. I pressed my lips fleetingly to his.

"What are you doing?" he asked, his mouth twitching in amusement.

"Making love to you. It's a beautiful night."

"You're trying to sidetrack me."

"Is that a crime? For a wife to sidetrack her husband?" I looped my forearms around his neck and pulled him closer, skimming my nipples across his chest and plucking at his lips coaxingly.

52

He opened his mouth slightly and I slipped my tongue in the crevice. He groaned, shifting his hands to my hips and then my buttocks. He squeezed gently, but insistently, until I backed away slightly and met his stare.

"Promise me, Anna. Promise me you'll be careful. That you'll let me know when you go out, and in what direction you're going at the very least."

"The last thing I want to do is worry you, Evan. Of course I promise."

A muscle jumped in his cheek. He looked appeased, if not relieved. Tension continued to harshly etch his handsome face.

He moved one hand, his deft fingertips releasing the buttons on my shirt with unerring accuracy. I held my breath, watching as he undressed me, his actions increasingly hasty. Forceful. Finally, he jerked open the fabric of my shirt wide, his stare in the dim light scorching me. Both of his hands again on my hips, he slid me along his thighs toward him. He planted his head between my breasts, his warm breath misting my skin. I held him to me, my fingers furrowing through his thick hair.

I would promise him anything.

The experience of the velvet viewing room had dimmed my desire to explore in the house, at least for the time being. We lived in only a small portion of the vast house and grounds, anyway: the big, warm kitchen and sunny terrace, the sitting area in front of the fireplace in the casual dining area, our bedroom, my overlook, and Evan's study.

One night shortly after we'd moved to Les Jumeaux, Evan built us a fire in the outdoor fireplace after dinner. Early summer nights at Tahoe could get chilly, despite the broiling heat of the daytime sun. That evening was particularly cool, but I was toasty warm and content in front of the fire, with Evan by my side.

"I'm going up," Evan said when the fire had dimmed to nothing but a few glowing embers. We'd been holding hands and talking idly, staring into the dying flames. He tugged gently on my hand. "Are you coming?"

"Yes, I'll be right up. I'm going to try to find something to read. I thought I'd look for something in the great room," I said, referring to what must have been thousands of books upstairs.

"I'll turn on the lights in the great room for you on my way up, then," Evan said before he released my hand.

A few minutes later, I stood in the middle of the huge main living space of the mansion, staring up at row upon row of books. They were arranged by genre, I soon realized. Here were all sorts of medical and anatomical books, here books on genealogy, psychopharmacology, psychiatry, and neurology.

"Not exactly the light reading before bed reading I'm looking for," I muttered under my breath.

I found the fiction section and after browsing a bit, picked a World War II drama-love story by a British author I liked. Two shelves down, I also located a Frida Kahlo biography I'd wanted to read. Satisfied with my finds, I headed over to the switch for the enormous chandelier that lit the room. Out of the corner of my eye, I saw a figure standing in front of the bookshelf. I had the distinct impression the person faced outward, and was watching me.

I cried out in muffled surprise. I turned fully, but nothing was there.

The hair on my neck and arms stood up. I was completely alone in the great room. My eyes told me that truth, but some other part of me, some primitive instinct, insisted that my vision couldn't tell me everything.

I stared at the place where I'd seen the figure, searching. When I'd thought I'd seen someone, I'd halted in front of the collection of medical and science related books. A dark red velvet book caught my eye. It was very large, and looked distinctly out of place among all the other scholarly-looking volumes. Approaching the bookcase cautiously, I set my books on a lower shelf. I went up on tiptoe and reached for the velvet book.

Cradling it in one hand, I opened it. The pages were made of thick parchment. I realized it was a kind of journal, not a traditionally published book. On the title page, someone had handwritten in lovely, elaborate cursive: The Madaster Family Tree and Bloodline, Theodore N. Madaster, 1982.

This time, the shivers went all the way down my arms and legs. Theodore Madaster? Could he have been Elizabeth's grandfather?

I began to turn the pages. Theodore had meticulously drawn out a tree that began on the left page and carried to the right, then resumed when the next page was flipped. As an artist, I admired his elaborate penmanship and well-thought-out design. He must have practiced elsewhere, perhaps many times, before he'd finally copied the pages into this book, because there were no smudges or errors. He'd used mostly black, dark bronze, and red ink, and the colors had held up amazingly well.

Theodore had also drawn several shields and various other heraldic symbols, presumably associated with different branches of the Madaster family. These drawings were concise and beautifully executed using additional ink colors of blue, gold, and green.

I was awed by the grandeur of it all, by the mystery and depth of meaning I couldn't quite grasp. I was also a bit envious. It was hard for me to imagine someone would put so much thought and care into his ancestry.

I myself was close to both my mother's parents and my father's mother—my dad's father had died when Dad was in his twenties. I'd always been told that my mother's roots were Irish, English, and Swiss, while my father primarily identified as being German-American. In essence, I'd always proudly considered us to be American mutts. What I knew about my great-grandparents could be said in a very short paragraph, a skimpy affair compared to *this* scholarly and artistic endeavor.

The first entrants on the Madaster family tree came from the thirteen hundreds. Most of Elizabeth's ancestors appeared to be from France, and someplace called the Holy Roman Empire, which in later pages became Germany. As I kept flipping the pages, each filled with so much detail that I couldn't fully grasp, I realized that as the years and the generations passed, the names entered had a sort of flourish beneath them of either a simple or complicated design. As the centuries wore on, the decorations beneath the names became increasingly complex. Sometimes the lines were etched in mere black, but a few of the designs were etched in flowery combinations of black, red, and bronze ink.

I realized I'd been flipping the pages for quite a while now, completely immersed. Evan would wonder what had happened to me. Wanting to cut to the chase, I flipped to the final entries.

Theodore Madaster was indeed Noah's father. Both of their names were underlined with complicated flourishes and quite a bit of red ink. And here was Lorraine Madaster, Noah's wife. Her embellishment was not as complex as her husband's or father-in-law's, but still contained a great deal of vivid scarlet and bronze ink.

Then I saw the last entry: Elizabeth Antoinette Madaster, born September 13, 1979. The embellishment beneath her name was the most lovely, and the most complex I'd spotted by far. It was also done almost exclusively in red. The scarlet ink glowed on the page, as if it'd been electrified somehow.

The date of death had not yet been entered.

"Anna?"

I jumped, nearly dropping the book at hearing Evan's voice at the top of the Y-shaped stairs.

"I-I'm coming."

I hurriedly replaced the red velvet book on the shelf. By the time Evan peered down at me from the landing, I'd grabbed my books and was walking over to the light switch.

"I'm on my way," I told him with a little wave before I plunged the enormous room into darkness.

When I reached the landing, I was breathless.

"What kept you?" Evan asked. His voice was low and relaxed, but his eyes searched mine curiously. He wore only a pair of black pajama pants, the drawstring tightened low on his ridged abdomen. My hunger for him—ever present, but sometimes banked—leapt up in me like a flash fire. I stepped into him and pressed my mouth against the crisp hairs on his chest and the dense muscle beneath.

"Nothing as interesting as this," I assured him as his scent entered my nose.

Chapter Four

I STARTED TO SETTLE INTO THE ROUTINE OF MY NEW LIFE.

In the morning, I would pack a picnic lunch in a basket I'd located in the pantry. Evan brought it up with him to the overlook at one o'clock or so, and we'd share it, looking out on the mountains and sparkling lake. He was always interested in my work. I reveled in his praise. Again and again, I experienced that wonder at being *seen* by him, valued. Cherished.

I was so in love, it was almost an exquisite ache, so difficult to describe. Always present.

One morning, I heard a knock down the kitchen passage that led to the driveway.

"Anna? Would you mind answering it? It's the groceries," Evan called from the distance.

He was working. I hadn't discovered his office on that first day, but had since. It was a woody, book-lined room on the same level as the kitchen. There was a pair of mahogany French doors that he often left wide open to the terrace, the sunlight, and the cool lake breeze.

The office had a definite masculine aura. I'd entered it only a few times, to bring him the morning mail. So in my head, I thought of it as the Male Room. I felt a little like an interloper, crossing that threshold. It wasn't Evan's fault. He was always kind to me when I knocked, but I could tell he was distracted by his work.

The bank acquisition was moving along, according to Evan, with only expected, minor bumps in the road so far. He was video conferencing or on the phone with his colleagues almost every time I tiptoed into the room. I felt a little guilty that the daily functions of being the owner and president of a private fund were such a mystery to me, especially when he seemed so interested and knowledgeable about my painting. But he insisted it was boring work, and usually deflected my questions about it.

Increasingly, I longed for that elusive study where I was not invited. Not the *room*, of course, but the man in it, the part of himself that existed in that space with whom I couldn't quite connect.

Among the many treasures of that morning's grocery delivery were peaches, golden and ripe. We ate them with relish that afternoon during our picnic on the overlook.

"Is this what I signed up for, then?" I asked him after I'd wiped juice off my chin. "We just live here in paradise, day after day. A maid service comes on Saturday, the groceries on Thursdays... everything provided like I was a princess in a tower?"

Evan smiled as he chewed his peach and swallowed.

"Are you complaining?"

"'Course not. I'm ridiculously happy. But I do feel a little... useless." I saw his slight scowl as he bit into his peach again with straight, white teeth. "Not useless, exactly," I clarified, thinking. "More like a boat without a rudder."

"Adrift in paradise?"

"Something like that."

"You have your painting."

"I know. And it's going so well. I'm amazed."

"I told you that you'd be inspired here," he said, tossing the peach pit aside and briskly wiping his hands with a napkin. "At the rate you're going, you'll have enough for a showing by the end of the summer. I'll contact Lauren whenever you say the word."

Lauren was the gallery owner he knew in South Lake Tahoe. He'd told me that he'd arrange a meeting with her whenever I was ready. Everything I could ever need, everything I could dream of, supplied to me on a silver platter.

"You really do spoil me," I said.

"Only because I like to so much. I'm a selfish man."

I heard the husky warmth in his voice. His mouth was there when I turned my face to him. He tasted like peaches. He cupped my face with one hand, drawing me closer. Our kiss deepened. Evan came down over me on the spread blanket, his hunger seemingly as great as mine. I worked my hand between our pressing bodies, finding a button on his shirt.

He covered my busy hand with his.

"No, Anna. Not now."

"Why not?" I whispered urgently. "There's no one around—"

He didn't reply. I saw him glance in the direction of the house, his light eyes gleaming in his dark face. His expression was hard. Unreadable.

"I have an important phone call at two fifteen. I should get back," he said, sitting up and brushing a pine needle off his jeans. He tossed some silverware in the basket in preparation to leave and glanced back at me. His face gave slightly.

"I'll make it up to you tonight?"

"There's nothing to make up for," I muttered, sitting up and brushing my hair out of my face. In a quick movement, he caught a tendril. I went still, watching as he ran the strands through his fingers.

"I'm neglecting you, aren't I? You're getting bored."

"*No*," I insisted truthfully. Bored wasn't the right word to describe my restlessness, my sense of being unanchored. "I'm so happy. So lucky. I shouldn't have said anything. I was being a whiner. It was stupid of me."

His gaze flickered to my face. "Not stupid. Honest. We're very isolated here. You're feeling lonely."

"No." The only company I wanted was Evan. If I could be with him more, I'd adore the isolation of Les Jumeaux. I was being incredibly self-ish. He devoted his evenings and nights to me. He joined me for lunch on this idyllic spot most days, even when I knew how busy he was.

But still, I wanted more. I was becoming insatiable. I wanted everything, including the Evan who shut himself off in his study. Who occasionally—rarely—seemed so far away from me, even when his skin touched my own.

"I'm spoiled," I said miserably. "And not in any good way." I reached out and put my opened hand on his chest. "It's just... I love you so much."

He leaned forward and kissed me.

"You are the most unspoiled person I've ever met in my life," he said against my lips a moment later.

One morning later that week, I grew disgusted by my progress on a painting. The sunlight was too bright, saturating every surface, making the mountains seem more one-dimensional than I knew them to be, the sky a flat, uninteresting robin's egg blue. I stood and walked out farther onto the promontory, squinting down at the water. A dark shadow hung over the large boulders of granite just below me, changing their usually benign appearances into a bed of wet, upturned blades.

Although I'm not usually afraid of heights, a wave of vertigo struck me. My eyes burned from fatigue. Holding my breath, I slowly backed away from the edge.

I haven't been sleeping well. That's the problem.

The nightmares had started a few nights ago. For the past few nights, I'd only fallen asleep at dawn. But I'd still gotten up at my normal time. No wonder I was so tired. I should take a break, maybe take a little nap up here on the overlook.

Evan had given me a blanket that I kept on the back of my chair. When I painted early in the morning, it could be chilly sitting next to the lake. I'd sit there like an old woman in a trance, huddled up under the blanket, my hand poking out of my cloak, my brush moving over the canvas.

I spread the blanket on the ground and lay down. The sunlight blinded my eyes, but was kinder on the exposed skin of my legs and arms. The warmth made me drowsy. I turned my face away from the sun's brilliance, putting my forearm over my eyelids.

Soothing darkness. A warm, gentle darkness, unlike the darkness from the nightmares I'd started having.

In those dreams, I lay in bed with Evan. Not in some vague, dream-like bed. In the very bed in the luxurious suite where we slept at night. Where we made love.

It shocked me a little, that I would dream so solidly and realistically about a room that I'd known for only a few weeks. I dreamed of rooms from my childhood home in Oak Park frequently. Occasionally, I dreamed of other places charged with some residue of anxiety or longing: a hallway in high school and my locker, for which I never seemed to remember the combination; the comfortable, cluttered high school art studio where I'd first felt a sense of pride and mastery in my work; the familiar roads, yards, and long-closed businesses from my hometown.

I rarely dreamed of my college dorm, apartments, or rental rooms I'd inhabited in the past few years. They were too impermanent, too inconsequential for my psyche to take notice.

That wasn't the case with the nightmare. This was reality within dream... or dream within reality? Horrifically, I believed completely that I was awake when the nightmare occurred. I knew it was a nightmare only after the fact though, because I could move again.

During the dream, I was paralyzed, forced to helplessly watch.

I didn't want to recall the nightmare as I lay there on the overlook in the blinding sunlight, but I couldn't seem to stop the images—or the fear—from flooding my brain.

I awake with a sense of dread. My head and body are like stones. No nerves connect those inert slabs of flesh to my brain. I find, in my rising panic, that my eyes can move, however. I make out the shadowed shapes of familiar furniture in the dim room. This is our suite at Les Jumeaux, I tell myself frantically. Of course it is. It looks completely normal. I sense rather than see Evan beside me, a warmth that should have been reassuring, but isn't.

In sleep, he's so far away from me. What dreams did he envision within the locked safe of his mind? He seems so unreachable. It makes me desperate, because I instinctively know that the visitor is coming.

My panic mounts. I'm trapped in this stone-body, and she would come. Nothing could stop her.

Evan's name burns a hole in my throat. My muscles spasm as I try to work them, but I'm incapable of sound. My gaze is fixed on the door of the suite, willing it to stay shut. But I know what's coming. Fear bubbles up into my throat like acid.

Then the door is open. One second, it's closed as I watch in rising agony, searching for movement, praying I see nothing. Then it's yawning open, a black void behind it. It opens in less than a second, in total silence.

I see movement emerging from the nothingness, and my heart seizes.

Her shadow moves toward the bed, slow, but steady. It's as if she knows my heart is threatening to burst with each oncoming step, as if she's playing with me. My cell phone is charging on the bedside table. The tiny light on it is inconsequential in the everyday world, but it's more than sufficient for a nightmare's purpose. I see her outline clearly. She is narrow waisted with round hips and the hint of full breasts. No clothes. She appears to be nude. Her skin is blacker than black, and appallingly... shiny? Wet? I can't make out her face. Her shoulder-length hair hangs in defined waves and ringlets. In my panicked, stone-like state, all I can think of is Medusa. I dread looking at her, but I have no choice.

She stands over me. My mind is a prison filled with silent screaming. My senses pour into me, but I can't react. I smell dampness and rotting flesh and the nuance of a perfume, a strangely familiar one. I hear a soft, raspy intake of breath. She's preparing to speak. To me.

I don't want to hear what the nightmare ghost says.

Water spatters on my cheek... one drop, two. I realize it's coming from her mouth. It's not just water. It's her blood. Her rotting essence.

Horror and revulsion swallows me up at this point, squeezing out every last sense of identity, of self.

My eyelids fly open (even though they'd been stretched open in horror, wider than they'd ever been in my life, just a microsecond ago). I inhale in a wheeze, as if choking hands had abruptly been removed from my throat.

The room is exactly the way it had just been, in the dream. But the door is shut fast. Evan sleeps silently next to me.

We're the only two people in the room.

Mentally, I scramble to believe it.

The warm sunlight and the gentle sound of the surf on the rocks far below me diminished the power of the remembered nightmare.

I drifted off to sleep, certain I wouldn't dream up here, in my special spot.

I awakened to the feeling of warm, dry fingers caressing my cheek.

"Evan?" I mumbled. The touch didn't feel like Evan's familiar one. But who else would be touching me so intimately?

When I opened my eyes, I stared for a moment, confused and groggy. Then reality hit. I gave a startled scream and scrambled like a crab on all fours backward on the blanket.

The old woman remained kneeling, her hand still outstretched. Long, lank gray hair fluttered around her narrow shoulders. Her blue eyes appeared filmed over. I had the crazy thought that she *saw* me, but was also as blind as a bat in this bright sunlight.

"Who are you? What do you want?" I demanded.

"You're burning," she said. When I just stared at her uncomprehendingly, she pointed to her nose. "The sun is burning you. Where's your hat?"

"My *hat?*"

To my amazement, she gave an exasperated shake of her head. She'd mistaken my bewilderment for backtalk. The tension in my muscles drained out of me. Her irritation had humanized her. This was no apparition, no daytime repeat of my nightmare. She stood up from the blanket. Her clothes—a food-stained pair of light blue pants and a flowered Hawaiian shirt—hung loosely on her frail frame. The buttons on the shirt had been fastened unevenly, so that several inches on one side drooped lower than the other. I realized her shirt wasn't the only thing about her that was *off*. A distinct air of madness hung about her. Another suspicion struck me.

No one is taking care of her. And she needs taking care of.

"No one does what I ask," she muttered bitterly.

"I... *wait*," I called when she turned and started to walk away, clearly miffed. Hurt? She stumbled on a stone and veered crookedly for a few steps, straining to keep her feet under her. I got up hastily, compassion and concern spiking through me. She seemed so fragile, so *crazy*. I reached for her upper arm to steady her. But she'd already found her balance. She looked up at me with those blind-seeming eyes, and again I saw that expression of exhausted annoyance.

"You *never* wear your hat."

She shook off my hold and walked away.

I asked Evan about the strange woman when I returned to the house. I found him in his study, as usual, staring at his computer screen with a particularly fierce expression on his face that faded when I called his name.

He listened to my story with polite attention, although I imagined I could almost feel the magnetic draw of his work pulling him back to it.

"Who do you think she was?" I asked him, leaning against his desk.

His gaze roved over me. He gave a small smile. "She was right. You are sunburned, honey."

"Don't you scold me as well."

He put up his hands in a surrender gesture. "There's a woman who lives down the coast a ways. I imagine it was her."

"That's strange. I've never seen another house while I was hiking." His gaze sharpened on me, and I imagined he was about to question me about my solitary walks again. I hurried to deflect him. "You're not concerned about her coming onto the property?"

"She's harmless enough. Even when I lived here, she was batty. She has some kind of dementia, I think. Rambled on about the craziest stuff every time I've run into her. I'm surprised she's still alive."

"Someone should be looking out for her," I said, irritated on the frail woman's behalf.

"I don't think she wanders over here often. I wouldn't worry about it," he said, standing and stretching. My focus latched onto his movements, his powerful chest and outstretched arms. I felt his inevitable pull.

"I'm sorry that work has gotten even worse lately," he said, crossing one arm over his chest and pressing it into his body with the opposite hand, loosening his tight shoulder and triceps. "I think I'll have a workout. Care to join me?"

"I exercised earlier," I replied. *Alone.*

"I've been thinking about hiring someone to come out to help with some light chores around the house and being a sort of... companion for you until this damn merger is finished."

My gaze jumped to his face. I was completely taken by surprise.

"What? A *companion*? You're thinking of hiring someone to be my *friend*?"

"Of course not," he said, dropping his hands to the desk. He leaned toward me, his expression serious. Earnest. "I feel bad because work is taking up so much of my time."

"You say you feel bad about me hiking in the woods on my own, but not bad enough to come and join me."

I immediately regretted my sharpness when I saw his expression flatten.

"I'm sorry," I said. "I shouldn't have said it like that. Or maybe I should have," I said, meeting his stare. "I don't need a watchdog, Evan. And *you* don't need to feel guilty. I'm *fine*."

"I wasn't thinking of a watchdog. That's ridiculous," he replied curtly. "We could use someone to do housework while you paint. And there are other things you'd like to do, things that I haven't been able to do with you because of this merger. Like see the local sights, or go kayaking or diving, for instance? You could be enjoying yourself a lot more if—"

"If I can't do those things with you, than I'd rather wait until I can."

He exhaled slowly. My guilt amplified at his slightly annoyed, weary expression. I felt like a grumpy child.

"Don't be mad at me, Evan. I don't know what I can do to convince you that I'm completely happy. We spend every evening and night together. It's more than most couples do."

He gave a short laugh. Relief swept through me when he reached for my hand and drew me around the desk. He wrapped me in his arms and pressed his face to the top of my head.

"I'm not mad at you."

"You were, a little," I mumbled against his chest.

I looked up at the sound of his gruff laughter. I couldn't help but smile at the warmth in his usually cool gaze.

"Don't look so smug," he cautioned. "I'm not convinced that hiring someone wouldn't be a good idea."

"I'll convince you," I whispered. I went up my tiptoes and pulled his head lower, brushing my lips against his. He pulled back several inches, regarding me with a heavy-lidded stare. I held my breath, waiting...

"You *are* very convincing, Anna," he said before his mouth closed on mine.

The memory of the old woman stayed with me. I couldn't help but be concerned about her.

A few days after our first meeting, I again glimpsed her rambling between the beach boulders in the distance. I called to her from the overlook. She paused, placing her hand on the surface of a granite boulder and looked around. I shouted hello again, and waved. A brisk breeze kicked up from the lake, plastering her print skirt and mismatched sweatshirt against her body. I saw her rib cage. Her thinness and frailty were uncomfortably obvious.

I thought of bringing her into the house and making her a hearty meal. Evan probably wouldn't approve, but I suddenly didn't care. I waved again, and then made a beckoning gesture to her. She was too far away for me to really say for certain, but I thought I saw her scowl as she squinted at me.

Then she turned, slipped in the sand, corrected herself gracelessly, and scurried out of sight.

Undaunted, I made a small basket of food before going up to the overlook the next morning. It took a few days before I saw her again, and could put the lunch basket to use. As I painted, I saw a flash of white out of the corner of my eye.

I glimpsed the woman near the boathouse, walking along the dock, the white smock she wore waving in the wind. I tossed down my brush and hurried to get the basket. I rushed down the slope, luckily not falling on my face in my haste.

She'd meandered toward the tree line on the south side of the property by the time I caught up to her.

"Hello!" I called between pants.

She turned and looked at me. Abruptly, she swung around and began heading again for the forest. I'd glimpsed her face. Her expression had been hunted, which made me feel guilty.

"I've made you a lunch. I thought you might be hungry. It's only peanut butter and jelly, an apple, and a granola bar, but the bread is fresh baked," I rambled as I stared at her retreating back. She disappeared behind the cover of thick pine tree trunks and manzanita bushes, the white of her shirt slowly dissipating into invisibility. *You lost her.*

But then, as I stood there, I experienced that uncanny feeling of being observed. I had an idea she'd paused twenty or so feet into the forest and looked back at me from the shadows as I stood in the bright sunlight.

"I'll just leave it here for you," I yelled, holding up the basket for her to see and then setting it down carefully on a stone.

I slowly backed away.

The next morning when I went up to the overlook, I found the basket placed in front of the storage unit. I smiled to myself when I saw it was empty.

My offering had been accepted.

The basket wasn't entirely empty, though. A maple leaf rested at the bottom. I would have thought it had just fallen there, but then I saw the edges of the leaf had carefully been placed into the weave of the basket, in order to keep it in place. I gently removed it, and saw the leaf was perfectly shaped and proportioned.

It was her thanks, I realized.

So I started leaving her a packed basket of food every day in the same location, in front of the storage unit. Every morning when I returned to the overlook, I found the basket with a leaf carefully placed into the bottom, and all the food missing. Maple, aspen, dogwood, alder: the leaf type varied, but the similarity was that each was perfect and obviously discerningly chosen by the woman. If it hadn't been for the deliberately chosen and placed leaves, I might have suspected that a wild animal was gobbling up my offering every afternoon.

For some reason, I felt no compulsion to tell Evan about these exchanges. It was a private little affair, between myself and the old woman. I pressed each of the leaves, side by side, in a thick sketchpad I kept in the storage unit.

I had no actual glimpse of the old woman again for quite some time. But at least I was fairly certain she was getting one square a day.

One afternoon, I left the overlook earlier than I usually did and went in search of Evan.

Usually when I approached his office I could hear him talking or the quick tapping of his fingers on his computer. That afternoon, however, everything was silent except for the distant, muted sound of the waves hitting the rocks that could be heard through the opened French doors. I crept farther into the room, calling his name and glancing around for clues as to his whereabouts.

The half empty cup of coffee on his desk and the fact that his computer monitor was still lit argued for the fact that he'd recently stepped away. Either he was taking a quick break, and would be back any moment, or he'd gone to the workout facility. I knew that he exercised daily, but he varied the times depending on his work schedule. He might return in a few seconds, or not for an hour.

My gaze landed on the pair of car keys lying on the coffee table in the sitting area. These were precisely the reason I'd come.

The same nightmare had continued to haunt me for a week and a half now. I'd grown desperate for a good night's sleep, frantic enough to decide to drive into the closest nearby town, Tahoe Shores, and get an over the counter sleep medication. I'd been like a zombie on the overlook trying to paint earlier. My work suffered, all because of that horror that came to stand over me every night.

And *that* was something for which I wouldn't stand. My work was too important to me.

"Evan?" I called again, but this time, in a quieter, muted tone, almost like I was afraid he would answer, which was ridiculous. When I got no reply, I went into quick action. I found a piece of paper and pen, scrawled a note, and left it on his computer keyboard, then snatched the car keys and rushed toward the door.

I wouldn't let myself think about why I was hurrying.

Ten minutes later, the answer blared in my brain as I maneuvered the car on the twisting mountain road, my hands aching from my vise-like grip on the steering wheel. Evan wouldn't have wanted me to drive this road until I'd gone out a few times with him in the passenger seat. In my head, his imagined response to my request to drive into town had sounded overprotective and cautious. That's why I'd been so keen to avoid it.

Now that I was here, terrified to let my foot leave the brake, a parade of cars and irritated drivers piling up behind me, Evan's caution didn't seem so unreasonable.

The nine or ten miles into town took me an eternity.

I'd just started to get into the groove of taking the tight mountain curves (although I'm sure the pissed-off drivers behind me disagreed) when I finally pulled into Tahoe Shores. I looked around, relieved for a straight stretch of road, but also curious.

This is where Evan had grown up.

The little town struck me as too sleepy and rustic to seem pretentious. But it was clearly affluent, nonetheless, with its sophisticated restaurants and boutique stores that catered both to ski and beach enthusiasts alongside Harrows, a mom and pop grocery store. Looking to my left and down the mountain, I could see the roofs of sprawling homes and the sapphire lake in the distance. Having gone a mile on what appeared to be the town "strip" and not seen a pharmacy, I backtracked to Harrows Grocery and parked the car in the busy lot.

The teenage bagger at the checkout was quick and graceful with his hands, dark-haired, and sporting an amazing tan. When I asked about directions to the pharmacy, he gave me a quick once-over that somehow wasn't offensive. Maybe it was because of his smile. I thought of a teenage Evan, so fresh, charismatic, and beautiful growing up in this idyllic town, his future unquestioned and golden. For some reason, a pain went through me. I guess it was that familiar longing, that wish... that *hunger* to know my husband better than I did.

"You're at the right place," the kid said, waving toward the back of the store and giving me a quick wink. "The *only* place. Mr. Harrow is also the town pharmacist."

I'd never had a problem sleeping, so I wasn't sure which sleep aids were the best. I waited for the gray-haired pharmacist—Mr. Harrow, presumably—to finish consulting with a customer, and then approached the counter to get his advice.

"Just a minute," he muttered distractedly, writing something in a log in a long, sloppy scrawl. He tossed down his pen, smoothed his pharmacist smock over a protruding belly, and glanced up at me. My first impression after observing him with the former customer had been that he was amiable and easy-going, even a little haphazard, given the stereotypical idea of the meticulous pharmacist. But from beneath shaggy eyebrows, his gaze was piercing and intelligent.

"I've been having some trouble sleeping, and I was wondering if you could recommend an over the counter sleep medication?"

He took a moment to reply. I shifted on my feet awkwardly as he stared at me. Were over the counter sleep medications suspicious somehow? Were they like those allergy medicines that had to be regulated because drug dealers used them to make methamphetamine?

"Vacationing here, are you?" he asked slowly, his gaze moving over my face.

"No—"

"But you don't live here? I've never seen you around."

"Not *here* actually, not in Tahoe Shores. I've recently moved here from San Francisco, after getting married. We live in a place down the shore a bit... "

I realized I was rambling, giving away more information than was warranted because I had some stupid idea that asking about over the counter sleep aides verged on criminal behavior.

"*Where* exactly do you live?"

I opened my mouth, about to automatically supply an answer, when I suddenly caught myself. Irritation swept through me. I didn't owe him any explanations. Even if the pharmacist was suspicious of me for some unknown reason, he should just get to the point. I tapped my hand once on the counter, straightened, and met his startled stare squarely.

"Is there a problem?" I asked.

I was a little confused at his manner, but also increasingly curious. Maybe this was typical behavior in a small town, to feel out strangers a little, chitchat before getting down to business?

"No, of course not," the man said gruffly, looking a little abashed now that I'd called him out. He gave me the name of a few medicines and pointed out where they could be found on the shelf. I felt his stare on my back as I walked away.

I left the store with the sleep aid. But I felt like I'd failed in my first small-town interaction.

By the time I returned to Les Jumeaux, late afternoon shadows hung thick on the narrow entry drive. When I reached the clearing at the back of the house, my gaze immediately landed on the stationary figure of a tall man on the front porch. He leapt into action, stalking down the steps and coming toward me.

I braked the car, staring all the while at Evan's tense, drawn face. His clothing seemed matched to his mood—black athletic pants, black running shoes, and a dark gray T-shirt that highlighted his muscular torso and powerful arms. If he'd been in the workout facility when I'd left, he hadn't paused to shower yet. There was a scruff of whiskers on his upper lip and jaw. He watched me steadily from beneath a lowered brow. He looked more than a little intimidating as he approached.

I lowered the window when he reached the back of the car, listening to the sound of gravel crunching beneath his shoes and the drum of my heartbeat.

"Where have you been?" he demanded, looking at me from what still seemed like a huge height despite his bent-over position. Both of his hands gripped the car door, like he thought I was going to try and get away from him.

"I ran into town to get a sleep medication. I tried to find you, but when I couldn't, I just left the note—"

"Damn it, Anna, do you have any idea how much I've been worrying?" he interrupted, gray eyes flashing angrily.

Despite feeling bad about upsetting him, annoyance bubbled up in me.

"I'm a grown woman, Evan. I've been able to drive a car for years now. It was a quick trip into town, not a journey up Mt. Everest."

"I had no idea you could be so impulsive."

"I had no idea *you* could be so controlling."

His mouth flattened. *If looks could kill.* I cringed internally, even as I held his furious stare without flinching. So *here* was the temper I'd hypothesized about so many times while studying his features like an artist absorbs a masterpiece.

"You're not used to driving these roads yet. Are you going to sit there and try to convince me it was a cakewalk for you?"

"I'm not trying to convince you of anything. It wasn't easy, but I made it there and back safely."

"With no incident," he stated flatly rather than asked, but his gaze was sharp. Searching.

"As you can see, I'm fine."

He straightened and took a step back. He flexed his hands at his sides, as though working the tension out of them.

"All you had to do was ask me. I would have gotten anything you needed immediately. You haven't said a word about having trouble sleeping." His tone had gone neutral. I'd witnessed the heat of his temper and now observed his tight control over it as well.

Regret trickled through the cracks of my irritation. It was true that I'd hidden my insomnia from him. Mostly because I didn't want to reveal the cause of it. I didn't want to mention the nightmare woman to him, or admit my primitive fear of her hitching breath, or dripping mouth... of what she might tell me.

If I let her.

"I didn't want to bother you about it. It's not a big deal. It's probably got to do with all the stress and excitement of our wedding and the move here. I haven't settled in yet, completely. I got an over the counter sleep aid. Once I get a few nights of decent sleep, I'll get back into a regular rhythm."

There was a long pause, in which I sensed him gathering the frayed ends of his restraint and tucking them back into place.

"I'd appreciate it if you'd let me drive you next time, or at the very least, let me go with you until you get more familiar with the road," he said in a careful, strained tone. "You have no idea how many tourists crash on the roads around here. You've seen the drop-offs. I assume you can imagine what could potentially happen if you made even a minor driving error. It's all I've been thinking about since I saw your note."

If I'd felt regret before, I experienced full-fledged guilt now. Why *had* I been so impetuous? I'd purposefully avoided him. I hadn't wanted him to know I was taking the trip alone, because I hadn't wanted him to talk me out of it. And he'd had good reason to be cautious. The road *had* been alarming the first time out, even if I did think I would grow used to it, eventually.

"Evan—"

"I'll see you inside," he said gruffly.

And suddenly the only view I had of him was his back.

Chapter Five

I THOUGHT OF LOOKING FOR HIM WHEN I GOT IN THE HOUSE, BUT figured maybe it was best for both of us to cool off first. I had planned to paint when I returned, but a wave of exhaustion hit me as I walked up the grand staircase. Maybe it was due to my insomnia, or maybe it was the adrenaline fading in my blood after the nerve-wracking drive and that spat with Evan.

I went to our room, drew the heavy curtains, and lay down. As I drifted off to sleep, the vision of Evan's face popped into my mind's eye. It struck me that he'd been angry, yes... but his concern had been almost wild.

He wasn't worried about me. He was worked up because of her.
Elizabeth.

It was a nasty hissing whisper in a distant corner of my mind. I choked it off, thinking about my painting with a furious focus, until sleep finally took me.

I awoke to the sensation of Evan's whiskered jaw lightly scraping my temple and his lips moving next to my ear. I turned. His mouth grazed mine. I opened heavy eyelids. The room had grown dim. Evan was an impenetrable shadow hovering over me, his touch and warm breath making my nerves flicker with pleasure.

"Dinner will be ready soon. I thought if you slept too much longer, you definitely wouldn't be able to sleep tonight."

"I'm glad you woke me up," I whispered, reaching to cup his shoulder.

He nuzzled me with his nose. Our mouths met again, clinging.

"Why didn't you tell me you were having trouble sleeping?" he asked against my lips, his voice a low, delicious rumble in the hushed, heavily shadowed room.

"I didn't want you to worry."

"I do worry about you. It comes with the territory," he said, nipping softly at my lips. I glided my hand along his back.

"God, you feel good," I said.

He kissed my neck. "You *smell* so good. Always. So sweet. Fresh."

"Evan, did Elizabeth die in a car accident?"

His tingling kisses ceased.

I bit my lower lip in inevitable regret when he slowly lifted his head. I strained to see his features in the dim light. All I made out was the gleam of his eyes.

"Is that why you think I'm concerned about your driving alone?"

"You seemed really worried. Unusually so. I thought maybe I'd struck a nerve because of something that had happened earlier... something with *her.*"

He straightened into a sitting position. I resisted a wild urge to take it all back... to pull him back down to me.

"Elizabeth drowned."

I started slightly at the harshness of the two words in the silent room. Shivers swept down my arms, causing my skin to roughen.

"How horrible," I whispered.

"Yes. It was," he said, still not facing me. "I thought maybe you'd read about it. You told me back in San Francisco that you'd Googled her name—"

"There was very little information on her."

"Her father pays a company to remove or bury most Internet search references to her... and himself, of course," he added, bitterness entering his tone. I came up on my elbow and stroked his arm and shoulder.

"Did she drown near the house?" I asked hesitantly. My imagination leapt to the idea of her drowning in that safe, protected little beach enclosure, and I just couldn't. Besides, wouldn't Evan be paranoid about me swimming there alone, if that were the case?

He exhaled, and I imagined I felt his emotion. I sensed dread in every cell of his being.

"No. It was a boating accident." He turned, resting his chin on his shoulder so that I could make out his profile in the evening light radiating from behind the curtains.

"I honestly wasn't thinking about Elizabeth when I worried about you this afternoon. I was thinking about you, Anna. Why don't you believe me?"

The bleakness of his question startled me. I sat up and came behind him. I wrapped my arms around his waist.

"I do believe you," I said, my cheek pressed against his back. "I'm sorry I ran off without telling you this afternoon. But I kept myself safe, Evan. Have a little faith in me."

He ran his hands along my forearms. "I have a lot of faith in you. It's the rest of the world about which I have doubts." He squeezed the back of my hands gently. "I'm sorry for snapping at you earlier. My imagination got the best of me, waiting for you to come back."

I kissed his spine through his shirt, and then nuzzled him with my nose. A feeling of sharp longing rose in me.

"We're both sorry," I whispered.

He patted the back of my hand. "Ready for dinner?"

I swallowed back that strange surge of emotion and swung my feet off the bed.

"Let's go. I'm starving," I said, reaching for his hand.

I took the medication that night and spent a blessedly dreamless night. I was a little groggy in the morning, but my lethargy disappeared in an instant when I entered the sunlit kitchen only to find Evan there, dressed in shorts, a T-shirt, and hiking boots. He was in the process of placing a chilled bottle of chardonnay in a portable wine cooler.

"What are you doing?" I asked him in amazement as he slid the cooler into a black backpack that already had a baguette sticking partially out of it.

"I'm taking the day off. I thought we'd go hiking to this little secluded beach down the way, have a picnic, swim... "

He faded off, lifting his eyebrows expectantly. I realized he was waiting to see what I thought of his plan.

"It sounds fantastic."

He grinned at my enthusiasm and resumed packing the bag. "Good. We should have done it sooner. *I* should have," he added under his breath.

It was a gorgeous sunny day with a light, cool wind... ideal conditions for hiking. Evan led me to a trailhead I hadn't yet located. It required a fairly strenuous hike uphill to a ridge.

When we got to the top, I gasped in pleasure between pants for air. We admired the scenery from our view at the top of the world.

I felt Evan's gaze on me. "I stole a good painting day from you, I think," he said.

I reached for his hand. "You gifted me with a day with you, which is something far better."

We hiked for another hour and a half or so, passing through dense woods, and then a rough terrain of rocks, brush, and boulders. I'd never thought of myself as being afraid of heights, but there were a few drop-offs that I carefully avoided even looking at, because they made me dizzy.

At one point, I spotted something high up on a cliff of limestone boulders. I started to scale them.

"Anna?" Evan called out sharply.

But I was determined, and didn't stop. He followed me up to a small cave inset into the rocks.

"Anna, there might be bats or some other animal inside," he warned when I ducked and entered the dark space. I looked around, delighted with my find, seeing no scary animals, only smooth, pale stone. Even the air was fresh instead of musty. The cave grew darker. I knew Evan had followed me in and was blocking the light. I put my hand back, and he took it.

He was far too tall for the cramped space, so at my urging, we sat side by side. We stared out at the sparkling, color-soaked view just feet away from where we sat in the darkness. The scene took on an extra vitality viewing it from the cave.

I laughed, strangely delighted by the moment. I mimed daintily drinking from a teacup and saucer. I really did feel like the queen of a kingdom up in that hidden place, with him by my side. Evan's rich laughter reverberated against the stone walls. He cupped my jaw with one hand.

His kiss at that moment struck me as exquisite: secret and sweet. Sacred.

By the time we reached the private, secluded sand beach and azure water, we were hot and dusty, and more than ready for a swim. We stripped to our skin and plunged into the crisp, cold water, me stumbling and squealing at the feeling of the small stones mixed in with the rough sand on my bare feet. I wasn't used to it. By contrast, the sand at the calm little beach at Les Jumeaux was smooth as silk.

Evan finally pulled me down into the water, more than likely tired of my yelps. I splashed enough to scare away all fish within a mile radius. I surfaced, laughing and spitting water out of my mouth, reaching for him blindly. When I pried open my eyelids, I saw that he was laughing, too, the image of his unguarded expression, light-infused gray-golden eyes, and wide smile slicing straight into me.

Later, he led me to the beach and spread a blanket. I'll never forget how he looked when he laid down next to me, and his gaze traveled over my naked body. His eyes narrowed on my breasts as he touched me with warm fingertips.

"You're different," he murmured. I heard the awe in his tone, and was confused and enthralled at once.

"How do you mean I'm different? I'm getting a good tan, that's all."

I sank my fingers into his thick, wet hair. He lifted his hand from my breast and grasped my wrist. Deliberately, he placed my arm on the blanket next to me. I realized I'd been partially blocking his vision of me.

Again, his stare scored me. He cupped a breast and leaned down to run his lips over a nipple. I shivered uncontrollably, clamping my thighs together.

"Evan?" I asked, unsure of what was unfolding at that moment, but fully in the grip of it nevertheless.

"I've never seen you in full sunlight. You're *so* beautiful, Anna," he said, sounding preoccupied as he kissed and then licked lightly at my beading nipple. Pleasure flickered inside me, and then swelled like a wave.

It was then that I realized—however fleetingly—that until that moment, he'd only made love to me in shadows.

Or pitch-blackness.

After we made love, we lay entwined, my head on his chest and his arms wrapped loosely around me while he idly stroked my shoulder. The soughing sound of the light surf and Evan's caressing fingers held me in a sublime trance. The light wind felt delicious skimming along my perspiration-damp skin.

"Would you consider going off the pill?"

I blinked, my awareness going from a blissful stupor to sharp disbelief in a fraction of a second. I lifted my head to examine his face. He merely stared back at me with that Evan-like calm that sometimes drove me crazy.

"You want to have a baby?" I asked shrilly. "*Now*?"

A smile broke over his face. Despite my sudden anxiety, I found myself smiling, too. Laughing, in fact. His stroking fingers turned into a deep massage of my shoulder and back muscles, as though he wanted to soothe me.

"I wasn't saying I wanted to *now*. I was just bringing up the topic. Do you ever think about it?"

"Having a baby with you?"

Upon hearing my own words, all amusement vanished.

Of *course* I'd thought about it. I was insanely in love with him. The very thought of sharing something so beautiful, so deeply intimate with him, took my breath away. It seemed to me like it would be a revelation, and a deepening of the mystery all at once.

"I've thought about it, but not in any..." I faltered for the right words.

"Don't worry about it, Anna," he said, a smile ghosting his lips. "I didn't bring it up to make you anxious."

"I know," I rushed to say, concerned he'd think I thought the idea reprehensible. "I love you, Evan. I want to have a family with you. Of course I do. I just didn't think that you were ready—or even *thinking*—about that yet."

He looked up at the blue sky, the ambient light turning his eyes into gleaming crescents of silver. "I think about it," he murmured thoughtfully. "It's like a dream, isn't it?" He ran his fingertip up my spine, and I trembled against him. "I suppose it's hard not to speculate about something so amazing, given the way things are between us."

I just stared at him for several seconds, a sense of wonder tickling at my consciousness.

"You mean that it's so good between us, so *big*, that it's hard not to imagine the outcome? The purpose of it all?" I asked in a small, hushed voice.

He met my stare. His stroking hand stilled. "There *is* a purpose, I think. And you're right. It's a bigger one than I ever imagined when I first saw your face looking back at me from that computer screen. Come here," he demanded gruffly. He put his hands on my upper arms and slid me up his naked body.

His mouth covered mine, and the hot need flooded through me again, burning away all the questions.

This thing between us wasn't rational. It blazed a trail. All we could do was follow it.

The hike back home seemed to go quicker, maybe because I was so relaxed and sublimely happy. We hadn't made any plans for having a baby, but his mere mention of the topic told me so much. It had added an extra luster to the future.

On the way back, Evan told me that he was thinking of having a construction crew come in as soon as he could schedule it in order to do a demolition on the viewing room.

"I meant to have it done before we arrived, but better late than never. Do you think the crew being here will interfere with your painting?"

"No," I assured him emphatically. I was as eager as anyone to have someone rip apart that awful room. Its presence in the house bothered me more than I liked to admit, even to myself. "It'll be more annoying for you in your office than it will be for me. I won't even be able to hear them up on the overlook."

As we entered the kitchen, I noticed that Evan was checking messages on his cell phone.

"You didn't check that thing the entire time we were gone," I said, smiling at the realization.

He glanced up, his gaze piercing me. He slipped the phone into his back pocket with a smooth movement and reached out for my wrist.

"I'm sorry, Anna."

I started in surprise at his intensity. "Sorry for what?"

"Sorry that the idea of me giving you my undivided attention for a few hours could make you smile like that. It's something you deserve every day."

"Don't be ridiculous," I said, trying to sound lighthearted even though my throat had gone tight at what I read in his eyes. "Neither one of us would ever get anything done if we went and did what we did today every day of the week."

"Maybe not every day. But you and I will make time to go out like that a few days a week. Maybe we'll go to South Lake on Friday and have lunch, then go and talk to Lauren at the gallery? Or we could spend a day in Carson City. Or go diving? I should order some paddleboards, and we could take those out—"

I went up on my toes and kissed his mouth. "Yes," I whispered. "To one of those things or all of them. But we don't have to do anything fancy. I'd be just as happy if you spent an hour with me once in a while out at our little beach here at Les Jumeaux."

He kissed my cheek, his expression somber. "I realize now it was unfair of me. To keep you so isolated here. You're young," he murmured distractedly, stroking my cheek with his thumb. "Full of life. You're used to socializing. You need more than just an introverted workaholic in your life."

"Wrong," I stated firmly, kissing him again. I pulled on several strands of his thick hair. "I *only* need *this* introverted workaholic in my life."

A few days later, I was up on the overlook in the midst of a two-hour marathon of concentrated painting. Whether it was because I'd slept for the past few nights without any nightmares, or because Evan and I had grown especially close following our fight about me taking the car, my mood and my focus had been exceptionally good lately.

I blinked, my trance breaking in mid-stroke on the canvas. I glanced around, unsure of what had interrupted my focus. I was sure there had been no sound. Three men had arrived yesterday to begin to demo the viewing room. I'd been right in thinking the construction noise wouldn't reach me here, though. No sounds of hammering or electrical saws penetrated the granite vault of Les Jumeaux and the stone cliffs.

A light breeze rustled the pines. Tranquility reigned absolute.

A tingling on my neck made me look over my shoulder and look at the turret of the South Twin. The hair on my arms stood on end. Someone sat at the tower window. I couldn't make out any specific features, except to say I would have guessed it was man. He stared directly at me. I'm not sure how I could testify to that with so much certainty, except for the goose bumps on my neck and arms.

That, and the queasy feeling of having my privacy violated.

Whether it was an intruder, a guest, or Noah Madaster himself, the South Twin was definitely occupied.

I'd have to tell Evan.

I had the impression of movement behind the staring man, and suddenly, his image receded. He didn't stand and walk away. One moment, he was there, and the next, he faded into grayness.

Oh no. Not another *ghost.*

I stood there holding my paintbrush, my pulse leaping at my throat. What the hell had I just seen?

The experience had been so eerie, I almost jumped out of my own skin at the sound of footsteps approaching the overlook.

Yesterday, I had seen the old crazy woman again. She'd been wandering on the boulders to the south of Les Jumeaux. As I stood there on the overlook, listening to the approaching footsteps, I briefly wondered if it might be her again. But the tread was too heavy and purposeful.

"Evan?" I called out shakily.

But it wasn't Evan who broke the tree line. It was a tall man with blondish brown hair wearing dress pants and a button-down shirt, the buttons at his throat unfastened. He paused several feet away and looked at me, his mouth hanging open, clearly as surprised to see me as I was him.

He had a nice face. Not Evan-quality handsome, but few faces were, in my undoubtedly prejudiced opinion. It was glazed with a light sheen of sweat, as if he'd found the climb to the outlook strenuous.

"So sorry to disturb you," he said quickly, walking toward me. "I'm Dr. Ryder... Wes Ryder," he added, stretching out his hand. "I'm old friends with Evan. I've known him since grade school in Tahoe Shores. He said I'd find you up here."

Why, if he'd been expecting me, had he appeared so shocked to see me? But then I started to suspect there was a perpetual look of surprise to Wes Ryder's expression, as if he couldn't entirely comprehend the situations in which he found himself.

"Hello. I'm Anna," I said, switching my paintbrush into my other hand so that I could shake with him. "So you've known Evan since he was young?"

"Since first grade," he said amiably, shoving both his hands in his pockets. "I've only just learned he was back at Les Jumeaux. With a new bride." He studied me through narrowed eyelids.

"That's me. I'm glad to meet you. I'm dying to hear more about what Evan was like as a boy."

"Best in class, best at sports... best with the ladies."

I looked away, made a little uncomfortable by his intense scrutiny.

"Sorry. I'd heard you were beautiful, but reality pales," he said in a conciliatory manner.

"Thank you," I said, moving away to my worktable. I pretended to busy myself with blotting excess paint off my brushes with a newspaper. I've never been comfortable with casual flattery. It always flusters me, striking me as too intimate coming from a stranger. Invasive, somehow.

"Is Evan coming up here, as well?" I asked.

"He's busy with something in his office, so I said I'd come up and get acquainted. You painted that?"

I turned and saw him staring at my work in progress. "I did," I said briskly.

"Beautiful *and* talented," he said after a pause. "Evan always did have all the luck."

I glanced back at him and our gazes briefly met. There had been a hint of longing in his tone—or had it been envy—only partially disguised by his charming, insouciant smile. I had a thought that he'd been referencing Elizabeth. I realized I had an opportunity here, having access to a person who had a long history with Evan... all while Evan himself was absent.

"I suppose you're referring to Elizabeth," I said with fake casualness as I turned toward him again. "Was she very beautiful?"

"You couldn't take your eyes off her," he said gruffly.

"Did she go to school with Evan and you?" I asked, taking several steps toward him.

"She came to Tahoe Shores when she was fifteen. But she wasn't in the same grade as Evan and me. Not in the same universe, you might say." His smile widened when he saw my questioning look. "She was two grades ahead of us."

"Was she? I hadn't realized she was older than Evan. Not by much, of course. I get what you mean. People two grades ahead of you when you're that age seem like they're gods."

"That's not the only reason Elizabeth Madaster seemed like a goddess. She floated while everyone else crawled. She always did seem like a creature from another realm." He smiled wryly. "An angel, maybe."

"Wow," I said with a nervous laugh. "You're going to make me downright insecure."

"You have nothing to be insecure about," he replied quietly.

I cleared my throat in the awkward pause that followed.

"What type of medicine do you practice?" I asked.

"Internal medicine."

"Is your office in Tahoe Shores?"

"Yep," he replied, rocking back on his heels, hands again jammed deep in his pockets. "Although I have patients who come from all over the area. But basically, I'm just your small-town doc who never wandered far from the place he grew up."

"You're lucky. Tahoe Shores is a lovely town, and who can complain about this?" I said, waving out at the incandescent lake and pine covered mountains. He merely shrugged. I had the impression that Dr. Wes Ryder himself might complain occasionally about the life he'd chosen.

"How long have you two been here? At Les Jumeaux?" he asked.

"Evan didn't tell you?"

He shook his head. "I only just learned he'd returned when he called me yesterday."

"It's been a few weeks."

"And what do you think of your new home?"

I looked around me. "It's just your basic heaven." I stated the obvious with a smile.

Wes nodded, staring out at the lake thoughtfully. "Evan says you grew up in the Midwest?"

"Oak Park. It's a Chicago suburb. But I went to art school in San Francisco."

83

"And that's where you met Evan. It's remarkable, really."

"Remarkable?" I laughed.

His teeth showed when he smiled. "That he was able to find love again. It's good to have him back. It's been seven years since he's been to Les Jumeaux. Seven years since I've last seen him."

Seven years since Elizabeth died, a voice in my head added.

"Evan never came back and visited, even for a few days?" I wondered.

Wes shook his head. "His parents moved back east a good ten or eleven years ago, so they weren't here for him to visit."

"And I suppose it was hard for him to be here at first, because of Elizabeth," I said slowly.

"In more ways than one."

I raised my eyebrows. "What do you mean?"

"Well, he *couldn't* be here until now. The courts only gave him legal access to Les Jumeaux earlier this year."

"I'm not sure what you mean. Why only this year?"

Wes hesitated for a moment, studying my face.

"Elizabeth's father hired a team of crack lawyers to prevent Evan's inheritance of the property. Evan hired better ones, apparently. But more to my point, Evan *couldn't* inherit until Elizabeth was officially declared as deceased. That only happened this year."

"I'm sorry?" I asked, squinting to bring him into better focus.

"The law states that a person can only be declared dead after they've gone missing for seven years."

"Do you mean to say—"

"Elizabeth Madaster's body has never been found. "

Chapter Six

I JUST STARED AT WES RYDER FOR A FULL FIVE SECONDS, TRYING TO compute what the news had meant to Evan, trying to understand what his suffering under those circumstances would have been. I came up against a great, black wall that my imagination couldn't penetrate. What would it be like, to never see your spouse again, to never have the closure of a memorial or a burial...

To never to have said goodbye?

"I'm sorry. I guess that Evan hadn't told you that yet?" Wes said.

I suddenly felt very warm. I untied the paint smock I was wearing, all the while willing myself to steady after being knocked off balance.

"No. He'd told me about her drowning in a boating accident, but I hadn't realized they'd never found her body," I said, pulling the smock off my arms and tossing it on the table. I looked out at the brilliant sapphire waters. The alpine lake had always struck me as sublime. But suddenly I sensed its unfeeling vastness, its uncompromising, frigid depths.

"She disappeared here, didn't she?" I asked, already knowing the answer.

"Yes. She was a very experienced sailor. She had a favorite boat—a restored wooden yacht her father had bought her. It was small, but top of the line. She called it *Survivor*," he said, his smile faltering slightly. I understood why. The name seemed ironic and sad, given the circumstances.

"Two days after she went missing, the boat was found miles from Les Jumeaux, foundering against some rocks near South Lake. There was only minimal damage to the boat. They searched for her body for weeks afterward, but it was never found. The search was eventually called off."

"Why did they say it was an accident?" *Couldn't someone have hurt her?* Something told me to keep that question to myself.

"Elizabeth was on the boat alone."

"How did they know she was alone?"

Wes glanced over his shoulder at the South Twin.

"Elizabeth's father is a control freak," he said after a pause in a quiet, confidential tone. "Back then, he had security cameras installed all over Les Jumeaux. After Elizabeth went missing, he gave the police full access to surveillance video. They saw Elizabeth leaving the boathouse that evening by herself. They studied video for the time period before she left, as well. They could trace the movements and activity on the boat for months before that night. There's no doubt that she was alone when she left. It wasn't unusual. She often went out on her own. She was fiercely independent.

"Anyway, after they found the boat, they searched for any sign of anyone being on board with her that evening, any signs of violence or anything irregular, and found none. Boating accidents happen. People hit their heads and fall in. There was alcohol on board, and sleep medication. Sedatives. She might have been intoxicated when it all happened. I suppose we'll never know. If she was only partially conscious or unconscious when she went in, well. . . "

He winced.

"Lake Tahoe is one of the deepest freshwater lakes in the world. They say you can stand up the Empire State Building in it, and never see the top of it. Many a body has been lost in that lake," he said.

Another shiver wracked him. He wrapped his arms around his waist. I realized he looked pale, as though discussing Elizabeth's death had made him physically ill.

"Are you all right?" I asked, concerned.

Wes blinked and attempted a smile. "Of course."

"You were close to her, too. Weren't you?"

"Close? No, I wouldn't say that. When we were younger, maybe. But Elizabeth made an impression on everyone. Her death hit a lot of people very hard." He glanced back toward Les Jumeaux. He seemed to hesitate.

"I suppose Evan won't appreciate me coming up here and gossiping like this."

"You weren't gossiping. I appreciate you talking to me. It's hard, speaking about these things with Evan. I don't want to... "

"Poke at his wounds?" Wes asked quietly.

I just nodded, thankful for his understanding.

"Well, I suppose we should get back?" he asked after an awkward pause. "Evan should be finished interviewing Valeria by now."

"Valeria?" I asked, completely confused as to why Evan would be interviewing a woman.

He grimaced slightly and again shoved his hands in his pockets, looking like a sheepish tween.

"Evan's going to kill me," he mumbled under his breath.

"Why?"

He shrugged and started to walk toward the path, but I lunged forward and caught his upper arm. He turned back.

"Wes? What's going on? Just tell me," I insisted.

He glanced at my face, seemed to sense my determination on the subject, and sighed.

"You're going to really like her, Anna. Valeria, I mean. When Evan described what he needed here at the house, I immediately thought of her."

"Why does it matter whether I like a complete stranger or not? And why is Evan interviewing her? What's she supposed to *do*?"

"He wanted someone to help do some light chores around the house, that's all. Run errands occasionally... "

"*And.*"

"He said you needed another soul around the house." He noticed my ominous expression. "I got the impression Evan is concerned about you being so isolated here. Valeria is close to your age, and she likes a lot of the same activities you do. She loves to hike and board and swim, and she's an expert scuba diver... teaches a class at the local community college—"

He broke off when I moved past him and stalked toward the path.

"Anna, wait. Evan is doing it only because he's concerned."

"He's only doing it because he's stubborn," I corrected, plunging down the slope.

You're an idiot, Anna.

And here I'd been thinking we'd soared past that spat we'd had, and moved on to some higher understanding in regard to our marriage.

I flung open the male room door without knocking.

"I *don't* want a companion, Evan. I'm a grown woman living in the twenty-first century, not some helpless female in a Jane Austen novel."

Evan sat behind his desk. His expression didn't shift at my outburst. The woman who sat in front of his desk twisted around in her chair, however, her eyes sprung wide.

"Ah, here she is now. Valeria Caro, I'd like you to meet my wife, Anna. She's not usually this loud, but there's always the potential for it, I'm learning," he said. He looked grave as he followed my progress into the room, but I saw the glint of humor in his eyes.

"Don't you dare laugh about this. How could you do this behind my back?"

Valeria stood from her chair and faced me. My anger fractured a little when I took in how disconcerted she was at my dramatic entrance. She was short, with long dark hair, smooth, golden brown skin, and small, delicately wrought features. She wore jeans and a short-sleeved tunic. I had the quick thought that Wes had been right when he'd mentioned the outdoor leisure activities she enjoyed. She had a great figure and the appearance of a woman comfortable in her own skin... a natural athlete.

At the moment, however, she appeared confused and unsure. I exhaled heavily.

"I'm sorry for bursting in like this, Valeria," I apologized, stepping forward to shake her hand. I threw Evan a dark look. "But I've told Evan I don't need him to pay someone to be my friend."

"Your *friend*?" Valeria repeated, laughing nervously. "We hadn't discussed that part of the job yet."

I stood there for a few seconds soaking in that information, my mouth hanging open.

"I was just explaining to Valeria that we need someone to do some cleaning, some light gardening on the terrace, laundry, errands, meal prep. Valeria takes classes at the local college on Tuesdays and Fridays, but she's available to come out in the afternoons the rest of the days of the week," Evan said, his tone light and conversational. *Reasonable.* His response stood in sharp contrast to my rude interruption.

He hadn't even mentioned anything to Valeria about being my companion. Maybe he'd changed his mind on that angle, after all.

I shifted on my feet. Now that some of my self-righteous fury was draining out of me, I was becoming more aware of my surroundings. I could hear the sound of pounding hammers and the buzz of a saw in the distance. The construction crew was hard at work, demolishing the viewing room.

My defiance hadn't entirely left me, though.

"I can do those things," I told Evan firmly. "Haven't we managed fine so far?"

"We've done okay, yes. But this is an enormous house, Anna. With extensive grounds. To be honest, I'm used to having far more than a cleaning lady coming in one time a week to help keep it all up. I have my work, and you have yours. This will free us up a little to not only do it, but to do other things as well."

I noticed the sensual gleam in his eyes, and knew he was referring to the idyllic day spent together yesterday. It was unfair on his part, alluding to it, no matter how subtly. He knew I'd be partial to that line of argument. He sounded so reasonable that I felt hysterical by contrast. For a strained few seconds, we just stared at each other.

"Excuse me. But does this mean the job isn't available after all?"

Evan and I blinked at the small voice. We turned our attention to Valeria. Her awkward uncertainty went through me like a lance. I suddenly saw myself through her eyes. She *really* must think she'd landed herself in the midst of a very unpleasant domestic situation.

"Of course it's still available," Evan said.

Valeria looked relieved. "Oh, good. Because I really need the work."

I cursed under my breath, feeling like an absolute bitch.

"I'm sorry, Valeria. Really. I'm not usually so rude. I misunderstood Evan's intent." I glanced at him. "But I still don't appreciate you doing this without telling me about it," I told him quietly. He just nodded once, and I knew he'd gotten my message.

"I see everyone's met." We all turned to see Wes enter the room. He looked disheveled, slightly sweaty, and out of breath. With a sinking feeling, I realized I owed him an apology as well, storming off and leaving him up there on the overlook.

"I'm sorry for running off like that," I said as he approached, sounding like a broken record of an apology. "I misunderstood when you told me about Valeria and the interview."

"I assumed there was *some* kind of mix-up," Wes said, his light brown eyes wide and sincere. There was a pregnant pause.

Evan gave a bark of laughter. I turned to give him a repressive look for laughing at such a tense moment, but noticed the hint of a smile on Valeria's lips as well. Embarrassment over my behavior swept through me. I must have looked ridiculous, exploding into the room like my head was on fire. Laughter burst out of my throat. Valeria gave me a wary glance, but then she started to chuckle, too. Wes appeared perplexed at our strange behavior, but after a few seconds, he grinned. He reached for Valeria and patted her back. Her long hair covered his hand, but I thought I saw him stroke her warmly.

Familiarly.

"So... difficult interview, Valeria?" Wes asked her cheerfully.

"Well..."

"She aced it," I interrupted, stifling my laughter. "Didn't she?" I asked Evan.

"Without a doubt. I already called all your references before you came, Valeria. According to them, you're hardworking and highly trustworthy. I'd be happy to offer you the job... if you're still interested?"

"I am," she said, glancing sideways at me. I rolled my eyes, and she laughed. She really did seem like a nice person.

"Then the job is yours," Evan said.

"Can I show you around the house and grounds?" I asked her, eager to give her a better impression of myself.

"I'd like that."

"That'll give Evan and me more time to catch up," Wes said amiably.

I wondered if Wes would confess to Evan what he'd told me up at the lookout about Elizabeth.

Valeria and I toured the house and the stone paths around the grounds. I found her to be warm and friendly. She was two years older than me, and lived in Tahoe Shores with three younger siblings, an older brother, and her grandmother, who was sickly.

Valeria had been working as a waitress at one of the North Lake casinos while attending college part-time. When the news had broken that the casino would be closing, it'd been a hard blow. She, her older brother, and a younger sibling were the breadwinners for the Caro household. I could tell she was very relieved about getting a new job, and one that worked with her busy life.

"This beach is fantastic. Look how calm the water is," Valeria enthused a half hour later as we walked on the white sand of the protected little harbor. "Do you paddleboard or kayak?"

"I've done both before, yes." I'd forgotten my sunglasses, so I shielded my eyes against the bright sun as I looked to the south at a gray stone building situated a ways down the rocky, natural portion of the beach.

"I'm pretty sure we don't have paddleboards, because Evan has talked about ordering some. But I think there are kayaks. I've never searched for any because I'm usually at the beach alone, and the idea of going out by myself didn't appeal. But I'm thinking they might be stored in that boathouse? I've never been in there. Do you want to walk over and see what's inside?"

Valeria nodded eagerly. We made our way down the beach, walking between, and sometimes over, the massive granite boulders along the water's edge.

The boathouse consisted of two buildings joined by a dock. One section was where motorboats or other craft could be moored. The other building looked like a large storage area. I tried the metal handle on the storage facility door, and groaned in disappointment when I realized it was locked.

An impulse struck me. I bent and picked up a corner of the mat in front of the door. The material crumbled to dust in my hand, but I still glimpsed what I wanted before the disintegrating mat flopped back into place.

"Well done," Valeria said when I held up a tarnished key.

The key took some fiddling before it finally released the lock. I walked into the boathouse first, peering into the shadows. There was only one little window at back of the building. It was covered with dust, making visibility poor. A musty scent suggested no one had been inside here for years. I fumbled for a light. I finally found a switch, and the room was illuminated.

"*Excellent*," Valeria breathed out.

I counted five kayaks mounted on one wall. In a large wooden box I could see partially deflated rafts and inner tubes. Dozens of paddles were propped up in the corner. On another wall, four mountain bikes hung from racks. What appeared to be two jet skis sat in the middle of the room, covered with gray tarps.

Valeria passed me and lifted the cover on one WaveRunner, then another. "These are in great shape," she said, smiling over at me. Something caught her attention on the wall directly next to me. "And *look*."

Hanging on the wall next to me, a modular storage system contained several wetsuits, boots, and fins. Inside a nearby closed cabinet, we found tanks, hoses, buoyancy compensators, regulators, flashlights... everything needed for a dive, and then some. I'd already told Valeria I'd learned to dive while I was in college, and she was apparently an expert. We felt like we'd hit the mother lode.

"We should try to go out sometime soon," I said excitedly, lifting one of the wetsuits off the wall. "I've heard diving in Tahoe is amazing."

"You're going to love it."

I sniffed at the wetsuit and winced at the musty smell. "These are still in pretty good condition, but the neoprene is a little dry."

"I'll come down after I start work, inspect the equipment, and get everything into good working order," Valeria said, closing the dive supply cabinet with a bang. "I mean... if that's okay with you and Evan."

"It's fine by me. There's some great stuff in here. I'm surprised Evan never told me about all the equipment. It'd be nice to inventory it all," I said, looking around the facility thoughtfully. "Clean things up, put a couple kayaks closer to the beach for easy access, throw away stuff that can't be used anymore." I reached for another wetsuit. "For the time being though, I'm taking all of these in to wash them."

There were five suits hanging there, two small ones and three large. I thought the larger ones had probably once belonged to Evan. Or Noah? I knew who had probably worn the smaller ones, but I didn't dwell on it. The discovery of the treasure trove inside the boathouse, in addition to

Valeria's enthusiasm and warmth, had me energized. Plus, my sleep for the past few nights had been deep and dreamless. It felt unusually easy to be optimistic. It felt *good* to effortlessly push aside thoughts of Elizabeth.

Maybe I owed Evan an apology about his idea to hire Valeria. She seemed to be having a positive effect already.

"When do you think you might start work, then?" I asked Valeria as we left the boathouse, our arms loaded up with wetsuits and boots.

"I can start tomorrow, if you guys want me to."

"That'd be great. I'd really like to get begin sorting that out," I said, nodding back at the storage facility as we made our way along the shoreline. "We could do it together, maybe after—"

I broke off at the abrupt sound of glass shattering. It was immediately followed by an animal-like growl, the sound making my skin tighten and prickle.

Valeria and I both froze in place and looked upward, to where the sounds had originated. We stared up at the South Twin's turret. From an upper window protruded a fist and forearm, both scarlet with blood.

Someone—a woman, I thought—shouted out in surprised anguish. I saw the outline of a man's upper body in the broken window, and then there was a fluttering of movement behind him.

I had the fragmented, irrational thought that whomever the hand belonged to had made such a fist of rage, it'd squeezed the blood right out of him.

In one fluid, swift movement, the glistening, red arm slid back into the room.

I ran into Evan's office, Valeria trailing after me. He and Wes were talking in the sitting area of his office.

"Evan," I gasped when he looked around with a startled expression. "Someone... a man... punched through a window at the South Twin. There was blood. I didn't know if I should call 911 or not? There was someone else there with him, helping—"

Wes stood. "Go ahead and call 911," he said to Evan. "I'm sure his nurse has already called, but it won't hurt to call twice. I'll head over there. He's still my patient."

"Evan? What does he mean? *Who's* still his patient?" I asked.

"Let me call 911 first," Evan said quietly.

Valeria and I exchanged an uneasy glance while Evan made the call. I wondered if she was thinking she'd taken on too much with her new job, given everything that had happened already. And today had just been the interview.

Evan hung up the phone. He seemed preoccupied as he stared out the window.

"Evan? Was that man who punched through the window Noah Madaster?" I asked shakily.

He blinked and focused on my face.

"I think it was, yes. Wes was just giving me the news that Lorraine and Noah had moved back to the South Twin when you two ran into the room."

"How long have they been here?" I asked disbelievingly, recalling how I'd felt watched several times while painting up at the overlook. Had it really just been this afternoon that I'd seen the definite outline of a man before the shadow had abruptly dissipated? The disturbing image of that bloody, punching fist flashed into my mind's eye.

That fist definitely hadn't belonged to a ghost.

"I'm not sure," Evan was saying. "Apparently, Noah had a bad accident years ago. He suffered a spinal cord injury and lost the use of his legs."

"You didn't know he was injured?" I asked.

"No. I've dealt with his lawyers in the past seven years, never him personally. Wes says he's hired a nurse to care for him here at Les Jumeaux. He's wheelchair bound, but insists on staying mostly in the top suite of the tower. There's an elevator in the house, but it only runs from the tower to the second floor. According to Wes, he rarely leaves the upper floors of the house anymore, because it would require someone carrying him down the stairs. That's not the kind of thing Noah would ever let happen."

Of course. That's why the shadow had swooped away so rapidly, it'd looked like a magic trick. He'd been on wheels. Someone had pulled Madaster away from the window.

I realized Evan watched me with a worried expression. Without thinking, I crossed the room and hugged him. He felt stiff in my arms for a moment before I sensed the give in his flesh. His arms encircled me. He pulled me tight against him. I felt him press his mouth to the top of my head.

"It must have been scary, seeing that," he said gruffly, his hand cupping the back of my head.

"Why did he do it?" I murmured against his chest. "Did that accident affect his brain or something?"

"I'm not sure," he said, kissing the top of my head again. "Where were you two when it happened?"

"We were coming from the boathouse. We'd just passed beneath that tower," Valeria said from across the room.

"You were over by the South Twin?"

I leaned my head back at the sharpness of Evan's question.

"We walked over to that boathouse to check out what equipment was inside," I said breathlessly. A horrible thought struck me. "Is *that* why Madaster had a fit and punched through the window? Were we on his property? Trespassing?"

A muscle twitched in Evan's cheek.

"Absolutely not. Don't worry about that," he said firmly.

"Evan... *is* that why? We found scuba gear in there, and we took some suits out to wash them. Were we trespassing? Taking property that belonged to him? Is that why Madaster got upset?" I demanded, sensing a crack in Evan's confidence.

"*No.*" He exhaled in obvious frustration. "Maybe Noah *thought* so, but in fact, you weren't. The boathouse was shared by both properties when they were joined, but if Noah had bothered to read the specifics of the most recent property allocations from the court judgment, he would know the boathouse belongs exclusively to the North Twin... to us," he added, giving me a pointed glance.

"So don't begin to imagine that you were responsible for him doing what he did, Anna. Maybe he did suffer some kind of brain injury that would make him impulsive or self-destructive. He always did have a problem with his temper. Maybe the injury worsened it."

I sighed. I suddenly felt exhausted, like everything had been going in super fast motion, and was now slowing to a burdensome crawl.

"What do you think we should do?" I asked Evan. "Should we go over and see if Wes needs any help?"

"No. Wes was just explaining before you arrived that he's hired a live-in nurse. And in any case, Noah wouldn't rest any easier having *me* walk in the room."

"A nurse. I'll bet that's whom I saw. Driving out of the South Twin that day," I said. I started. "If that's true, then the Madasters having been living at the South Twin since before we arrived."

As I stared up at Evan's tense face, I heard the far distant sound of a siren through the opened French doors. We remained silent, listening closely.

"It's close. His nurse must have called 911 after all," I said. "Do you think he could have hurt himself badly?"

"Broken glass at your wrist can never be a good thing, especially for a frail man." He squeezed my shoulder. "I need to go and activate the front gate so the ambulance can enter. I think I better jog out to the fork in the road, too... make sure the ambulance doesn't waste any time by taking the wrong direction and coming our way."

"I'm coming with you," I said, starting toward the door before he had a chance to argue with me.

"I'll wait here for Wes," Valeria told me as we passed.

By the time we reached the front steps, I could tell by the sound of the siren that the ambulance had reached the mountain road turnoff to Les Jumeaux. "We'd better run," Evan said.

So we did. Inevitably, I fell behind his long-legged, athletic pace.

"Go ahead," I panted when he glanced back at me over his shoulder. He took off like a jet.

I reached the fork in the road just in time to see Evan waving the ambulance in the correct direction. They barely slowed upon seeing him, just swerved to the left and disappeared into the pine forest.

I bent over, bracing myself with my hands above my knees, trying to catch my breath. The air felt unusually heavy and humid for typically arid Tahoe. I wondered if we'd get rain later.

In the distance, the siren abruptly stopped. When I straightened after my breathing had evened a little, I saw that Evan just stood there at the fork in the road, staring in the direction the ambulance had just taken with the oddest expression on his face.

"Evan?" I asked uncertainly.

He blinked and looked at me.

"What's wrong?"

"Nothing," he said quickly, walking toward me even though his gaze was glued again to the road that led to South Twin.

"Ready to head back?" I asked, turning toward the house.

"Wait."

My feet froze at the terseness of his tone. He gave me a brief apologetic glance, informing me he'd been aware of how sharp he'd sounded. He came to me and put one arm around my shoulder, hugging me against him.

"Let's wait for them to pass."

"All right," I agreed uneasily.

I stared up at his stoic profile. I wanted to ask him if he was upset at the idea that the Madasters had been living next to us the entire time we'd been there... to inquire about how he was feeling about the fact that his one time father-in-law and apparent enemy had become so incapacitated that he was wheelchair bound, and now was headed to the hospital with a possible serious injury.

But he seemed so preoccupied, so far away from me. I couldn't bring myself to do it at that moment.

The ambulance approached us silently. I had the fleeting impression that perhaps Madaster's wounds weren't as bad as we'd worried, because while the vehicle traveled with good speed, it was nowhere near as fast as it had when it had arrived.

After it passed, Evan grabbed my hand and we walked into the center of the road. We stood side by side, Evan staring fixedly into the rear windows of the ambulance.

Wes and Valeria were on the front porch waiting for us when we returned to the house. I thought they were holding hands when we first broke the tree line onto the circular drive, but couldn't decide for certain as we got closer. Maybe it'd been a trick of the fading light. Storm clouds darkened the eastern sky.

"How is he?" Evan asked Wes.

"He'll need a few stitches, but it's his heart I was concerned about. I was about to leave, to follow the ambulance to the hospital."

"Does he have heart problems?" I wondered.

"He's had a few minor heart attacks in the past few years," Wes said, looking uneasy.

"Did he seem upset?" Evan asked.

I found myself studying his profile and intent expression.

"He seemed wound up. Tense. He wasn't saying much by the time I got there, but that may have been because of his heart. His pulse was thready." Wes looked distinctly uneasy. "I probably shouldn't say anything else. Patient confidentiality and all."

"Did he say why he punched through that window?" I asked.

"Anna is worried that he did it because she and Valeria were in the boathouse," Evan said. "I told her that Noah has no right to be upset about that. The court documents clearly allocated that property and all its contents to the North Twin. Anna had every right to be in there."

"Maybe Noah hasn't read through the details carefully yet," Wes said diplomatically.

"Since you're still acting as his physician, and apparently you two are so close, maybe you'd be kind enough to tell him," Evan said.

I glanced at Evan, trying to read his expression, but found little to go on. Wes, on the other hand, seemed determined not to meet Evan's stare.

"I'm heading over to the hospital now. I'll mention it to Noah, if he's in any state to hear it." He turned to Valeria. "I guess we should get going."

I volunteered to walk them out to the car, which was parked on the entry drive. On the way, Valeria told me that she'd report for work the following day at noon. She asked for the entry code for the garage. I hesitated. I felt very unsettled by the events of the afternoon. The thought had occurred to me that Valeria's employment might be cast in doubt by the events of the last half hour. I wasn't at all certain Evan would want to stay at Les Jumeaux, given the fact that his ex-in-laws were living next door.

"Can I text you the code this evening? I've only used it a few times myself, and with everything going on, I can't think of it at the moment."

I saw the flicker of uncertainty on her face. I'd never been a good liar. I realized she was probably wondering if I'd reverted back to my hostility toward the idea of Evan hiring her. I felt I owed her some kind of explanation. Or warning? As Wes got into the driver's seat, I grabbed by Valeria by the elbow, halting her.

"Listen, I just want to be honest with you about something," I said quietly, trying to keep the conversation muted from Wes, who sat in the car waiting.

"Is something wrong?" Valeria asked.

"I don't know for sure. It's just that you've told me all about your family, and how you and your brothers look out for everyone. I know how important getting a new job is for you. I thought maybe... maybe you shouldn't tell the other places you interviewed with that you're unavailable just yet."

Valeria looked stunned. "So you've decided you don't want me for the job, after all?"

"No, it's not that," I said in a rush, hating this whole situation. I wasn't used to being in a position where my opinion made the difference in the finances and well-being of an entire family. "I think you'd work out perfectly, to be honest. If we end up staying at Les Jumeaux, that is."

"You're *leaving*?"

"I don't know," I whispered, glancing at Wes's shadow in the driver's seat of the car. "This whole thing with Madaster might have thrown a wrench in things. Evan hadn't realized they were living at the South Twin. These houses are so large, they're completely separated by the landscape, and with Madaster being unable to go outside... Well, we just hadn't realized they were here. Wes was just telling Evan the news that they'd retired here when Madaster... did what he did," I said, grimacing at the unpleasant memory of that bloody fist of rage.

"It's uncomfortable." I tried to explain. "Evan and Noah Madaster don't get along at all. I'm not sure Evan will want to live here, knowing the Madasters are just next door."

"Oh, I see," Valeria murmured.

"I tell you what," I said. "I call you just as soon as I speak to Evan. I promise. I wouldn't have brought it up, but I thought it'd be better to keep you in the loop instead of surprising you with news that Evan and I might be leaving Les Jumeaux, after all. I didn't want you to cancel with another job opportunity, at least until I can check with Evan."

Chapter Seven

EVAN WAS IN THE KITCHEN WHEN I RETURNED, POURING SOME RED wine into two glasses. He handed one to me silently when I approached. I took a sip from the heavy crystal goblet and sighed.

"What a weird day," I said.

"Are you all right?"

I nodded. "Are you?"

He gave a small smile. "I'm not the one who saw a man punch his hand through a window."

"No. But you did find out that your former in-laws have been living next to us since we arrived. Evan... did you know they were there?" His expression flattened. "I mean... did you even *suspect* it?"

"Of course not."

The silence that followed seemed to swell and pulse against my eardrums. Evan took a sip of his wine and waved in the direction of the two deep leather chairs situated in front of the fireplace. We sat and set down our glasses on the table between us. I reached for his hand.

"Do you want to leave Les Jumeaux?" I asked.

He started slightly, as though he'd been surprised by what I thought was the most obvious unspoken question at that moment.

"Do *you*?" he asked.

I gave a little gasp of disbelief. "I don't see how my opinion matters one way or another."

"Of course it does. Would it bother you? Knowing they live in the South Twin?"

"*I* don't know them, Evan. It would bother me if it bothered *you*. Does it? You've said yourself you don't like Noah Madaster. You've been in a court battle with him over your inheritance of the North Twin, and just got your rights to the property earlier this year."

His gaze sharpened on me. "Did I tell you that? About gaining rights to the property earlier this year?"

I paused with my mouth hanging open. I'd been caught.

"No. Wes only told me earlier today. Up at the overlook, while you were interviewing Valeria."

God, had that unsettling conversation with Wes only occurred hours ago? It seemed like weeks, so much had happened since then: Learning about Evan's plan to hire Valeria, discovering the treasures of the boathouse, witnessing Noah Madaster punching his fist through a pane of glass in a fit of rage, finding out the Madasters were our neighbors...

. . . Wes telling me how Lake Tahoe had swallowed up Elizabeth's body, keeping her, and all of her secrets, for an eternity.

The image that had haunted me for so many nights in a row—the menacing, wet figure of a woman hovering over me, opening her mouth to speak—suddenly leapt into my mind's eye. The nightmare took on a whole new level of horror. I shivered.

Why was Elizabeth haunting me?

She's haunting you because your insecurity is allowing her to do so, I told myself with frustrated annoyance. I didn't believe in ghosts. (Did I?) But I was becoming irritatingly familiar with my lack of confidence when it came to my husband.

"Anna? What else did Wes tell you?"

I turned at the sound of Evan's voice. He'd sat forward in his chair and was giving me a narrow-eyed stare. I swallowed thickly, willing away that cold, nauseated feeling that had come over me at the mere memory of that nightmare-woman.

Elizabeth. May as well call that ghost created by your own unconscious mind what it is. *She's* not real. But your insecurity *is*. Had Wes's admission that her body had never been found somehow made the elusive threat of Elizabeth worse in my mind?

"Here."

I blinked at Evan's terse tone, and realized he held out my wineglass for me. I took it and drank, eager for the chance to distract myself.

"Thanks," I said hoarsely, setting down the glass. I took in Evan's sharp stare, and knew he was still waiting. He was concerned, but still expected an answer.

"Wes told me Elizabeth's body was never found."

Evan didn't move a muscle. I had the horrible thought that his handsome, compelling face appeared frozen in that moment. Lifeless.

"I'm so sorry, Evan. That must have been awful."

It still must be.

For a few seconds, I was panicked he wasn't going to say anything, that this moment of me gazing at his frozen grief would stretch on forever. But then he nodded and leaned back in his chair, staring at the empty fireplace.

"She was supposed to meet me out for lunch in San Francisco the day she disappeared," he said finally. "We'd been living in San Francisco for several weeks at the time."

"You weren't living here, at Les Jumeaux?"

"No. Elizabeth had been ill. She'd had a recent hospitalization. Work required me to be in San Francisco a lot during that time period. Although she was much improved after her hospitalization, I still didn't want her far away from me.

"It was the oddest thing," Evan continued, sounding distracted. "There was security video footage from our condo building of Elizabeth leaving for our lunch meeting. After she disappeared, it was reviewed by the police. But she never arrived at the restaurant. Instead, the surveillance video here at Les Jumeaux showed her getting on her boat four or five hours after that. She'd driven here instead of meeting me."

"Why did she do that?" I asked, breathless over the fact that he was talking openly to me about a topic that usually was taboo between us.

He blinked and focused on my face. He'd been so lost in his thoughts, it was like he'd forgotten our conversation. Forgotten my presence.

"I don't know for certain. I called when she didn't arrive at the restaurant, but she wouldn't answer her cell."

"Was that common? For her to just change her mind like that? Take off without telling anyone?"

"She was fiercely independent... or at least she liked to believe she was. She wanted to be in control of her own destiny so much. So *yes*. Because of that, Elizabeth could be very erratic at times."

I thought it was a strange thing to say. He must have noticed my confused expression.

"Elizabeth was trying to decide what she wanted in her life during that time period. Things had been rocky in our marriage. We'd become estranged. Elizabeth was trying to decide about her future. About who she wanted in it." He picked up his wineglass and took a swallow.

"And then she came to Tahoe and disappeared," I said. I was trying to absorb the fact that he and Elizabeth had been estranged, wondering where that piece of crucial information fit into the whole equation.

There had been a hint of wistfulness in his tone when he spoke of her. Despite the fact that Elizabeth and he hadn't been getting along, Evan clearly had hoped she would choose him to be part of her future.

Evan's gaze sharpened on me. He set down his wineglass so hard, the crystal rang.

"This is why I didn't want to discuss it with you."

"What?" I asked, taken aback by his blazing stare.

"You're as white a ghost," he said, standing abruptly. "Let me get you some water."

"I don't *need* water," I protested, flying up from my chair as well. I grabbed his forearm, halting him. "Evan, I'm *fine*. Why do you always treat me like I'm so fragile, when clearly I'm *not*? Was Elizabeth delicate? Is that why you always jump to that conclusion?"

He winced. "Why are we even *talking* about Elizabeth?"

"Because we just found out that her parents are living next to us," I replied just as heatedly. "Because I'm *trying* to figure out why you would want to stay here, given everything you found out today! And the only thing you seem concerned about is that I'm going to shatter like a piece of dropped china."

His mouth pressed into a flat line. I took a deep breath, trying to calm my choppy breathing.

"Why would you want to live here, knowing they're next door?" I asked, forcing my voice into a calm, even tone. He was keeping things from me. I understood that instinctively, but imagined that he did so because he didn't want to burden me. Hurt me.

Or maybe I just wished that.

"We won't ever see them, Anna. Madaster is in a wheelchair. He can't even leave the house... unless it's by ambulance."

"That's not an answer, Evan."

He raked his fingers through his thick hair. For a few brief seconds, he looked alarmingly distraught. But then he dropped his hands to his sides and gave a little bark of exasperation.

"Something was taken from me, Anna. Maybe things won't ever be the same." He gave me quick, fierce glance. "I don't *want* them to be the same. I want a whole new chapter. But I don't want to run away from this place, either." He turned to me, grasping my elbows and pulling me into his body. "I want to stay, but I'll go if it's what you want."

"I'm not sure what I want."

"Maybe I'm wrong, but I had the impression you were coming to love it here. That you'd fallen under the spell of this place."

"It's true," I admitted uneasily. "It's the most beautiful place in the world. I wake up here every morning freshly amazed that I actually live here."

"Would it really bother you that much? To stay? The residences are completely separate. There's no connection, like there used to be. I made sure of that. You understand that, don't you? Madaster can't touch you."

I gasped in surprise. "*Touch* me? You make it sound like he'd want to hurt me."

"I just mean that you won't ever have to deal with them. You won't ever have to lay eyes on him. This is our home. I hate the idea of him running us off it."

He looked so intent... so desperate for me to understand. But I sensed he wasn't giving me all the pieces to completely comprehend. Maybe it *wasn't* intentional, on his part? He was just so caught up in the private world of his own memories and motivations, he didn't even realize he left me alone in the dark half of the time.

"I don't understand how you can do it, Evan," I said bluntly.

"Do *what*?"

"Live in this house. Exist in a place where your wife... the woman you loved disappeared."

His hands tightened on my upper arms. I looked up at his shadowed face as he loomed over me, the ache in my chest amplifying.

"Do you know, when I looked at you the first time, I was shocked to the core? And you're talking to a man who doesn't surprise easily.

Not anymore. I was stunned to see something so wholly new. So fresh. Honest. *Rare.*"

His deep voice vibrated with emotion. Rarely had I heard him speak this way. I stared up at him, speechless.

"I loved Elizabeth once, that's true. I used to think she was the most perfect thing in existence. But the years matter, Anna. Maybe you're too young to understand that yet. My point is, she's gone. And I've fallen in love with *you*. God, can't you feel that?"

Light flickered around us. His question roared in my brain alongside crashing thunder. Distantly, I realized that the kitchen had grown dark. The storm had crept up on us silently, but arrived with a fury. Its power was nothing compared to the man who held me.

"*Yes*," I admitted honestly. "I can feel how much you love me."

He swooped down and captured my mouth with his. Thunder crashed around us. I clutched at his shoulders, surrendering to the heat. To the truth.

I realized in some distant part of my brain that *this* was the reason he didn't feel the need to tell me the miniscule details of his thoughts: This inescapable attraction between us, this magnetic draw. It was so big, so overwhelming, so *obvious*, it trumped everything else.

He put his forearm under my thighs. My feet left the floor. Our kiss continued, voracious and desperate, even as he threaded me through the obstacles in the kitchen and carried me up the stairs.

That night was the one where I think I started to believe in ghosts. Truly believe. Maybe ghosts were supernatural.

Maybe they were just the haunts of our minds.

That night, the dream returned. It was the same as before... terrifyingly the same. There was the similar dread and anticipation as I stared at the closed door in our room as it disappeared, transforming into a black void. There was the familiar horror at seeing *her* figure emerge from the absolute darkness, the smell of rotting flesh, the paralysis and mind-melting fear as she stood over me and slowly opened the hole of her mouth to speak. Water dripped on my cheek, the essence of her, the sensation horrifyingly real.

All of it was the same.

Except for the ending.

Someone gripped my shoulder and shook me.

"Anna. *Anna*, wake up."

My eyelids flew open at his command. I winced at the bright light, gasping. I reached out blindly, my flattened hand slapping against Evan's chest. He felt warm and solid. I dug my fingertips slightly into his bare flesh, trying to ground myself. I realized he sat up partially in bed, the sheet draped across his lap, leaving his upper body exposed. He stared down at me, his dark eyebrows slanted in concern. A shudder went through me.

"What happened?" I asked, still disoriented and agitated by the light and the residue of the nightmare.

"You were screaming," he said, his hand transferring to my upper arm. He squeezed slightly, as if, like me, he needed to feel my flesh. "No, not screaming exactly. More like you were *trying* to, but someone was choking you. Are you all right?"

I glanced around the room. When my eyelids had first opened, it'd felt like a searchlight had been directed at my face. Now, I realized that Evan had only turned on a bedside lamp. It gave off a warm glow, casting our bedroom in a soft light. I had just been in this exact same place, in the nightmare. But this was an entirely different world.

Still... that other world, that nightmare world existed. I knew that somehow, deep in my bones. It lay just beneath this one, a menacing shadow-world to the one where I lay here with my husband.

I saw Evan's concern, felt the tension of his body. But the vestiges of the dream still gripped at me. I rubbed my hand across my face, trying to clear away my weird thoughts like I would a clinging cobweb.

"Anna? What were you dreaming about?"

I opened my mouth to tell him about the nightmare woman who had taken to haunting me.

His first wife.

Instead, something else came out of my mouth.

"Evan, why are we here? Just *tell* me."

He flinched back slightly. I thought I understood why, at least partially. My voice had sounded strange, like the nightmare had infused it with some otherworldly authority. I waited, holding my breath, sure he was about to repeat his former explanations. His face looked gray as he peered down at me, like the soft lamplight wasn't strong enough to touch it.

He released me, sat up, and swung his legs to the side of the bed. For a few seconds, I just watched in wonder and rising concern as he placed his elbows on his knees and his face in his hands.

"Evan?" I sat up and scooted toward him. I put my arms around his waist and pressed my cheek against his back. Still, I was ruthless. I craved an answer, or so I told myself. I kissed his bare skin.

"Tell me why we really came to Les Jumeaux."

He inhaled, his ribcage expanding beneath my lips.

"Do you really want to know?" he asked roughly.

"*Yes.*"

But I was lying. I know that now.

"Because I'm sinful," he mumbled.

At least that's what I thought he'd said.

I stilled. I might have misunderstood his muttered words, but the grief that rang in his tone was obvious. Heartbreaking, somehow. I shivered and pressed closer to him, tightening my hold around his waist, trying to give him my heat, longing to absorb his pain. I didn't understand what he'd meant. I suddenly didn't want to.

All I knew was that he was despondent, and I had made him feel that misery.

"It was just a nightmare," I whispered between kisses on his back. "I was still in it, I think, even after you woke me up. It's better now."

He remained as still as a statue, locked in grief. I couldn't stand it. I wanted him to confess his supposed sins to me, but I dreaded it, too. It struck me that the nightmare woman's obscenely opening mouth made me feel the same way as I did in this moment: panicked. Like the ground was falling away from me, like my entire world was.

"Come back to bed, Evan. Please."

He eventually lifted his head, as if he were awakening from a trance. I scooted back. Just as he was about to make eye contact with me, he turned out the light. We lay side by side in the darkness. He took my hand in his.

"We'll leave tomorrow, if you want to," he said woodenly.

I rolled onto my side and put my arm around him, cuddling close to his naked body.

"I don't want to go. I need to finish the series I'm painting, and I can't do it anywhere else. But I'll leave... if you want to," I whispered.

"We'll stay, then," he said after a pause. "For now."

I knew he didn't sleep for a long time, because I was awake, too. I was glad for the sound of the wind howling and the rapid click-click-click of raindrops on the windows.

It helped fill the gaping silence between us.

Chapter Eight

THE NEXT MORNING BRILLIANT SUNSHINE BATHED EVERY SURFACE OF the house, defying last night's shadows and the fury of the storm. Evan came up behind me while I stood at one of the kitchen islands, my phone in my hand.

"Who are you texting?" he asked, his gruff, warm voice near my ear causing a shiver to run down my neck and roughen my skin.

"Valeria. I told her I'd text her the entry code to the garage and house this morning."

He cupped my hips with his hands and pressed his lips to my neck. I felt his body behind me, ghosting me elusively. I moved back, molding against him. I sighed.

"Thank you for understanding about Valeria," he said, kissing the shell of my ear.

I turned my chin and nuzzled his jaw, seeking his lips. He found me. Our mouths fused, he turned me in his arms.

"Are you okay?" he asked me a moment later between kisses on my cheeks and lips.

"I'm great," I told him. With the sunshine streaming around us, and in his embrace, I'd never been more sincere.

He leaned back and met my stare.

"I have told you before, and I mean it more now than I ever have. I want you to be happy, Anna."

"I am happy."

He regarded me soberly, his gray eyes softened by the sunshine.

"Will you tell me about your nightmare?"

I shook my head and buried my face in his chest, inhaling his spicy, clean scent. "I don't want to think about that." I rubbed my nose against his cotton shirt. He opened his hand at the back of my head, cradling me against him.

"I'm sorry about last night. I was really out of it when you first woke me up," I muttered.

"Anna."

I heard the question in his voice and reluctantly looked up at him.

"You don't have to apologize. Just tell me about your nightmare."

"I don't remember it."

His eyes had narrowed to gleaming crescents. "Have you had the nightmare before? Is it the reason you've been having trouble sleeping?"

Two phone alerts chimed at once, one of them coming from Evan's pocket. I raised my cell and saw that it was Valeria, texting me back.

"She texted you as well," I said, backing slightly out of Evan's arms as I read Valeria's message. I looked up at him and smiled brightly. "She'll be here before noon. I want to get up to the overlook before the light changes much. It's incredible right now, after the storm."

He caught my hand as I started to turn away.

"I'll ask Valeria if she can make us lunch. Come back to the house at twelve-thirty, and we'll have it on the terrace?"

"Why don't you come up to the overlook? I miss our picnics. You hardly come up to see me anymore, like you used to," I said, reaching to stroke his jaw. I refused to be somber on this incandescent morning. I would not be reminded of the shadows... or Evan's suffocating grief. "You'll have me thinking you're turned off by my paint smock."

"I happen to find your paint smock very sexy, especially since you wear next to nothing underneath it," he murmured, leaning down to cup one of my butt cheeks beneath the edge of the shorts I wore and kiss the corner of my mouth, his stare going smoky. "But humor me, and come back to the house to have lunch with me today."

"It's a date," I murmured, caught by the warm promise in his eyes.

Painting up on the overlook that Friday morning, it was hard to maintain my determined carefree attitude. I continually felt that tingle on the back of my neck, that telltale sign of being watched. But it was strictly my imagination. Every time I turned to peer at the South Twin, the windows remained empty. Noah Madaster was likely still at the hospital. I wondered how serious his condition was, and experienced that vague feeling of guilt that I'd contributed to his anguish and possibly worsened his health.

By the time I set down my brush a little after noon, I was frustrated at my lack of concentration on my work. If we were going to stay at Les Jumeaux, I needed to forget about Noah Madaster. It was like Evan said. I had just as much a right to be there as Noah did.

That's what I was repeating to myself when I hit the stretch of rocky beach and started up the steps to Les Jumeaux. Out of the corner of my eye, movement caught my attention.

"Hey!" I shouted, startled by what I saw. Two men were walking out of the boathouse, their arms filled with tanks and hoses: The scuba equipment we'd seen yesterday! I couldn't believe it. They paused at my shout.

"What are you *doing*?" I yelled over the sound of the surf.

I hadn't even got out the question before they were moving again, taking long strides along the beach and disappearing behind some boulders. I started to take off after them, but then recalled how big they'd seemed, even at a distance. Did I really want to confront two possibly dangerous thieves on a desolate stretch of beach, by myself?

"What the hell?" I muttered, furious and disbelieving at the intrusion. Then it dawned on me that maybe Evan had hired someone to come down and get the equipment to make sure it was safe to use.

When I walked into the kitchen, I saw Valeria standing behind the stove, holding a spatula. She greeted me warmly.

"Welcome! Have you been finding your way around all right?" I asked, walking over to the sink and washing my hands.

"Everything's good so far," she said before she confidently flipped what appeared to be two grilled sandwiches and set down her spatula to toss a salad. My mouth watered. "I hope grilled cheese sandwiches and salad is okay. Evan said supplies are a little low, since your grocery delivery doesn't get here until tomorrow."

"It sounds great," I said.

"Valeria told me she'd go shopping in town for us, if we'd rather have someone pick out our produce and meat with a more discerning eye," Evan said from behind me. I felt his arms encircling my waist. I spun in time to catch his kiss on my mouth instead of the back of my head.

"I have a cousin who runs a stand at the weekly produce market. I'll go there this afternoon, and then to the grocery store for the meat. The market is the best for first rate veg and fruit, though, and my cousin will give us a discount," Valeria was saying behind us.

"Produce market," I said, looking over my shoulder. I could pick up some nutritious things for the old woman's basket. "I'd love to go with you. Sounds nice."

"It is. They have great stuff there besides the produce: jewelry and flowers and crafts... "

"Where is the market?" Evan asked.

"Just in Tahoe Shores," Valeria said as she removed the golden brown sandwiches from the pan and placed them on plates. "We'll have time to start inventorying the things in the boathouse after we get back, if you still want to, Anna."

"Oh, I nearly forgot," I said, turning back to Evan. "Did you happen to send someone to the boathouse to get the scuba equipment cleaned and checked out?"

His relaxed expression went hard. "What are you talking about?"

"I saw two men hauling all the scuba equipment out of the boat-house just now, as I crossed the beach."

He hissed a curse, and without another word, headed toward the stairs and beach entrance to the house.

"Evan?" I called, stunned by his furious intensity.

"Stay here," he barked in a perfunctory manner over his shoulder.

"Why would someone take all the scuba equipment?" Valeria asked from behind me.

"I have no idea," I said, listening to Evan's rapid footfalls on the stairs.

I was on the verge of going after Evan when he didn't return after ten minutes. But just when I started for the back entrance, and Valeria was calling she'd come with me, I heard the downstairs door open and close.

Evan explained what had happened over lunch.

He'd come upon the men, loading up the scuba equipment into a pick-up truck parked in the South Twin's driveway.

"I asked them what they hell they thought they were doing, hauling away my property right under my nose. I'll be damned if they didn't just keep going about their business, like I wasn't even there," he said, eating a mouthful of salad. I could tell by the slant of his jaw as he chewed that just the memory made his blood simmer all over again.

"So what'd you do?" I remembered how I'd hesitated about going after the two men alone. They'd been in their thirties or early forties. They hadn't had the bodies of athletes, necessarily. But they were big, beefy, rough-seeming guys, not the kind of men I'd wanted to confront about stolen property alone... or have my husband tangling with, either.

"I told them that I knew who they were, and I'd report the theft to the police straightaway if they tried to leave with it," Evan replied. "I said their license plate number out loud for good measure. I told them wouldn't get ten miles out without being stopped. Maybe that was a bit of exaggeration on my part in regard to the local police department's abilities. But it worked. I doubt either one of them wants to come face to face with the police with stolen goods in their truck, given their likely criminal records."

"Likely criminal records? You *knew* them?"

He gave a little shrug, his eyes taking on a hard, silvery gleam.

"I knew *one* of them. I recognized him, anyway... some stoner thug three years ahead of me in school, Frank Sharpton. He was already dabbling in theft, assault, and small-time drug dealing back in high school. He's turned out even worse than I would have predicted he would. The other one looked rougher than Frank did."

"What happened after you said what you did?"

"They brought the stuff back to the boathouse and put it back where it belonged."

I gave a short laugh at his matter-of-fact response.

"Just like that? They just followed your orders?" I asked disbelievingly. "I would have thought a guy like the one you're describing would have done the exact opposite of what you wanted, once you confronted him."

"Men like that are much more obliging to authority than you would think, once the rules are made clear."

"And the rules involve... what? Money? Intimidation? The threat of prosecution?"

"All three, I'd say," he said briskly, eating another bite of salad. "In this case, I guessed correctly that the latter would be the best place to apply pressure."

I set down my fork. I'll admit to being a little amazed—intimidated?—by his casual show of ruthlessness in a confrontation with two men who were probably very familiar with violence and crime. He glanced at me and did a double take.

"What? Don't tell me you're feeling sorry for them?"

"No, of course not. I agree with you. My impression of them was that they were pretty rough. Not to mention the fact that we caught them in the act of stealing. *I* didn't want to go out after them."

"I'm glad you didn't," he said with a sharp glance.

I chewed thoughtfully for a moment. I realized I was startled at seeing this new side of him. Evan was very fit, confident... physically tough. I'd never for a second imagined that he didn't get precisely what he wanted in most cases. I hadn't previously imagined him being conniving or cold-blooded, as I supposed he'd had to be, going head to head with men like that. But of course it made sense. Evan must have a hard, aggressive side to his persona. He hadn't gotten to be an extremely successful businessman being a pushover.

"They are the type of men motivated by money or power, you say," I said as I fiddled with my salad. "So it follows that Noah Madaster must have paid them to remove the equipment, doesn't it? He saw me going inside the boathouse yesterday, and he believes I trespassed. He might believe I stole from him, and was trying to move the valuable property to another location before I returned for more."

"I don't care what he believes. He's wrong."

"I realize that. But still... Madaster must have hired those men to come here."

He didn't respond for a few seconds until he'd swallowed.

"That's the assumption I'm going on, yes," he finally said.

"Evan, do you think Madaster is going to continue to try and undermine us living here?"

"How is everything?" Valeria asked brightly, walking through the terrace doors holding a pitcher of ice water.

"I think we've hired the right person for the job, if this lunch is any indication," Evan said, wiping his mouth with a napkin.

"It was just grilled cheese and salad. I'll get fancier for your dinners," Valeria said to me with a wink. "Would you guys like some coffee or dessert? Fruit, maybe?"

"No," Evan said before I could get out a reply. He tossed his napkin on the table and scooted back his chair. I thought he was about to say that he needed to get back to work, given his familiar manner of purposeful determination. But instead, he stood and held out his hand to me.

"I've made plans for Anna and me to go to Sapphire Bay for a weekend spa getaway, and we should pack straightaway. We'll be back Sunday afternoon by dinnertime," he told Valeria.

"How *nice*. Sapphire Bay is supposed to be amazing," Valeria said, grinning.

"But... I didn't know anything about this." Evan reached for my hand and I gave it to him.

"Of course you didn't. It would haven't been much of a surprise if you had," he told me, his light eyes going warm.

That weekend away with Evan was like a perfectly distilled honeymoon.

The suite he'd reserved took up the entire top floor of the boutique hotel, giving us access to a large terrace overlooking Tahoe. The owner of the hotel herself came and served us our exquisitely prepared meals there. I loved taking in the breathtaking view, appreciating the differences in light and perspective afforded by switching my angle on the lake.

We took advantage of the spa, hiked, and even dived on Sunday morning. Evan hired someone from South Lake to take us out for my first official scuba dive at Tahoe... my first dive with him, in fact.

The scuba guide took us to Hurricane Bay, explaining on the boat trip there that this particular spot was famous for diving because of the crystalline water and a bonus: a twenty-five foot sunken sailboat.

At the mention of a sunken boat, I glanced uneasily at Evan. Would it make him think of Elizabeth? But he merely grasped my hand and asked the guide a question about dive site elevations. I remembered that Elizabeth's boat had been found, undamaged.

The uncomfortable moment passed.

I had told Evan I considered myself an intermediate diver, but I think he wanted an expert on hand for our initial dive, just to make sure I hadn't overestimated my abilities.

Afterward, he complimented me by saying he thought I'd actually downplayed my skill and knowledge.

"Have I done something to make you believe I'm a braggart?" I teased him as we removed our gear on the boat. It'd been a successful dive. We'd not only found the sunken sailboat, but also had swum past a huge, spooky submerged pine tree that had grown in some prehistoric drought, its trunk six feet in diameter, its branches coated in a white sediment that only added to its ghostly appearance.

Evan looked a little taken aback by my question. "Fair point. You're always modest about your abilities. Maybe I just wanted to see your skill firsthand. Now, I don't need to worry if you decide to dive while you're at Les Jumeaux."

"Good. You need to do less worrying, when it comes to me. And it's not like I'd ever be alone diving. If you aren't there, Valeria will be. And she's a scuba instructor."

He just nodded in an offhand way, but I wasn't buying his nonchalance. I had the feeling that Valeria's scuba diving credentials had factored into his decision to hire her.

I was so overwhelmed with love for him at that moment, even more so than usual because of the idyllic surprise weekend he'd given me. I found it easy to forget about his tendency to over-protect.

We couldn't stop touching each other on the drive back to Les Jumeaux. I stared out of the car window onto the sparkling lake, holding Evan's hand between mine and resting it in my lap. The usual feeling of being on a rollercoaster, given the twists and high elevations on the road, had vanished. I was secure and steady, not to mention ridiculously happy, with the sensation of his hand between mine.

My euphoria burst like a pricked bubble a minute after we passed the fork in the entrance road to Les Jumeaux. Evan braked abruptly. I was thrown against the restraint of the seat belt.

"What the—"

"I'm sorry," Evan said as the world settled from the jarring halt. At the same moment he'd slammed on the brakes, he'd instinctively reached to brace his right hand against my left shoulder, holding me even more firmly in place in the seat.

I looked out the front window where he stared fixedly. Six to eight feet of soil, rock, and dislodged underbrush blocked the road directly in front of us. Evan's quick reflexes had prevented us from driving directly into the wall of sediment, but only just.

"What happened?" I asked, shocked. "A landslide?"

Evan didn't immediately respond, but removed his hand from my shoulder. He unfastened his seatbelt and opened the car door. I followed suit, still feeling rattled and disoriented by the near collision.

"Anna," he called sharply. I paused in the action of stepping out of the car. "Stay inside. Please," he added tersely. I sat back down in the seat, glancing anxiously up the slope of the ravine to my right. The trees, rocks, and underbrush seemed ordinary just next to me, but gravity had certainly pulled aggressively at the soil just feet away. Who knew how secure the earth really was? I closed my car door very carefully, afraid of sending off vibrations into loose soil. I had a brief, vivid vision of being buried beneath tons of earth, of blackness swallowing us whole. Evan was out there, without the benefit of the armor of the car to hold off the pile of dirt and rock. I bit my lip to stop myself from screaming at him to get back in the car.

He walked the width of the road, inspecting the pile of earth. He stared up in the direction from where the earth had fallen, and then in the opposite side of the ravine, toward the creek.

I exhaled in relief when he finally returned to the car and sat in the driver's seat.

"Do you... do we get a lot of landslides around here?" I asked him.

"We do in Tahoe occasionally, yes. But not at Les Jumeaux. Never before, anyway," he said, his mouth set in a straight line. "Feeling up for a walk? We're going to have to get to the house by foot. We'll go down to the creek and hike past the slide. I'll call someone to come out later and clean this up, and reinforce the sides of the ravine, if need be."

So we hiked down the creek bed past the landslide, and then made our way back to the road. "What do you think caused it?" I asked, staring over my shoulder at the pile of earth, now from the opposite direction.

I came to a halt on the road. "Could there have been an earthquake while we were away?"

"We would have heard about it if there had been a quake," Evan said, his hand coasting up my spine, and pausing to rub between my shoulder blades. He always seemed to know instinctively where tension tightened my muscles. "I'd say human beings were responsible."

"Human beings? Like... someone caused it on purpose?"

"I'm not saying that, no. It was probably hikers. People could have wandered over from the public beach and accidently kicked it off. It only takes one tumbling rock in the wrong location to start a debris avalanche. I don't want you hiking around here until we get a geologist to come out and inspect the road and the land around it. We'll get a professional opinion on what caused it, and then we'll know for certain. Don't worry, we'll make things safe again." He patted me gently. "Come on. Let's get back to the house so I can make some phone calls."

But I saw the trace of worry on his face. The recollection of that grim, tense expression he wore as he we walked back to Les Jumeaux stayed with me the rest of the evening.

I hadn't dreamed during our idyllic getaway. But that night, I had the nightmare again. And this time, I didn't wake up when the ghost woman opened the sickening black void of her mouth. Through the thick waves of my terror, I thought I heard her gurgling voice.

After I'd awakened, wet with sweat, I realized that maybe I'd misunderstood what I'd heard. It'd been like listening to a crow underwater. It didn't make sense, what I thought she'd said.

Light in the darkness.

Chapter Nine

THE NEXT FEW DAYS PASSED PEACEFULLY. EVAN CONTACTED BOTH the construction crew that had been working on the viewing room and Valeria, informing them not to come to Les Jumeaux until the ravine could be inspected and the road cleared of the landslide. We were stranded at the house, but happily so. Evan swam with me at the beach several afternoons. We took out the kayaks one evening, gliding along the coast during a glorious sunset.

My mom called one afternoon during our isolation, while Evan and I were exercising in the workout facility. She was full of questions about my new life at Les Jumeaux, all of which I answered with genuine cheerfulness and excitement. The tentacles of the nightmare couldn't reach me during the daylight hours.

We talked about my latest series of paintings, and how I'd be showing them to Evan's friend in South Lake very soon. Then she put Jessica on the phone.

I got off the treadmill for what was bound to be a more serious, involved, sisterly conversation. I sat down on a weight bench, losing myself talking to Jessica. She told me about the apartment she'd rented for her graduate school program, and complained about the process of interviewing potential roommates. I consoled her, knowing from experience what a crapshoot the roommate game was.

God, had I really been single and living through that very unpleasantness just months ago? It seemed impossible... like I taken on someone else's identity. I felt deeply grateful to be living the life I was versus that of a typical young woman, struggling to make her way in the world.

When I finally hung up, I turned around to see Evan toweling off his neck after a grueling run, a small, very appealing smile shaping his mouth. It struck me, as it had before at our wedding, that he was fond of my relationship with my family. Observing our familiar, boring, yet unique domestic interactions pleased him in some way.

"Everyone doing well?" he asked.

"I wish Jessica could come and visit us sometime," I told him impulsively.

He tossed aside his towel and came toward me.

"I'd like that. But not now," he said gruffly, reaching for my chin and tilting up my face. His thumb pressed against my lower lip. "Right now, you're still exclusively mine. And I'm not willing to give that up for a while yet."

He leaned down. His kiss was warm. Possessive. It made me dizzy. A moment later, he straightened, giving me that blazing stare I recognized. He went over and locked the workout facility door, even though we were alone at Les Jumeaux. When he returned, I held out my arms. He grabbed my hands, drawing me up against him.

On Wednesday evening when we sat down to have dinner on the terrace, Evan told me that he'd received a report form the geologist he'd hired.

"Did she think the landslide was caused by hikers?" I asked.

"Most likely," Evan said, looking down as he cut his steak. Since we hadn't been able to get any groceries due to the landslide, I'd raided an icebox I'd noticed in the garage. I'd discovered it was packed with frozen meat, so we'd been especially carnivorous for the past few nights. "She recommended a crew to do some reinforcements in a few key areas. After that's done, I'll have someone come out to clear away the debris."

"Evan," I said quietly.

He glanced up, blinking at my serious tone.

"Are you even a little bit worried that Noah Madaster is somehow responsible for the landslide?"

He set down his steak knife with a clinking sound.

"The thought crossed my mind," he said after a pause.

"Is he really that awful?"

"To my mind, he's one of the foulest men whom ever lived. Still, I have my doubts about him orchestrating a landslide. Even I have to admit that isn't really his style."

"His style?"

Evan nodded distractedly, picking up his knife again. "Madaster is subtle. He's a snake, not a bull." His stare briefly met mine. I felt a shiver pass through me. "He's a *poisonous* snake, Anna. He's dangerous. I don't want you to forget that. I don't want you to ever get within speaking distance with him. There's no telling what damage he could do with that forked tongue of his."

"Why do you say that? What did he do that's so horrible?"

"You've never heard about why he was drummed out of the governor's office?" Evan asked as he resumed cutting his steak. I wasn't fooled by his even tone or calm manner. I sensed his usual tension churning just beneath the surface when it came to the topic of Noah Madaster.

I shook my head. "No. Like I said, I couldn't find very much online about Madaster—or Elizabeth," I added, more hesitant to say her name than I ever had been. "The only articles I did find were mostly political: stuff about his campaign and his inaugural ball, or bills he'd signed into law... stuff like that."

"All glowing references, no doubt," Evan muttered, and this time he couldn't hide his bitterness or anger. "It's amazing, how a man can rewrite history by paying enough money to a company to fix his online reputation. To create his own reality, in other words. Noah has had negative news about himself buried so deep, I'd imagine you need to go to page fifty or sixty to find some of the more controversial articles about him and his crimes. *Some* of his crimes, anyway. The most serious ones he committed never reached the light of day."

He looked down at his meal distastefully, as if his food had suddenly made him ill. He pushed back his plate. I felt bad for ruining his dinner by bringing up the topic.

Still, that didn't stop me from pressing it further.

"What did he do?"

For a moment, Evan didn't respond. I saw a muscle working in his jaw.

"Are you really going to make me do a Google search to page sixty?"

He gave me a quick, cool glance, but then he sighed. I knew he was going to give me what I wanted.

"In looking up information on Noah, you may have found out he was a neurologist before he entered politics. By all accounts—including my own, I'll admit—he's a brilliant man. It's what he's done with that vast intelligence that's infuriating. Horrifying," he added quietly under his breath.

He paused. While I waited anxiously, he took a sip of water.

"What you have to understand about Noah Madaster is that he's an absolute control freak. It's why he went into politics. He couldn't stand the idea of being on the sidelines, allowing other people to influence his financial and private affairs. He'd inherited an enormous estate from his parents, a fact which allowed him to go to medical school and specialize in neurology without ever once having to think about expensive tuitions or paying a single bill. Medical school and practice were all a lark to Noah.

"The Madaster lineage and wealth goes back a long way. I've never known anyone who is as much of an ancestry freak as Noah. It was like he thought Madaster genes were purer than everyone else's... *greater*, somehow. It was just one of many facets of his narcissism," Evan continued, his manner grim.

I thought of that ornate Madaster family tree I'd found in the great hall. Noah Madaster must have inherited his snobbishness and pride from a long line of Madasters.

"The American branch of the Madasters made their fortune in real estate, oil, mining... a lot of extortion, graft, and shady dealings, as well, but Noah never talked about those things. Every generation compounded the family fortune, feeding its children more and more wealth. More and more corruption.

"Noah became the ultimate gentleman physician, rich in knowledge and skill, but scarily short on empathy for other human beings. Most doctors enter the medical field, at least partially, because they want to help and heal people. But that was *never* what motivated Noah.

"Once he became a physician, he never really treated patients. Not for their benefit, anyway. Research became his forte. He was obsessed with the idea of control, more specifically, the goal of perfectly revealing human lies. He created a lie detector that read brain waves, as opposed to monitoring other physiological responses, like a polygraph does, for instance. He called his machine the Analyzer. He used to say he put people 'to the test' with it."

Evan paused, staring down at the flickering candle I'd lit for our dinner.

"Noah Madaster would be cast perfectly as the head of the Spanish Inquisition or the Gestapo. A cult leader," he said.

"*Cult* leader?"

"The man never wavers in his belief of his *rightness*. Time passed, and Madaster continued to perfect this piece of equipment—or at least that's what he believed. He peddled it at doctor's conventions and medical conferences, and for a while, his invention was hailed as an exciting new option for criminal investigation, a significant improvement over current polygraph tests."

"I wonder if that's where Madaster met Tommy," I said, referring to our mutual friend from San Francisco. "Remember, I told you that Tommy said he met him at a medical conference?"

"Maybe it was where they met. I didn't even realize they knew one another until you told me."

"Tommy didn't like him much. I think he didn't mention knowing Madaster to you, out of respect for the fact that he was your father-in-law, and he didn't know how you felt about him."

"Tommy must have seen him for what he was. A few people saw through Noah's facade, but most were completely taken in by him. He was the ultimate snake oil salesman. He had so much money, and so much polish, and so many friends in high places, it took time for a few people to finally see through his act. Most never did. They're still fooled by him today."

"You don't think the Analyzer worked?"

"Do I think it could tell if people were lying? Yes, I believe it did that, if inconsistently. It certainly wasn't any more reliable than existing polygraph equipment that uses blood pressure or respiration as measures. The true power of the Analyzer was Noah himself. He had such a large personality, such charisma and magnetism about him, that when he informed people that they were lying—because he had the scientific proof in front of him, didn't he, given his machine?—people *believed* him. He actually convinced them that *he* knew their truth better than *they* did, that he knew they were lying, even when they weren't. Eventually, they'd confess to all manner of supposed lies, betrayals, and sins, all because Madaster *said* they'd committed them. All because it served *his* purpose."

"He was practicing brainwashing," I said softly. "Not lie detection."

"Exactly. He would have created a slave race around him if he could have, their entire purpose being to prove that he was the rightful authority of whatever sick little world he'd created. I know it sounds like I'm being melodramatic, Anna, but I'm not."

Emotion vibrated in his deep voice. For a few seconds, our stares locked. I almost tasted Evan's disgust in that moment.

His hatred.

"The Analyzer was his downfall, though. It was the reason he eventually had to step down as governor," Evan said after a pause. "He was absolutely paranoid about anyone who worked for him. But his need for complete control escalated to epic levels with his staff and advisors once he reached the governor's office. He constantly suspected leakers, that he was being undermined by someone in his inner circle.

"That's when he began to insist staff members submit to questioning, using the Analyzer. I know it sounds unbelievable, in this day and age. But I swear to you, it happened. He set up his own miniature Inquisition in the governor's office. And he got away with it for years.

"From what I've come to understand, the working environment at the governor's office was nothing less than pure misery and fear. Still... people did exactly what he wanted for years. It may have been hell, but Noah managed to always convince people things *could* be worse, if Noah decided you were no longer loyal to him.

"His authority wasn't inviolate, though. He made the mistake of pushing too far, growing too bold... too drunk on his own power. A young—very courageous— female aide broke her silence to the press. She reported that Madaster had touched her inappropriately during the questioning process. After she spoke out, several other employees went public about both emotional and sexual abuse by Madaster, sometimes while he used the Analyzer on them, sometimes not."

"What happened to him?"

Evan frowned. "All charges were eventually dropped."

"You're kidding."

"Madaster has a way of silencing his enemies."

"You mean... he just got away with it?" I asked, outraged at the idea.

Evan shrugged. "Charge after charge came in against him, and he was eventually forced to resign. But he never went to court for any allegations. One by one, the charges were dropped. The news stories faded."

He glanced up and noticed my disbelieving anger.

"He's got a powerful team of lawyers who will do anything short of murder for him, and I'm not entirely convinced they wouldn't do that. Trust me, I've been doing battle with them for seven years over my ownership of the North Twin. But in answer to your question: Yes. Noah Madaster got away with it. He's never been punished for his crimes. Not one."

"That's outrageous," I said, sitting back in my chair, stunned at the unfairness.

Evan leaned forward, placing his elbows on the table. I got the impression he really wanted me to understand something.

"It is outrageous, yes. But remember I told you Madaster is a snake? A spider? He taps into people's weaknesses and ultimate fears, and spins those vulnerabilities to his benefit. He does it as easily as he breathes. A man like him will never be trapped by the black and white language of the law."

I swallowed with difficulty, my mind churning over everything Evan had told me. Finally, I exhaled.

"I suppose he has been punished though, hasn't he?" I asked quietly.

"What do you mean?"

"That fall that he had," I said, staring out at the black lake and star-dusted sky. "He's like a prisoner in his own body, isn't he? Living in that huge mansion, up in that tower... bound to his wheelchair. For someone who thrived on power and control, he's lost the ability to manipulate even his own legs."

"You sound like you're feeling sorry for him."

I blinked at the sharpness of his tone. *Had* I been feeling sorry for Madaster, for the owner of that bloody, clenched fist protruding out of that window? One thing was for certain: I'd never witnessed a more distilled image of helpless, frustrated rage in my life.

"No, not feeling sorry for him. I was just thinking how ironic and ruthless fate can be, how sometimes it gives a person exactly what they've earned during their lifetime."

Evan grunted softly. "It'd take Noah Madaster a thousand lifetimes to ever begin to pay for his crimes," he said with a tone of finality before he stood and picked up his plate and half-eaten dinner.

The entry road was cleared. A maintenance crew came out to set up reinforcements in the areas where the geologist had recommended.

I'd grown increasingly uneasy painting up at the overlook, ever since discovering that the Madasters lived next door. My work had suffered because of my discomfort about being observed from the South Twin's tower. I often turned and looked over my shoulder at the circular row of windows in the distance. The one Madaster had punched had been covered with cardboard and duct tape. I was a little amazed, given their wealth and means, that no one had been there to repair the glass yet.

But despite that telltale prickling on the back of my neck, I never saw any movement or the outline of anyone in the windows. It must be my imagination at work.

Still, that feeling of being watched persisted.

The days flew by. I had an appointment next Tuesday to show a series of my Tahoe paintings to Lauren Dewerson, the gallery owner Evan knew. Despite that deadline, I found myself setting aside my brushes and leaving the overlook before I'd made any decent progress on the last painting for the series.

Evan was sipping coffee in the kitchen when I trudged inside one morning. Upon seeing him standing there next to the counter, I smiled to cover my frustrated expression and feeling of failure.

"Taking a break?" I asked him, coming around the island and going up on my toes to kiss him. He cupped my shoulder with the hand that wasn't holding a coffee cup.

"Kind of," he said, his manner relaxed as he rubbed my upper back and arm. I always loved the feeling of his big, massaging hand on my body. He gave me so much pleasure without ever seeming to realize he did it.

"I was about to walk up to the overlook to find you."

"Why?"

"I just got news that I'm going to have to be in San Francisco this weekend. One of the bank's chief legal officers is flying in from the

Netherlands. A meeting has been planned between him, the chief legal officer from the U.S. bank, and me, unfortunately. I couldn't get out of it. But we can stay at the condo for the weekend. I'll take you out to dinner Saturday night after the meeting. Anything you like."

"I can't leave, Evan," I said anxiously. "I mean... I want to, but I have that meeting with Lauren on Tuesday, and I'm having a horrible time with this last piece."

His expression grew somber as he studied my face and continued to massage my shoulder muscle.

"You're having trouble painting up there, aren't you? Knowing that the Madasters are living in the South Twin?"

I didn't respond, finding it difficult to put my discomfort into words.

"I can imagine me telling you about Madaster's character didn't help your uneasiness any," Evan said.

"I'm *glad* you told me about him. I wish you'd talk to me *more* about what's going on in your head."

He stared down at me, his gaze thoughtful.

"I'll show you another spot where you can paint," he finally said firmly, as if he'd just come to a decision. "It's not quite as picturesque as the one you're on now, but the view is beautiful there, and trees will shield you from the tower."

"Really?" I asked hopefully at first. Then reality hit. "But I wanted this series to all be from the same perspective."

"Is it really that important? It doesn't matter if one of them is from a slightly different angle or not."

"It *does* matter. The concept for the series is to paint the same view at the same time period everyday, and try to show the differences in light caused by weather, cloud formations, and the gradual alteration of the sun as the season slowly changes. It'll ruin *everything* to have a painting from a different perspective. It doesn't make any sense."

"Hey," he said gruffly, because I'd been staring at his chest while my mind spun anxiously. I looked up at him. He squeezed my shoulder. "Lauren is going to love your stuff, honey. You're incredibly talented. I know you're a perfectionist, but you're going to have to trust me on this."

I smiled, a feeling of relief penetrating my anxiety. That was the effect his praise and reassurance had on me. No one else could have soothed me about that topic. He was right. I was a perfectionist when it came to my painting.

"But what about San Francisco?" I asked.

"I don't like the idea of leaving you here alone."

"I'll be fine. Our security system could work for Fort Knox," I said dryly, referring to the fancy, high tech wireless system that covered every square inch of the mansion. Despite my assurance to him, however, a vivid picture of the nightmare woman standing by our bed jumped into my mind's eye.

I would be alone with Evan gone.

Alone with *her*.

I didn't think I showed the slight shock of fear that went through me. Nevertheless, Evan resumed his casual massage on my shoulder, as if to calm me.

"How about if I ask Valeria if she can come out and stay while I'm gone?" he suggested. "That way, you can paint all weekend if you want."

"That'd work," I said, brightening at the idea.

He watched me for a few seconds from beneath a lowered brow.

"Maybe. I don't know. It still makes me uncomfortable, the idea of you being here without me."

I went up on my toes and pressed my mouth to his.

"Come on, Evan. What could possibly happen?" I whispered against his lips.

Chapter Ten

EVAN PLANNED TO LEAVE FOR SAN FRANCISCO THAT FRIDAY AFTER lunch, but I noticed he lingered over his coffee extra long after we'd finished eating.

"Don't you need to get on the road?" I asked him.

He shrugged and took another sip of his coffee, flipping his newspaper. I'd watched him pack a suit earlier for his meeting. But for the drive, he was dressed casually—and very attractively—in a soft-looking, light gray running shirt that emphasized the breadth of his shoulders and the unique color of his eyes.

I'd felt a powerful urge to run my hands all over him during our lunch, but had refrained, of course. His imminent departure weighed heavy on me, even though I was determined not to show it. It would be the first time we were separated since we'd been married.

"I'd forgotten Valeria couldn't be here until after her class was finished. I'm not crazy about leaving you here alone with the construction crew downstairs," he explained after a pause.

I rolled my eyes. "Come on, Evan. You know I'll be fine. You yourself have told me that you know the supervisor—Keith Vankamp, isn't it?— personally. You went to school with him, didn't you?"

"Yeah. He's a good guy. Very thorough. Trustworthy. But that's the thing. Keith is off today. He texted me this morning that his seven-year-old fell off the jungle gym at the park and broke his arm and nose."

"Ouch. Poor kid. But still—you said Keith is trustworthy. He'd only hire good guys for his crew, do background checks, the works. I'll be fine, Evan. You should go now. You're already going to be hitting evening traffic as it is."

I thought I'd convinced him when he stood. But it seemed that between getting his suitcase and finishing up a few things in his office, he still was there by the time Valeria arrived. Once she was there, he suddenly was raring to get on the road. I wasn't fooled. He'd hung around intentionally until Valeria came.

"I'll text you just as soon as I get to the condo," he said as we stood next to the car. "Don't forget to set the security system just as soon as—"

"The construction crew leaves and Valeria and I are in for the night. I *know*, Evan. Stop worrying, and just drive safely," I insisted, going up on my toes to kiss him. He opened his hands at my waist and pulled me closer.

What began as a short goodbye kiss grew steamy. Hungry.

"You're not making it easy, Evan," I panted softly a moment later as he ran kisses along my temple. He nuzzled me with his nose and I tilted my mouth up again.

"Maybe I don't want you to think it's easy, separating from me," he said gruffly. He gave me one last kiss; it was swift, hard, and guaranteed to make me bereft when he moved away a few seconds later.

It felt like a hole slowly opened up in my chest as I watched him drive away.

I suspected he'd been teasing me about not wanting to make our separations easy. But if he *had* wanted to make this hard on me, he'd succeeded in spades.

Valeria and I spent a productive afternoon. We inventoried the storage contents of the boathouse, and made a big pile of things to throw away. Valeria did a thorough check of all the scuba equipment.

During our search of the boathouse, we discovered four different sets of keys in a box, each of them with a tag and boat description on it, like Cuddy Cabin, Cruiser, and Speed.

One set merely said, *The Survivor.*

An uncontrollable shiver passed through me upon seeing the name of Elizabeth's boat. It again struck me as especially sad... *tragic*, that she'd chosen that name.

"Should we take some of the boats out, to see what kind of condition they're in?" Valeria asked me.

"Sure," I replied, because I didn't know what else to say. I imagined what I'd do when we came upon Elizabeth's wooden sailboat. Did I *want* to walk the boards where her bare feet had passed? Did I *need* to see the last things she'd witnessed before she'd gone overboard into the deep, cold waters?

I honestly didn't know if I was attracted to or repelled by the idea.

Nevertheless, I left the storage facility with Valeria to inspect the boats. We followed the dock to the covered boat slip.

I felt self-conscious walking out on the dock, just like I had earlier when we approached the boathouse from the beach. Truthfully, I hadn't been able to forget Noah Madaster the entire time we were at the boathouse, even when we were behind the closed door. I wondered if Wes had given him the message about the boathouse and its contents being allocated to Evan's property. And if Wes *had* told him, had the information calmed Madaster, or upset him even more?

Whatever the case, there were no incidents coming from the South Twin that afternoon. All was quiet. The big, brooding mansion might have been as deserted as we'd once believed it to be.

When we entered the boat slip, I had my answer as to whether or not I was morbidly curious or disgusted by the idea of getting on Elizabeth's boat. Only the three motor craft were moored side by side. The fourth birth remained empty. I heaved a sigh of relief.

I wondered if her boat had been sold, and if so, by whom? Did Evan even realize Elizabeth's boat was absent? Surely he did, since he said the boathouse and its contents had been allocated to him. Although Madaster hadn't known that. I thought of the men hauling out the scuba equipment, mostly likely at Madaster's request. I doubted he'd have any compunction about selling or destroying his daughter's boat, no matter to whom it legally belonged.

We found that all three of the crafts had gas in them and were ready to use. I was comfortable piloting the cuddy cabin and the speedboat. My parents had owned a summer cabin on a lake in downstate Illinois, and we'd gone there during summers for most of my childhood. Jessica and I were both proficient at driving a speedboat. But I felt less certain about the enormous cruiser, which contained two berths, a galley and large lounging and dining area. Valeria took over for the cruiser's test run. I was comforted to see how confident and easy she was, piloting the big boat with all the complicated looking controls.

"Ever since we were fifteen or sixteen, my brother and I both worked at the local resort's dock during the summers," she explained from behind the wheel of the cruiser as we glided along the cerulean blue Tahoe waters. "We valeted people to the resort once they'd buoyed their boats, but they used to pay us to get their boats out of dry dock and into the water, as well. They'd give great tips," Valeria said with a grin and a wink.

It was such a gorgeous afternoon, we decided to take the cruiser for a longer ride. I laid out on the deck as Valeria drove, soaking in the amazing views and hot sun.

"Doesn't Evan like to go out on the boats?" Valeria asked me later as we walked along the beach toward the North Twin. She noticed my sideways glance. "I just asked because you didn't seem to know anything about the boats, before we went out there today. I would have thought you and Evan went out on them regularly."

"I don't know why we haven't for sure," I said, frowning. "Evan loves yachting and diving. A friend of ours from San Francisco—Tommy—and he used to crew together on a yacht. But Evan's first wife died in a boating accident, here at Tahoe," I admitted slowly.

"Wes mentioned something about that. That's so sad. Maybe that's why he doesn't go out to the boathouse much."

"Maybe," I said doubtfully.

Evan and I had gone out on a boat to go diving during our getaway at Sapphire Bay, I recalled. Evan hadn't seemed nervous being out on the guide's boat. In fact, he'd seemed extremely at ease and entirely in his own element out on the water.

Thankfully, my brief mention of diving changed the direction of Valeria's and my conversation. We decided we'd try a dive tomorrow. Valeria said her brother Manny could take us out on one of the boats while we dived.

"One of the sharpest drop-offs on the lake happens right here near Les Jumeaux. I've dived it before, but not near your house," Valeria explained. "Just fifty feet or so from the shoreline, the water depth goes from thirty feet to over a thousand. From that overlook where you paint, you could throw a rock, and it'd sink eleven hundred feet to get to the bottom. They call it the Great Wall. There are boulders the size of houses, and some pretty big underwater caves. Maybe we should do that dive tomorrow, since it's so close?"

"Absolutely," I said.

Once we reached the house, Valeria went to the kitchen to start meal preparations. I went upstairs to double-check that everything was prepared in her guest room. Afterward, I decided to do a workout in the exercise room, and then sauna.

I heard the muted sounds of hammering in the distance later as I stripped out of my sweaty workout clothes and wrapped a towel around me. It was good to know that the construction crew was keeping it honest, and weren't cutting out early on a Friday, just because their supervisor wasn't on site.

The workout facility at the North Twin contained both a wet and dry sauna. Evan preferred the wet one exclusively, while I loved the dry heat, especially from this particular sauna. It got satisfyingly hot, and always melted every trace of tension out of my muscles.

Once inside, I turned up heat to the highest level and stretched out on the cedar planks on the top bench.

Fifteen minutes later I was slick with sweat. I'd forgotten to bring a bottle of water in with me, and now I was feeling dehydrated from the combination of being in the hot sun out on the lake this afternoon, my workout, plus the intense sauna heat.

My legs felt a little rubbery as I stood and descended down the benches. Spots scattered at the periphery of my vision. Fantasizing about drinking quarts of ice water and then taking a cool shower, I reached to push open the door.

It didn't budge.

I pushed harder, but the door was fixed in place. I stared blankly at the solid cedar door. An adrenaline rush cascaded through my whole body. There was no lock on the door. I knew that for a fact.

I pushed again, then threw my hip against the door once, and then twice in mounting frustration and fear. The impacts caused the black spots at the sides of my vision to scatter toward the center.

"Hey!" I yelled, pounding on the door with my opened hand. "Let me out of here."

What the hell was going on? Was Valeria out there, playing a practical joke on me?

Even as I thought it, I knew the idea was ridiculous. I realized I didn't know Valeria well, but she absolutely did *not* seem like the type to do something as crazy as to hold the door of the sauna shut on her new employer on her second day of work.

Besides, Valeria was even smaller than I was. Even if she had thrown her entire weight to block me inside, I would have felt a give in the door when I pushed. But that absolutely wasn't the case. It was as if the door had become frozen, an utterly unmovable stone slab. Even if there *had* been a lock on it, I would have felt more give in the door than I did presently as I pushed, pounded, and shouted.

Recognizing the pressure in my chest as the prelude to panic, I forced myself to pause and try to slow my breathing. It was hard, with what felt like a wall of fear pressing in on me from every direction. It was hot. *So* hot. I couldn't breathe the heavy air. Just the distant echo of the word *suffocation* in my head made it feel like my heart had been pinned outside of my chest, exposed, vulnerable, and convulsing grotesquely.

Think, Anna.

No one is holding the door shut. It just got stuck somehow. You need to stay calm. What should you do until you can get Valeria's attention?

Clutching the towel around my breasts, I went over to the temperature control and slid the dial all the way to the lowest setting. I couldn't shut the sauna off entirely, though. The power button was just outside the door. Unfortunately, I'd turned up the temperature up so high upon first entering that it would take quite a while to cool down.

Don't think about that.

I just needed to make enough noise that Valeria would hear me from the kitchen. Unfortunately, I was feeling so weak-kneed from the intense heat, I hardly felt up to making the necessary ruckus.

Cursing myself for not bringing in a bottle of water, a thought struck me. I dipped my hand in the wooden pail with the dipper we used to throw water on the heating element to create steam. There were several inches of water in it, even if it was probably old and dirty. I lifted the dipper and drank several mouthfuls of water. It was almost too hot to swallow, but I hoped it'd give me the energy I needed.

Then I went over to the door and hammered with my fists and screamed my head off. I called Valeria's name. I begged. I cursed. When my hands and forearms grew sore from pounding, I got the wooden ladle out of the pail and banged on the door with that.

Every minute or so, I'd try to open the door again, each time wondering if I'd been temporarily insane by imagining it was locked tight.

At one point in this waking nightmare, I climbed the sauna benches and banged on the ceiling with the ladle and shouted, thinking sound might carry through the house to Valeria in the kitchen better that way.

It was much hotter toward the ceiling, though. So I staggered back down the benches, my legs nearly folding under me when I leapt to the floor.

I'd been leaving the last of the water in the pail for an emergency, but it seemed like the crisis was upon me. The water wouldn't do me any good if I passed out.

How long had I been in here? I wondered after I drank the remaining mouthful of water. It felt like an eternity, but was probably closer to an hour. I usually could only tolerate fifteen or twenty minutes or so in a dry sauna. I pounded on the door again, but my banging sounded weaker. My throat felt cracked and sore. I couldn't shout anymore.

How long can I survive in this hot, airless room?

The thought nearly undid me. I sagged against the door, weakness and fear overwhelming me. Seconds dragged by. Minutes. The temperature of the room hadn't decreased much. The air felt like it scorched my throat and lungs. It hurt to take it in, but I had no choice but to inhale. I realized that while I'd been wet with sweat before, my skin was now dry. I'd grown so dehydrated I couldn't perspire anymore. My tongue and lips felt parched and swollen.

Fear pounced, holding me at its mercy.

I was twenty-three years old. I had never really considered death with any seriousness. Now, I felt like it'd latched onto me unexpectedly. A haze swam across the dim room. I was blacking out. I found I didn't have enough energy to care overly much. I realized I was sinking toward the floor.

Was this really how things would end? They would find me shriv-eled and desiccated, dead on this wood floor? It seemed ridiculous. Pitiful.

Evan's face leapt into my mind's eye, the vision shockingly realistic, as if he stood in front of me... as if I could touch him.

I won't get to say goodbye to him.

I heard a raspy sound of protest, and realized it was coming from my own parched throat.

Distantly, I became aware that I sat on the floor now, my back against the obstinate door. How much time had passed? Again, I was uncomfort-ably aware of how fast my heart beat in my chest, as if I were running the race of a lifetime.

It can't keep going like that. It will give out soon in sheer exhaustion.

My towel had slipped off me. I could feel a sliver of cool air against my upper buttock and lower back. It came from the crack beneath the door, I realized with the barest glimmer of excitement. I told myself to move, but nothing happened. My limbs were like lead posts.

I forced myself to conjure up the image of Evan again.

With a gargantuan effort, I heaved myself onto my belly. Fingers digging into the wood planks of the floor, I managed to scoot forward several inches. I put my mouth to the crack under the door and drank in the cool air from the changing room in wild desperation, my lungs heaving. It felt divine, intoxicating... almost as glorious as the idea of chugging down a glass of deliciously cold water.

I opened my eyes, still sucking madly with my lips pressed to the bottom of the door. The crack beneath it was tiny and nearly indistin-guishable. Nevertheless, at such close proximity, I could make out two distinct shadows beneath it, two obstructions blocking the light from the changing room.

They were *shoes*, I realized in dull amazement. Someone stood just on the other side of the door, inches away from my lips.

As I stared, the shadows wavered and then vanished.

I inhaled more air. Minutes passed, as I tried to decide if the cool, refreshing blasts of oxygen had restored me enough to get off the floor.

The door swung outward. Light and cool air washed over me.

"Anna? My *God*, Anna? What happened?"

I recognized Valeria's anxious voice, even though the light had blinded me, and I couldn't see anything but her small, quick shadow kneeling in front of me.

"Door was blocked. Someone was holding it shut," I tried to say, but my words came out like I had a mouth and throat stuffed with sandpaper.

Valeria wanted to call an ambulance, but refrained when I demanded that she just help me to sit down in the changing room. The next thing I knew, she was handing me a glass of water and pressing a cold washcloth to my head. I'd never tasted anything so good in my life as that water. I handed her the empty glass, and she immediately went to get me more out of the water dispenser, and then more again.

After several minutes, the haze of misery that had enveloped me began to loosen its clutches. Valeria asked if I thought I could stand to get into the shower. I agreed, and with her help, made it over to one of the two shower stalls. Once there, my legs shook from weakness. Fortunately, there was a shower seat to which she guided me.

Cool water rushed over me, bringing down my body temperature. I sat there for I don't know how long, fisting the ledge of the seat, my head down and my wet hair streaming down around my face.

Finally, I lifted my head, feeling reasonably comfortable for the first time in what felt like an eternity. I stared up at Valeria. She stood in the shower stall with me. She was every bit as soaking wet as I was, but fully clothed, her face pulled tight in wild concern. I gave a bark of regretful laughter.

"God, Valeria, I'm sorry. I didn't mean for you—"

"It's okay," she said quickly. "Anna, are you all right?"

"I'm fine," I said automatically. I took a few seconds, focusing on my body. My skin felt cool, my heart had stopped its crazy, dangerous charge into the unknown. I shuddered, recalling how I'd wondered while I was stuck in the sauna how long the organ had before it just stopped from sheer exhaustion. Fear had made me exclusively, *repulsively* aware of my heart and its function, more so than I'd ever been in my life.

More so than I ever wanted to be again.

"Anna?" Valeria asked anxiously. I realized she'd seen my shudder of fear.

"I really am fine. I feel okay now. How did you find me?" I asked, realizing that she'd come *after* I'd ceased my banging and shouting.

"One of the construction workers came upstairs to the kitchen, looking for Evan. He said they'd found something in the viewing room when they were ripping down a cabinet there—a box of some kind. Here, let me help you," Valeria said when she saw me start to stand. "Hold on, Anna," she warned when I wavered.

I sat back down while she turned off the shower and stepped out of the stall to get towels for both of us. When she was satisfied that I was strong enough to stand and keep myself steady, we walked back out to the changing room. I sat down while I toweled off my hair.

"Did the construction workers hear me banging?"

"The guy who came up to the kitchen mentioned that he'd thought he'd heard some banging, and he didn't think it was from the crew. When he said that, about the banging, I realized how long you'd been down here. I started to get worried, and came to look for you."

"Maybe it was him," I breathed out. "Maybe he was the one who was holding the door closed."

Valeria blanched. "I can't imagine why he would do that. I *know* him. Kind of, anyway."

"Who is he?"

"His name is Jesse... Jesse Martin, I think? He's my younger brother's age, like twenty? Twenty-one? They were both on the football team. He's a good kid. Why would he try to lock you in the sauna?"

"I don't know," I said, just as confused as Valeria appeared to be. "You didn't see anyone else when you came to the dressing room? Anyone near the exercise room, or anywhere else they shouldn't have been?"

"No. The only person that wasn't where he usually would have been was Jesse, but he'd already returned to the viewing room to work by that time."

"How long was it after he left the kitchen before you came down here?"

She shrugged, thinking. "Almost immediately. I thought about what Jesse had said about the pounding for maybe a minute before I decided to check on you."

"I couldn't get out of there. I almost passed out from the heat, but the door wouldn't budge," I said, staring around the changing room, looking for some sign of an intruder's presence there. I saw nothing out of place. It took me a moment to realize Valeria hadn't responded.

"What's wrong?" I asked her when I saw her uncertain expression.

"But... there's no lock on the door. Anna, it opened easily for me the second I got here."

"Someone was holding it closed," I insisted. "I'm telling you, Valeria. Someone was out here, holding that damn door shut. I could see their feet under the door!"

"Okay, I believe you," Valeria assured, holding up her hands, her eyes wide in alarm.

"I saw movement. Or at least... I *thought* I did."

At that moment, I'd recalled the black spots I'd been seeing as I started to pass out, and the shimmering haze over my vision. Had those spots been responsible for what I'd thought were shadows on the other side of the door?

"But who would do something like that? Are you saying someone was trying purposefully to hurt you?"

Kill you?

Valeria didn't say the last, but I heard the voice in my head. It sounded melodramatic. Ridiculous. I stared at the sauna door, my mouth sagging open. Valeria hadn't shut it all the way when she'd helped me up off the floor. It hung open several inches, the exposed, smooth side of it making it clear there was no lock. It appeared benign. Innocent. Even if a very strong man had been holding it shut, I would have felt a give in the wood when I pressed against it. Wouldn't I have? Instead, it'd been like pushing against a ten-ton slab of rock.

"It happened," I said, but my voice shook as my confidence wavered.

Valeria nodded. "Then we'd better call the police," she said, digging in her shorts pocket for her phone.

"No... wait."

She blinked at my terse command.

"Do you think the door could have just been stuck?" I asked hesitantly. "I had the temperature in the sauna up really high. Maybe there was some kind of heat expansion on the door, and it made it stick?"

"I guess it's possible," Valeria admitted slowly. "I mean, *something* had to have happened. But still... it opened so easily for me."

I nodded, thinking, replaying the sequence of events in my head, and trying to make sense of the nonsensical.

"But at some point, I turned down the temperature as far as it could go, even though I couldn't turn it off all the way. It didn't feel like the air temperature went down that much afterward, but maybe that's because I was so overheated to start with. Maybe it'd cooled enough by the time you got here, and the door had contracted again?"

Valeria frowned. "If that's true, then the manufacturer of that sauna ought to be sued. Of course there's going to be expansion and contraction of the wood with the heat. You'd think they'd have that factored into the design."

"You're right," I said, standing. Thankfully, my legs held firm this time. "I'm going to call the manufacturer first thing tomorrow and tell them what happened. That was so scary."

"I'll bet. If I hadn't shown up, you could have been killed."

I glanced at her uneasily, shocked by hearing her say out loud what I'd feared the most while locked in that hotbox.

"Maybe you shouldn't mention this to Evan," I said. "I'd better be the one to tell him. He already worries enough about me as it is."

"If you think so," Valeria said, but I heard the anxiety in her tone.

I nodded, pretending confidence. "And I'm going to go and check with the work crew... ask that guy, Jesse, if he saw anything unusual when he came back from the kitchen."

Valeria did a double take. "You mean you're still not convinced? You think it could have been a person who was responsible for holding the door shut?"

"No, not really. It's just... I thought I was going to die in there," I admitted, laughing uneasily when I heard the words. They sounded strange. Surreal. A distance was already growing between the Anna who stood here chatting with Valeria, and that scared-shitless woman desperately sucking air from a tiny crack beneath the door. Maybe confronting death was just too big, too *awful* for my normal, everyday consciousness to dwell on for long, let alone comprehend.

"It'll just make me feel better to cover all the bases and hear what Jesse has to say," I assured, smiling in the face of Valeria's obvious concern.

She probably was starting to suspect I was crazy.

I was beginning to wonder about the same thing myself.

Chapter Eleven

THE EMOTIONAL DISTANCE BETWEEN MY SHARP FEAR OF WHAT HAD happened in the sauna and my typical, everyday sense of safety and normalcy continued to grow. So much so that by the time Evan called at around six thirty that evening, I didn't have to try overly hard to sound light and carefree in our conversation.

I'd tell him about what had happened in the sauna eventually. But I didn't want him to worry about it while he was away and had those important meetings on his mind. Especially since I'd gone to the viewing room earlier and spoken to Jesse.

Jesse had been just as Valeria described: friendly and unassuming. I couldn't have imagined a less likely candidate for attempted murder. The idea had never seemed more ludicrous than when I looked into his frank, open face.

It was the first time I'd been in the viewing room since that day after we'd arrived at Les Jumeaux. I was pleased to see the garish fabrics and the sickening odor were long gone. The space had been completely gutted, even the drywall torn out, leaving the wood beams exposed. Piles of rubble dotted the room. In one, I noticed a strip of vivid scarlet fabric amongst the torn white drywall and splintered wood planks.

A man in his late forties greeted me when I cautiously entered the large room, apologizing for the intrusion. He said his name was Dave Sanchez, and he seemed to be the second-in-command, acting as supervisor in absence of Keith, the man who owned the construction business and Evan's acquaintance.

"I'm the one who asked Jesse to take the box upstairs to Mr. Halifax," Dave explained after I'd stated my case and he'd called Jesse over at my request. "I hope that it wasn't a problem that I sent him up to the main house?"

"No, not at all," I assured, smiling at Jesse who stood awkwardly next to Dave.

"Something happened to me over in the workout facility at around the same time you went upstairs. It wasn't a big deal. But when Valeria mentioned that you'd been up to the kitchen at around the same time, I just wanted to ask: did you see anyone or anything out of place on your way to or from the kitchen?" I asked Jesse.

"No, ma'am," Jesse said, his Adam's apple bobbing as he swallowed. "I did hear some pounding. It was coming from a different part of the house, so I didn't think it was us," he said, holding up the hammer he clutched in his hand. "I mentioned hearing it to Valeria, when I gave her the box."

"Yes. She told me you'd mentioned it, thank you," I said.

"You didn't give the box to Mr. Halifax, like I told you?" Dave asked Jesse sharply.

Jesse started to open his mouth to defend himself, but I spoke first.

"Evan was away for the afternoon," I explained, keeping it vague. There was no need to tell people Evan was away for the entire weekend. I started to thank them for talking with me when I noticed Dave's troubled expression.

"Is everything all right?" I asked him.

"Yes. But that box... "

"Yeah, what *about* that?" I wondered frankly. The shock of being locked in the sauna, and my physical recovery afterward, had dampened my curiosity about this mysterious box. Until now, anyway. "Valeria mentioned that you found it here, in this room?"

"Yeah," Dave said, shifting on his feet. "The bar and the cabinet were one of the last things we tore down. We found it in there in a locked compartment. I thought it should go to Mr. Halifax right away. I didn't realize he wasn't here, at the house."

"I'll make sure he gets it the second he comes back. Well, thanks for taking a second to talk to me."

As I came downstairs after talking to Evan on the phone, a divine scent entered my nose.

"Whatever you're making smells fantastic," I told Valeria as I entered the kitchen.

"Coq au vin and oven roasted asparagus," Valeria said. "Do you want to eat out on the terrace?"

"No, why don't we just sit here at the counter," I suggested, pointing at several stools situated next to the island.

"We?" Valeria asked, straightening with a pan in her hand, her eyes wide. "You want me to eat with you?"

"Uh... yeah, is that okay?"

"I guess. I don't know," she laughed as she set down the asparagus. "I've never really had a job like this before. I don't know the rules, exactly. I don't want to break any accidentally."

"Well, I've certainly never had someone... you know, cooking and doing things for me before," I confessed. "It feels really weird for me, too." I realized Valeria seemed as uncomfortable as I did, and rallied.

"Look, there's no doubt that Evan didn't hire you to be a typical cook and maid. I think he wanted you to be another friendly face around the house. And you've really been that so far. You were nice enough to come out here and spend the weekend with me, and that's not at all part of your job duties. Maybe we should just sort of figure things out as we go along?"

"Sounds good to me," Valeria said gamely.

"And in that spirit... can we just open up a bottle of wine and eat this amazing dinner you made at the counter?" I asked hopefully.

Valeria laughed and nodded.

I spent half the meal gushing over how delicious the food she'd prepared was. I wasn't lying. Valeria clearly possessed layers of talent.

In retrospect, I think we both wanted to avoid the topic of what had happened in the sauna. For me, the whole memory had become charged with fear, embarrassment, and doubt. For Valeria, I imagine it was just yet another weird thing she had to deal with in regard to her new employers.

Instead, we talked about our planned dive tomorrow.

"I talked to Manny, and he says he can take us out on the boat," Valeria said.

"That's great," I replied, taking a sip of wine. The Languedoc red I'd chosen to go with dinner had a real kick to it. Maybe that—or the unusual stress of the day—was responsible for what I said next.

"So… you and Wes Ryder?" I said with a little twitch to my shoulders and a grin. "What's the story there?"

I immediately regretted my off-the-cuff comment when Valeria's smile vanished in a split second. I set down my wineglass.

"I'm sorry. I didn't mean to pry." I rolled my eyes. "Jesus, this wine is strong. Forget I said it. I just thought—"

"It's okay," Valeria interrupted. She gave a shaky smile. "I'm not the one who wanted to keep it secret."

"Just forget I mentioned it," I said, mortified.

"No, it's okay. Wes and I met at the casino I used to waitress at, a couple months ago. He was a regular."

"At the bar?"

"No, at the tables," she said evenly.

"Oh," I said, sitting back slightly and trying to picture it. Valeria smiled at my reaction.

"Don't look so shocked, Anna. This is Nevada. People gamble. Besides, gambling isn't even the worst of Wes's habits. But as to why we're keeping it secret, I think Wes didn't want me to mention it because of Evan."

"Evan?"

"Because Wes and Evan are old friends? And Evan asked him for a recommendation for the job here at Les Jumeaux, and Wes suggested me… "

She trailed off, looking uncomfortable.

"I see. You guys were worried Evan would think Wes recommended you, just because—"

"We're sleeping together. Yeah," Valeria said, her voice sounding rough. She glanced up at me from beneath lowered lashes and sighed.

"Sorry. Didn't mean to be sharp. It's just that… well, that's all there really is between Wes and me. Sex, I mean. That's all he wants there to be," she added under her breath.

"And you want there to be more?"

She shrugged and moved some chicken around her plate.

148

"He's way out of my league. He's a doctor and he comes from a really old, good family in town."

"Whatever *good* means. Your family sounds every bit as good, in my book."

She gave me a little smile.

"Anyway, it doesn't matter about the job," I told her bracingly. "Wes was right to recommend you, whatever the status of your relationship. Forget the fact that you saved my life earlier. I would have hired you for this meal alone," I told her, taking another succulent bite of chicken. Something caught my eye.

"Oh," I cried out, swallowing and setting down my fork. "Is that the box?"

I pointed at a dusty mahogany box on the shelf adjacent to my knees. It was about two feet wide and nine or ten inches deep, with elaborate carving on it. It was really more of a small chest, I realized. I hadn't noticed it when we first sat down at the island.

"Yeah. That's what Jesse brought upstairs. I wasn't sure what to do with it, so I just stuck it there for now," Valeria said, sounding relieved to change the subject.

I leapt down from my barstool. "Have you opened it yet?" I asked Valeria, bending down to get the box.

"No... I wouldn't."

I straightened, holding the heavy box in my hands. Valeria's cheeks were flushed even more than they had been before. I shook my head once in regret. I was rotten at dealing with a paid employee in the house.

Lady of the manor I was *not*.

"Of course you wouldn't," I said, giving her an apologetic glance before I set the heavy box on the top of the island. I ran my fingers along the seam and over the bronze clasp. "I'm not sure I know how to open—Ah," I said in satisfaction when I felt the fastener give. I flipped open the box.

For several seconds, my brain didn't entirely comprehend the contents.

They were sex things—handcuffs, a leather lasher, a ball gag, leather straps and restraints and other things I didn't immediately recognize. I also saw a clear bag filled with various colored capsules.

There were a dozen or so Blu-ray discs with hand-written abbreviations on them and dates. I read one: A, E, J &W, June 2003.

I slammed the lid shut. Valeria jumped where she sat across the island. One glance at her face and I knew she hadn't seen what I had. The lid had blocked her view.

"It's some files and documents," I said, lifting the box. "I'll just take it over to Evan's office. Back in a second."

I felt strangely numb as I walked down the hallway, burning box in tow. Maybe it was naïve of me. Evan and I had a very active, extremely good sex life, after all.

At least I'd *thought* we had.

But we'd never crossed the boundary into the *box* territory. We'd never restrained each other up with cuffs or leather straps, or whipped each other, or taken drugs to enhance our response... or made movies.

Again, I pictured that garish viewing room as it had been, its air of cloying decadence and decay.

To whom had the box belonged? I wondered as I entered Evan's office. He'd left a lamp on near the couch. I walked through the shadowed room and set down the box on his desk. It felt weird, like I didn't know whether I was leaving him something he'd find offensive, or something forbidden.

Exciting?

What would Evan think when he saw it? How would he feel about me having seen it? I resisted a wild urge to open the box again. There had been an "E" in that list of letters and a date. Had that "E" referred to Elizabeth?

Or Evan?

Maybe both of them had been involved? My assumption was that the other initials referred to other participants.

A wave of nausea swept through me. I choked back a strong urge to vomit.

That old feeling of immaturity and inadequacy that I'd felt frequently at the beginning of Evan's and my relationship plunged through me again, seemingly a thousand times sharper this time. It was as if it'd been there all along, but held at bay by Evan's obvious desire for me.

By the fact that he'd made me his wife.

But what did I really know about him? What kind of cravings did he keep locked inside him?

Because I'm sinful.

I heard his muffled, deep voice echo around my head, shame and anger knitted into every uttered word. I gripped the edge of his desk and swallowed back my nausea.

You knew he had a past when you married him. You can't hold things over his head that he did in another lifetime.

But what if those cravings remained, and he's stifling them. For me?

Had Elizabeth shared in his desires at one point in his life... fulfilled them? I recalled him speaking with so much emotion. *"I loved Elizabeth once, that's true. I used to think she was the most perfect thing in existence."*

I groaned softly and pushed myself away from the desk. It was too much.

I walked away from the box.

Inevitably, I'd have to deal with it when I showed it to Evan after he returned. I'd have to cope with his response to it, whatever that might be.

But at that moment, that box represented mysteries I was too inexperienced—or maybe too unwilling—to confront.

Chapter Twelve

I THOUGHT I'D DREAM THAT NIGHT, BUT MAYBE MY BRAIN COULDN'T handle any more stress after what I'd been through that day. I awoke feeling surprisingly refreshed to a pristine summer morning like only Tahoe can produce. Fears and doubts wilted and crumbled on a day like today.

Valeria's brother arrived at around noon, just as I was coming down from the overlook after a decent morning of painting. Manny Caro reminded me of a male version of Valeria: compact, cute, and charming, with that athletic ease and comfort in his skin that I admired so much.

Valeria did another careful inspection of the dive equipment we planned to use. After she gave the okay, Manny, Valeria, and I hauled everything we needed out to the cruiser. Ever since Valeria had mentioned this drastic drop-off close to the shore—the Great Wall, as she'd called it—I was eager to explore it.

As I'd already discovered with Evan, scuba diving in Tahoe is not like diving in the ocean. There are no cute fish zipping around you, or colorful coral, or seaweed. The clarity of the water is stunning, but the underwater world is strangely barren.

My dive with Evan had been fantastic. I hadn't told him this, but I'd also found it eerie. Beneath the surface, Tahoe was a beautiful but haunted place. As Evan and I got to a depth of forty feet or so, the sunlight penetrating the crystalline water turned an inky blue. There was a strange stillness that made me feel watched by some vast, cold consciousness.

Today, Manny used the sonar onboard the cruiser to find a good spot for our dive. We didn't go out far. As I sat on the edge of the boat with Valeria, I could easily see the rocky shore and Les Jumeaux, and even the beige, waterproof locker up on the overlook where I stored my painting supplies.

Valeria gave me thumbs-up. We went over the edge into shallow water, only twenty-five feet or so deep. Once I'd gotten my bearings in the cerulean, sunlight-flooded waters, I spotted Valeria. She waved, and I followed her lead.

The surface below us consisted of a whitish-gray, rough sand. Everything looked bleached and clean. Dead. Sunlight poured around us, but I saw no signs of life. There was something skeletal about diving in Tahoe. Something secret.

Suddenly, the floor dropped out beneath us. We swam over a cliff into a yawning, black depth. A thrill passed through me. Coldness immediately penetrated the neoprene of my suit.

Valeria turned in the water in front of me and pointed down. I nodded and followed her down the vast, vertical stone wall. I'd never seen anything like it. It was epic in size. We were like little ants scurrying in the water in front of it.

We descended along the wall, forty feet, fifty feet. It gave me some kind of primitive, primal feeling of mingled awe and fear. I remembered how the scuba guide Evan had hired had told us jokingly about the famous diver Jacques Cousteau. Rumor had it that years ago, Cousteau went scuba diving in Lake Tahoe. He emerged from the water and appeared to be emotionally shaken. "The world is not ready for what I have seen," Cousteau allegedly said.

I had no problem believing that rumor as Valeria and I swam deeper along that enormous stone wall, Valeria slightly ahead of me. The light deepened to a gloomy cobalt blue. Despite the sound of air gurgling from my buoyancy-compensating device, I was struck by an overwhelming sense of silence and stillness.

At around sixty feet below the surface, Valeria paused ahead of me and waved her arms in excitement. I swam deeper and realized why. We'd come upon a break in the wall. The underwater cavern opening must have been thirty feet long. I couldn't even tell how wide it was because the entrance spread so far. Valeria pointed into the hole and made a dive hand signal. I understood. She'd asked if I wanted to enter the large cave opening—not far, just a few feet to look around.

I gave her the "okay" sign in response.

We took out our dive lights. Valeria entered the large cavern first, her light beaming a path. I was relieved to see that the walls were wide and spacious. They shone a ghostly white. I had the brief impression I swam inside a giant stone whale. Adrenaline spiked through me, making my flesh tingle with heat despite the cold just outside my suit.

The tunnel of gray boulders narrowed some, but still, there were no tight spaces that made me claustrophobic or cautious. I shined my light all around the tunnel, seeing smooth stone, cracks, and fissures of various sizes. But I swam in wide-open space. Where my dive light didn't penetrate, the blackness was so thick it seemed to have weight.

I don't how long I swam, but suddenly, I realized I was alone. Valeria was nowhere around me. I abruptly stopped swimming, disoriented. How far had I gone? It was almost like I'd lost time there for a moment.

Almost.

I turned. I saw the cobalt blue of the lake beyond the opening of the cavern in the far distance. The cave opening wavered eerily behind Valeria's oncoming dive light. I blinked and shook my head to clear it. What I saw bore no similarity to what Valeria had suggested with her sign language: a cautious, short entry a few feet into the cave to look around.

Valeria had to be a good forty or fifty feet behind me. I hadn't even been aware of passing her. I shone my light at her as she swam toward me. She winced as the direct beam hit her face. I quickly tilted my light upward, hovering in the still, icy cold water.

The roof of the cavern went up and up, smooth stretches of granite interspersed with stacks of boulders. I thought I saw something. Acting on impulse, I switched off my dive light.

Up at the very top of the vertical tunnel above me, a light glimmered. I blinked, sure I must be imagining the solitary light.

At the same time, it was almost like I'd *expected* that light to be there.

Was it somehow a reflection of Valeria's dive light as she neared me? But no... Valeria shone her dive light downward, just below my fins. Her light dispersed, while the one above me was a solitary pinprick of illumination, like a lit bulb.

That steady light made no sense.

I felt a touch on my shoulder and glanced down, only to see Valeria's anxious eyes behind her dive mask. A shiver tore through me. She looked strange hovering just a foot or two away from me, the whites of her eyes showing. I couldn't shake this feeling of eeriness... of the almost preternatural.

She gestured rapidly with her arm toward dark blue mouth of the cave. I nodded, and started to follow her out of the pitch-black cavern. I saw her turn, as if to make sure I followed her. I felt like a naughty child.

I had no idea why I'd swum so deep into that impenetrable darkness alone, or why I'd outdistanced her. It wasn't at all like me. I'd been a cautious diver from the first, always following a more experienced diver's lead.

Maybe this whole thing with the discovered box filled with all those sex things had me more bothered than I'd thought.

We surfaced into the blinding sunlight. Once Manny had helped us back onto the cruiser and we were taking off our gear, Valeria demanded to know what I'd been doing.

"Did you see something in the cave?" she asked tensely. "You took off like a torpedo."

Confronted with her puzzled concern, I couldn't think of what to say. I didn't know *why* I'd swum away from her like that. Everything had gone black there for a period of time. Or it hadn't, really... I couldn't explain it. I distantly recalled swimming with a feeling of sure confidence, decisiveness.

Excitement.

"I saw a light," I blurted out.

The lie had just popped out of my mouth. It wasn't entirely a lie. I *had* seen a light, but not until I'd come back to myself and stopped swimming.

"A light?" Valeria asked, shrugging as Manny helped remove her tank.

"Yeah. The ceiling of the cave opened up, and way up high, there was a light."

"That's weird," Valeria mumbled, her gaze on me odd, like I wasn't exactly what she'd expected.

"I'm sorry, I don't know why I swam ahead of you. I won't do it again."

"It could have been dangerous," Valeria said, her eyebrows knitted together in concern and irritation. "We should stick together when we dive."

Don't let her see you sweat it. It's not for her to judge you.

I'm not sure where the voice came from exactly. But I recognized it as one that I heard sometimes when I felt put on the spot or awkward. I thought of it as some kind of "confined lady of the realm" part of my personality that popped out of her closet every once in a while when I felt cornered and defensive.

"I know. Like I said, I won't do it again." Somehow, I knew that edge in my voice would silence her.

And it did.

Chapter Thirteen

I FELT UNUSUALLY TIRED AFTER WE RETURNED TO LES JUMEAUX AND stored the dive equipment. I told Valeria I was going to take a nap. Ignoring her concerned expression, I headed up the stairs and fell into bed, where I immediately dropped into a dead sleep.

I awoke to elongated shadows in the bedroom. My cell phone was ringing. I sat up, feeling extremely disoriented. I picked up the phone and checked the caller ID.

"Hi, honey," I said groggily.

"Hi. What's wrong?" Evan asked me, concern in his tone. I realized my voice sounded very ragged.

"Nothing. We went diving this afternoon. I think I overdid it a little. I was wiped out when we got back. I was napping when you called."

"Sorry for waking you. You must have been tired. You don't take naps often."

"I know."

"Did you have a good time diving?"

"Yeah. Manny, Valeria's brother, took us out on the cruiser. We dived near the shore here. It was amazing. How are your meetings going so far?"

"Fine. Nothing out of the ordinary." There was a long pause. "Anna? Are you sure you're all right? You sound strange."

I laughed. "I feel a little strange, to be honest," I confessed, rubbing my itchy eyes. I stood and headed toward the bathroom, desperate for a glass of water. I started to suspect that the stressful incident in the sauna, the discovery of the box, and my strange behavior diving today wasn't all adding up.

I felt as if I was getting sick.

Valeria agreed with me that the experience in the sauna might have worn me down more than we'd thought. She was very sweet, insisting I take it easy and bringing me dinner in bed. I had no interest in arguing with her about it, which seemed to me further proof that I was a little under the weather. So I did a little Netflix bingeing and ate Valeria's delicious supper of mandarin orange chicken and salad.

I was asleep by ten o'clock.

The nightmare woman came to me again that night, her presence once again turning my body into a locked prison. This time, much to my horror, I heard her gurgling voice more clearly. Not, *light in the darkness,* as I'd previously thought.

Light from my darkness.

And then:

Swim deep.

That's what I heard in the ghost's rattling throat.

The message left me highly unnerved. The most obvious reason was that I'd seen a light in the darkness when I'd swum impulsively into that cave. But something else left me uneasy about those ghostly words... something I couldn't quite put my finger on.

I spent a good portion of the night sleepless, that disturbing, inexplicable message lying heavily on my consciousness. I didn't fall asleep again until dawn had broken.

I awoke to sunshine streaming around the curtains. I experienced a familiar sense of urgency about my work. It wasn't the time for me to be puzzling out the bizarre message of a nightmare. I wanted to finish my painting today, and the light appeared to be perfect for it.

While I was in the bathroom, I heard my cell phone ringing. I sprung for it when I saw it was Evan calling.

"Morning. Feeling better today?" he asked.

"Much. A good night's sleep is just what I needed. I think I might have been coming down with something when we talked yesterday, but hopefully I've licked it. There was a little incident the day before yesterday. Maybe it ran down my immune system."

I hadn't planned to tell him about getting stuck in the sauna until he returned. Maybe at that moment, it seemed safer to bring up the sauna than it did my inexplicable, irrational behavior diving with Valeria yesterday.

Or the box.

"Incident?" Evan asked, his tone going sharp.

"It was nothing. The door on the dry sauna got stuck. I was locked in the heat until Valeria saved me. Damn... I meant to call the manufacturer yesterday to tell them about the door expanding and contracting—"

"Anna, what the hell are you talking about?"

"The door on the dry sauna expanded from the heat and got stuck," I repeated.

"With you in it?"

"Yeah."

"That door shouldn't get stuck. It never has before."

"Well, it did," I said with a little laugh. Given his apprehension, I felt a necessity to keep things light. "I'll admit, I had the heat turned up as high as it could go. Anyway, the door contracted again eventually, and Valeria got me out. I think it dehydrated me, even though I drank an ocean of water afterward. My immune system must have taken a hit. But like I said, I feel much better today."

It took me several seconds to realize he hadn't replied.

"Evan?"

"Don't go back into the sauna until I have someone out to check it," he insisted tensely.

"I wasn't planning on it, trust me. That was *not* a fun experience. So... you think you'll be home in time for dinner tonight?"

"Yes. I think we need to talk about something," he said.

I silently agreed, grimly thinking of that taboo box I'd set on his desk.

In the kitchen, I saw signs of Valeria—a full pot of coffee and diced vegetables on the cutting board, presumably for an omelet—but no Valeria herself.

When she didn't return after I'd drunk half a cup of coffee, I began to look around a little. Some instinct pulled me to the front entryway. I opened one of the heavy wooden doors.

Sure enough, there was Valeria, standing on the front stone steps wearing a pair of running shorts, a tank top, and tennis shoes. She started at the sound of the door opening. She wasn't alone.

"Hi, Wes," I said, sounding as startled as Wes Ryder looked. He looked especially pale this morning, and a light sheen of sweat covered his handsome face. *For a doctor, he doesn't look like he's in very good shape.*

"Anna," he said, shoving his hands in his pockets and peering up at me like a guilty eight-year-old kid. His gaze stuck on my face, and I experienced that feeling of self-consciousness I often experienced in his presence. "Sorry to bother you this morning."

"Is everything all right?" I asked.

"Yeah. I got a call from Noah's nurse this morning. He's back from the hospital today, so I came out to make sure he got settled all right."

"He's been at the hospital this whole time?" I asked, shocked. I'd assumed Madaster had returned at some point, not because I'd seen anything to prove it, one way or another. The only thing I was basing my suspicion on was that feeling of being watched I'd get sometimes at the overlook.

"No, not the entire time. Noah actually returned to Les Jumeaux the evening of the window incident," Wes explained, grimacing slightly when he said *window incident*. "But he had chest pains a few days ago, and I recommended to Ima that she take him in to the emergency room. They ended up keeping him for a few nights for testing."

"Is he better now?"

Wes frowned. "He had a very minor heart attack, but he's recovered. He's stabilized on some new meds. Noah is usually stronger than a bull, despite the spinal cord injury, but he's been having a bit of a rough go lately." His gaze ran over my face again. I couldn't help but wonder if Madaster was worse off than Wes implied.

"Anyway, I came over to see Evan just now, but Valeria told me he was out of town," Wes said. "And then, we got our own visitor."

He waved uneasily to his right. I realized I couldn't see what he was referring to, and opened the door wider.

There, standing on the stone pavers of the circular drive, was the old, demented woman. She stood several paces away from the steps, her manner extremely wary. I was glad to see her. I knew it was unusual for her to come so close to the house or to other people.

"Good morning. Are you out walking?" I asked her warmly. "Are you hungry at all? Would you like some breakfast?"

She didn't reply. I had the impression she'd bolt at the slightest move. She just stared at me with those filmed-over blue eyes I recalled so well. Today she wore a faded flower print dress, which hung on her loosely and was slipping off one bony shoulder. Beneath the dress I spotted a grayish tank top that had once been white.

"Have you two met?" Wes asked, looking surprised.

"Yes. We ran into each other up at the overlook a few weeks ago," I said, speaking directly to the old woman. "But I didn't ever find out your name."

I noticed Wes give Valeria an uneasy glance.

"Anna, this is Lorraine Madaster," Wes said.

I started.

"No. No, that's not right," I insisted.

"Wait... are you *sure*?" I asked Wes when I saw his blank incredulity. He'd clearly been taken aback by my flat denial of what he'd said.

"Yes, I'm quite certain," Wes said with an awkward little laugh. "I've been her physician on and off for seven years."

"I'm sorry, it's just that Evan said—"

"Worthless piece of shit," the old woman hissed.

While all three of us stared at her in open-mouthed surprise, she turned in her dirty high tops and stalked away in the direction of the road. Her stride was much steadier than it had been that day on the overlook.

Had she been talking about Wes or Evan?

Before I could elaborate on the thought, or think of anything reasonable to say to call her back, she disappeared around the bend in the road.

"Anna? Are you all right?"

I blinked, focusing on Valeria.

"I guess. When I met her before, Evan told me she was—"

A harmless demented woman who lived down the coast a ways, and who occasionally wandered onto the property.

"How long as she been like that?" I asked Wes.

He shrugged. "Ten years? It started around then, anyway, and has gotten progressively worse every year. Early onset Alzheimer's."

A roaring sound like a muffled high wind had started up in my ears. Ten years? Evan must have *known* who she was when I described her to him. He'd lived here at Les Jumeaux when she'd first been diagnosed.

Of course he'd known.

Which meant that he'd known the Madasters were living in the South Twin all along. He must have known when we came there.

Evan had been lying to me all this time. But *why*?

The only answer I got to that question was a black, enigmatic coldness. It was that same void I saw in Evan's eyes sometimes.

My heart gave an uncomfortable jump in my chest. I put my hand over it, pressing down as if trying to keep it in place.

"Valeria? Do you think you could drive me somewhere this morning?" I asked. I saw her and Wes exchange another uneasy glance.

"Sure. But I thought you wanted to try and finish your painting today."

"It'll wait," I said distractedly.

"Do you think you need to see a doctor?"

"A doctor?" I asked her in blank non-comprehension. "*No*... no, I was wondering if you could take me to the library. In Carson City?"

The roaring in my ears had grown louder.

Suddenly, it was if I'd been transported in time back to that evening I'd gone to meet Evan for dinner in San Francisco, determined to break up with him because I knew there was something not right, something *unnatural* about our relationship.

I needed to face facts. I'd suspected that Evan was keeping things from me. Things about Elizabeth, perhaps. Things about his past with her... his heartbreak about the breakdown of their marriage, and her disappearance and death. It struck me as I stood there that I'd partially been responsible for his silence. I understood his suffering at the loss of a wife, or at least I thought I did. But the thought of hearing him elaborate on his grief pained me.

But this was different. He'd brought me here, knowing full well that the Madasters lived in the South Twin. Why would he do such a thing? I was being left in the dark, like the naïve, helpless ingénue he seemed to imagine I was. The Internet had been unhelpful.

The only way I was going to get any answers as to the mystery of how I'd ended up here at this moment in my life was to find those answers on my own.

When we got to the library entrance in Carson City later that morning, I told Valeria that I didn't know how long I'd be.

"Do you have any errands or shopping you need to do?" I asked her from where I sat in the passenger seat. "You could pick me up here in say... two hours? If I think I'll be longer, I could text you?"

Valeria agreed, but I could tell she was concerned. I'd been vague in my explanations about what I hoped to accomplish at the library, and distracted and noncommunicative during the half-hour drive to the city.

For my own part, I wasn't sure what I was feeling. A strange chill had come over me that I associated with fear or panic, but it wasn't like any kind of dread I'd ever experienced. A cold, hard kind of sensation accompanied it. As I entered the library and searched for the information desk, I distantly recognized it as determination.

I felt sick with dread, but the idea of ignoring the truth seemed as impossible to me as cutting my own throat.

The woman sitting behind the circular desk at the center of the main room had gray, short hair. She looked at her computer screen when I approached her and began to speak. She glanced at me, did a double take, and peered at me more closely. I noticed how sharp and assessing her blue eyes were behind her glasses.

"I was hoping you could help me? I need to access some old newspaper articles and I really don't know how to do it," I said regretfully.

The librarian gave a little smile. "You don't have to be apologetic. Nobody your age knows how to use microfilm anymore for research. Why would you, when you've always had computers?"

She stood up and started to come around the desk.

"Can I ask what you're looking for?"

I hesitated.

"I'm interested in a family—the Madasters. Specifically, anything about Noah Madaster's career." The librarian just nodded matter-of-factly and waited patiently to see if I said anything else. I had no doubt she knew who the Madasters were. They were a prominent family in the area, after all. Her nonchalant reaction was so unlike anything I'd experienced with Evan. I hadn't realized until that moment, standing there with a stranger, how charged the atmosphere always became at the mere mention of the name Madaster.

"I'd also like to find all the articles available about Elizabeth Madaster's disappearance seven years ago," I said.

"Follow me," the librarian said. She began walking at a brisk pace. "For Noah Madaster's governorship, you might want to start off with the *Las Vegas Review-Journal* or the *Reno Gazette-Journal*, although anything on his early career as a physician might be more easily found in our local paper, the *Nevada Appeal*. Same for anything on Elizabeth Madaster, seeing as how she grew up and lived in the Carson City-Tahoe area. How are you related?"

We'd left the large entrance area of the library and were walking down a wide corridor. The librarian glanced over her shoulder at me inquiringly. It took me a few seconds to replay what she'd said in my head, and respond.

"How am I related to the topic?" I asked, thinking she was asking me why I held an interest in the Madaster family.

The librarian's eyebrows pinched together. "No, I meant how are you related, family-wise? I'm sorry, I just assumed."

"Oh, *no*. I'm not related to the Madasters. I'm just doing some research, and it's very hard to find anything online."

The librarian's footsteps slowed. "Like a photo of either of them, for instance?"

"Yes. I couldn't find even one photo."

We'd come to a stop in the corridor. The librarian glanced behind me uneasily.

"Is something wrong?" I asked, looking over my shoulder, but not seeing anything out of place behind me.

"Elizabeth Madaster was the head of the charitable organization that spearheaded the building of this library. Did you know that?" the librarian asked me, her tone gentle. Cautious?

"I didn't. I did know she was very involved philanthropically." A thought occurred to me. "Does that mean you knew her?"

The librarian nodded.

"But you *do* realize that you and she—" She waved her hand circularly in the vicinity of her chin, giving me a pointed look.

"I don't have any idea what you're talking about," I told her with a nervous laugh.

"I may as well show you," she said after a pause, pointing behind me and walking in that direction. "You'll find out soon enough when you look at the microfilm."

I followed her fifteen or so feet down the corridor. A low row of bookshelves ran along the length of the hallway. Above the bookshelves, various commemorative plaques and photos associated with the library had been mounted on the wall.

"This is a photo of Elizabeth Madaster," the librarian said, turning to watch my reaction. "You can see why I assumed... "

I looked into the dark blue eyes of the woman in the photograph.

Everything seemed to fly away from me. Only the photo and my body remained fixed in time and space.

The woman in the portrait was myself.

Chapter Fourteen

SOMEONE WAS TALKING, EVEN THOUGH THE SPEECH WAS INSIGNIFI-
cant, like the patter of raindrops on the window during an earthquake.

The first urge that rose up powerfully inside me was to laugh.

I'd been so caught up, so consumed by all my insecurities about
Elizabeth. Every time I'd fantasized about what she was like, the camera
in my brain remained unfocused. I glimpsed her enigmatic smile before
she turned away in my imagination, or experienced the magnetic, dreaded
allure of her dark sexuality. I breathed her, that's how omnipresent she
was at Les Jumeaux... or when I was with my husband...

When we were in our bed.

Always in my imaginings, she was *more* than. I stood in her shadow.

But I'd never once dreamt that my appeal to Evan was that I *was* her.

Not completely, of course. No one could ever truly fill her shoes.
But the photo I stared at could have been a glamour shot of me—a
more polished, more confident, slightly older version of Anna Solas with
shoulder-length hair.

If it weren't for the age difference, we might have been identical twins.

"Damn. I shouldn't have shown you, should I have?" I blinked and
focused on the librarian's face. Her eyes were wide with alarm.

It felt as if an hour had passed as I stared at her face in the portrait,
but it was more likely just the longest minute I'd ever lived. I realized
vaguely the librarian had been speaking to me the whole time, and that
her lined face appeared very concerned.

"Of course you should have shown me," I said, my voice sounding surprisingly level.

"You... you honestly didn't know, did you?"

"No, I had no idea."

"But your interest in the Madaster family? I just figured it was related."

I'm interested in Elizabeth Madaster because she's my husband's former wife. I'm obsessed with her because she's my husband's obsession. Apparently, he chose me on an Internet dating site because of Elizabeth. He's married me because I'm her physical double.

Everything I thought was true sixty seconds ago, including the fact that my husband loved me for who I am, is now a complete and utter lie.

I didn't say those things, though. Instead, I said neutrally, "They say we all have one, you know."

"Have one?"

"A doppelganger," I told the librarian with a dry smile. I couldn't believe I sounded so normal. "Someone out there in the world who is our double. Myth has it that when you see your doppelganger, you're about to die."

The librarian started slightly. Maybe I hadn't sounded as normal as I thought I had.

"Are you sure? There's no way you are related to the Madasters?" she asked.

I shook my head.

"I'm from the Chicago area. My parents are the polar opposite of the Madasters. It's just some freak of nature."

A random arrangement of genes. An anomaly that had fallen onto my life like a mile-wide asteroid.

"Do you mind if I take a photo of the portrait?" I asked the librarian.

"Of course not," she said. She seemed very startled by the sequence of events, but I could feel no empathy toward her in that moment. I was operating on automatic. After I'd taken a couple shots, and read over the plaques and framed articles commemorating Elizabeth's dogged and dedicated service in getting the library built, I turned to the librarian.

"I think I'll come back another day, if you don't mind? To finish the research?"

It was a lie. I doubted I'd ever be to this part of the country again in my life.

"Of course," she said. She surprised me by reaching out and squeezing my forearm. "I am so sorry. I didn't handle this very well at all. I made an assumption about why you were interested in the Madasters."

"It's all right. I'm glad you showed me."

The librarian nodded. I turned to leave. I had only my next move in mind, the next one hundred or so steps to the front door. My brain and body buzzed with uncomfortable energy. Walking to the front door was all I could plan at that moment.

"I mentioned I knew her."

I spun around at the sound of the librarian's voice.

"Elizabeth Madaster," the librarian said. "She was the kind of woman that you could tell had a lot on her mind... the type of person you suspected had been through a lot. But she was always kind to me. She was a real lady. She told me in the beginning we were going to get this library built, and she never wavered in that promise, even when the odds were stacked against us. Elizabeth Madaster could have moved a mountain with the force of her charm and sheer will."

Of course she was, I thought resignedly. *She was a saint, a lady, a mystery, and a whore. All of the things men found irresistible.*

Including my husband, apparently.

So here it was, I thought as I sat in the passenger seat of the car and we began the climb back up into the mountains.

The truth at last.

Evan had married me because of my shockingly strong resemblance to his dead first wife.

"It looks like we might get rain tonight," Valeria observed as she drove. I sensed her glance over at me. "Anna, are you sure everything is okay?"

"Did you know that I look almost exactly like Evan's first wife, Elizabeth?"

"*What?*"

My hand went out reflexively to handle on the door when we swerved on the road.

Valeria quickly corrected the car. "What are you talking about?"

"I saw a picture of her, there at the library. We might be twins," I said. I studied Valeria's profile as she stared ahead at the road. I thought her incredulity was genuine.

But then again, what kind of a judge of character was I, really? What kind of discerner of the truth?

It was an epic joke to think I could see behind a person's façade to their true self.

"Wes never said anything to you about it?" I challenged. "Or Evan? Because they both knew. All along. They've both been playing some kind of game with me." At that moment, a vivid memory popped into my brain of Wes Ryder topping the rise of the overlook, and starting in surprise when he'd seen me. I'd thought his shock was strange, since he'd gone up there in search of me. But my presence hadn't been what had taken him aback. The fact that I was the spitting image of Elizabeth Madaster had.

My mind went back to the first moment I'd met Evan, face to face. Now his careful reserve combined with those sudden flashes of heat and desire took on a whole new meaning.

"No, Anna. I swear I didn't know," Valeria said breathlessly, clamping the steering wheel hard.

Fury suddenly swept through me. It felt like a handhold. I grabbed at it in desperation. I recalled how Evan had claimed to fall for me through my art, and how I'd believed him, because I'd wanted to. I'd needed to believe he saw me like no one else had... like no one else *could*. In reality, he'd been seeing another woman the entire time. I—Anna Solas—had been invisible.

Insignificant.

That he'd manipulated me in that *particular* way, using my art, my unique means for expressing myself to the world, felt like the most infuriating betrayal to me at that moment.

He had noticed my similarity to Elizabeth through the dating site, found out about my life. I'd handed myself to him on a platter by using that dating service. He realized I worked for Tommy Higoshi. How convenient that'd been, that we coincidentally shared that mutual contact.

Evan had *schemed* to meet me.

That's why Tommy had felt compelled to tell me on the eve of my wedding that Evan had made of point of asking to see my paintings even before he'd joined the dating site. At the time, I recalled thinking Tommy's manner had been odd when he'd told me that, like he'd been trying to give me some kind of coded message. Now I understood.

Tommy had worried something was unusual about Evan's focus on me. But he hadn't been able to put his finger on *what*, exactly. Tommy and Evan had become friends after Elizabeth passed. Tommy had never seen Evan's first wife.

He'd never realized we looked almost exactly alike.

Evan had used Tommy as well.

Anger burned in me so uncomfortably that I pushed my fist against my gut.

"Are you sure there isn't some other explanation for all of this?" Valeria asked me anxiously.

"I don't see how," I said, staring the grayish, steel-blue clouds crouching menacingly over the mountains. "I have a picture of a photo of her on my phone. I look exactly like Evan's first wife. How many explanations could there be for why he'd want to marry me?"

Valeria was probably worried about the job she'd taken, but I'd passed the point of believing I made a difference to her happiness. I was inconsequential.

I would be gone tomorrow.

We didn't say anything else to each other on the trip back to Les Jumeaux.

The Gothic lines of Les Jumeaux's pitched roofs and towers looked much the same to me. But the house and its beautiful mountain and lake landscape had forever changed. How could I have ever believed that I was a unique part of this place, that my life would become intertwined with it? I was barely a blink of the eye in the grand scheme of things.

My stupidity hurt almost as much as my acid anger at Evan.

Ignoring Valeria as she called out to me, I climbed the grand staircase. Not until I sat securely in the seating area of our suite did I allow myself to ask the questions.

What would I do? Where would I go?

Should I confront Evan? Demand answers?

Would it give me even an ounce of satisfaction to do so?
No, it wouldn't.

That answer came to me, swift and certain. It would *not* help me to confront him about his lies and manipulations, about how he'd turned my life upside down just to gratify his obsession. In fact, it might make matters worse, to discover the truth.

Vividly, the memory of him holding my hands and trying to convey to me the importance of the prenuptial agreement leapt into my mind's eye. I recalled the crass irritation of his lawyer.

"Evan has provided you with much, much more than the clothes on your back, even in the case of divorce. You're a very fortunate young woman, Ms. Solas."

Lucky. That's what that lawyer bastard had called me.

I realized dully that Evan had insisted upon providing for me, even in the case of me filing for divorce, because he'd known he'd been using me. He'd insisted upon the clause in the prenuptial agreement providing for me because he'd known this day would come.

His thoughtfulness in that regard only highlighted his premeditation. His deliberate cruelty.

"I don't want to ruin your life."

Pain seized my whole body. I clenched my eyelids shut and braced myself against it. It tore through me like fire anyway.

"But you *have*, Evan."

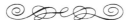

I sat there for I don't know how long, my muscles clenched tight as I tried to fight off the pain and anger and rising panic.

Finally, I stood and walked over to the closet. I found my large suitcase. Had it really only been a month or so since I'd stored it away there?

It didn't matter. I had to get out of here. It was like I'd become aware that the house exuded some kind of foul, noxious gas. How had I not realized I'd been breathing it, slowly poisoning myself all along?

Evan had said he would return this evening. I had to get out of there as soon as possible. The thought of seeing him made my mind go blank with rage.

Why the hell did you make me fall in love with you? Was that really necessary to your plan, you fucking, heartless bastard?

I threw my suitcase on the bed so hard, it bounced up several inches. I unzipped the case and started throwing handfuls of clothing straight from the bureau drawers into it. In my fury, I accidentally shoved the Tsang sculpture of the lovers kissing, making it scoot several inches all along the bureau.

"It's my wedding gift to you. Do you like it?"

Rage clamped down on me. I dropped the clothing, picked up the priceless porcelain in both hands, and hurled it against the wall. It hit with the impact of a small explosion.

"Anna, what the hell are you doing?"

I turned around to see Evan standing just inside the door.

Chapter Fifteen

EVAN'S GAZE APPEARED STARTLED AND SHARP ON ME. WHISKERS darkened his jaw. The appeal of him, even under these circumstances, horrified me.

"What are you doing home so early?" I asked.

"I was worried after we talked this morning. Rightfully so, I'd say."

He entered the room, long legs motoring toward me.

"What's happening?" he asked tensely, his gaze landing on the shattered pieces of sculpture. He grabbed me by the upper arms. I made a muted sound of furious misery and jerked out of his hold.

"Anna? Tell me what's happened," he demanded.

My throat burned. I was so angry—so hurt—I didn't have the energy or desire to try to spell it all out for him. I just reached in my back pocket and extricated my phone.

I held up the image of Elizabeth Madaster.

His expression froze, altered somehow. The light didn't fade from his eyes. It went out like a snuffed candle.

"Valeria told me just now she took you to Carson City. She said you were upset, but she wouldn't say why. You saw this at the library?" he asked, his voice infuriatingly calm.

"That's right," I said, still holding the incriminating evidence up to his face.

"You don't have to keep showing me the picture, Anna. I know what Elizabeth looks like."

"Sure you do. You're looking at her right now."

For several seconds he just stared at me, his face ashen.

"I realize there's very little I can say in a few seconds to make you understand. I knew this moment would come, eventually. I hoped to be the one to tell you, though."

"Tell me what, exactly?" I seethed. "That you married me because I look exactly like your dead wife? That you're a sick motherfucker who decided to ruin a stranger's life, all because it gave you some sense of happiness—some perverted thrill—to have your obsession in the flesh?"

He winced. "Anna, you don't understand."

I gave a hysterical bark of laughter. "Understand? What's to *understand*? It was my *life*, Evan," I yelled, thumping my chest with my fist. "You manipulated me from the first! You lied to me. You made me think you cared about me, but all along, I was just a face. A body... something you filled up with your fantasies for someone you couldn't have—"

"*No.*"

I started at his shout. His face twisted in what appeared to be genuine anguish.

"Let me try to explain, Anna. Please." He turned and walked to the door.

"No, leave the door open," I insisted, panicked at the idea of being shut in the room with him. "I'm leaving," I said, striding over to the bed and squashing down the clothes I'd thrown into the suitcase.

"You can't leave. Not without letting me explain why."

"I know why, Evan."

He grabbed my upper arm. "No. You don't."

I paused, searching his face and eyes, trying to discern the truth. It took me a few seconds to realize I was doing it. I did it from long habit. I *always* hunted every nuance of his expression, looking for clues, searching for answers, so hungry for the truths he withheld. *Yes*, I saw a wild desperation on his face; I saw an entire universe of grief and anger.

But what did it mean, really? I couldn't trust what I saw. Not anymore.

I shook off his hold.

"I don't believe a word that comes out of your mouth. That photo of Elizabeth is all the proof I need. You ruined my life because you're sick and selfish." I flung my suitcase closed and tugged on the zipper tab. A piece of clothing got stuck in the zipper. I tugged at it, tears of frustration stinging my eyes.

"What I don't get," I bit out angrily, "Is why you tried so hard to make me fall in love with you. Was that really necessary? Maybe so. You couldn't really imagine that you were living happily with your dead wife if she didn't worship the ground you walked on."

"That's not what I was doing, Anna. I didn't mean for it to happen. But I did fall in love with you."

Smack.

The sound of me slapping his face echoed in my ears. I stood facing him, panting. My tingling hand fell to my side.

"Don't you ever... *ever* say that to me again."

Beneath the deepening pink hue from my slap, a muscle jumped in his cheek.

I jerked the zipper past the bit of clothing, tearing a hole in the fabric in the process. My head felt like it'd become my heart, the drumbeat was so loud in my ears. I heaved the suitcase off the bed.

"I can't let you go like this," he said when I turned to look for my purse. I saw it on a chair.

"You don't have any choice," I told him, walking past him to get the purse.

"I agree that you have the right to be furious. I *have* wronged you. I won't deny that. I realize I've lost you. But please just let me explain. You think you understand, but you don't."

"Did you or didn't you notice my similarity to Elizabeth on the dating site, and then manipulate our meeting?" I asked, avoiding his stare as I walked back to my suitcase.

"No. I didn't notice the similarity. I hired a private detective agency to do that."

My breath hitched. I stared up at him in open-mouthed shock. Misery etched his face.

Get out. Get out now.

"I'm sorry. God, Anna, I'm so sorry. You have no idea. Every day that's gone by, every hour, I've fallen further and further into this hell of my own making, knowing what I've done to you."

"I don't care if you do burn in hell. I don't want your apology. I don't even know who you are."

179

I grabbed the handle of my suitcase and started for the door. My lungs had locked. I couldn't breathe. All my focus and energy was being channeled on forcing my feet to walk away from him.

"I know you think that I married you because you look like Elizabeth. You believe that I was so in love with her that I wanted her double after she died. But you're wrong, Anna. Things had gotten so painful and toxic between Elizabeth and me toward the end. The last thing on earth I wanted was to be reminded daily of her, of the ashes or our marriage, or how helpless I was in stopping how *bent* she'd become."

My feet stopped moving. I didn't make a choice to look over my shoulder, but suddenly I stared at his face.

"I didn't fall in love with you because you look like her. I fell in love with you *despite* that, Anna. Please," he said, coming toward me slowly. "I know you feel like you can't trust me right now, and I don't blame you. But pause a moment. You're angry now, and hurt. But that's not *all* of your feelings. Once you walk away, once time passes, you're going to realize that. And you're going to want to understand. You're going to want to make sense of it all, at the very least. If even a tiny bit of what you've felt for me was real, couldn't that be enough for you to listen to my explanation for why I did it?"

"My feelings for you have nothing to do with this. This is about what you've done. This is about how you've manipulated me."

"Yes," he agreed emphatically. "I have manipulated you. In the beginning, I was coldhearted and ruthless about it, too. But that was before I met you. Before I understood how honest you were... how talented... how clean of spirit. God, you were everything that my life wasn't, everything that could have been before I came here, before I met Elizabeth," he gave a wild glance around the room. "Before I'd begun to breathe and eat the corruption and sickness of this place."

I almost looked away, his misery—*Pretended misery. It's faked suffering, Anna*—was so palpable. But at the same time, wasn't this what I'd longed to see for so long? My husband without his guard up? Evan exposed?

Witnessing it now was horrible, but riveting.

"What have you got to lose by hearing my side of the story?" He waved toward the window. "It's raining out right now, anyway. You should at least wait until it stops before you travel."

The last tactic struck me as ridiculous, given the enormity of our situation. I laughed bitterly. "That's what you bring up at a moment like this? My safety driving in the rain?"

"I bring it up, because believe it or not, I care about you. More than I've cared about anything in my life."

"I told you never to talk about your supposed feelings for me again." I turned to go, but he grabbed my elbow.

"I say it because it's true. I've been worried sick about you ever since I brought you to Les Jumeaux."

I rounded on him. "But not worried enough to tell me about your twisted plans to replace your dead wife with a double."

He gave a rough moan and abruptly released my arm. He pressed his hands to his face, before fisting them into balls and dropping them to his side.

"It *is* twisted, all of it. Me. Elizabeth. Noah most of all. That much, I'll admit with no argument. But it kills me to hear you say I wanted to replace Elizabeth? Why would I want to replace her? Elizabeth *repulsed* me, toward the end of our marriage."

A shiver tore through me.

"That's the real kicker of all this, Anna. The single most amazing fact, the one thing I still can't wrap my head around? I fell in love with you, even when you look so much like the woman I'd grown to hate at times, and pity at others. You're genuine and kind and unspoiled. You're the type of light that could never touch her. No, *he* had choked off the possibility of anything truly good coming from Elizabeth years before I ever arrived on the scene."

Chapter Sixteen

DESPITE MY ANGER, I FOUND HIM CONVINCING. IT TERRIFIED ME, MY vulnerability to him. He may be telling me the truth. He may be lying, as he'd clearly done before.

But the only tool *I* possessed was honesty.

"I don't want to be hurt by you anymore, Evan. Let's just say for the moment that you do care for me, which I doubt," I added sharply. "Why wouldn't you just let me go now, if that's true? You've admitted that you've drawn me into something you shouldn't have, that you've come to regret involving me in... God knows what? If you really cared, you'd let me go."

One second passed. Two.

"You're right. If you really want to go now, I'll take you to the airport in South Lake. I use a private plane service out of there. I'll arrange to have you taken anywhere you like."

It felt as if someone pulled a plug on me. My legs went weak. I clamped my eyes tight against a surge of emotion.

"Anna?"

I fought against the thick concern I heard in his voice. I struggled against the warmth of his hands on my shoulders.

"I'll listen to you," I got out in a choked voice. "But I'm leaving as soon as you're done. And I don't... " I sobbed raggedly, pushing at his forearm, "want you to touch me." I backed away from him. "You've lost any right you had to do that."

We went to the seating area, Evan taking the chair and me sinking straight-backed into the corner of the couch. For a few seconds, he just stared blankly at the empty hearth of the fireplace. I thought of how many times I'd imagined us being in this exact spot come fall or winter, of relishing the warm fire and each other's company.

I hated myself for my stupidity. I despised myself in a way I hadn't known was possible before I'd looked at that photo of Elizabeth Madaster today.

"I'm sorry," Evan said hoarsely. "I don't know where to begin. I've never spoken out loud about most of this to another person."

"If we're going to do this, then do it completely. Start at the beginning. And Evan." He glanced over at me with those quicksilver eyes of his. "Don't leave anything out. Don't give me anything less than the truth. If you lie to me again, and I find out about it... "

I shook my head, unable to say exactly what the consequences of that action would be.

"It'll make things worse," I said simply at last. "If that's possible."

"I have no desire to keep you in the dark. Not anymore."

A thought occurred to me. I laughed, the sound seeming shrill and off-balance in my own ears. Who cared? It was either laugh or go insane, given the thought I'd just had.

"What is it? Anna?" Evan asked, sitting at the edge of his chair, his elbows on his knees, looking like he was ready to spring off the seat.

"You wouldn't make love to me in the daylight. Not at first, you wouldn't."

He inhaled slowly, as if the action pained him.

"I couldn't stand to touch you and see *her* face. At first, anyway," he admitted. "But part of me knew, even from the beginning, that you weren't the same. In reality, you might as well have been from another planet, you were so essentially different from Elizabeth."

Even though his expression appeared fixed and grave, I saw the difference in him. I sensed it. His grief, even if I did question its veracity, was openly, unbearably, on display.

Rain peppered the windowpanes as Evan began his story. He told it uneasily, but doggedly, like each word, each morsel of knowledge had to be dug out of the dark places of his soul where they'd been wedged, and where they now festered.

"I realize you think that my feelings for you are associated with Elizabeth... that everything goes back to her. In a way you're right, but not in the way you imagine.

"I was thirteen when I first saw Elizabeth. It was at a junior women's golf tournament at my parents' country club. I'd heard the name Madaster before. Noah was a member of my parents' club. But at that time, they still lived on their ranch in the Carson Valley. Elizabeth went to school in Carson City. But that summer, the Madasters moved permanently here, to Les Jumeaux. They started showing up at the club regularly.

"I remember the exact moment I first laid eyes on her to this day. I was in the crowd with some of my friends. We all gawked in stunned silence while she holed out of a sand trap on the sixteenth.

"I'd never seen anything like her before. Every move she made, it was like a goddamn movie sound track started playing in my teenage brain." Despite the self-derision in his tone, I caught that faraway hint of residual awe.

"She was graceful, but also purposeful. Forceful, even. Her will was like a brand on you. Beautiful doesn't come close to describing her; she was something more. So full of—I don't know—style, I guess. You *felt* her confidence. Her influence. Her charisma.

"And Elizabeth *knew* you felt it. Even then, she was extremely aware of her power over people... especially men. She knew perfectly well on that day that she held the crowd at that tournament in the palm of her hand. She was older than I was by two years. To a thirteen-year-old, she seemed like an adult. Like something from another world."

"Was Wes with you on that day? At the club?" I asked.

He blinked at my question. "He was. What makes you ask that?"

I shrugged, trying to mask my bitterness. "It was the way you were talking just now—like you'd witnessed a goddess or something. I heard the same tone with Wes on the first day I met him, when he talked about Elizabeth."

"You asked me to tell you the truth. I'm just trying to give you the full picture. Elizabeth's allure... her sexual power. It's key to understanding this story. Little did I know that my attraction to her, which started innocently enough, would become like a cancer that slowly started to eat away at me.

"I know that now, but back then, I was just a stupid, blind, dumbass kid. I worshipped her. It hurts more than I can explain, as I sit here right now, to have to admit that."

"Why was she so special?" I asked. I'd been listening to all of this with a mixture of anger, jealousy, and absolute fascination.

"She wasn't like anyone I'd ever known. She didn't care what other people thought. I assume because most people either adored or envied her. The few who didn't, hated her, more than likely because they'd encountered her venom in some way. But she just laughed at them. She saw their hatred as a weakness, a sure proof of her victory over them.

"She was wild. Daring. Noah had given her a rare, vintage Ferrari Spider when she got her driver's permit. Cherry red. She wasn't even old enough to get her license yet, but he let her drive it without adult supervision. It was a hugely inappropriate gift for a fifteen-year-old. He'd just smile when anyone—including his wife—brought up the fact that she was driving without a license. Noah would say that Elizabeth drove with more skill than 99.9 percent of the drivers on the road. *He* knew she was safe to drive it, and to hell with what the law said.

"A few weeks after I first met her, Elizabeth took me for a ride around the lake in that Spider. Noah was right, at least about her skill. She handled that car with the precision of a world-class race car driver. I don't know where she got her instincts, but they were sharp as a knife. She knew perfectly well she was scaring the hell out of me that day, driving as fast as she did." He paused and shook his head. "But she'd just smile and accelerate through the next twist in the road."

"She didn't just scare you. She excited you."

"She did. I'll admit it. My only excuse is that I was a child in the beginning. By the time we married, I was almost twenty-three. By then, some of her glamour had started to fade. I'd begun to see her complexities and vulnerabilities. Her many scars."

"What, Evan?" I prodded when he paused, a shadow crossing his face.

"Unfortunately, understanding her complexities and her pain only made her more attractive to me. I wanted to protect her. Worse, I wanted to save her," he admitted, his harsh tone telling me that he recognized this as a personal shortcoming, a deep flaw in his character.

"It was a new hold she had over me, an even stronger one than my desire for her. And she knew how to use this hold to her advantage every bit as well as she knew how to manipulate for attention and sex."

My stomach burned at what I heard in his voice at that moment. Not just bitterness.

Hopelessness.

"Why did she need to be saved?" I asked.

"She needed saving from her father," Evan stated bluntly. "At first, I just thought it was his unhealthy hold over her, a grip that Elizabeth both fought against and seemed to relish at the same time. Later, I understood it was much more."

He glanced up, and saw my confusion. He grimaced.

"Noah had been abusing Elizabeth. Since she was nine years old," he said.

"Sexually?" I asked, not really sure I wanted to know.

"Sexually. Emotionally. Physically. He regularly drugged her, all for the sake of his sick 'research.' What he did to that girl... that woman..." The muscle in his cheek flickered again. "It was diabolical. It was torture. I can't think of any other way to describe Noah and his intentions. He didn't want to just control Elizabeth. He wanted to *own* her. Body and soul. Every thought she had. Every desire. Every dream, he wanted to stamp himself on it. He even wanted to own her occasional rebellion against him."

"I don't understand," I told him honestly.

"No," Evan said dully. "I wouldn't expect that you would. And I'm not sure I want to tell you, now that the time has come."

I stared at his gray face, a visage of bottled misery.

"You brought me here, Evan. You brought me here and made me part of this story. You owe me the truth. Make me understand about Noah Madaster. Make me understand Elizabeth. Make me understand why you *did* this to me," I demanded. I was a little taken aback by the authority in my voice, but it seemed to cut through the cloud of misery that surrounded us in that moment.

"I'm not sure I want you to understand, Anna. The cost might be too high." He noticed my angry, determined expression and exhaled in defeat before he continued.

"Noah Madaster was an intimidating giant of a man. When I was a kid, he scared the hell out of me. As I got older, I realized he scared and manipulated nearly everyone he met, adult or child. With most people, he was charming at first. Smooth. Sophisticated. But he was never that way for me. He seemed to sense something special in my relationship with Elizabeth, something innocent maybe... somewhere he wasn't allowed to tread. Somewhere he had no authority. It threatened him.

"He was strict and controlling with Elizabeth when she was a teenager, but also strangely permissive, as well. It was like he constantly swung between spoiling her, and then punishing her for enjoying herself and escaping his authority. He monitored her interactions with boys and men obsessively while at country club parties or events, for instance. He wouldn't allow her to date anyone unless he approved of him first, although he rarely granted his approval. But Madaster also gave Elizabeth that ridiculously expensive Ferrari when she was only fifteen. He supplied her with plenty of cash and credit cards. Elizabeth used them to escape his net of control, but he knew what he was doing all along. Because he'd given her those things—the car and the money—he always retained ultimate control. They were *his* tools, not hers. He seemed to enjoy seeing her push at the confines of her invisible prison. He seemed to love the moment when he reeled her back within his grip."

"And Elizabeth's relationship with you? Was that an attempt by Elizabeth to escape her father's influence?"

"Yes, I suppose it was. But our relationship was unique, too. Innocent. Or maybe it wasn't. That was the thing with Elizabeth. Just when you thought you understood her, just when you thought the connection between you was sound and genuine, she would turn around and do something completely inexplicable. She'd break the link willfully. Spitefully. Grotesquely. I *used* to think that our initial connection to each other was special. But as in all things, Elizabeth left you swimming in doubt. I still doubt, even today. Who really knew what she thought or wanted? Her desires had been forged and culled by her father, meticulously fashioned into the shape of *his* desire. Can the slave ever truly break free of the slave master? I don't know. That was the problem. I never truly knew. I still don't.

"But all those doubts only came later. I was in awe of her in the beginning. I didn't understand why she chose me, out of all the other boys and men who constantly surrounded her. But after we'd spent some time together, the layers of her—that outer cold, hard armor she wore—seemed to peel away. It was like my youth and inexperience rubbed off on her. Instead of seeming like fifteen going on forty, she started to act like a teenage girl: funny, impulsive, painfully insecure at times. Sweet."

He uttered the last gruffly. The look in his eyes brought a hard lump to my throat.

"The first summer we met, we would hike out to this overlook a few miles from my house and talk about stupid things. Kids' things. Or so I'd thought at the time. We'd play this game: wish upon a star, where we'd pick a star for the other person. If it was a bright star, you could make a big, important wish, if it was a small, dim one, you could only wish for a little thing... a passing fancy, like that when you got home, you found out that your mom had gotten all the stuff for ice cream sundaes, or that when I joined Elizabeth at Tahoe Shores High School in a year, we'd have the same lunch hour. Stuff like that.

"I remember once, I picked the brightest object in the sky for her, even though it wasn't a star. I picked the full moon. And I waited, wondering what Elizabeth Madaster's biggest wish in the world could possibly be, the one that surpassed every other."

"What did she say?" I asked breathlessly when he paused.

"She said that she wished she belonged to another family... a boring, regular family," Evan said quietly, his expression grim. "She'd live in Kansas, or Iowa, or anywhere, really, as long as people didn't look at her with so much expectation. Some place anonymous. Some place safe. She wished she could be invisible, for the most part. That she could blend into the landscape whenever she chose."

A foul taste had started at the back of my mouth. "She didn't want other people to have an effect on her. Unless she chose it."

He nodded. "She'd been *effected*, nonstop, by her father since before she could remember. It was the first glimmer I had of the truth, but I was too young to understand. The hell that she went through day in and day out wasn't something a thirteen-year-old kid from a happy, reasonably well-adjusted family could begin to comprehend. And the thing was, Elizabeth didn't consider it hell. For her, it was all normal operating procedure. The air she breathed."

"When did you understand? That her father was abusing her?"

"Not for a long time. Not until after we were married. Elizabeth always avoided the topic of Noah. But he was always *there*, a brewing storm on the horizon."

"When we were young, Noah tried to separate us. He'd forbid her from seeing me. I was a thorn in his side, the one thing he couldn't erase from Elizabeth's consciousness. Although I'll bet he tried like hell to do just that with that damn Analyzer of his.

"When I got to high school, Elizabeth and I would be together every chance we got. We used to meet in this old, unused stairway behind the gym. Sometimes, she'd escape out her window at night, and I'd do the same. She'd pick me up in her car, and we'd drive aimlessly. Or park. Anything, as long as we were together."

He paused here, the silence making me see it all. The beautiful girl and the young boy speeding through a starlit night, their faces alight and alive as they thirstily drank in the rare intoxicant of freedom.

"Because he couldn't completely control her when it came to seeing me, Madaster eventually sent her away to private school to separate us. But Elizabeth and I managed to remain in contact for years, all through the rest of high school, and then college. When we eventually announced our engagement, when I was twenty-two and she was twenty-four, Noah seemed to resign himself. He welcomed me into the family with open arms."

"You didn't believe him, though?"

"I wanted to. But no, I never trusted Noah. He'd made the mistake of showing me his true colors early on. He'd never bothered to charm me, and that was his mistake. To me, he was my enemy from day one. No matter how supportive and benevolent he began to act toward me, I understood on some elemental level that the only thing that mattered to him was Elizabeth, and that he considered me a barrier to her. Or at least a partial one."

"You didn't know at that time of the engagement Elizabeth's father had been... "

"Abusing her?" Evan asked when I faded off. "It wasn't a matter of *had* been, Anna. Elizabeth and Noah never stopped their incestuous relationship. It continued from when she was nine years old to—presumably—just before she died."

My mouth dropped open. "But how could Noah possibly force her into something like that when she was an adult?"

He shook his head. "Noah didn't have to force Elizabeth into anything. She went to him willingly. The thing you have to understand is that Elizabeth was Noah's greatest triumph, on so many levels. But one of the main reasons he coveted and prized her so passionately was that she represented his greatest victory. She was his main test subject for that Analyzer he'd created, the lie detector that was really a means for mental programming. He'd warped her since she was a child, even since before he'd first raped her. When Elizabeth went to him, she genuinely believed she did so of her own free will. Why? Because he'd brainwashed her until she didn't know the difference anymore between her own desires and his."

Chapter Seventeen

THE SURFACE OF MY SKIN SEEMED TO STING, AS THOUGH I'D RECEIVED some chemical burn. I noticed Evan's narrowed eyed gaze on me.

"I'm sorry, Anna. I'm sorry to have involved you in something so ugly."

"I don't want your apologies," I hissed, feeling vulnerable from his knowing stare. "I just want the truth."

He nodded, his face smoothing into a mask. Then he continued with his story, his manner reminding me of a man walking his last steps to the gallows.

"I never fully answered your earlier question, about whether or not I knew when Elizabeth and I got engaged about Noah's abuse, about the true nature of their relationship. The answer is no. I didn't know it consciously, anyway. It's hard to imagine something like that, when you don't have any prior template into which to shape the thoughts. Over time, the outline became clearer and clearer though, even though it was years before Elizabeth admitted to me that he'd been abusing her—but of course, Elizabeth didn't couch it in those terms.

"But even before Elizabeth's admission, there was always a vibe that Noah gave off with Elizabeth that made me highly uneasy. It was proprietorship. I got the message, loud and clear. I may become her *husband,* but that title was a far second to that of *Father*. And Elizabeth did her part to fan those flames. She'd be flirtatious and knowing with both of us, in turn. Noah didn't seem to mind. He saw how much it bothered me, when Elizabeth paid attention solely to him. But why should it bother him if she occasionally made me her sole focus? He was confident about to whom she belonged."

I looked away, feeling nauseated.

Evan noticed. "It's not a pleasant story to hear. It certainly wasn't pleasant living it, either."

"I'm listening. Go on," I said, avoiding his stare.

He exhaled heavily.

"Noah offered to assist me in setting up my first fund when I finished college. I had serious doubts about accepting his patronage. I didn't trust him. But at the same time, I wanted... no, I *needed* to become established if I wanted to marry Elizabeth. The only thing I had to support us was a very modest trust fund that my parents had given me. It wasn't enough, not if I wanted to give Elizabeth even a little of the lifestyle to which she was accustomed. So in the end, I agreed to have Noah help me."

"You wanted Elizabeth that much? That you agreed to work with a man that you claim is right on par with the devil?" I asked, anger in my tone.

His spine stiffened. "I don't need you to tell me I was stupid, Anna. It didn't take me long to recognize it would be an epic mistake, aligning myself with him. Not just potentially for my career. For my life. My identity. Noah's influence was toxic from the outset.

"At one point, he suggested I make a big splash with my first clients, using their money to invest outside the original parameters and specifications of the fund in order to spread the word of the fund's success. He urged me to invest in a risky hedge fund in order to make enormous profits. I refused, recognizing the danger to my customers' investments. When I wouldn't do what he advised, Noah threatened to withdraw all his support. But this time, I managed to avoid the trap. I was adamant. Thankfully, I was able to make the fund a success despite Noah cutting off his patronage and refusing any further support.

"Noah's aim was to get a hook in me all along. It was a means for blackmail, a standard operating procedure for him. If the hedge fund gamble failed—which there was a high likelihood of it doing—I'd be forced to rely on Noah to cover the losses. Do that, or face financial failure and ruin and possible federal prosecution. If that gamble didn't fail, then the next one he suggested *would* have. He had the power of odds on his side. Plus, he had the threat of exposure if I stepped out of line at any time. If I played his *first* game, that is. When I refused the bait at the outset, he was furious," Evan said, his speech clipped now.

His eyes had gone hard and silvery. I understood that the encounter he described had been a sort of watershed moment for him. At twenty-two, he'd stood up to a formidable, more experienced, and ruthless enemy. And he'd won the battle.

The question was, who had won the war between Evan and Noah Madaster? Or was it still raging?

I suddenly knew for certain that it *was*, silently and furiously.

"That's why I'm here, isn't it? You brought me here because of this vendetta... because of this war between you and Noah Madaster."

"Yes."

That swift admission sliced through me, the pain of it impossibly worse than all the previous blows. He stood abruptly, his expression growing anxious. I realized that tears had sprung out of my eyes, wetting my cheeks. He reached for me. I flinched back.

"Goddamn it, Anna," he muttered, pacing back and forth several steps. "Goddamn it. What do I do? This is me. It's still *me*. What can I do to make this better?"

But I was lost in misery, unable to respond to his agitation. I'd been transported back to that night he'd awoken me from my nightmare, that night when I'd demanded he tell me why we'd come to Les Jumeaux, and his answer: *Because I'm sinful.*

But that's not what he'd said. I knew that now. I'd misunderstood him, perhaps purposefully, because I didn't want to face his real answer anymore than I had the false one.

Because I'm vengeful.

"You almost told me," I said, wiping my cheeks with the back of my hand. "That night, when you woke me up from the nightmare. You told me we were here because you were vengeful. But you never said anything else."

"Only because you seemed to not want to hear it. You changed the subject," he said, desperation in his tone. "I offered to take you away from here. If you only knew how hard this has been, how much I've been drowning in regret. I've wanted to tell you the truth for weeks now, but I didn't know how—"

"You hired a private investigator to find someone who looked like Elizabeth," I interrupted, unwilling to hear about his feelings. It was difficult enough, bearing witness to his sins against me. Hearing his

195

emotion—his regret and pain—was intolerable. "How long did it take you to find a double? How long have you been planning this, Evan?"

He froze in his pacing. He opened his mouth, but nothing came out.

"Tell me the truth. Or whatever you've convinced yourself the truth is," I grated out.

His expression went stony. Unreadable.

"I started planning about a year after Elizabeth disappeared. At first, I tried to come up with some kind of scheme that would expose Noah for what he is. I tried to meet with some of the people who had worked for him in the governor's office. I got to know a few of them... a couple better than others. At one point, I thought the young female aide—the one who had first come out to the press about the fact that Noah had touched her inappropriately while he was using the Analyzer on her—would agree to tell more of her story to the press, putting his crimes in the limelight again.

"In the end, Noah somehow silenced her, though. She started to refuse to take my calls. I don't know how he did it. I'm sure it was related to how he silenced her after she told the press her story the first time. I told you that blackmail is his forte."

"I had to try another tack. For a year or so, I did exhaustive research into Noah's financial holdings and contracts. I thought maybe I could find a way to expose any dark business dealings, contrive a way to bring about his financial ruin. Nothing ever paid off, though.

"Finally, I realized that the only way to get to him was through his one weak point, his most single-minded obsession."

"Elizabeth," I said.

He merely nodded, that faraway, haunted look once again in his eyes.

"I believe that at the end of her life, Elizabeth and Noah had a big blowout. I suspect that my pleas, and then my *insistence*, for her to sever her relationship with him had finally gotten through to her. Before she died, I'd told her that if she didn't break off all ties with her father, I would divorce her for good. I couldn't stand to see her debasing herself anymore. I couldn't bear watching her kill herself slowly."

"You think that Elizabeth told her father that it was either him or you... and she chose you?" I asked in a hushed voice.

"I think that when she told him that his days of manipulating her every move were over, he ended her life."

My brain seemed to slam against a cold steel wall.

"You're saying Noah Madaster *murdered* his daughter?"

His wintry gaze met mine. "Noah *did* murder Elizabeth. That's why I'm here. That's why *you* are. Because every day that passes that Noah goes unpunished for all that he's done, the burn inside of me gets hotter and deeper. I can't rid myself of the fury. The only thing that will give me peace is to see Noah Madaster finally face justice."

Chapter Eighteen

I FELT THE FULL FORCE OF HIS FURY AT THAT MOMENT, THAT ANGER that he'd always carefully hidden from me. It awed and frightened me. Evan was right.

His rage burned.

"But how do you *know*?" I asked. "You yourself have said that Elizabeth was unpredictable. How do you know that she ever confronted him about his abuse and threatened to cut ties with him? How do you *know* that Noah killed her? The police never came up with any evidence like that, did they?"

"No. The police had their suspicions about Noah, but never enough to make a substantial case against him. You ask me how I know. I can only answer from my experience with Noah Madaster all those years, and my experience of Elizabeth. I've done any number of stupid things in my life, Anna, but I'm not a stupid man."

"No," I said, panting slightly, trying to catch my skittering, flickering thoughts. I was completely confused at that moment, but I completely agreed with that. Evan was the opposite of stupid. He was patient, hard, and ruthless.

I, of all people, had come to know that firsthand.

"I believe that Noah killed Elizabeth when they had that last confrontation, because I know *Noah*. He would believe it was his only course of action if she insisted upon cutting all ties with him. It would be the only thing he *could* do, being the narcissist that he is, and given those circumstances. In Noah's eyes, it would have been like Frankenstein realizing the monster had become something he hadn't expected, that it had evolved into something uncontrollable. Once the monster took on a life of its own, once it obtained a will of its own... it had to be killed at all costs. Elizabeth's only use was in being precisely what Madaster wanted her to be. And once that was finished, once she demonstrated a will of her own, and wouldn't back down from it? That was the end. He terminated her very unhappy life."

I didn't want to believe him. But the story had a raw, tragic note to it that struck a cord somewhere deep inside me. It had the terrible, clear tone of the truth.

In that moment, I had never seen Elizabeth so clearly, and it was a painful image. I had envied her, once. I had hated her for her seemingly effortless, powerful influence over everyone in her sphere. I had feared what I'd believed to be her ghost in my nightmares.

Now I pitied her. It was somehow worse than my envy.

"My point is," Evan continued, his recitation of the facts striking me as merciless in that moment, even though he was only doing what I'd demanded. "Even though I believe Noah murdered Elizabeth, I also knew from all those years of experience that he would insist until his dying day that he adored and loved her above anything else.

"I confronted him with my suspicions before I left Les Jumeaux seven years ago, and that's exactly what he did. He insisted no one on this planet came near to loving Elizabeth like he did. But in typical Noah-fashion, which is in a sly, elusive way, he admitted to me that he *had* been responsible for her disappearance."

"What did he say?"

"He agreed with me that he'd never seen his daughter in so much pain as she'd been in recently. He accused me of her unhappiness, for stirring her up, for confusing her about what she wanted. And then he said that his love for her was greater than mine, because if *he'd* ever seen her so unhappy, he would certainly have done *anything* to stop it."

"Even kill her?"

"She was his absolute obsession, the reason he rose from bed in the morning, the ultimate motivation for every decision and action that he ever made. Including snuffing out her existence."

For a few moments, an uneasy, poisonous silence settled. But then Evan continued.

"A couple years ago, I first heard about Noah's accident and the resulting spinal cord injury. I learned that he'd become a virtual captive in the tower at the South Twin, a prisoner in his own body, as you put it once. I started to realize that possibly the only way I could ever expose him for the rapist, abuser, manipulator, and murderer that he was, was to make him somehow admit his sins himself."

"And that's when your plan took shape. You'd find someone who looked like Elizabeth. They say we all have a doppelganger in this world. At this point in history, everyone is putting their photo out there some-where. You had the whole world to access, given the Internet. You just had to have the time and resources to find that face. Once found, you would bring the double to Les Jumeaux and parade her in front of Noah. With his damaged body, and more than likely damaged mind, Noah would be forced to look at the image of his daughter day in and day out, the one that you say was his ultimate obsession... the child he loved above all else. The daughter he murdered."

Realization struck. I gasped like I'd been hit in the solar plexus. My throat swelled.

"That's why you situated me up on the overlook, first thing. It was so that Noah would see me painting every day. See you kissing me... touching me. You did it all just out of his reach. You did it all to drive him mad, to force his confession."

"I stopped visiting you up there. At first, I thought it might drive the knife deeper if he was forced to see us together, but then I couldn't make myself to do it. More and more, I hated the idea of him watching you, even though it's what I originally planned as a means to force him into some kind of action... some admission or revelation. My feelings for you kept evolving and deepening, and I started to doubt myself more and more. I never believed he could actually *harm* you, made helpless as he was by his injury. But I knew just seeing you could potentially do a great deal of damage to his psyche. Enough so that it might break him. Expose him.

"But I began to have a change of heart about that. I didn't want him to even *see* you. It came to strike me as deeply wrong... possibly dangerous, even, from a distance, like those electrical transformers that cause cancer with constant exposure. I'd sit in my office and worry about you up there on the overlook. I knew it wasn't rational, my worry, but I couldn't seem to shake it. That's why I suggested you move to a different spot to paint, a place where he couldn't watch you anymore. And when I said I'd leave if you chose it, I meant it, Anna."

"I'm so lucky, to have you thinking of my welfare."

He winced at my sarcasm.

"I deserve that. I know. But believe me when I say that I never planned to put you in harm's way. I always wanted you to be happy. I told myself that while I knowingly used you for my own purposes, I would make your life better for it in the end. I wouldn't have done this if I weren't confident I could give you what you wanted, after this business was finished. By the time we married, I didn't want you to leave me. Far from it. I dreaded the idea. I hoped, maybe stupidly so, that once we spent more time together, you'd realize my feelings were true.

"But *if* you left me—something I tried to resign myself to, difficult as it was—at least I would have left you the financial resources to give you freedom. I knew how much you wanted the time and opportunity to paint."

"I didn't come to Les Jumeaux to *paint*. And I never wanted your damn money. God, I believed you," I said, freshly terrified by the words.

"You should have believed me. You believed that I loved you because I *did*. I do. I think I loved you without knowing it since the first time we met... before, even, when I looked at your paintings. I defended myself against that feeling, of course, given my plan. The realization of how much you meant to me, the full extent of my feelings, didn't hit me until we came here, though. Until the threat of Noah was so near. I am completely and hopelessly in love with you, Anna. I wouldn't have married you, otherwise. I didn't need to, in my original plan... before we even met. I just needed to get you here."

"A clueless double of Elizabeth. You were confident you could seduce somebody so stupid. That was the easy part," I bit out, fury spiking through the thick emotional fog that had settled from hearing this tragedy. I saw him open his mouth to defend himself. "Just finish, Evan. Finish telling me about your little story of revenge."

He took a moment to gather himself. I waited, impatient now, increasingly desperate for this to be over.

"I put all my resources into finding a double," Evan said. "I'd almost given up hope by the time the private investigator I'd hired sent me your dating profile. He and two other people, whom he'd hired specifically for this case, had been combing sites for years, everything from Facebook to Twitter to professional social media sites to dating sites. They did a worldwide search. For a few years, we came up short, though. I'd already taken steps to hire an actress if need be... to find someone with a passing similarity to Elizabeth who might be willing to have some minor surgery done in order to look more like her.

"When the private investigator finally sent me the link to your profile, and I saw your photo, I was stunned. You might have passed as Elizabeth at twenty-three. And when I say that, I mean you might have passed with people who knew her *well*. It was amazing to think you were right there in San Francisco the whole time. We'd been searching the globe, and you were only a few miles away from me. Then I met you in person."

"And you were shocked to the core," I said bitterly, repeating what he'd told me once about how he'd felt upon our first meeting. "Wasn't that what you said? That you were stunned to see something so new. So fresh. Honest. *Rare*. You fucking liar."

I stared at him with blistering defiance, but fresh tears spilled down my face.

An angry glint flared in his eyes. "When I told you that, I was being honest. You *were* unlike anything I'd ever expected... anything I've ever known. I *get* the irony of that, Anna, given what I was planning. I *get* the screaming bad luck of it all. I'm being punished. Not for wanting to see Noah Madaster exposed for what he is. But for plotting to use *you* to get justice against *him*. I fell in love with you, against my will and against my better judgment. Fate sent me a gigantic *Fuck You, Evan Halifax*. I deserve your scorn, and I deserve for you to leave me and never look back. But *don't* try and make out I was lying about my feelings for you. Don't twist this story any more than it already is. God knows it's sick enough."

"I'm not the one who has been twisting things, and you know it. You realize that your plan for revenge is working, don't you?" I asked him in a high-pitched voice. "Your plan to torture Madaster? First, he punched his fist through that pane of glass when he saw me. And he's spent the last few days in the hospital because of a heart attack."

I saw his expression shift subtly.

"You didn't know about his most recent heart attack? You must be so pleased. He's been suffering and weakening, just like you'd planned, seeing me on the grounds of Les Jumeaux."

"Anna, please try to understand. Elizabeth's body was never found. There was no means for finding the truth... for serving justice."

"I'm not your *means*, Evan," I shouted.

I stood and headed toward the bathroom. The full knowledge of what he'd done, how he'd manipulated me like a piece on a chess board, made my legs rubbery and my head feel like it was about to explode.

"Anna—"

"I'm getting a tissue and a drink of water," I snapped, meaning to come off as defiant, but in fact, only sounding peevish and tired.

It was too much to take in, all in a matter of hours, too much to absorb. The husband whom I'd loved with all of my spirit, and whom I'd believed loved and cherished me equally as much, had really been plotting to bring me into his life for the sole purpose of revenge.

And I told Jessica that I loved him so much because he'd seen me. It seemed so ridiculously naïve and embarrassing in retrospect.

I stared at my pale, tear-damp face in the bathroom mirror.

You thought you were so special, didn't you? But you knew, deep down, it was too wonderful to be true. All he saw when he looked at you was a means to an end.

It had happened. The floor had dropped away from my known world.

But I was still standing.

When it came down to it, I realized that you just kept going in the face of impossible pain. Why? Because there was nothing else *to* do. The heart kept beating doggedly. The cells kept up their chemical function.

The feet kept moving.

"Anna? Are you all right?" Evan asked anxiously when I came out of the bathroom. He stood five feet outside the bathroom door. His face had a strained, pinched look.

"No. I'm not all right," I replied evenly. "I'm going now. I'm taking the car. I assume you're okay with that."

"*No*, Anna. You can't go yet," he said loudly, taking several steps toward me. I swung my body out of the reach of his outstretched hand and walked past him.

"I haven't explained everything yet. You still don't understand the whole story."

"I understand enough. I understand how ridiculously out of place I am here," I said, my gaze glued to my suitcase. *One step at a time. I've got to get out of this house. This hell.*

Because if he touches me, I honestly don't know what I'll do. Hit him? Once I get started, I might never stop pummeling until he's a bloody mess.

Or worse, I might sink into his arms and beg him to tell me that it was all a mistake? That I really am the love of his life?

That I really am special in his eyes?

The thoughts, heavily laced with a brutal self-disgust, were just what I needed. My vision cleared as I grabbed my suitcase and purse.

"Anna, please."

"I'll leave a text as to where you can pick up the car," I said through a throat that was closing. "And for Christ's sake, if it's true that you ever cared even a little bit about me, don't say anything else, Evan. Just leave me be."

Storms in the Sierra Nevadas can be capricious, saber rattling and booming threats over the distant mountains, but never quite launching a full out attack.

As unpredictable as Elizabeth Madaster herself, I thought as I pulled Evan's sedan out onto the drive.

It was unusually gloomy and dark for this time of day because of the hovering, undecided storm. Or was it? I wondered hazily. What time *was* it? How much time had passed in this nightmare of an afternoon? A quick glance at the dashboard clock told me it was four thirty.

At least I'll have daylight for a few hours while I make my escape.

Escape to where, exactly?

I had a quick, vivid image of me driving Evan's car across the country to my parents' house... of my mother holding out her arms as I crossed the threshold of the front door, of my father's concerned face as he patiently listened to my woeful story.

I gasped loudly at the image, my body convulsing, more damned tears spilling down my cheeks. Or maybe it wasn't the imagined scene that made me cry out and grab the wheel in a death's grip. It was more the sure, slicing knowledge that it would never happen.

I could never go home again. I could never be comforted. Not in that way. If there was one thing Evan had done by maneuvering his way into my life, he'd made me grow up.

He'd aged me.

I forced myself to focus on the road in front of me, squeezing unwanted tears out of my eyes. The giant pines waved and frothed, stirred up by the storm that hung and rumbled at the top of nearby mountain peaks.

Fairyland doesn't want you to leave.

I mentally scoffed at that random thought. Not only was Les Jumeaux the direct opposite of a magical place. It could never care about me. I was a glitch here, a curious interloper, a freak meeting of random genes and a vengeful, single-minded man.

What would she *think? What would Elizabeth think of Evan's plan for revenge?*

I gripped the wheel even harder, amazed at the thought. It'd popped into my head seemingly out of nowhere.

I passed the fork in the road, forcing my increasingly buzzing, churning mind away from the charged memory that flashed into my head of Evan waiting for the ambulance to pass, of him holding my hand and pulling me into the center of the road—

He'd wanted *Noah to see us together there.*

Just like he'd tried to keep me from driving into Tahoe Shores, because he knew the locals would recognize my resemblance to Elizabeth.

I pushed aside the volatile thoughts, because it was necessary to drive, to move foot by foot, yard by yard, away from Evan.

I passed the gatehouse, recalling against my will our arrival at Les Jumeaux, how I'd taken the card key and rubbed it against my shorts, Evan's small, slightly incredulous and yet accepting smile when the card had opened the gate.

I should have known it only required a sprite's touch.

I braked the car hard at the turn off to the mountain highway, gravel popping beneath the tires. Lightning flashed. Thunder answered in a fury.

The storm had stopped its prevarication. It raged down the mountainside.

Right or left?

I released my clamped jaw. *Right.* Turn right.

I started to turn left, done with trusting with my own instincts. I broke so hard, my seatbelt snapped against my chest.

Another car raced by on the mountain road. *Not* there one second; *there* the next. Startled, I watched openmouthed as it passed. My first impressions were of speed, and vivid *red* amongst the muted gloom of the oncoming storm.

The ends of a white scarf fluttered around the female driver's shoulders as she sped past. She wore the scarf tied around her head like Grace Kelly or Audrey Hepburn might have in old movies, to keep their hair from blowing about in a convertible.

And this *was* a convertible, I realized dazedly as the car zoomed by. This was a convertible that would show up nearly every convertible on the planet. The top was down, despite the impending storm. Chic, sleek, and fast. I caught the prancing horse emblem on the shiny red of the paint, and then the car zipped around a curve and behind a mountain.

I gasped, my lungs unfreezing. Only a split second had separated us from crashing together in a fiery mess of metal, but she'd been unfazed. She'd never even glanced around. The *red* replayed in my mind's eye like a speeded up, repeating film clip, played faster and faster, the mechanics of the recorder losing control.

Chic. Red. Fast.

Elizabeth.

"Noah had given her a rare, vintage Ferrari Spider when she got her driver's permit. Cherry red."

Light from my darkness.

You are no outsider to this place, Anna.

The thoughts came at me like mortar fire. I didn't know if they were mine, or someone else's. That's what scared me the most at that moment.

Thunder shattered the very air around me, seeming to split atoms in half. I cried out, grabbed the wheel tighter, and butted my forehead hard against it.

I welcomed the jolt of pain.

Chapter Nineteen

THAT'S HOW EVAN FOUND ME, GRIPPING THE WHEEL LIKE I THOUGHT it was a life preserver in a stormy sea, my forehead pressed against it, my body shuddering.

At first, I didn't register much of anything from the outside world: not the rain pounding on the windshield like it was being hurled in buckets by some giant above me, not the roar of the wind, nor the sound of Evan opening the car door and calling my name.

I didn't come back to any sense of reality until he touched my shoulder.

Turning my head on the wheel, I met his stare. His palpable alarm cut through me. I started and straightened. The hand on my shoulder moved, kneading the muscle, doing that dance of reassurance with which I'd become so familiar.

"Take it easy. Keep your foot on the brake." He reached in front of me. I watched, as if from a distance, as he moved the gearshift to the Park position. I'd had the vehicle in Drive the entire time, my foot jammed on the brake.

How long had I been sitting there, gripping that wheel?

I turned to Evan, searching his face and body, as though they could give me clues for my own bizarre behavior. My strange thoughts. I learned nothing. He looked reassuringly solid standing there, bent over and staring at me, even if he was soaking wet, his dark hair plastered to his head, the fabric of his shirt clinging to his shoulders and chest.

"I think I just saw Elizabeth," I said.

He glanced out the window where I pointed before giving me an odd glance. Then he touched my forehead. His brow furrowed. "You've hit your head, Anna. Are you hurt anywhere else? Are you in pain? Are you dizzy?"

I shook my head.

"Can you get out of the car all right? I'll drive us back to the house."

"But... how did you get here?" I asked, my feet swinging to the side of the seat as he straightened and took my hands in his.

"I ran," he said simply. "Something told me I should."

He pulled me gently out of the car, and I joined him in the torrential downpour.

I don't remember much about returning to Les Jumeaux in that storm. I don't think it was because I'd purposefully hit my head on the steering wheel during a fit of bewildered grief. Maybe my partial amnesia was emotional overload. All I recall is walking down the wood floor hallway upstairs, Evan's arm around me. He guided me toward our bedroom, and my feet halted.

"No. Not in there," I stated flatly.

Evan paused only for a second before we continued down the hallway. He opened the door to another room. I'd seen it before, when I was choosing a guest room for Valeria. It faced the pine forest at the back of the property. Like our bedroom had been before we arrived, it was devoid of personal photos or keepsakes: comfortably anonymous.

I pushed on Evan's forearm. His hold fell off me. I walked like a robot to the en suite bathroom and shut the door.

The rain had chilled me to the bone. I turned on the shower, stripped, and got in, all without thinking. When I got out, I wasn't surprised to see a towel and a robe laid out for me, obviously by Evan. I felt dull and heavy.

He sat in a winged chair, waiting, when I plodded out of the bathroom. He stood and came toward me. I meant to step away, but I was caught by his stare. My feet wavered, undecided. He grabbed my elbow, as if to steady me.

"I can't stay here," I said.

"I know. But you can't leave now, either. The storm is bad." He paused, as if to make a point. I heard the sound of a hard rain and the eerie, creaking sound the tall pines made as they swayed in the wind. "And you've hit your head."

He urged with me his hand. I followed him over to the bed. He'd already pulled back the sheet and comforter. There was a glass of water on the bedside table and a bottle of aspirin. I sat on the edge of the mattress, undecided, but suddenly so tired. Exhaustion weighed down every muscle in my body. My cheek pressed against the soft, clean cotton of the pillowcase.

"Do you need some aspirin? For your head?"

"I did it myself."

"You did *what*?" Evan asked, covering my shoulder with the comforter.

"I hit my head against the steering wheel on purpose."

His hand paused. "Why?"

"I don't know. To stop thinking, maybe," I said hoarsely. My tongue felt thick and uncooperative. "To stop myself from seeing that car in my head. The red Ferrari. Elizabeth driving it."

His hand started, then slid along the top of the comforter, seemingly smoothing the fabric, but in fact, soothing me. I remembered I'd told him he'd lost the right to touch me. Maybe he'd recalled that, because he comforted me now only through the barrier of the thick blanket.

"Go to sleep, Anna. Things will be better when you wake up."

"Don't go," I whispered.

I shut my eyes. Shame swamped me at my pitiful request.

Thankfully, the exhaustion was even more powerful.

When I awoke, the first thing that struck me was the dead silence. The storm had run its course.

I'm alone in this big house. It'll swallow me whole.

The thought was stupidly irrational and terrible at once. I thought of the ghost in my nightmare, and had the crazy idea she now had the power to pierce the veil... to step into my waking reality. A dim light shone behind me. I flipped over in a rising panic.

Evan sat in a chair next to the bed, the soft lamplight shining on the opened book he held in his lap. He looked up at my abrupt movement. I saw that he'd changed out of his wet clothing. He wore a pair of jeans and a button-down white shirt that made his skin look dark by contrast, his light eyes yet another layer of juxtaposition. He still hadn't shaved, his whiskers adding to the rugged angles and shadows of his face. Our stares locked: one second, two, three...

I saw his concern, and something else in his grave gaze. A fragile, hesitant thread of hope. Distantly, I realized that hope might be coming from the way I was drinking in the vision of him like a parched woman.

"What time is it?" I asked him, just for something to say.

"A little after nine," he said.

I glanced uneasily at the windows, confirming there was no light peeking around the curtains. I'd slept for over four hours. Evan had been right, about things being better after sleeping. The memories of that day seemed clearer, but more distant, too.

Safety barrier.

Yes. That's what my sleeping mind had done. It'd put up a safety barrier, of sorts. I could still see all the heart-shattering moments and revelations from that day, but I did so from behind a thick, mental insulation.

Evan set aside his book on the bedside table. "Do you have a headache?"

"No," I murmured.

Again, our stares held. And despite the newly installed safety barrier, I felt my throat swelling. I shut my eyes and swallowed away the discomfort.

"Why did you say you were repulsed by Elizabeth at the end of your marriage... that you hated her, at times."

Had that been *my* voice asking that question in the oppressive silence? It must have been formulated in my unconscious mind, while I slept. I opened my eyes and saw that Evan, too, had been surprised to hear it.

"You're sure you want to talk about this again now?"

I saw his gaze flicker up to my forehead. I silently cursed myself for impulsively admitting I'd hit my own head on the wheel. After several hours' sleep, it seemed bizarre that I'd both purposefully injured myself and then confessed it.

I nodded, my cheek brushing against the pillowcase.

"It's a complicated question to answer in a few sentences, when the reason built up over years, over tens of thousands of little encounters, small observations and a dozen or so big, scary experiences," he began slowly. "If I were to choose one moment when my hatred of Elizabeth began, I'd probably say when I realized that she was unfaithful to me. I was completely sideswiped by that. I was about twenty-seven or so when it happened."

"You mean that you realized she and her father—"

"No, I didn't understand about her and her father until about a year before she died. I'm talking about a more run of the mill infidelity. She slept with more men than I could count over the years. Guys we'd grown up with and gone to school with. My friends. Men her father knew. Men *my* father knew. Random men in bars. To say she was promiscuous doesn't capture the reality. She needed sex. She needed the desire of men like an addict needs a drug.

"But I didn't understand the depth of her cheating immediately. When I first found out, I thought she'd been unfaithful to me one time. I confronted her about it, and she was remorseful. We reconciled, but it wasn't easy. After a few years though, I was forced to admit the truth: she'd never stopped having affairs, even during that time period we went to counseling, and supposedly were working on our marriage after I'd discovered the one affair. She couldn't seem to stop herself.

"But as time passed, I couldn't ignore the evidence anymore. My wife had slept with a good portion of men in the surrounding towns. Sometimes, she went through them two or three at one go." I heard something in the gruff sound he made, and realized uneasily it was shame mixing with his misery. I thought of that discovered wooden box in the viewing room, with all of the sex-things inside it, and the discs with initials indicating several people's involvement. Sex recordings. Elizabeth Madaster had taped herself having sex with men.

"I know you must be wondering why I stayed with her," Evan said, voicing my exact thought. "I wondered the same thing hundreds of times a day during that time period. The sexual part of our relationship had ended."

"Then why *did* you stay?" I whispered.

He grimaced. "Sexual promiscuity, sex addiction, and risky sexual behavior aren't uncommon with people who have been abused. It's a symptom, just as classic as mood instability or suicidal ideation."

"But I thought you said you didn't find out about Noah until later."

"I didn't. But sexual promiscuity can be symptomatic of mental illness, as well—depression, bipolar disorder, personality disorders. She was so fragile. I stayed because I was the only thing standing between her and almost certain destruction. I may have come to hate her at times for making a complete farce of our marriage, but I could see she was spinning out of control with her drinking and drug use, her affairs, her sheer *franticness*. I'd loved her since I was a kid. There was so much history between us. When you've loved someone so much, for so long, it's hard to just not care, to let go when you see her suffering. Because that's what I saw when I looked at Elizabeth, no matter how much she partied and drank and screwed every man she saw.

"I worried she'd destroy herself, eventually, no matter what I did. Her illness was cyclical. It escalated gradually, until she became increasingly out of control, drinking more heavily, having affairs while I was working in San Francisco. As her mania escalated, she wouldn't bother waiting for me to leave town. She'd bring her men here, entertaining them in the viewing room even while I was in the house. She drank and took prescription drugs to excess, drove intoxicated, swam drunk—once she nearly drowned. Noah and she went scuba diving once at night for some inexplicable reason no one could ever really explain to me. She passed out when they surfaced. Drug overdose. Thankfully, they were near enough to the coast that I heard Noah's shouts. We were able to get her to shore. I did CPR, and she revived before the ambulance arrived. For a while, I thought for sure she was dead, lying there on that beach. It was terrifying.

"She had a psychiatric hospitalization after that. She was hospitalized four times during our marriage, in addition to having one substance abuse rehab stay."

"If she was that out of control, didn't you, or the police, consider the possibility that she'd committed suicide when she disappeared?" I asked.

"It was a consideration for the police, yes. I believe that because of Noah's stature in the community, they never seriously followed up with that possibility. *Best not to go down that path, if it would only bring more grief to the family.* That's what I imagine the police were thinking."

"But *you* never seriously considered she'd committed suicide that night?" He shook his head. "Why?"

"For several reasons. For one thing, I was familiar with her cycles. Too familiar. Her behavior would escalate until it came to a climax, for lack of a better word." He winced and shut his eyes before rubbing his bunched forehead.

Despite my uncertainty about Evan in that moment, I pitied him. The pain of what he'd endured all those years was fully exposed now. I sensed the cold, relentless fear he must have lived with, given his wife's condition. She might self-destruct at any given moment. Every day when he woke up, he must have wondered if today would be the day. I couldn't imagine the hell he'd been through, being married to such a damaged, fragile woman.

And yet he'd stayed.

"She was diagnosed as bipolar," he said. "I'd take her to psychiatrists and counselors, but she'd eventually stop her medications, and I couldn't force her to stay in therapy. As a neurologist, Noah was no help in that. He had a strong distrust of psychiatrists and psychologists, spouting all kinds of nonsense about how unscientific mental health treatment was. I was constantly fighting against his influence on her, against its effect on her non-compliance with her treatment."

"He was the cause of her dysfunction, in large part."

Evan's eyes flashed. "Yes. He certainly didn't want *that* coming out in her therapy. Plus, it suited him best to keep her vulnerable. Desperate. He hated outsiders interfering with her life. Interfering with his influence over her. He was even jealous of Lorraine, Elizabeth's mother. He'd poisoned their mother-daughter relationship from the cradle. Maybe Lorraine does have Alzheimer's, but I've always thought she would have eventually gone mad in some fashion, regardless, just from being exposed to that man, day in and day out."

His bitterness and anger seemed to hang like a mist in the air between us. I knew by now there was nothing I could do or say to make it better, so I just watched him, waiting for him to continue.

"When Elizabeth's manic cycles would fizzle out, she would become regretful. Depressed. She would come to me and break down. Confess all her affairs, all the sordidness and depravity in which she'd drowned herself. She'd be filled with self-hatred. It was nearly unbearable to witness, given what a confident, strong, and dynamic person she typically was.

"It became *our* cycle. Just like when we were kids, she seemed to find comfort and some kind of *redemption* in our relationship. For a period of time—for at least a few months, sometimes for up to four months—she'd stabilize. She'd become the generous, hard-working, charismatic woman that I remembered. It was just enough for me to hope that things could be better for her. For us. Then she'd slowly start to spin out of control again."

"And at the time of her disappearance, what part of her cycle was she in?" I asked.

"She was in an unprecedented period of stability and health. She'd just undergone an extended hospitalization, and then a substance abuse rehab stay." He exhaled heavily.

"Of course, I began to see the destructiveness of our cycle, as well," Evan said. "I was enabling her, acting like some kind of catharsis for her shame. I started to see a therapist myself, in order to help me establish some limits with her. It was during my own therapy that I started to realize the sheer depth of Elizabeth's pain and agony. I began to wonder and have my suspicions about the source of her dysfunction."

I sat up in bed, propping myself up on my elbow. "You began to suspect Noah of abusing her?"

"Yes. At first, I thought it'd all taken place in the past. I didn't realize it was ongoing," he said, sounding weary. *Looking* weary. I had a fleeting thought that I should tell him to stop, to keep the rest of his explanation until tomorrow. He needed to sleep, too. But he kept talking, sounding tired but determined to tell this story, ugly as it was.

"Maybe four months or so before she disappeared, I was having a bout of insomnia. It happened a lot, the years before Elizabeth died. So I got up, planning to go down to the kitchen to have a drink or some warm milk... anything to help me sleep. I hadn't even turned on the light yet in the kitchen when I saw Elizabeth... saw the paleness of her nightgown moving in the darkness."

"Didn't you notice she wasn't in bed with you before you came downstairs?"

"We weren't sleeping together in those last years. That part of our relationship was finished. It'd been killed by some of the things Elizabeth had done. I stayed because I wanted to see her reasonably healthy and stable before we separated. But you can't go back. Not after some things."

We stared at one another. In the silence, I heard my heartbeat thrum in my ears. Is that what's happening to us now? Surely what Evan had done to me was one of those unforgiveable things.

Evan blinked and swallowed thickly. I found myself wondering if he'd had a similar thought.

"While Elizabeth and I still shared a bed at the beginning of our marriage," he continued gruffly, "I would often wake up and find her gone. A few times, I looked all over the house for her. I checked the garage. The boat slip. But all the cars and boats would always be there. At some point upon returning, I'd find her, either back in bed or going up the stairs. Of course, she always made an excuse as to where she'd been. 'We must have just missed each other,' she'd say, and laugh it off. I'd let it pass, but it always struck me as odd.

"But on this particular night when I saw her up out of bed, I knew more. I knew about her mental illness, and her infidelities. I knew how she'd used that viewing room in the past, for her little drug and sex parties. Orgies, to put it bluntly."

His mouth went very hard at that. I sensed his outrage. It couldn't have been easy for any man, no matter how compassionate he might be, to endure something like that.

"She'd been going through a relatively stable period at that time. But when I saw her, moving so excitedly and secretively in that dark room, I recognized immediately that she was manic again. Sexually compulsive. It was like a little explosion went off in my brain. How dare she do this to me again? What kind of a monster *was* she?"

His eyes blazed as our gazes locked. He'd been asking rhetorically, in part, but another part of him—a small, wounded part—wanted an answer, *craved* an answer so badly. I stared at him, speechless. I didn't know the answer to his question. I couldn't even fully imagine the things he was telling me, couldn't make sense of how someone survived such suffering.

"So I followed her. Before, I'd always dreaded the idea of catching her in the act with one of her lovers. She'd confessed things to me, things that would turn your stomach, Anna. Things I can't even bring myself to repeat," he said, breaking our stare.

"Her actions were hers, Evan. She was sick, and she acted out. You did your best to try and protect her, but you couldn't completely control her decisions and choices. Not unless you turned into a Noah Madaster."

His gaze flickered over to me. I sensed his surprise at my compassion. Maybe I was weak for offering it. But it was hard to withhold simple honesty, in the face of so much sorrow.

He inhaled, seeming to take courage to continue from my words.

"That was the night I discovered the corridor. The one between the North and South Twin."

The hair on my arms and the nape of my neck stood on end. "You didn't know it existed before?"

"No. No one ever mentioned it to me. The entrances were concealed. There's a hidden door at the back of a storage room. It's on the same level as the workout facility and the viewing room. You have to know where to access it. I'm sure Lorraine never knew of its existence, either. I'm willing to bet that a good portion of people who lived at Les Jumeaux over the past century didn't know about it."

"Did you follow her into the corridor?"

"Yes. She didn't realize I was behind her. I stayed back and watched her open the door."

"Where did it lead?"

"To a concealed room on the lower floor of the South Twin."

"That's how Noah and Elizabeth were meeting for their... trysts?"

"If that's what you want to call them," he said flatly, that bitter-taste expression once again on his face. "Madaster would claim that's where he was carrying out his research." He made an angry quote-gesture around the word research. "But in fact, it's where he was regularly drugging, brainwashing and raping his own daughter."

My chest felt very tight when I tried to inhale. "He was using that thing—the Analyzer on her?"

"Yes," Evan replied gruffly. He blinked and looked at the table. He picked up a water glass and drank half of it thirstily before setting down the glass with a jarring bang. "That monster would have her wear the sensor cap of the Analyzer while they had sex."

He said it like he was giving me a reluctant, necessary blow to my head. But I was only confused by his revelation.

"I don't understand," I said.

He explained to me that Madaster had turned the visual feedback on his brainwave lie detector into an auditory function, which he could hear through a small ear bud. Another supposed "advancement" of the Analyzer was an easily donned "sensor cap." With it, no difficult individual attachment of sensors to the skull was necessary.

"Noah could ask questions of the person wearing the sensor cap and supposedly determine from the auditory tone in his ear if the person was lying or not. It was his 'hands free' option for the Analyzer," Evan explained, his tone rife with sarcasm and anger. "Or at least, that's what Noah and Elizabeth believed. But I think it was the force of Noah's personality, the use of drugs—scopolamine, sedatives, LSD and other psychedelic drugs—along with his cruelty and mind games, that were really made the Analyzer 'work.' Not as a lie detector or mind reading technique, but purely as a means for control and brainwashing.

"He would give Elizabeth drugs that were meant to free her consciousness. Then he'd make her wear the sensor cap during...." He winced and gave me a quick, reluctant glance. I merely nodded once, trying to assure him it was all right. "Various torture and bondage activities. She'd wear the cap during sex, and he would demand that she tell him the truth about whatever he was doing to her. He would insist she was lying, even when she was honest. Eventually, Elizabeth believed whatever he told her was the truth. He made up into down, Anna," Evan said, his voice cracking. "Wrong into right... pain into pleasure and love."

I covered his hand in mine. It killed me, seeing him like this. He glanced up, my touch pulling him out of his misery. I hadn't even told myself to sit up in bed and try to comfort him. His anguish had been so tangible, I'd responded without thinking.

"You *saw* it. You saw them *doing* that?" I whispered shakily. The idea of him having to witness something so abhorrent firsthand was unthinkable.

He shook his head. "Not all of it, no. Not that night. I heard later about most of it, from Elizabeth herself. That night, I just saw her enter a room. There was a bed in the background, with some wires and equipment on it. A lamp was lit. Noah was there, and I could tell he'd been

219

waiting for her. He embraced her, and she embraced him back. There was something so familiar about the way they touched each other. So charged. I remember he grabbed her hair and pulled on it, stretching back her neck. He jerked at the straps of her nightgown so that it fell down to her waist. I was horrified. I started to run forward to stop it all.

"But then I saw her expression. She stared up at him, not just with adoration. With lust.

"That was when I understood that she hadn't only been sexually abused by her father. The abuse continued. And Elizabeth didn't consider it abuse in the least. Then he kissed her, and Elizabeth reciprocated. In fact.... she became the aggressor... "

His deep voice broke. I squeezed his hand tighter when he faded off, his jaw clenched tight. He squeezed back.

"It was like... part of me froze, and has never unthawed, to this day. Abomination. That's what it was. That's what *he* was. I can't think of a better way of describing it. He'd corrupted her to the point that very little of her original self remained.

"But seeing them together like that, it changed me. Suspecting something and seeing the truth are two very different things, Anna. I'd hated Noah before that night. But after that... that's when my obsession began, to see him pay for what he'd done."

Chapter Twenty

EVAN SIGHED HEAVILY, BUT THAT HARD, DETERMINED SET TO HIS mouth remained.

"Then Noah closed the door," he continued. "And I heard a lock click into place. I didn't confront Elizabeth until she returned to her bedroom, early the next morning."

"What did she say?"

"It was a lot like so many times before. The tears. The confessions. The remorse. It was the same on her part, anyway. For me, everything had changed that night. Elizabeth cringed with shame and regret when she understood I'd seen her with her father and knew they were sexually involved. She cried. She admitted everything: how they'd first had a sex when she was just nine years old, how the abuse had continued since then, how their activities had grown in depravity, how he used the Analyzer on her. She insisted that she wanted it all to end, and begged me to help her put a stop to it all."

"What did you do?"

"I insisted she check herself in for a long-term psychiatric hospitalization, and then for substance abuse rehab. I knew nothing could change until she got away from Noah and Les Jumeaux, and admitted what had been happening to her for most of her life to mental health professionals. I only had a vague idea of the effects of brainwashing and mind control at that time, but I understood that she required professional care, an expert to help deprogram her from all of Noah's deliberate brainwashing.

"I also insisted that we go to the police," he said.

"So that she could report Noah?"

He nodded. "She was willing to do everything I asked in regard to treatment. But when I mentioned going to the police, she got frantic. Panicked. Did I want to see her charged with something? Did I *want* to see her family and herself, ostracized publicly?

"When I persisted, she turned angry. Spiteful. Vicious. She said she'd refuse treatment if I insisted upon her going to the police to report what Noah had done to her... what he continued to do. Then... "

His eyes looked hollow as he hesitated.

"She laughed at me for wanting to save her from her father," he said gruffly. "She told me that *she* was the one responsible for what went on between Noah and herself.

"It wasn't until then that I realized she believed it; she *honestly* believed that she was as much at fault as Noah. *More* than equal in blame. I found out that Noah had convinced her that their first sexual encounter was initiated by her—Elizabeth."

I cringed back. "But she was a child."

"*I* know that. *You* know that a child can't give consent for something like that; the idea is ludicrous and sick. She was completely at her father's mercy. But that was the real terror of his brainwashing. Elizabeth *didn't* understand that. She believed, body and soul, that she'd wanted what her father had done to her. Craved it. She was convinced she was warped sexually. That she'd been born depraved. Noah had her convinced he was trying to stamp the twisted gene out of her. *That's* what she believed he was doing to her while she was hooked up to that Analyzer, and he was abusing her. The whole thing was so screwed up. It boggles the mind, to consider the evil one human being can force onto another. Worse, this was a father corrupting his daughter to the core.

"When I couldn't convince Elizabeth that the fault was one hundred percent Noah's, I realized the best I could do at that point was send her to treatment... get her away from the devil, free her from drugs and alcohol, and hope that professionals could deprogram her from the lies and filth he'd imprinted into her brain. Her soul. I hoped that after that, she'd be able to condemn her father for decades of abuse, separate from him—both physically and psychologically, and begin the long process of healing."

"Did she agree to the treatment?"

"Yes. She had an extended psychiatric hospitalization where they were able to stabilize her on medications for her bipolar disorder. She attended regular therapy. After that, she checked into substance abuse rehab. Upon discharge from both the psychiatric hospitalization and the substance abuse rehab, I'd never seen her so healthy. Her doctors and I had to work on convincing her, but while she was still in rehab, she agreed to come with me to San Francisco. Our marriage wasn't what it was—it never would be—but it was enough that she was growing stronger during those weeks we lived in San Francisco, away from the influence of Noah."

"You never did tell me how you reacted toward Noah after you saw the two of them together... after Elizabeth told you what he'd been doing to her."

Our hands were still clasped together. I felt a tremor pass through him. He glanced at me reluctantly.

"Evan?"

"We had a blowout. I hit him. Hard. He went down. It felt fantastic, Anna," he admitted with a quiet, terrible intensity. "I wanted to do more."

"Did you?"

"No. I regret it. Sometimes. Noah managed to pick himself up off the floor."

"Did he admit to his abuse of Elizabeth?"

His mouth slanted angrily in memory. "Yes, essentially, although he didn't consider it abuse, of course. For a narcissistic sociopath like Noah, there's always a good defense for his behavior, even when the behavior is utterly indefensible. It was an ugly war of words between us after that. I won't go into all the details, except to say that Noah took off his mask during our confrontation. I threatened him with public exposure. He threatened me with sabotaging Elizabeth's treatment and separating us, and eliminating what he considered to be my unhealthy influence over her once and for all."

"How did he plan to do that?"

"He claimed he had the power to do it, just by speaking to her. One phone call to the hospital. A brief visit after she was discharged. Not only that. He insinuated that if Elizabeth ever revealed his abuse, if she turned on him and went to the police, he would stop her. End her."

I stilled. "He *admitted* to you he would kill her if she told the truth?"

"Not in those words. I'm telling you just what he said. He said he'd end her. It was the look in his eyes when he said it that made me think he meant it literally. He wasn't talking about cutting her off from her trust fund, or ruining her reputation socially. He meant end her life. I was afraid he was telling the absolute truth. No... part of me was *certain* he was. But at that point, I'd only started to realize the depth of his power over Elizabeth.

"So we left things at a standoff for the time being. Elizabeth's continued stability and the hope of improvement had to be my one goal. Noah wouldn't try to contact Elizabeth and interfere with her treatment or life as long as I didn't publicly expose him for what he'd been doing to his daughter for nearly her whole life. I hated having to agree to that, but I didn't know what else to do to keep her safe."

Evan lowered his head at that point, his weariness palpable.

"After Noah and I fought," he said, "and while Elizabeth was still in the hospital, I had the corridor between the twins filled with rock and soil, and the doors sealed."

"Did Noah know that you'd done it?"

"Yes. It would have been impossible to disguise the construction crew onsite."

"He didn't confront you about it?"

Evan lifted his head slowly. "No. Part of me wanted him to. I wanted to finish that fight. But he never did. I just saw him once while the men were working. He was standing on the grounds, watching. You should have seen the look on his face."

"What was it?" I asked, reaching to brush back his hair.

"Smug contempt. Like the bastard knew something I didn't."

He abruptly caught my stroking hand in his. "God, I hate him, Anna," he said with such fierce intensity, for a split second, I was frightened. But then I felt the trembling in his flesh. It nearly undid me, to experience my strong, virile husband shaking with rage.

"You're going to go on with this, aren't you?" I asked him. "You're going to continue with this vendetta until either Madaster is exposed, or you're dead."

"*No.*" He said it so passionately, that I started back.

"That's what I've started to realize, being here with you. I crave seeing Noah punished for what he's done. I wanted it so much that it consumed years of my life. I grew bent on revenge. That's what he does to the people around him. He makes us *bent*. Twisted.

"When I came up with this plan, I thought there was no way he could harm *you*, though. But now, given what happened to you yesterday in the sauna, and the rock avalanche on the road... even the fact that those two thugs were here on the property, removing stuff out of the boathouse—likely at Noah's request—I'm starting to think I've overestimated Noah's vulnerability. I've underestimated his potential *reach*."

"You think Noah was responsible for those things?"

"I'm not positive. But I can't take the chance. Let's leave Les Jumeaux, as soon as we can. When I came home early from San Francisco, that's what I had in mind. This is what I've learned in the past few months, being with you. I hate him. But I love you more, Anna."

"Don't say that."

"It's true. I know I've wronged you. I'm sorry for dragging you into this, and that you found out about the truth from someone other than me. I know you'll need time and space to sort through all this. But don't separate us. Please. We'll go wherever you want. We'll go to Tiburon. God, I wish I'd listened to you, that day after our wedding, and stayed there with you there. Or we could go to San Francisco if you like... or to Europe... "

"You would just forget about Noah? About making him pay for what he's done?"

"If it would help."

My fingers tightened in his hair. "Help *what*?"

"For you to begin to forgive me."

I exhaled shakily, tears stinging my eyes. I'd reached a wall again. I was pressed against it so tight, I couldn't fill my lungs. I wasn't sure about anything. Evan. My feelings. My future.

The only thing I knew for certain was my pain. *Our* pain. Evan and I were co-sufferers in that moment.

I reached for him, my hands under his elbows, urging him to stand. He rose slowly. Our stares locked as he looked down at me.

"Come to bed," I said through a raw throat. "You're exhausted, and so am I. We'll see how we feel in the morning."

"Anna—"

I shook my head, cutting him off. I pulled on his hand and scooted back on the mattress. I put out my hands for him.

"I can't believe you did this to me. I'm furious at you, Evan."

"I know, I wish I could—"

"No more talking. I can't absorb anymore right now. I can't decide anything. The only thing I know for certain is that we're both hurting. Come to bed," I repeated softly.

He stood there for several seconds, just looking at me. Then he came down on the mattress and took me into his arms.

I let him.

We held each other tight throughout the night, our embrace our only ward against a world of bitterness, uncertainty, and loss. We were alike in that way, Evan and I.

Neither one of us could bear to see our spouse in pain.

That night, I dreamt of a world of water.

And that water was *so* cold.

Chapter Twenty-One

THE NEXT MORNING WHEN I AWOKE, I WAS ALONE. I EXPERIENCED
none of the terror I had last night when I'd awakened and thought I
was alone at Les Jumeaux with only a ghost for company. I lay in bed,
surveying the strange room through these new eyes I'd acquired since
yesterday. I saw that Evan had brought me a stack of clothing and my
toiletry bag, and had set them on the bureau.

Memories from yesterday and last night swam around in my brain,
but the one that stood out the most was Evan's face when he'd said, "God,
I hate him, Anna," and the alarming feeling of his strong body quaking.

I got up, a little amazed at how relatively calm I felt. I'd grown rootless in the past twenty-four hours. My life wasn't what I'd believed it
to be. But rootless or not, I still looked much the same in the mirror. I
still went through the mundane activities of daily life, of showering and
brushing my teeth and dressing. I discovered that those basic, unquestioned actions grounded me, anchored me to the moment, and kept
me from spinning off into oblivion.

In the kitchen, I saw that Evan had made coffee: another common-
place routine. If we heard on the news that a nuclear bomb had exploded
nearby, and that all life would end in a day or two, would we still make
coffee in the morning? I thought we would.

A gorgeous, sunny Tahoe day reigned outside on the terrace, oblivious to the sordid, ugly little details and heartbreaks that occurred inside
Les Jumeaux's walls.

"Anna?"

I blinked the sunshine out of my eyes and turned at the sound of Evan's voice. He walked toward me, wearing a pair of fitted gray slacks and a blue button-down shirt. The weariness that had shadowed his face last night had vanished. He'd shaved. He looked tense, but still freshened from his night's sleep. Crisp. Achingly attractive...

And concerned, I realized.

"Are you all right?" he asked quietly, stepping close and peering down at me in the bright sunlight.

I nodded and held up my cup. "Just trying to clear my head." I stared up at him and felt my throat tighten. I laughed and looked away.

"What?" he asked me, and I heard the uneasiness in his deep voice. I understood why. My laugh had sounded brittle. Odd. He probably worried I was going mad.

Just like Elizabeth.

"Nothing. I was just thinking about how we'd probably make coffee even if a nuclear bomb dropped nearby," I said thickly, blinking unwanted tears out of my eyes and taking a giant gulp of my coffee, burning my throat to distract myself. He didn't say anything for a moment. Then he touched the inside of my elbow lightly.

"That's how this feels to you, isn't it? Like a bomb has dropped on your life."

I tried to laugh it off, but it sounded like I was choking. I felt him taking my coffee cup out of my hand. He put his arms around me, his chin resting on my head.

"I'm so sorry. God, I'm sorry, Anna."

We just stood there, my arms at my sides, his arms wrapped around me in the warm sunshine, until I brought myself under control. I sniffed and snuck my hand between our bodies, wiping off an unwanted tear or two from my face. He must have sensed me breaking the connection, because he loosened his hold on me and backed away.

"Will you come into the office? I want to talk to you about something." He waved behind him, and I saw the opened French doors that led to his office. I hadn't entirely been aware of walking out onto the terrace, or where I'd gone. But I'd stopped at the stone parapet just outside of his office.

I followed him inside, thinking how strange it was, entering the male room from this door. Same room, different perspective.

The world turned upside down, I thought, and nearly laughed out loud again.

All traces of hysterical humor vanished when I saw the wooden box on his desk, just where I'd set it the other night. I experienced a strange sense of time stretching into eternity and then collapsing closed violently, like a snapped rubber band.

"It could *not* have been only two nights ago that I put that thing on your desk," I muttered.

"Where did you find it?"

"I didn't. The work crew did while they were doing demolition in the viewing room. One of them brought it up to the kitchen, and Valeria showed it to me later."

"You opened it," Evan stated flatly rather than asked.

I nodded.

"I'm sorry. Again," he exhaled in obvious frustration. "Always."

I didn't say anything for a moment. My emotions were bubbling up to the surface again. I wasn't as calm as I'd convinced myself I was.

"You apologize. Does that mean you had something to do with it? The box?" I asked him.

"No, of course not. The things in that box were from Elizabeth's domain, not mine."

"Then why did you apologize?"

"You know why. Because I brought you here. I exposed you to it all."

"Could you put it away?" I asked, my voice sounding unusually high.

"Of course," he said, moving quickly. I saw him whisk Elizabeth's box—the Sex Box—as I'd come to think of it in my mind, off his desk and open a cabinet all through the periphery of my vision.

"I'll get rid of it later," Evan said a moment later.

"You shouldn't," I said, turning to face him. He stood behind his desk. I noticed his questioning look. "Get rid of it. Maybe there's some kind of proof on those discs."

"Proof?" Evan asked blankly.

"Clues. I don't know. Information about Elizabeth's disappearance. Something about Noah that you could take to the police," I tried to explain.

"I told you. I don't care about that anymore," he said, coming around the desk. "All I'm thinking about right now is you."

I laughed again. I honestly don't know why I kept doing it, except to say it seemed to be my body's natural way of expelling tension and distress. Maybe there was a good reason that crazy people laughed so eerily.

"You can't honestly expect me to believe that you're going to abandon this whole... *mission* you've been on," I said.

"I'll prove it to you. We'll leave now. Today. We'll never speak of Les Jumeaux again, Anna."

"Never speak of Elizabeth?" I asked softly.

"If that's what you want."

I found myself staring out at the sunlit terrace. *Was* it what I wanted? For some reason, a vision flashed into my mind's eye of an old, disheveled woman hovering over me.

"You never *wear your hat."*

"She thought I was Elizabeth that day. Lorraine Madaster," I said. "She saw me up at the overlook, and in her confusion, she took me for her daughter." I met Evan's stare and saw his discomfort. "You lied to me after that. You made it seem like she was some random crazy lady who wandered around here. One of many lies you told me. When Wes told me she was Lorraine Madaster, I was forced to face the fact that you'd been lying to me about other things, too. That's what made me want to go to the library, to try and figure out what other lies you were telling me."

His mouth tightened and then opened.

"Don't," I said, stopping him. "I don't want more apologies right now."

For a moment, neither of us spoke.

"Did Elizabeth love her? Her mother?" I finally asked.

"Like I said, Noah poisoned that relationship. Lorraine became a shadow... a cutout figure of a wife and mother. She'd served her purpose by giving him Elizabeth. After that, she was something to be tolerated. Elizabeth and Lorraine's relationship was distant. Cold. But to answer your question: yes," he added after a pause. "I think down deep, Elizabeth loved Lorraine."

I thought of the gentleness of Lorraine's touch on my cheek, at her impatience and hurt when she thought she was being rebuffed for the simple act of nurturing, for worrying that her daughter was getting a sunburn. *No one does what I ask.*

She had been eliminated from the basic, biological right of mothering her child.

"What about you?" I asked him. "Did pity for Lorraine ever figure into your need for revenge?"

"Yes."

I blinked at his quick, concise reply, not expecting it. Maybe I'd been imagining, at least in part, that his vendetta with Noah was purely a testosterone-driven thing, a primitive male right to show who was the alpha of the pack.

"I came to care for Lorraine in the years I was living here. She seemed so alone. Maybe I realized our similarities, given Elizabeth and Noah's exclusive relationship." He shrugged. "We never spoke of it directly to each other, but I think we both knew that the other one suffered. Anyone would, being in the vicinity of Noah. And maybe we understood instinctively that we'd both lost Elizabeth. Or that we'd never had her."

Our gazes locked in the silence.

"Lorraine was a distant Madaster cousin, you know. She married Noah when she was very young, in some medieval-like, dynastic alliance," he said bitterly. "She had Elizabeth within a year and a half, and then was cast off, for the most part. She lived here but was unacknowledged, except as a nuisance. Like I told you, it's no wonder she went mad. After Elizabeth disappeared, I asked Lorraine if she wanted me to take her away from here. But her deterioration escalated a lot after Elizabeth went missing. I don't think she ever really accepted her death. She flatly refused to leave Les Jumeaux. She wasn't talking all that much, by that time, but I had the impression that she seemed to think it would mean abandoning Elizabeth somehow, if she left."

I sat down heavily on the couch behind me. My feelings of sadness and pity for Lorraine Madaster went deeper than I realized or understood.

"What is it, Anna? What are you thinking?"

I blinked and glanced up, amazed to see Evan kneeling in front of me.

"She deserves better," I said honestly. "Lorraine Madaster. I thought it, even that first time I woke up to see her hovering over me. She's completely alone in the world. No one is taking care of her. It's not right."

He nodded. He touched my cheek, very softly. I held my breath.

"Evan... Anna."

I jumped at the unexpected interruption. Wes Ryder stood at the entrance to the room, looking typically rumpled and frazzled, but also worried.

"I'm so sorry for barging in like this. I tried to call," he said, giving Evan an entreating glance.

Evan stood slowly. "What is it, Wes?"

"I was wondering if I could speak with you, Evan? Privately?" he asked, his glance striking me and then bouncing away.

Evan stared at his old friend with narrowed eyelids. "How the hell did you get in here?"

"When I heard the... uh... news," he faltered, his gaze shooting to me again. "I thought I should come. I spoke with Valeria this morning, and she said you'd called and asked her to take a few days off. I talked her into giving me the entry code. Can I talk to you, Evan? Privately?"

"Not now," Evan said in a clipped tone.

"It's all right," I said, standing up from the couch. "I told Valeria yesterday that I'd found out Elizabeth and I were doubles... That you'd married a replica of your first wife. Valeria undoubtedly told Wes that the cat's out of the bag," I said to Evan, giving Wes a weary, irritated glance. I retrieved the coffee cup Evan had brought in from outside and held it up. "I'll just go warm up my coffee."

"No, Anna. I don't want you to go," Evan said.

"It's all right," I told him, holding his stare for a second so that he could see I meant it. "I'm not going anywhere, except to get some sunshine on the terrace."

I gave Wes a cool glance as I passed him. I had the impression he wanted to back away from me... give me a wide berth, but that he held his ground with effort.

He sees a ghost when he sees you.

And then quick on the heels of that: *Wes slept with Elizabeth.*

Lake Tahoe was cobalt blue on this late summer morning. I stared out at that perfect alchemy of water and sunlight, wondering about those seemingly random thoughts that had popped into my brain while I looked into Wes Ryder's big, glassy eyes as I passed him a few minutes ago.

Maybe my thoughts weren't as random as I'd initially thought they were. I recalled the way he'd talked about Elizabeth up at the overlook, the obvious admiration and more subtle tinge of longing and loss in his tone.

I remembered something Evan had told me last night: *"She slept with more men than I could count over the years. Guys we'd grown up with, and gone to school. My friends... She needed sex. She needed the desire of men, like an addict needs a drug."*

I didn't second-guess the knowledge that Wes Ryder had been one of Elizabeth's conquests, any more than I doubted that she'd left an indelible mark on the doctor. Elizabeth may have considered Wes to be a passing fancy—a quick fix—but Wes would remember her until his dying day.

Poor Valeria.

The thought was distant and somehow unconnected to me.

Movement to my left caught my attention. I was so numb that I wasn't surprised when someone rose up a stone stairway to the left of the terrace. I didn't think much of anything at all as the dark-haired woman with a stocky build walked toward me, as though she'd known she would find me there. She looked solid and real enough in the blinding sunlight. Her white Velcro tennis shoes gleamed on the gray stone pavers.

She wasn't a particularly attractive woman. But the expression on her face as she glared at me made her appear downright ugly.

"You ought to be ashamed of what you're doing," she accused.

I blinked at the sheer venom in her tone. I found myself staring at the thick, tight bun on her head. I recalled seeing the outline of it in the car leaving South Twin.

"You're his nurse, aren't you? Noah Madaster's nurse?"

"This is from him," she said. She shoved an envelope toward my midriff. I reached for it unthinkingly. The nurse turned and marched away, disappearing down the steps as rapidly and inexplicably as she'd arrived.

I became aware of the envelope in my hand. It felt warm, like the heat from the woman's anger had been absorbed by it. I lifted it and stared at the writing scrawled on the paper.

Anna Solas, it read.

A chill passed through me. *Not* Anna Halifax. It was inscribed with my maiden name.

Which meant that Noah Madaster had been researching who I was.

"Anna?"

I turned to see Evan walking across the terrace. I folded the letter in half and shoved it in my shorts pocket before I faced him.

"I'm sorry for the interruption," he said as he approached me. He hitched his thumb back toward his office. "Wes is still in there, making some phone calls."

"It doesn't matter."

He blanched slightly at my indifference. "It does matter. Everything—all of it—matters."

"I suppose Wes knew all along? About your vendetta against Noah Madaster? I guess he'd have to be told something, given the fact that I look exactly like Elizabeth. You'd have to tell Wes, or he'd blurt out something stupid when he saw me."

Evan squinted at the lake. "He doesn't know about my plans in regard to Noah, no. He just thinks that I met you and... "

"Fell in fake-love with me because I look like Elizabeth?" I finished for him.

"I'm not sure what he believes, exactly. I haven't been very forth-coming on the subject of you. I just told him about the resemblance, and asked him not to show shock, because you didn't know about it yet. And yes, I told him that I was in love with you. In love. *Not* fake love, Anna."

I laughed harshly. "Wes wouldn't have any trouble believing that, I can imagine."

"What do you mean?"

"I look like Elizabeth. And Wes was in love with her, just like you were," I said recklessly. "He slept with her. Right?"

I liked his startled expression. It was nice, not to always be the stupid, naïve one.

"How did you know that?"

"I see the way he looks at me. Like I'm a ghost. Like part of him wishes like hell I really *was* her, while the other half wants to turn tail and run. I heard the way he talked about Elizabeth."

For a few seconds, Evan didn't respond. The narrowed crescents of his eyes glittered as he stared out at the sun-gilded lake.

"Wes was the first," he admitted gruffly. "Not the first ever—I doubt there was a time that Elizabeth was ever faithful to me—but Wes was the first I found out about. He was the one we went to therapy for... the only one we really ever worked as a couple to get past. Or so I believed at the time. After that, I didn't really focus much on the identity of Elizabeth's men anymore. It wasn't the individual man who mattered. It was her desperate hunger. Her need to be desired. It gave her a semblance of control over men. Over her world."

"A control that her father had stolen from her years before," I added.

I absorbed it all for a moment. Wes may have been a blip on Elizabeth's sexual radar, but she'd been a game changer for him. Somehow, I just knew that.

"How can you still be friends with him?" I asked Evan.

He seemed unsurprised by the question. I realized it was because he'd probably asked himself the same thing many times before.

"Wes and I have a long history. Our friendship goes back, even before Elizabeth entered the picture."

A thought occurred to me. "You knew he was Madaster's physician, didn't you? Before we ever came here?"

He met my stare squarely.

"I did, yes."

"Of course you did. You called Wes and renewed your friendship because you knew he could offer you inside information about Madaster and what was going on in the South Twin. You were using him, like you used me. How else could you possibly find out what effect your plan was having on Madaster? What effect I was having on him."

"In part, yes."

"So actually, your long history with Wes has little to do with you ever contacting him. You're tolerating him because he fits into your plans to drive Madaster crazy with my presence. You'd even put up with one of Elizabeth's ex-lovers, if it meant getting your revenge."

"I know that you're angry with me, Anna. But you're wrong to think that I resent Wes's affair with Elizabeth, to this day. I forgave him for it years ago. She made a fool of any number of men, including me. It's hard to hold a grudge, when you understood what she could be like... the kind of power she could wield."

That irritated me.

"Wes is having an affair with Valeria, you know," I said dully.

"I suspected it. After seeing them together. Anna—"

"I need to get out of this sun. I have a headache," I said, cutting him off.

He caught my hand as I started for the door that led to the kitchen. "Maybe I should take you to the doctor." He seemed to read the alarm on my face. His forehead furrowed. "Because of your head," he explained rapidly. "Because you hit your head, and now this headache—"

"It's not from hitting my head. It's a migraine. I don't get them as often as I used to, but I definitely recognize one. Stress can trigger them."

Stress also can trigger hallucinations and other forms of madness, can't it?

I forced the vision of the woman in the red Ferrari out of my head with effort.

"Do you still want to leave today?" Evan asked me.

The feeling of his large, dry, warm hand enfolding mine distracted me, making it difficult to gather my thoughts. The truth was, I didn't know what I wanted at that moment.

"I do. I think."

He nodded. "I'd like to take you." He noticed my frown. "I know you need time. I'm not going to crowd you. But let me take you away from here. You need time to think. To process. I realize how much I've hurt you. But please don't send me away from you. I want to be there for you, to answer any questions you might have. To do whatever you need. I'll do anything to make this right, Anna."

I made the mistake of looking into his eyes. I sensed his honesty.

But I didn't trust it.

The pain behind my right eye throbbed. I pressed my fingertips against it.

"I don't know. Right now, I just need to be alone."

"Of course. I left the aspirin on the bedside table. Lie down and get some rest."

I distinctly felt the edges of the letter pressing against my thigh. I nodded and tugged on my hand, *needing* to get away from him at that moment.

But at the same time, I hated the feeling of my fingers sliding from his grasp.

Chapter Twenty-Two

ONCE I WAS IN THE SAFETY OF THE BEDROOM SUITE WE'D SLEPT IN LAST night, I left the curtains drawn. I hurriedly swallowed a couple aspirin, then went over to the seating area and turned a lamp onto its dimmest setting.

I looked first at the bold signature at the bottom of the second page.

Noah Madaster.

A surreal feeling went through me.

I thought of Wes's report of Madaster's recent heart attack. This script was *not* the writing of a frail man. Instead, the large, bold scrawl, screamed vitality and strength... along with something else. Blazing confidence. It reminded me of the sumptuous, unflinching writing in the detailed Madaster family history I'd discovered in the great room. That had been written by Theodore Madaster, Noah's father. Could the appearance of handwriting be passed on through the genes? Could a confidence so great that it looked like self-righteousness and narcissism be coded in DNA?

My fingers felt chilled as I clutched the pages.

Anna,

My name is Noah Madaster. Knowing my one-time son-in-law as well as I do, I have no doubt that by this time, when you read my name, you will equate it with the devil himself: horns, hooves, pitchfork and all.

I have not had the pleasure yet of meeting you. But I get the impression from my observances that you are not a foolish woman.

Nor are you an untalented one. Evan Halifax may try to paint me with his typical slashing, black and white strokes.

But I've seen your paintings. I was quite moved by them. I believe that you are more subtle and complex in your rendering of reality than your husband can ever fully comprehend.

I am aware of how Evan has wronged you, leading you to believe that he is in love with you, marrying you under false pretenses, and bringing you to this place in order to exact his revenge on me. I can't begin to tell you how much this angers me on your part. I'm not sure how much of the truth he has told you at this point. But I can tell you this: Whatever he's told you is not the truth in its entirety.

Evan has made a terrible misjudgment, Anna. One that even he, sitting in his self-erected throne of judgment, doesn't understand.

I have seen the way you look at him, while you two were up at the overlook. I saw my daughter look at him in much the same way. I know, more than anyone, the effect Evan Halifax can have. He poisoned my Elizabeth against me. Sadly, I know he's likely been doing the same to you. His web around you is thick, but I hope not impenetrable.

I realize that you must be in very much pain right now, learning what you have about your marriage. But I beg of you. Don't leave Les Jumeaux without coming to see me, as soon as possible, in the South Twin. Come today, if possible.

You have only learned half of the truth, Anna. As an artist, you're struggling to see the whole landscape. But Evan can't give it to you. I can. I have discovered something that is of vital importance to both of us.

Come quickly.
Noah Madaster

I sat still for a stretched moment after finishing the letter, staring off into space. Who had told Noah that I'd found out I looked like Elizabeth Madaster? Wes via Valeria? The librarian, possibly? The librarian had seemed to know Elizabeth well. For all I knew, she also was an acquaintance of Noah's as well, and had called him to tell her story about my visit at the library.

I didn't trust Noah Madaster. I couldn't trust much of anything associated with Evan and Les Jumeaux at that point. But my distrust of Madaster didn't come from Evan. Not entirely, anyway. It came from the feeling of his gaze on me, when I'd been up at the overlook. It came from the vision of his bloody fist of rage.

(He's dangerous. He's a cancer. Never underestimate him. But you have to face him.)

It was my voice in my head... but it wasn't. Some note in it was off, familiar and yet different, somehow. I didn't have the energy to puzzle it out at that moment.

I got up and went over to the pile of clothing Evan had brought in for me. I secreted the letter between a couple T-shirts.

As an artist, you're struggling to see the whole landscape. But Evan can't give it to you. I can.

Evan had said that Madaster was subtle in his manipulations. I wasn't kidding myself. I recognized the cleverness of his mentioning my art to convince me to his cause. Somehow, he'd intuited the exact language to sway me. Both Evan and he had targeted that vulnerability in me.

Ever since Evan had singled me out on that dating site, I'd felt as if my senses were only half operating. No matter how hard I tried, I couldn't quite focus on the truth. Before yesterday, part of my refusal to see reality had been my own denial. Some psychological reflex had kicked in, willing me to see only the fantasy of my picture-perfect marriage to Evan versus reality.

But now the stage and the sets had been ripped down. The horror and pain of seeing the truth had happened right in front of my eyes. I wouldn't flinch from that pain anymore. I wanted to see the entire picture.

No matter how ugly that portrait was.

When I opened the bedroom door, I did so silently. I crept down the hallway, wincing at the slightest squeak on the wood floors.

Evan would go ballistic if he knew I planned to visit South Twin.

I don't know what I expected when I lifted the heavy wrought iron knocker on the South Twin's front door. But it wasn't that Lorraine

Madaster would be the one to respond. It seemed strange, to see her within the confines of a house.

She looked afraid when she saw me standing there, her filmy blue eyes sprung wide.

"It's okay, Lorraine. It's just me, Anna. From next door."

"You should go." Her voice sounded hoarse, like she didn't use it much.

I started when she reached and pushed me back on the shoulders—hard. I lost my balance.

A shout that was almost a roar emanated from above us. I regained my footing only to see Lorraine freeze in the process of shutting the door in my face.

"Let her in, you imbecile. Don't you dare touch her again!"

Lorraine now looked terrified. Regret swamped me. I rushed forward and touched her upper arm, stroking her to try and soothe her.

"It's okay, Lorraine," I whispered. "Please don't be afraid. I just came over for a quick chat with him."

"I was weak. I'm sorry." Her ragged, broken whisper was unlike anything I'd heard from her while she rambled about in the outside world, wild and a little fierce. In here—in the South Twin—she was cowering and helpless. A prisoner. A feeling of profound sadness went through me. I knew instinctively she was seeing Elizabeth when she looked at me.

I squeezed her shoulder softly, my pity amplifying at the realization of how bony and thin she was. I needed to do a lot better than a sandwich a day.

"You have nothing to be sorry for. Nothing." The desolation on her face didn't ease.

"I understand," I said gently. "I understand how difficult it was for you. I'm safe now. You don't have to worry anymore. And... " I swallowed thickly in the midst of my dissembling. "I forgive you."

Part of me was stunned that I said it. But then I saw relief break over her thin, ravaged face, and I knew why I had.

Lorraine had known, deep down, what Noah Madaster was doing to their only child. She'd believed she'd been powerless to stop it. And so she'd consigned herself to waking up to a fresh hell every day of her life. I understood in that moment that Lorraine's madness was an escape from Madaster. But it was an escape from the monumental guilt of a mother who could not—or would not—protect her child, as well. I cringed inwardly, recognizing the pit of pain and despair inside her.

Inside this house.

In the distance, I heard the sound of someone descending the stairs rapidly. I looked behind Lorraine, and peered for the first time into the South Twin.

It was darker here than in the North Twin. Heavy drapery covered every window that I could see. It was laid out differently, as well. The first thing that I saw was an impressive mahogany grand staircase almost immediately outside of the entry foyer. It wasn't Y-shaped like the one in the North Twin.

This one went straight up.

Straight *down*.

The staircase was so steep, I couldn't see the top of it. But surely that's where the shout—Noah's shout—had come from. I pictured him sitting impatiently at the top of the stairs in his wheelchair, the shadows clinging around him.

It was Noah's nurse who currently descended the steep steps. She stopped around halfway down the stairs, a frown plastered on her face. She beckoned to me. I gave Lorraine another stroke of reassurance and started to move past her. Lorraine grabbed my wrist, her grip surprisingly strong.

"Be careful on the stairs. They're more dangerous than a knife," Lorraine whispered heatedly. And then I saw it: a knowing, malicious gleam in her rheumy eyes. I started. Seeing the blank surprise on my face, Lorraine gave a small nod, affirming the flash of truth I'd seen.

Lorraine Madaster wasn't the helpless pawn I'd imagined. It played out in my mind's eye like a film clip: the frail, forgotten woman with a lifetime of regret, loss, and hatred boiling inside her. She creeps up behind Noah Madaster.

(Not so weak in that moment, was I?)

I started. It'd been like Lorraine had said the words, but her mouth hadn't moved.

Madaster had been talking on the phone in that loud, firm, superior tone, oblivious to everything but whatever he was demanding of the person on the other end of the connection.

She *hated* the sound of his smug, authoritative voice. Years of suppressed rage exploded to the surface.

A mighty push.

And the all-powerful Noah Madaster was falling and falling, his body breaking before her gleeful gaze.

I blinked, cutting off the imagined film clip.

Only it wasn't my imagination. I knew that, somehow, as I stared down at Lorraine's flushed face. Noah's fall had been no accident. Lorraine had been the one responsible for Noah Madaster's spinal cord injury.

Just like Evan, she'd wanted revenge. And she'd gotten some measure of it. But he'd lived. Why hadn't Madaster punished her for pushing him?

"He doesn't know," Lorraine whispered as though she'd read my mind. She pointed to her temple, her face full of madness. "His head got broken a little on those stairs, too. Not as much as his back. But enough to make him forget."

"*Miss*. If you just walk away from her, she'll leave you alone."

I threw a frown over my shoulder, fuming. That Nurse-Bitch had made Lorraine sound like an annoying dog.

I gave Lorraine another shoulder-squeeze. "I'll be okay," I said softly.

I felt her grip fall off my wrist. Steeling myself, I walked toward the stairs.

I passed the nurse, not even sparing her a glance. All my attention was focused like an arrow on the presence I sensed at the top of the stairs. As I neared him, nausea flared in my stomach. It was very dark, and I couldn't quite make him out in the shadows.

Keep back, I ordered that encroaching panic angrily. *I won't let him see me afraid.*

I stopped ten feet from the top of the stairs.

"Turn on l light, or I'm not coming up any farther," I said.

There was a pause, in which I thought I heard his breathing above me. There was a rasp to it, as if there was liquid in his lungs. But his voice had been strong and hard earlier when I'd heard him shout down the stairs at his wife.

"Turn on the light, Ima. She's not used to this dark old house the way we are."

I felt Ima rumbling heavily up the stairs behind me, her disapproval wafting past me. A moment later, a light illuminated the landing on the second floor. It was an old, elaborate wrought iron chandelier, I saw. My gaze zoomed to Noah Madaster.

His wheelchair looked too small for him. Not to small *for* him, I realized. Too small to *hold* him.

Noah Madaster was an intimidating giant of a man, I recalled Evan saying. That hadn't changed, spinal cord injury or not. He was tall and thin, but far from frail. He must have been very muscular, once. Now he'd faded to a kind of wiriness.

Electric wiriness.

The thought popped into my brain as I met his blue-eyed stare. An idea came to me that he'd been manically powerful in his youth, his electric personality finding focused outlets in multiple directions. When his injury had stilled him, he'd somehow channeled that feverish, frightening energy inward.

Now he seethed with it.

His hair was a thick, blondish-gray mane, a shocking reminder of his former virility. Light colored whiskers dusted his chin, jaw, and upper lip. His face... I found myself compelled by it. Repulsed by it. I didn't know which. It was like a skeleton with a wax covering, only his eyes glaring furious, electric life. The only other feature that wasn't bone-like on his face was his lips, which were surprisingly full.

I realized a silence had descended as we inspected each other.

He grunted, as though passingly satisfied with what he saw.

"Follow me," he said. His hand moved on a control on the arm of his chair. He whizzed backward, and then forward down the hallway. I realized the hand he used to power the wheelchair was bandaged. It was the fist he'd used to punch through the window.

Noah led the way, his nurse following, and me trailing along in the back. (*This is how it always is with him. He must take the lead in all things. Subordinates must fall behind.*

Only a Madaster can lead. That's his mantra.)

I'd given up even questioning where my thoughts came from. I would marginally accept them until they proved wrong.

Madaster paused outside two curving metal doors. He punched a button, and the doors slid open to reveal an elevator.

A very *small* elevator.

Madaster adroitly backed himself in, and Ima followed. I just stood in the hallway while they both stared out at me. *I can't get in there,* I thought. *It's too small, and I'll be too near him.*

I'll suffocate.

I felt a pressure tightening around my throat. I opened my mouth to tell them to send the elevator back down after they'd gone upstairs, when I saw the little smile on Madaster's fleshy lips.

He knew what I was about to say. He saw my fear.

I walked into the small, circular elevator, holding his stare. I think I held my breath for the entire ride upward. When the car came to a halt with a slight jarring sensation, he made a deep, raspy sound in his throat.

I realized he was chuckling at my show of defiance.

The door opened. I backed out of the elevator so fast that I ran into the wall in the hallway. The jolt popped the held air out of my lungs. Madaster got off, Ima following him. I once again brought up the rear in our bizarre little parade through the dark hallways of the South Twin.

"Bring us something to drink, Ima," Madaster ordered when we crossed the corridor into a large, circular room. It was blindingly bright after the darkness. I saw banks of windows that looked out onto the brilliantly blue lake and mountains in the distance. One of them was blacked out with the cardboard they'd inserted into it after Madaster had punched through the glass.

I was in Madaster's tower.

Ima hurried to a swinging, wooden door in the back of the room and disappeared. Madaster manipulated his chair to a seating area around a coffee table. There was a luxurious but worn leather couch and two upholstered chairs around the table. I approached him cautiously.

"So. You do like the sunlight," I said, glancing around the illuminated tower-room.

"It's why I chose this suite after my injury. Do you think I turned to ash in the sunlight? I'm sure your *husband* had you convinced of that."

Irritation spiked through me at the ironic way he'd said *husband*. I started to give an irritated response when my gaze landed on the coffee table. An electronic box lay on it, about twelve by four by eight inches. There were wires... and a cap of what looked like electrodes or sensors.

I glanced up at him in stark disbelief. It was the Analyzer. *Surely* it was. He'd placed it brazenly on the coffee table, for me to see. He'd done it to set me off balance. To taunt me.

Test me.

Chapter Twenty-Three

"YOU ACT AS IF YOU'RE OFFENDED BY THE FACT THAT EVAN MIGHT call you a monster." I glanced down at the equipment on the table with disgust. "Or a vampire. But you're not really, are you? You *know* what you are."

"I know exactly what I am, Anna. Self-knowledge is power." His blue eyes blazed at me through that skull-face. "The question is, do you know what you are? I don't believe you do."

"I couldn't care less what you believe."

His smile seemed like it would crack his face wide open.

"But you should," he said. He turned, and I realized Ima had entered the room. She carried a tray with two iced teas on it. He waved vaguely at the coffee table.

"Set them down and go."

"Yes, Dr. Madaster."

Anger spiked through me at the demonstration of his casual superiority and Ima's submission. Did Madaster use the Analyzer on his nurse? The thought disgusted me. I hated this place.

I hated *him*, even though I barely knew him.

He leaned forward and placed a glass in front of one of the upholstered chairs next to him. He glanced at me expectantly.

"You aren't going to have this conversation standing, are you?"

"I'm not going to stay for long."

"However long you stay, it will be enough. Please, join me," he said, waving gracefully with his left hand toward the chair.

I *hadn't* come here to just to stare at him. Feeling highly uneasy, I walked over to the chair.

"You take it without sugar, I assume?" he asked, nodding at my glass of iced tea.

I didn't know why he would assume any such thing.

"It doesn't matter," I said, even though I did, indeed, drink my iced tea straight. I took a gulp of it to soothe my raw throat and set down the glass, keeping my gaze averted from that ugly device on the table. I laced my hands over my stomach, trying to still the panicking butterflies in there.

"You seem upset, Anna," he said, his brow creasing in concern. False concern. Anyone could see that. "Learning that you're the double of my daughter Elizabeth must have come as quite a blow to you."

"How did you find out about that?"

"I have my ways."

"Don't be so dramatic. Wes Ryder told you, didn't he? I said something to Valeria, his girlfriend. She must have been alarmed enough by my shock that she mentioned it to Wes. And he told you. Or maybe that librarian called you?"

"It doesn't matter how I found out. It only matters now that the truth is out. How did Evan explain his manipulation of you?"

"He told me that he's been planning revenge on you, ever since Elizabeth disappeared. He believes that you murdered your daughter," I admitted bluntly. "Did you?"

His laugh had nothing to do with mirth.

"I knew he couldn't resist turning me into the villain of this affair. I *knew* it. The man is so predictable," he said, shaking his head and taking a healthy swallow of his iced tea. "Did Evan say anything to you about the tunnel? The one between the Twins?"

I was set off balance by his abrupt question. "He told me that he filled it in and sealed it, when he found out what you and Elizabeth were using it for."

His widening smile confused me. The bastard seemed infuriatingly satisfied by everything I said.

"He was always missing the point, your *husband*. The fact of the matter is, Elizabeth would be alive today if Evan hadn't inserted himself into our lives." His gaze ran over my face. "She would be sitting where you are right now, happy."

"Happy?" I asked incredulously. I glanced at the Analyzer on the table. "You mean controlled, don't you?"

"If Evan gave you the impression that Elizabeth could be controlled in anything, he was dead wrong. It was just easier for him to imagine she was being coerced, when in reality, Elizabeth never did anything she didn't want to do. She was a force of nature."

"One that you created and fashioned. You disgust me. You're the vilest man I've ever imagined."

He made a fake "sad face" and gave a little shrug. Still, I had a feeling that his sarcastic, flippant display was a show.

Madaster *did* care what I thought of him.

"So... you've decided to take Evan's side, despite the fact that he's been using you? You're miserably in love with him, aren't you?"

"Yes. I love him," I said. I didn't hesitate, although I probably should have, given what Evan had done to me. It just struck me in that moment that speaking honestly about love was a weapon against which this man couldn't defend. But instead of seeming taken aback by my declaration, he again appeared alarmingly self-satisfied.

"I'm not saying that I trust everything Evan says," I continued. "But you... I trust *you* far less."

"And how are you making that judgment?" he asked, suddenly very interested. Focused. *Fascinated*, even.

"I don't know what you mean."

"How are you coming to this certain conclusion about me and my character, when you just met me a few minutes ago? You *must* be swallowing Evan's story, wholesale."

"I'm not."

"Then answer my question!"

I started at his shout... at his abrupt cruelty.

"I'm coming to my conclusions by sitting here in your disgusting presence," I found myself shouting back. My face felt very hot. "I decided what I thought of you by meeting your wife, whom you and that witch-nurse of yours ignore and half-starve, when she's clearly in need of care. I understand all I need to know of your *character* by the fact that you've taunted me by putting that... "—I pointed at the Analyzer on the table as if it were a live snake—"that *thing* on the table for me to see."

His smile ratcheted my fury up another notch.

"I came to my conclusions about you because I *know* how rotten you are to the core."

"*How* do you know?"

"I just know. I don't know how, but I know *you*," I seethed.

"*I* know how you know," he said. His blue eyes shone with blazing confidence.

He didn't move in his chair, but I had the vivid impression that in Madaster's head, he danced with excitement.

"It's a little known fact, revealed only to the highest echelons of society—a chosen few," he said. "It's why Egyptian kings took their sisters as their wives. It's why European royalty intermarried. They did it to keep the genes pure. Because if the bloodline can be kept pure enough, certain gifts are given... gifts that yield natural leaders. Psychic abilities, for one thing, most notably with living relatives. The faculty to communicate with and see the deceased ancestors, for another."

I must have started in shock, because his stare on me grew even more avid. Hungry.

"You *have* heard her, haven't you?" He studied my face like he thought it held the secrets to the universe. "You've *seen* her."

It struck me at that moment, what I heard ringing in his voice. Envy. He *envied* me, because he thought I'd heard and seen Elizabeth.

Abruptly, I laughed.

"You're *crazy*," I declared, feeling incredulous, but also oddly fevered and light-headed. I picked up the iced tea and took several swallows, then pressed the cool glass against my cheek. I panted, trying to bring myself under control. I met his manic, electric stare, dread creeping into my awareness when I fully registered what I saw. "God, you *are*. You're crazy as a loon. You don't know anything."

"You wouldn't have come here if you thought I didn't know anything. Tell me why *you* came here, Anna. Tell me, and if it's in my power to give you answers, I will."

"I wanted to meet you myself. I wanted to see if Evan's hatred of you was justified. To know if he has even a tiny bit of a decent defense for what he's done to me."

"You've decided that he does?" Madaster said. "But you've hardly given me a chance yet to tell my side of the story."

"You never wanted to defend yourself," I said with certainty, glancing down at the Analyzer on the table, my lip curling in disgust. "That not why you asked me here."

"No, you're correct. It isn't," he said, his pleasant manner infuriating me further.

"I want to know what you did with her body. Elizabeth's. Tell me," I ordered him. Determinedly, I held his stare, willing him to do it. To confess.

His eyes widened slightly at that. Then he grinned again, pure triumph in his expression. "My God. You *are* like her. You look so soft, but you could probably have men jumping off cliffs for you, if you put your mind to it. So alike. And to think... you never even knew her. It's all a matter of genes. Those amazing, perfect genes," he mused. His avid stare ran over me, making me feel hot. Dizzy.

"I don't know what you're talking about," I told him frankly. I hadn't expected him to be insane. He was crazier than Lorraine, but in a much more frightening way. Madaster's lunacy was horrifyingly lucid and focused.

"No, I realize you don't understand me. But you *will*. Tell me about your family. They live in Illinois, don't they?"

I leaned back in the soft chair, trying to still my spinning head. The idea that Noah Madaster knew about my parents and sister, the very thought of his spidery, poisonous reach touching them from so far away, had hit me like a blow.

"How do you know about my family?"

Again, that chafing laugh.

"I had to do my research, Anna. What else was I supposed to do, when I saw you standing there, down at that overlook? It was like seeing Elizabeth sprung to life again. At first, I thought it *was* her. But no," he muttered, his expression darkening. "She will not come to me. You were flesh and blood. A living woman, brought here by Evan to torment me.

"Evan hired people in order to find you. He enlisted the help of friends, like Tommy Higoshi, in order to draw you into his plot of revenge. So *I* hired people, too. I talked to Tommy Higoshi. Rather, I forced Tommy to talk to me, so that I could find out about how you two ended up together."

"Tommy talked to you?"

Madaster shrugged. "Evan had launched an attack. What else was I supposed to do but launch a counterattack? Evan brought you here to make me crack like an egg in his fist. He thought I was helpless and easy prey, all because he'd learned that these don't work anymore," he hissed, viciously slapping at an immobile, atrophied leg. "But he underestimated me, as usual. God, his idea of revenge isn't only weak and ineffectual, it ended up being the opposite of what he intended. It really is hysterical."

"Shut up," I said, because he was laughing again, and his laughter hurt like a fingernail scratching on the same spot on my skin, over and over.

"He intended for you to be *his* tool of revenge, but you've ended up being mine. You're *mine*, Anna."

"Stop it. I'm not your anything," I seethed. I spun. No, the *room* did. Noah Madaster's hateful, leering face swam in my vision. Pain sliced through me. It took a few seconds for me to compute that Madaster had grabbed me. I cried out, trying to pull my hand from his grip. He pressed tightly on the nail bed of my thumb, the pain shockingly precise.

"You have it, too," he gloated. "I knew you would. They call it the murderer's thumb, you know. But that's just an ignorant fortune-tellers' misnomer. Elizabeth had it on both hands. I have one, too. Right thumb. Just like you."

"Let *go* of me," I yelled, pulling on my hand. Nausea bloomed in my stomach. He applied more pressure on the thumb, and I cried out.

"BDD. Brachydactyly type D. Shortened thumb. Stub thumb, some people call it. It's a harmless little genetic anomaly. It's a little ugly, but at least yours is subtler than Elizabeth's. Yours is barely noticeable. And of course, it causes no dysfunction. Surely you've noticed you had one? A stub thumb? This one is two thirds the size of your other one."

I jerked on my hand, wincing in sharp pain. I barely absorbed what he was saying. All I wanted to do was escape his vise-like grip on me... make the pain and the spinning in my head stop. I had the crazy idea he was transferring his madness to me through his touch.

"I'll wager your parents don't have a stub thumb. How did they explain yours to you, Anna?"

"Let go of me, you bastard. Help! Someone *help* me," I screamed. My body shook. It seemed to be short-circuiting. I fell on my knees onto the floor, but Madaster refused to relinquish his hold. I clawed at him with my free hand and hit at his arms, but he only squeezed tighter on the nail bed. I dug with my fingers on his forearm. Blood seeped up to the surface of his parchment-like skin. It ran under my fingernails. Madaster appeared not to notice.

"They say it's common among European royalty, which makes sense, because the Madaster family tree is entwined with that of kings and queens. You should be proud. It's a sign of superior genes, Anna, that ugly little thumb. It's the mark of a Madaster."

I stopped clawing at his arms. I tried to focus on his face, but it was nearly impossible through my vertigo. I vaguely realized that tears ran down my cheeks in a steady stream.

"Madaster?" I muttered.

"Yes," he said. "You're Elizabeth's child. I'm almost certain of it. But we'll just check to be certain. Ima!"

He abruptly released his hold on me. I had struggled to be free of his grip, but with it gone, I sagged onto the carpet, weak, dizzy, and sick.

(They drugged you, darling. Daddy loves his drugs.)

"What did... what did... you give me?" I asked, using all my energy and will to get out the words. The world had become a nauseating smear, like someone had taken their hand and swiped over it, blurring it, and then wickedly spinning it like a top.

"You'll be fine after a rest. Don't panic. Just be still for a second," I heard Madaster say.

Then someone was pinching my lip, forcing open my mouth. I cried out in protest, and felt something swipe the inside of my cheek. I slapped at the hand near my face, holding onto the wrist. I forced my eyeballs to focus utilizing a monumental effort. For a split second, I saw Ima's face just a foot away from me.

"Get away from me, you bitch," I said, but it sounded more like, "Gid away frod me, y' bid."

Ima punched at my forearm, releasing my useless grip on her. Suddenly, the disdain on Ima's face segued to alarm and fear. As if by magic, Ima flew to the side. I heard her body thump heavily on the floor.

"How dare you hit her, you pig. She's a *Madaster*. Get out of here before I smash your ugly face to a pulp," I heard Madaster shout.

"*No.*"

But my shout sounded feeble to my ears. I struggled against those three words—*She's a Madaster*—harder than I fought not to lose consciousness. Surely, he hadn't meant *me*. Suddenly, Madaster's face swam into my sight. Blackness edged my vision of him.

"I'm not Elizabeth's. I'm not yours," I managed to get out.

His smile slid over straight, yellow teeth.

"Oh, you're not Elizabeth's and *mine*. You're Elizabeth's and *Evan's* child."

I heard his laugh as if it echoed through a long stone tunnel.

"That holier than thou husband of yours brought you here to break *me*. But how do you think he's going to take it when he learns that he's every bit as foul as he supposes *I* am. He's judged me for sleeping with Elizabeth. He holds a vendetta against me, but *he'll* be the one punished when he realizes what he's done. He not only slept with *his* daughter. He *married* her. God, the brilliant irony of it all."

Blackness narrowed down my vision until it was just a pinpoint. Than, there was only darkness. My hearing remained intact though, at least for a little longer than my vision did. I heard a furious shout.

"I'll kill you for this, Noah," I heard Evan roar.

Chapter Twenty-Four

THE FIRST TIME I WOKE UP, IT WAS THROUGH A FOG. I SAW A NARROW bed and white sheets, and the form of a body beneath them. It was all disjointed, though. The body didn't belong to *me,* it was just an inanimate thing, like the railing on the bed or the white sheets.

The next time I opened my eyes, I was back inside myself—if that makes any sense.

I looked around, not recognizing anything about the small, confined space where I lay. I searched backward in my memory, clawing for some handhold as to why I lay on a skinny bed with ugly, industrial-looking light blue curtains all around me. I couldn't find anything to grab onto as to why I was here. There was only darkness: a black hole.

It horrified me.

"*Evan,*" I shouted, sitting up abruptly. I winced in pain, glancing down at my arm. Blood shone at the juncture of my forearm and upper arm. A few drops had spilled on the sheets, the scarlet color on the snowy white fabric shocking my stunned vision.

"Evan," I screamed, in a complete panic now. I scrambled to get up out of the bed.

The blue curtains whipped back. A blonde woman in her forties wearing pale green scrubs rushed to the side of the bed, placing her hands on my shoulders as I tried to stand.

"Calm down, Mrs. Halifax. You're in the emergency room. Everything is going to be all right. *Please,* calm down. You've torn out your IV."

"Where's my husband? Where's Evan?" I demanded, still struggling to stand.

"I'm here. *Anna.*"

I froze. I found myself staring at Evan's face.

Oh no, oh no, oh no.

The floor of the known world really has *dropped away out this time.*

I had no idea what those skittering thoughts meant, but my heart beat uncomfortably loud in my ears. I heard a whimpering sound and realized it came from my throat.

"I'm here, Anna. It's okay," Evan repeated, his anxious gaze glued to mine. I don't think it was possible for him to look *pale*, per se, but he looked more washed out than I'd ever seen him beneath his tan. Drawn. He reached around the nurse, touching the side of my face, stroking me. I gasped at his touch, so warm and solid against my skin.

"You're in the emergency room at Barton Memorial Hospital. You're going to be fine. They were just waiting for you to wake up and getting you hydrated with the IV."

"But... what happened?"

"You were drugged. Ketamine. The doctor was telling me just before you woke up. The lab results had just come back. It's a powerful, very fast-acting drug. You don't remember what happened?"

"No, I can't seem to make sense of it—"

"Ketamine causes memory problems," the nurse said. I realized that she'd let go of my shoulders, now that I wasn't struggling anymore. She'd removed the IV completely and stepped aside. Evan saw the blood on my arm for the first time.

"*Jesus.* Is she going to be all right?" he demanded of the nurse.

"She'll be fine. She was disoriented and pulled out the IV. I'll be right back to get that bandaged up. Can you stay with her for a minute, Mr. Halifax?"

"Of course."

Evan and I were alone in the little cubicle. There was something in his eyes I'd never seen before. Anxiety... yes, I recognized that. But there was something else. Wariness, I realized.

"Evan, what happened? Please tell me."

"Noah Madaster happened."

In my mind's eye, I saw a bank of windows in a circular room flooded with sunlight. I inhaled sharply at the vivid abruptness of the memory.

Why the hell had I ever gone there?

"I found you in his suite. He drugged you. Do you remember the letter he sent you?" Evan asked me.

"Yes. He sent me a letter," I said slowly, remembering Madaster's large, bold script. I blinked, refocusing on Evan. "You found it?"

He nodded. "I came looking for you, and couldn't find you anywhere. I got worried, and started going through some of your things, to see if anything was missing... if you'd taken anything, and then left Les Jumeaux. That's when I found the letter."

I strained to recall more, but the memories were isolated patches, a mosaic of separated pictures on a mostly pitch black background. I had a vision of Lorraine Madaster's frightened face as she opened the door of the South Twin. I tried to force more memories, but the effort made me feel like I'd vomit. I pressed my fist against my stomach.

Against my will, I remembered Noah Madaster's ugly, triumphant smile. I shuddered.

Who had he triumphed against? Evan. I was somehow sure of it, but I couldn't recall why.

I didn't want to.

Evan's hands opened at my back, stroking me. He reached for my hand. After a few seconds, I realized his eyelids were narrowed. I looked down, to see what he was looking at. My thumbnail had turned an ugly purplish black color.

"Oh, *Jesus*." Pure fear swept through me at the sight. I jerked my hand out of his, gasping.

"Anna? What is it?"

"I don't know," I mumbled, gasping for air. I wasn't lying. I didn't have a clue why I'd cringed when I'd seen the blackened nail, or why I'd jerked my hand from Evan's touch as if it repulsed me.

Oh no, oh no, oh no. The feeling again of the world dropping out from under me. Nausea so strong, it was like a wave of overwhelming pain rather than a stomachache... like my whole body could vomit.

Another memory struck me with the strength of a two-by-four to the temple.

"You said you would kill him. Madaster."

Evan blanched. "*That*, you remember. I thought you were unconscious when I ran into that room."

"Evan?" I prodded anxiously.

255

"Of course I didn't kill him. I *might* have, to be honest," he said after a pause, grimacing. "But I was too preoccupied once I saw you, lying on that floor. I thought he'd murdered you, at first." That haunted look had returned to his eyes in full force.

"What did you do?"

"I checked to make sure you were breathing, of course. Found a pulse. Noah was ranting. I called an ambulance, and then Wes. He was still over at the North Twin, and I thought he might be able to help you. Then the ambulance came and they brought you here."

"But Madaster—"

"I contacted the police. A cop came here to the ER, and I filed a report against Noah for drugging you. I'm assuming the police have gone to the South Twin to question him, by now. I hope he's been arrested for what he did."

"Why did Madaster *do* it, though? Why did he drug me?" I whispered, rubbing my eyelids. "Evan?" I asked, opening my eyes when he didn't immediately reply. That wariness I'd seen before was back full-fledged on his face.

"You don't remember anything that he did when you started to lose consciousness?"

I realized that while I was searching his face, looking for answers, he was doing the same thing to me.

I don't have any answers, Evan. I'm most worried about what you *know... about what Madaster revealed to you while I was unconscious.*

The curtain twitched behind him, and the nurse reentered the cubicle, carrying some first aid supplies.

"Excuse me, please," she told Evan briskly.

"I don't know why Noah did it," Evan said, before he stepped away from me to make room for the nurse.

But by that time in our relationship, I had experience with Evan's sidestepping of the truth. With a sick, sinking feeling, I realized he was lying to me now.

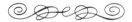

Evan stood aside to let the two police officers pass him. He closed the door with a muted click behind them. He turned to face me across the luxurious hotel suite. We'd checked into it yesterday, after I'd been discharged from the hospital.

At that moment, I sensed all of my own frustrated helplessness mirrored on Evan's face.

"Madaster said that his nurse was the one solely responsible for drugging me. And that crazy bitch said it was *true*." I paraphrased part of what the police had just told us. My voice rang hollow with disbelief and outrage. Ima Butler, the nurse, had confessed to putting the ketamine into my iced tea. She'd claimed she'd done it out of anger at the fact that Evan and I had been purposefully upsetting and agitating Madaster ever since we'd arrived at Les Jumeaux. Madaster himself had posted bail for Ima, and she was currently free on bond. I was still stunned by the turn of events.

"Why would she do that? Why would she take the blame?"

Evan shut his eyes briefly and stepped further into the room. The suite we were in wasn't huge, although it was at a luxury hotel on the waterfront with a balcony. A big electronics convention was taking place in town. Evan had had to do some finagling to get us a room in South Lake on short notice. He'd made it clear upon leaving the hospital that we would not be returning to Les Jumeaux, under any circumstance.

"She's become one of his creatures," Evan said, raking his fingers through his thick hair. "I can't say I'm surprised she did it. I told you. It's how Noah operates. He makes slaves, or the equivalent of them. It's the type of person he wants around him: subservient. Eager to please. I'm pissed as hell that she took the fall for him. But I'm not surprised."

Feeling deflated, I sat down at the corner of one of the queen beds in the room.

Two beds.

I'd slept in one last night, Evan the other. I'd been exhausted upon being discharged, wrung out and numb with everything that had happened in the past few days. I'd slept with Evan's arms around me on the previous night, even when I'd discovered his betrayal.

But last night, I'd insisted we sleep separately in the hotel room. I didn't understand why I did it, and that frightened me even more. And despite my exhaustion, I'd been restless in that bed; unmoored and drifting away from everything that had once counted to me.

"Anna, are you all right?"

The fierce concern on his face made my throat swell uncomfortably. I placed my hand on my throat and lightly rubbed the straining muscles. I'd been the witness of his raw, wild worry dozens of times since yesterday. It was unbearable, because I knew I couldn't comfort him. I certainly couldn't take solace from *him* anymore.

"Anna?"

He sat down on the bed next to me. My panic expanded in my chest when I felt his hand on my back. I cringed, and immediately tried to tamp down the instinctive response to avoid his touch. But Evan felt me flinch. He exhaled and dropped his hand onto his thigh.

"You've pulled away from me again. I'd hoped that after last night, well... I don't know what I was thinking," he said heavily. "That there might still be a chance between us, I guess. But there isn't. Is there?"

I clamped my eyelids shut. How could I tell him that I felt like my heart was breaking every time I looked at his face? That his touch—once craved so much—now made panic claw at my insides. I got the same feeling every time I looked at the ugly bruise under my thumb.

How could I tell him why I felt that way, when I was having trouble understanding myself? The memories nibbled at the edge of my consciousness, threatening to bite viciously into me at any moment. I was barely holding it together.

It was all his fault. Madaster's. He laid ruin to everything he touched.

"It's so much, Evan. I can't just act like everything is fine between us."

"I know. I don't want to press you. But, Anna—"

I heard his hesitation and turned to look at him.

"There *is* something I have to ask you."

"About Madaster?" I asked uneasily. "I don't remember much more about what happened than I did yesterday."

It was *kind* of true. I didn't have that many more flashes of concrete memory than I'd had after ten minutes of awakening in the ER yesterday. But increasingly, I strained to hold back that thick, sickening feeling of dread. It was that sinister horror that slinked closer whenever Evan touched me.

"No. Not about Madaster. Anna—"

"Just say it," I prompted, feeling irritated at his reluctance. Trapped. The dread edged closer now, an insidious, hungry shadow. It crept forward, even without Evan touching me.

"Is it possible you were adopted?" Evan asked me.

Chapter Twenty-Five

I'D THOUGHT THE DAY BEFORE YESTERDAY—THE DAY AT THE LIBRARY, and then hearing Evan's confession—had been the longest, most miserable day of my life. Then I'd visited Noah Madaster in the South Twin, and *that* day had moved into first place.

Now I knew this day in the hotel room with Evan would be the hellish new winner.

It was enough to make a girl prefer oblivion to tomorrow.

When he said the word *adoption*, it triggered a wave of emotion in me. I shuddered uncontrollably.

"Of course not," I cried out. "What would make you say something like that?"

"I'm sorry," Evan said, clearly taken aback my reaction. "It was something Noah said while I was in his suite yesterday."

The only thing that kept me grounded in that moment, that allowed me to stave off panic, was the weight and history of my happy, mundane childhood. I couldn't allow that to be ripped away from me as well.

"I'm *not* adopted. That's ridiculous. Don't you think my parents would have told me?"

"I suppose," he said slowly, and I could feel his gaze on my face: studying, gauging. Worried. "Although I'd imagine it's a decision adoptive parents make early on and try to stick to: whether to tell the child, or let the child assume they are a natural part of the family."

"You're suggesting I'm unnatural?" He reached for me, and I struck his hand away. I stood—too abruptly, because dizziness hit me. *Unnatural. Adoption. Unnatural. Adoption.*

"What are you trying to do to me, Evan? Tear me apart, piece by piece?"

"No. God, no, I'm sorry—Anna!"

I rushed to the bathroom and slammed shut the door. When I heard him call my name again, I locked it.

I turned and stared at the pristine white bathroom. It was a blank canvas, blazing in my eyes. They say nature abhors a vacuum. Upon that clean, white canvas, the memories started to slash and splatter.

I believe that at that moment, if I could have ripped my heart from my chest in order to stop the pain, I would have.

I sat back on my haunches, gripping the toilet seat. The dread had been too much for me to contain. I'd vomited it up violently. There was a continuous roar in my ears. Maybe that's why I didn't hear Evan breaking through the lock on the door.

I looked up at him when he burst into the room.

"Madaster told me that I was Elizabeth's child. I remember that now," I told him dully. I couldn't voice the other part... couldn't possibly name whom Madaster had said was my father. Of *course* I couldn't speak of Madaster's monstrous claim. It'd be like sending a sharp knife through my own flesh. Self-preservation won out, I guess.

Evan stared down at me, horror plastered on his face.

My husband's face.

My *father's?*

My stomach and ribcage heaved again. Impossibly, more bitter fluid came out of me. I felt Evan's hand on my back, stroking my body as it convulsed.

A moment later, my arms limply circled the toilet seat. I pressed my cheek against my biceps.

I'd read something else in Evan's horrified expression when he'd looked down at me a moment ago.

"You think it's true. Don't you?" I asked him weakly. "You believe that somehow, some way, I'm Elizabeth Madaster's daughter?"

Evan stood. I heard the water running at the sink, and then he knelt next to me. He pressed a cool, damp washrag against my forehead and cheek. Then he carefully cleaned my mouth.

"Anna? Look at me," I heard him say firmly.

I forced my tired eyes to focus on him.

"It's true that Madaster told me yesterday that he believed you were Elizabeth's daughter. He was spewing all kinds of filth while I tried to get you out of that tower. But because Madaster said it... because he *wants* to believe it's true, that doesn't mean it is."

I lifted my head off my arm. "Tell me that you didn't believe I was Elizabeth's daughter when you set out to seduce me."

Tell me. Please, tell me.

He opened his hand on the side of my head, his fingers sliding through me hair.

"I never, *ever* thought such a thing. Why would I? You can't think that I would have allowed what's happened between us to happen if I believed that."

"You never suspected it? Given how much Elizabeth and I look alike?"

"Of *course* not. Elizabeth told me everything, eventually. She was *never* pregnant."

"She told you things only after you discovered her lies, or when she was trying to cleanse her consciousness of everything she'd done."

"Anna, I know how old you are. I saw your birth certificate when we got the marriage license. Elizabeth would had to have been sixteen when she had you. I knew her then. It didn't hap—"

"Didn't you say she went away to school? When she was sixteen? Couldn't she have been pregnant then?"

He looked taken aback, but only briefly. "*No.* There's no way. It's true that Elizabeth became secretive and evasive when she got older, but she told me everything when we were kids."

"Except that Madaster had been abusing her since she was a child."

He flinched slightly at that.

"Evan, what if I *am* related to him... to that monster?" I whispered, feeling the nausea rise in my throat again.

"No. I'm telling you, it's not possible," he said with a slashing gesture of his hand. I sensed he wasn't angry at me. He was angry at Madaster for putting the idea into our heads. He was angry at himself, for even considering the possibility. Or for *not* considering it before.

"You don't understand. Elizabeth couldn't have children," he stated harshly.

I sat up straighter. "She *couldn't*?"

"No. She had an abnormality in her uterus. We tried to have a child at one point, but she never got pregnant. We went to specialists a few years into our marriage, but—" He shook his head, avoiding my stare. "She couldn't have children, Anna."

"But you've thought about it, haven't you? You've wondered if it could be true, ever since Madaster claimed it yesterday. That's why you immediately said the thing about my birth certificate, because you've been going over it all in your head since then, reassuring yourself it was impossible."

"I spoke with the doctor back then, Anna. About Elizabeth's medical tests, I *know* she couldn't have children."

"Then why did you ask me if I was adopted?" I asked bitterly. "Evan?" I asked again when he didn't immediately respond. "Did Madaster tell you who he believed my father was?"

His face became that death mask I hated with all my soul. His shook his head once, as if to clear it.

"Noah Madaster is a *liar*. He's trying to get to you. To us. We have to try to resist it. This is all my fault. I should never have brought you here. I should have known how dangerous it would be, for you to speak with Noah."

My head dipped and wavered. My neck didn't feel strong enough to support it anymore. My throat felt raw from being sick. I felt so sore. All the certain truths, and the possible truths, battered at me from every direction.

"I'm the one who went to meet him, even though I promised you I wouldn't."

"What's done is done. You've been sick, and you're weak," he said, gently cradling my head. "You need to lie down. Can you stand?"

He helped me get to my feet and escorted me to the bed. I lay there, appreciating how hollow I felt. How empty. Evan came out of the bathroom carrying a glass of water. He sat down on the bed next to me.

"You've remembered other things, haven't you? About your meeting with Madaster?" he asked me reluctantly.

I experienced a sharp pain in my thumb, and winced. Tears sprang to my eyes, as if Madaster was there, cruelly pinching it all over again.

"Noah lies easier than breathing," Evan said. "You're safe now. And you're never going to have to see Noah Madaster again. Or listen to his lies. He wanted to poison you. Not just with a drug. With ideas. Delusions." Evan's gaze drifted over me, anger hardening his jaw. "And he's succeeded, Anna. Partially. Don't continue absorbing the poison by believing him."

"He's been doing his research. He knew about me. About us. He said you launched an attack on him by bringing me to Les Jumeaux, and he had no choice but to launch a counterattack."

His expression darkened. "I know. I got that, from when he was ranting at me."

Did he tell you what he told me? Do you loathe me now, Evan? Are you forcing yourself to touch and comfort me? Is that why I see that new wariness in your eyes?

Because I'm unnatural.

The thoughts were too heinous to dwell upon for long. Instead, I landed on a memory—a suspicion— that was nearly as terrible.

"Do you know when I first fell in love with you?" I asked him.

His head jerked up. I saw his surprise at my question. His vulnerability.

"No," he replied gruffly.

"When you took me, with so much confidence, to my favorite painting in the museum. It was the most incredible moment of my life," I said with stark honesty. "I felt *seen* by you, Evan."

His mouth fell open. His eyes shone with emotion.

I leaned up on my elbow and took the water glass from him. I swallowed some of the cool liquid, trying to steady myself against a truth I didn't want to hear, but knew I must.

"One of the things that Madaster told me yesterday was that he'd been in contact with Tommy Higoshi," I said. "That part of his research into us was getting information from Tommy about how we met... how you put your plan into place."

"Tommy talked to Noah? Why wouldn't Tommy tell me that Noah had contacted him?"

"I don't know," I said, handing the water glass back to him. "Madaster said he *forced* Tommy to talk to him. You said that Madaster either manipulates or blackmails everyone he meets. Maybe he had something on Tommy. Something business-wise. They're both in the medical research field, and Tommy had met him before at a conference, remember? You'd have to call Tommy, to know for sure. That's not what I'm trying to find out," I said. I saw Evan's puzzlement, and got to the point.

"*Did* you enlist Tommy's help in bringing me into your life? Did you ask him things about me, things to give you an inside track? Things to make me fall in love with you? More specifically, was Tommy the one who told you what my favorite painting in the museum was?"

"*No,*" he roared. I was so empty, so exhausted that I didn't even jump at his furious response.

"Dammit, Anna, this is *precisely* why I didn't want you to see that devil. Don't let Noah do this. Don't let him poison you against me. You see he's already got his hooks into Tommy somehow, in order to give him another weapon to fight me? Us? I *swear* to you, Tommy never told me anything, or did anything, to give me an 'in' with you. The only thing he did was show me some of your paintings, at my request, before I ever contacted you on that dating site."

"You asked to see my paintings, after you'd gotten my name and information from that detective agency you used."

"Yes. But I didn't need to pretend amazement when it came to your work. You're brilliant. I was mystified, and half in love with you, just by looking at your paintings. I don't believe I'm being hyperbolic by saying that, either. And as for your favorite painting at the museum, Tommy *never* told me anything about it. What I told you was one hundred percent true. I just knew somehow it would be a favorite, because I *knew* you."

Maybe it was odd for me to be so preoccupied on this aspect, out of all Madaster's claims. But somehow, if I didn't clear up *this* incident in my head—if I couldn't believe in that *one* thing in my life I'd held so dear—I wondered if I could ever untangle *anything.*

I wondered if I could ever believe in anything again.

Evan saw my doubt.

"Think about it, Anna. Did you ever even *tell* Tommy what your favorite painting at the museum was?"

I saw his point. I didn't think I had mentioned it to him. Tommy would have known that particular painting, it's true. He was an art expert and a huge donor to the San Francisco Museum of Modern Art.

But I don't think I'd ever discussed my partiality to that painting with Tommy.

"I don't think I did," I said slowly. "No, I'm sure I didn't," I said with more confidence.

Evan exhaled, clearly relieved. He'd seemed to guess how important the whole issue was to me. It seemed to me that it was just as crucial to him.

"You can't let Noah insert himself between us," he said.

It's not just Noah Madaster who has done that.

I wanted to ask him what other things Madaster had told him yesterday. But I was afraid of his possible answers. It overwhelmed me. As if Evan had sensed that, he reached into his pocket and took out a white pill.

"The doctor prescribed you a sedative. He said that one of the side effects of the ketamine can be insomnia. I know how restless you were last night. This will help you to sleep easily, so you can recover more quickly. Are you okay to take one?"

I nodded, more than willing to surrender to forgetfulness for a period of time.

I swallowed the pill.

Chapter Twenty-Six

I WOKE UP AT AROUND TWO THAT AFTERNOON, FEELING GROGGY.
A nasty fuzz had grown inside of my mouth. Evan was there, sitting on one of the chairs in the small lounge area. He wore his glasses and was reading a page in a thick binder. When I rustled beneath the sheets, he looked over the top of his glass frames and met my stare.

"The merger," I murmured, glancing down at the binder he read. "You must have fallen behind on it all."

"I haven't fallen behind on anything," he said, taking off his glasses and setting the binder on the coffee table. "And if I had, it wouldn't matter." He walked toward me. "How do you feel?"

I stretched, considering his question.

"Not bad, I guess."

It was kind of true. Some of that glorious mental insulation had been erected while I'd slept. I'd never consider denial a bad thing again in my life. It saved me, during those dangerous days.

"I'm hungry," I said.

"That's a good sign," Evan said, a small, wonderful smile shaping his mouth. It kicked me, that smile. I looked away, anxiety rising in me like a flash fire.

I showered and dressed, and we went downstairs to the hotel restaurant for a meal. I started out ravenous. I'd been nauseated on and off since awakening in the hospital, and hadn't eaten solid food in two days.

267

Now, I was lightheaded with hunger. I asked the waiter if he could bring me bread before my entrée arrived.

After three quarters of a roll and butter, the nausea returned.

Nevertheless, I forced down a portion of my meal when it arrived. I worried I might throw up at any moment, but was highly aware of Evan's concerned gaze on me. Aside from trying not to worry him, I needed the strength food would give me.

I sensed this whole catastrophe wasn't over yet.

"How long were you planning on staying here?" I asked Evan after we left the restaurant and returned to the hotel room.

"Just until you can recover a little. I'll get someone to go to Les Jumeaux and have our things forwarded, including your paintings," he said, locking the door and walking toward me. He stopped in front of me. "Have you thought about where you'd like to go?"

I shook my head, avoiding his stare.

"I'll take you anywhere you want to go. I'll make sure you have whatever you need. I'll do whatever you want, even leave you, if that's what you decide. But not yet. Not until you're stronger."

I studied the design on the carpet, holding my breath.

"But please know this," he continued, his deep voice washing over me. "I love you. And I will never leave you willingly."

My lungs burned. I exhaled in a lurching gasp.

"I don't understand how you can walk away from this whole thing with Madaster."

"Don't you?" he asked. I saw his hand rise, as though he were about to touch me. I took a step back, instinctively avoiding him. His hand fell to his side. I saw the desolation on his face.

Madaster had plunged a knife into both Evan and me in that tower yesterday. He'd wounded us both, and triumphed in our pain.

He'd abused and neglected Lorraine for her entire adult life.

He'd peeled back the very skin of my existence and scooped out my identity.

(*He murdered me, choked off my life like he'd snuff out a candle. Light from my darkness, please help me.*)

I trembled, recognizing the speaker in my head, and yet denying it, at once. Believing, and all the while knowing it was ridiculous to believe a smidgeon of Madaster's ravings.

"You have heard her, haven't you? You've seen her."

I silenced the charged memory with effort. Evan had said that Elizabeth was barren, after all. It made no sense for me to be so over-whelmed by Madaster's claims.

I focused on Evan's face. It made no sense that this man could be my biological father.

"Of course I understand that you want to leave," I told him.

But it was a lie. I didn't understand how Evan could walk away from Les Jumeaux. Because somehow, in the past few days, Evan's obsession with seeing justice served in the case of Noah Madaster, Evan's hunger for revenge, had transferred to me.

(You will be the wielder, darling. And you will be the weapon.)

I smiled to reassure Evan.

"I think it's time I called my parents, don't you?" I asked.

Evan seemed very uneasy about the idea of me speaking to my par-ents. But he didn't try to postpone the call, for which I was thankful. In fact, he offered to take a short walk, to give me some privacy. When he went to leave the hotel suite, he hesitated with his hand on the door.

"Are you going to tell them everything?" he asked me quietly.

"Do you mean am I going to tell them about how you married me to get back at Noah Madaster? And Madaster's claim that I'm somehow Elizabeth's daughter?"

I saw his regret at my blunt questions. Would there ever be a time when I didn't see guilt and wariness and pain in his eyes? I used to see heat, desire, and love. Or at least I *thought* I did. Now, the memory of his hunger cuts at me even more than his regret.

"I don't know what I'm going to tell them exactly, to be honest," I admitted. "But I have to find a way to ask them if there's any chance what Madaster claimed was true."

"And you're sure you'll be okay if I go?"

He saw my impatient expression and put up a hand, as if to surren-der. He left the suite, closing the door quietly behind him.

In the end, broaching the complicated topic of possible adoption wasn't as difficult as I'd imagined. My father wasn't home yet from work when I called, so I had my mother all to myself. We talked about my painting and what was going on in Jessica's life. She told me that she and dad had joined a gym. But after ten minutes or so of idle chitchat, my mother was the one who cut to the chase.

"Okay, tell me what's going on," she said. I could hear pans clanging in the background, and pictured her in our bright kitchen, with the blue barstools pulled up to the oak countertop island. My mom ritualistically had a cup of tea and unloaded the dishwasher when she got home from work. I imagined her favorite pink mug steaming as it sat on the counter. A sharp feeling of homesickness went through me.

"What do you mean, get to the point?" I asked her.

"I don't know. Something in your voice. Call it a mother's intuition. You didn't call to hear about your dad's and my ab workout, did you? Is something wrong, honey?"

"I wouldn't say wrong, necessarily, no. But something happened to me recently," I began carefully. "I was at a local library, and there was a photo on the wall of someone who helped build the library. Anyway, this woman looked almost exactly like me."

The pans stopped rattling.

"That's odd."

"I mean, she was almost my double, Mom. And it got me wondering... Do we have any relatives out here? I know you and Dad went to school in Northern California and lived there for a few years. But we don't have family here, right?"

"No family that I know of. We're all scattered around the Midwest."

I heard the caution in her tone, though.

"Mom?" I asked softly. "I know it may seem strange for me to ask this... but is there any chance I was adopted?"

I heard a scraping sound and knew she'd just pulled out one of the blue barstools and was sitting down. I, too, suddenly felt a need to sit. I sank down heavily onto one of the chairs in the seating area.

"I don't know who that woman in the picture you saw was, Anna," my mom said. "But... Jesus, I wasn't expecting this," she continued under her breath. "I wish your father was here."

"Mom?" I asked, because she'd faded off.

"I've imagined telling you before, but never like this. I never thought you'd be the one to bring it up. To ask me point blank." She sighed. "We never wanted you to feel less than... never wanted you to feel that you weren't one hundred percent one of us, our beautiful, treasured little girl—"

Her voice broke. I just sat there, clutching my phone to my ear, my heart fluttering like it wanted to escape from my ribcage.

"You know that your father met me when he was in law school and I was an undergrad at Berkeley. We eloped before I even graduated, and lived in this grubby little apartment in Oakland while your dad clerked for a local judge. Hardly a similar scenario to your marriage and living situation, but it was wonderful. Some of the best days of my life." Her laugh sounded wistful. "Then I graduated and got a job as an art teacher at a local high school, and your dad got a good job as a human resources attorney at Kaiser. And we saved up enough to buy ourselves a little house in Emeryville."

I'd heard this story a hundred times before—the little dive apartment in Oakland with the heater that always gave out on the coldest nights, and the rickety winding stairwell that was such a pain for carrying up groceries. And how after a few years of marriage, they'd bought their first home. They'd felt like royalty in their new little house.

Their thoughts had turned to starting a family.

"You said that's where I was conceived," I inserted at this point. "At the new house you'd bought. That's where I was born. In Emeryville. It's on my birth certificate. Then Dad was offered a new job in Chicago. When I was a few months old, we moved."

"I know that's what we've told you, honey. But the truth is, we had trouble conceiving a baby. We tried for almost a year before we went to a specialist. And we were told that we'd probably never successfully have a biological baby that was both of ours."

"So I am adopted."

"Yes." She made a sound of frustration. "I wish your father was here. He'll be so upset, knowing I told you like this, on the phone. But

I've been thinking about it a lot lately, now that you've finished school. Now that you're a married woman. I've been thinking about telling you the truth... and now, this call. I hope you're not angry, Anna. Maybe you think it was selfish of us, not to tell you, but I truly believe we didn't do it for us. Not entirely, anyway. You were *ours,* from the moment we laid eyes on you. And we were yours. Forever. I never wanted you to believe anything different."

Her small sob cut through my stunned state. In the suspension I'd existed in between belief and disbelief, I'd half expected she might confirm my suspicion.

But at the same time, you can never really prepare for being told that your entire past wasn't at all what you thought it was.

"I'm not mad, Mom. I'm not. You and Dad will always be my parents, no matter what. I'm just trying to understand. Is Jessica adopted, too?"

"Oh, honey," my mother sniffed. "No, that's one of the strangest things about it. Ten months after we took you home with us, I found out I was pregnant. It floored us. But we learned that it happens that way sometimes, in cases of adoption. When the stress of getting pregnant goes away, after the couple adopts, things just resolve naturally. It was the damndest thing. We couldn't believe how lucky we were, to have one beautiful little girl, and then to be blessed with another one."

So. Jessica was the natural one, then.

Me, the unnatural.

I pushed the thought aside, recognizing it as self-pity. My mother was clearly very emotional. I wanted to understand, not spread my sense of rising alarm at the news onto her.

"But my birth certificate says that Dad and you are my parents—"

"It was amended. It's common, to have an amended birth certificate with the adoptive parents' names on it. The amended copies are the only ones we have."

"Do you know the names of my biological parents?"

"I don't. I'm sorry, again, if you think that was selfish of me. But I didn't want to know. I never did. You came to us when you were only two days old, and I wanted it to be a clean slate. Like I said, you were ours from the moment we laid eyes on you."

"But Mom... someone has to know who my biological parents were. Does Dad?"

"No, honey. He felt the same way about it that I did. But there would be a sealed copy of your original birth certificate somewhere, inaccessible to the public. If it's something you would want to pursue, you could, Anna. I think it takes a court order, for you to see it. But I don't know why the courts would deny you, given that you're an adult now."

I just sat there, thinking of that document locked away in some dark file, the names typed in on the form.

Mother. Father.

"Anna?" my mom asked weakly. "Are you okay? You *are* angry, aren't you," she stated rather than asked, dread in her tone.

"No, I'm not," I insisted. "I mean... it's shocking, that's all. I'm spinning."

"Of course you are. But it doesn't really change anything. Not the essentials. Not about the way we feel about you. About your childhood. Everything. You are and always will be Anna Marie Solas, our beautiful, talented, adored daughter."

(Light from my darkness.)

I realized the phone shook next to my ear.

"I love you, Mom," I said.

"I love you, too. So much. And so does your father. Can I have him call you? As soon as he gets in? He'll want to hear your voice. He'll want to know you're okay. Anna? You *are* okay, aren't you?"

I heard the doubt in her voice. And the congestion. There was no doubt, she was crying. Just like I was, I realized, touching my wet cheeks.

"I'm fine," I insisted thickly. "I just... " I swiped at my cheeks. "I'm feeling kind of emotional, that's all."

"Course you are. And you must have a million questions."

I gave a bark of laughter. "You know, I really don't, at this point. Well, one I guess. Jessica—"

"She doesn't know. I'll leave it up to you, whether or not you want her to know."

"Okay," I said in a muffled voice.

"If you decide you want to get access to the original birth certificate, I'll completely support you. I'll take time off and come and try to help you with the process. I'll take time off, either way," she added decisively. "I'd like to come and visit soon. Spend some time with you."

"I'd like that too. We'll work something out, after I've had time to let things settle a little," I said, even though I wondered if anything would ever be *settled* in my life again.

"Is Evan there with you? I don't want you to be alone right now."

I briefly imagined my mother's horror if she ever heard Noah Madaster's accusations. I *certainly* wouldn't allow her to be there to see those names printed on the newly revealed birth certificate. She and Dad would blame themselves for not telling me I was adopted, and then inadvertently sending me into the arms of my own—

STOP. Don't go there.

Mother. Father.

For a few seconds, my lungs locked. I struggled to inhale. I covered the receiver on the phone, and finally took a lurching breath. I removed my hand from the phone. A bizarre calm overcame me.

"Yes. Evan is here, Mom," I said.

Chapter Twenty-Seven

EVAN RETURNED JUST AS I WAS SAYING GOODBYE. I WATCHED HIM AS he removed the sporty black jacket he'd worn for his walk. Autumn had come to Tahoe unexpectedly during these past few days. It'd snuck up on me while I'd been so self-absorbed in the mess of my life.

I hung up the phone as he came toward me. He immediately noticed my wet cheeks. He lowered to the chair facing me and took my cell phone out of my hand. He placed the phone on the table and took both of my hands in his.

"They told you that you were adopted. Didn't they?"

I nodded. "My mom did. Yeah." I gave a shaky laugh. "I can't believe it, and yet I can, you know?" I shook my head. More tears fell down my face. My laugh sounded brittle. "This whole thing is so fucked up. Do you still believe that it was impossible for Elizabeth to have children?"

"I can only tell you what the doctor told me, Anna."

"Doctors can be paid off. Besides, just because Elizabeth couldn't have kids at twenty-five doesn't mean she couldn't have at sixteen, right?"

He squeezed my hands. "Anna... there's something we need to talk about. I've been trying to put it off, because you haven't been well."

"I'm fine, Evan."

I could tell he doubted that, but had decided the topic needed to be broached anyway.

"After I found you in Madaster's suite, I called Wes, thinking he might be able to do something to help you before the ambulance got there."

"Yeah, you told me that."

"It was only a minute or two before Wes got to the South Twin, and maybe ten minutes at the most before the ambulance arrived. But during that time, Madaster was... " His strong throat convulsed as he swallowed. "Ranting about a lot of crazy stuff."

"Yeah," I whispered. "He was with me, too. I had no idea he was *that* mad. That fall he had messed up more than his spinal cord."

His gaze sharpened on me. "What do you mean? What did he say?"

"He said that I had a stub thumb," I said, holding up my bruised thumb. "It's supposed to be some kind of genetic anomaly. Brachydacty? Something, I can't remember exactly. It just means that one thumb is a little shorter than another."

For a few seconds, Evan didn't speak. He didn't seem to breathe. Then he gently ran his fingertip over my thumb's purple nail.

"Did Noah bruise you?" he asked, and I realized that while he was lost in his own private thoughts, he was also furious in a still, ominous fashion.

"Yes. He grabbed it and squeezed it. He said that Elizabeth had the same thing, but that she had two shortened thumbs. Did you notice? Elizabeth's thumbs? When you were married to her?"

"I noticed. I never noticed yours, though," he said, still caressing my thumb softly. He seemed far away, caught up in his private thoughts. "Elizabeth's were more pronounced."

"He said it was a sign of a Madaster. That it was an indication of pure, superior genes... that it ran in the royal families of Europe, and it signified the ability to lead and... I don't know. All kinds of nonsense." Evan remained grim. "Evan? It is nonsense, right?"

"Of course. I told you that Noah is obsessed with the supposed nobleness and superiority of the Madaster line. His father was obsessed before him, and his father before him. He believes some pretty delusional things."

I watched him breathlessly as he stroked my thumb. "And the fact that he believes Elizabeth was my mother?" I asked weakly. "Is that delusional, too?"

He exhaled heavily, released my hands, and leaned back in his chair. He regarded me in silence for a moment. "One of the things Madaster told me—and Wes, too, once he arrived—was that he'd taken a genetic sample from you. I think that was the reason he drugged you. In order to get some of your cells, so that he could have them tested."

"To see if Elizabeth was really my mother?"

He nodded.

"How did they do it?" I asked, feeling ill at the news. Violated.

"They swabbed the inside of your mouth."

I blinked, that particular memory not coming back to me until that moment. "I remember," I whispered. "I was blacking out, and he called for his nurse. And she pinched my lip, and I felt something in here," I said, pointing inside my mouth to my cheek.

Evan nodded.

"What did you say, when Madaster said he'd done it?" I asked him.

"I insisted he return the sample. I more than insisted. I grabbed him and nearly threw him out of his chair. But Noah refused. His nurse wasn't there by the time I got there. We couldn't find her in the house. She must have taken the sample with her. When things started to get out of hand between Noah and I, Wes intervened. He pulled me off Noah. He suggested that both of us turn over the sample to him."

"What did Wes want to do with it?"

Evan met my stare squarely. "He said he'd handle the testing, act as a neutral party to the whole thing. He knows someone at a lab in Carson City who could put a rush on the results. Noah said he could supply some of Elizabeth's DNA, for comparison. Noah said he'd agree to that, if I did."

He hesitated, avoiding my stare.

"Evan?"

"I told Wes to do it, Anna."

He saw my stunned expression.

"I'm sorry. I know Noah stole the genetic material from you without your consent. But after some of the things Noah was claiming, and your similarity to Elizabeth—"

"You thought it would be better to clear up any doubts. And you *are* having doubts," I said, staring blankly into space. "In the past few days, you've grown to suspect that I could be Elizabeth's child."

"I suspected Noah had been telling you some of the same lies he told me. I thought there was a possibility you'd want proof that his claims were unfounded." He winced and glanced away. "That was before—"

"We knew for certain that I was adopted. Or you knew about this," I said, holding up my bruised thumb.

277

"I've told you. I don't see how it's possible that you're Elizabeth's child."

"You mean that you never thought it was possible *before*. Until yesterday, in Noah's suite," I corrected.

I saw his jaw tighten.

What about the paternity? a voice in my head screamed.

But the possible answer was too sickening... to reprehensible to say aloud, let alone consider for long. I realized it must be precisely the same situation for Evan.

So we both existed in frozen horror.

"No matter what the test results show, it won't change how I feel about you," he said.

It took me a few seconds to absorb his words. When I finally did, I laughed harshly. It scared me, because I couldn't stop. I laughed until more tears ran down my cheeks and Evan stood over me, looking alarmed.

"I'm sorry," I managed between jags of laughter. "It's just all so insane, I think it's making me crazy, too."

"No," Evan said resolutely, grabbing my upper arms and helping me to stand. "You're overwhelmed and exhausted. Come lie down, Anna."

I was too dismayed to argue. It felt like my heart was being crushed inside my chest. I found myself avoiding Evan's eyes at all costs. The pain of meeting his gaze, of thinking of what had been between us and could never be again, overwhelmed me.

I curled up on my side on the bed, my back to him when he sat on the edge of the mattress. I jerked away from him, and then took a twisted comfort in the fact that he didn't move. He remained next to me, solid and warm.

Slowly, the wave of hysteria ebbed out of me.

"How long will it take for the testing?" I asked, sniffing.

"Wes told me today that he should have the results by tomorrow, Thursday at the latest."

God, let me wake up from this nightmare.

Evan touched me on my back.

"Don't."

His hand sprang away. A moment later, I felt him get up from the bed. I perfectly imagined his hurt, his barren distress. I lay there unmoving with my eyes closed, locked inside a slowly constricting tourniquet of grief and horror.

Hours later, Evan finally turned out the light and got into the other bed. I knew how he sounded when he slept. It took what felt like an eternity before I heard his slow, steady breathing.

I willed my sore, tight muscles to unclench.

I couldn't bear to be in that room any longer. I had to get away.

But not before I heard the news from Wes. It would be wrong to be rash, when I didn't have anything but Madaster's allegations.

(*Are you sure he's delusional? Sociopathic, to be certain. Cruel. Selfish beyond belief. But I wouldn't say delusional.*)

Of course he's delusional! He believes that his family is some kind of example of a pure race, and that intermarriage and incest should be encouraged because it creates psychic abilities and the capability to speak with the ancestors.

(*If that's a delusion, then what are we doing right now?*)

I started, a whimper leaking out of my throat. Evan moved restlessly in the other bed, and then quieted.

(*He's such a good man. I never deserved him, but you do. You're pure. Untainted. You shouldn't be so harsh with him.*)

Shut up!

I sat up in the bed and clutched at my head, desperate to stop the voice.

(*Do you want to escape, Anna?*)

Yes.

(*Then go. Get up right now, take the keys from Evan, and drive. Drive until the road runs out. But you'll never be able to escape the memories. You'll never be able to escape your husband. Your father. There's only one thing that will bring you any peace now. Us any peace. Swim Deep.*)

I squeezed at my head now, my fingernails digging into my scalp. I clamped my eyelids tight. My throat burned from a silent scream.

(*Wait for the test the results, if you must. But you already know you're mine. When you get the results, you know what you have to do. Find me, and you'll find yourself. Light from my darkness.*)

"Anna," she said.

Her voice resounded, substantial and real within the confines of the shadowed hotel room. I heard authority, gentleness, love, and an ocean of regret; all of it in that single utterance of my name.

I opened my eyes, and saw *her*—Elizabeth—standing at the foot of my bed.

The scream exploded from my throat. I banged my head back on the wooden headboard, wild to get her *out*.

What penetrated my horror were the sound of Evan's voice and the light going on in the room. Both seemed to cause Elizabeth to disappear. Despite that, I couldn't stop screaming.

"Anna... God, Anna, please stop. You're safe. Tell me what it is. *Please* tell me."

His obvious anguish finally silenced me. I leaned my head back and brought him into focus. He sat on the bed next to me, his tight embrace holding my arms next to my sides. In my panic, had I been swinging at him as he tried to comfort me? He looked as panic-stricken as I felt. Now that I'd stilled, he reached up and cupped my face.

"Whatever it is that's scaring you the most, just say it, honey. You need to let it out, or it's going to kill you."

"Don't you know what's terrifying me?" I whispered hoarsely.

He winced. "I... I think I do. You're afraid that if you are Elizabeth's, then you might be Noah's, too." I just stared at him in mute amazement. His brushed his fingertip over my wet cheek. "But even if that were true, it doesn't matter, honey. It doesn't matter."

"That's not what I'm most afraid of," I said. "I'm most afraid that *you're* my father."

His stroking fingertips stilled on my face.

"That's what Noah told me yesterday before you burst into the room. He seemed certain," I said.

His frigid gaze thawed in an instant. I saw a fire spark where the cold desolation had been.

"That fucking bastard." He started shaking his head furiously. "No. No. *No*, Anna. You have to believe me, that's a complete impossibility." I felt him shudder. He put his hand over his face. "Oh God, that's what you've been thinking? You've been imagining that *I* was... "

Another shudder went through him. He grabbed my shoulders.

"Anna, listen to me. I never *once* considered you could be my child. Never *once*."

"But you knew Elizabeth lied—"

"I knew you couldn't be my child because I never slept with Elizabeth until I was seventeen years old," he shouted.

I paused with my mouth hanging open.

"The private investigators I hired had told me your date of birth," Evan said. "Later, I saw your birth certificate with my own eyes. The dates didn't match up, Anna. If they had, maybe I would have had the crazy, unlikely suspicion of paternity. But they *didn't*. I would have had to have had sex with Elizabeth when I was thirteen or fourteen years old—"

"And you didn't?"

"*No*. God, no. I know I told you that Elizabeth and I were close, and we were. But I thought you understood that it was innocent at first. Our relationship as kids was platonic. I think Elizabeth wanted to keep it that way. She could relate to me differently than all the other men in her life. Anna?" His hands tightened on my shoulders. "Do you believe me?"

I stared up at him. The wild sincerity in his eyes struck me like a lightning bolt. But I couldn't believe him entirely. Because I'd learned I couldn't trust my own instincts.

"Yes," I said.

Why did I lie? I suppose it was the same, obvious answer. I loved him, no matter what. I couldn't bear seeing his pain.

"I didn't understand," he said thickly. He leaned forward and pressed his forehead to mine. He cradled my face in his hands, rocking me gently. "God, I'm sorry, Anna. I knew you were horrified and traumatized, but I thought it was because you were worried it was Noah—"

"All I could think of... " *All I can think of.* "Was what if it was true? What if I'd slept with my own father. Fallen in love with him?"

"Do you see?" Evan entreated desperately, his stare willing me to believe him. "Do you see why I warned you? Noah lies. He lies to control. He lies to *hurt*. Please don't let him in, Anna. Please."

Chapter Twenty-Eight

THAT NIGHT, I FINALLY FELL INTO A DREAMLESS SLEEP IN EVAN'S ARMS. In the morning, I awoke feeling blessedly numb. I told Evan I was feeling claustrophobic, and that I needed to get out of the hotel room. I saw the whites of his eyes showing as he looked around at my declaration. I could tell that he was still worried about me to the point that he was having difficulty focusing on anything else.

"I'll come with you," he said.

"No. I'm going alone. I'll be back in an hour. I'm fine. I feel much better today. Talking last night helped. I just need some fresh air and a little exercise."

I saw him considering, searching for reasons why I shouldn't go. Obviously, he couldn't come up with anything. I wasn't an invalid or a prisoner.

"Take your cell phone, in case you need me for anything," he said, handing me a card key for the hotel room. I put it in my purse. I'd already secreted his car keys in there, while he'd been in the shower earlier. I wasn't sure if I would use them to make an escape or not.

I just wanted those keys, like a safety line. In case the sheer panic hit me again.

Even though I'd stolen the keys, part of me knew I wouldn't go. Not until I'd heard the truth about the genetic testing, anyway. I left the suite, determined to ignore the worry I sensed pouring off of Evan. There was nothing I could do to comfort him besides tell the lie again that I was fine.

That I believed him.

The sun and cool air revived me a little. I distracted myself by browsing through some of the luxury shops on the bottom floor of the hotel and walking along the beachfront. I temporarily forgot the car keys in my purse. For a few blessed minutes, I didn't think about escape, or Evan, or Noah, or the fact that I wasn't my parents' biological child... Or the horror of Elizabeth leaping out of my dreams and from inside of my head into the concrete reality of the hotel room last night.

Thankfully, that insulated cocoon that made me into the equivalent of a walking, talking zombie stayed with me when I returned to the hotel room forty-five minutes later.

I needed that protection for what was to come.

I heard distant male voices as I quietly entered the suite. I paused a moment just inside the door.

"... a bloody mess," I heard Evan say. "She's so fragile, after everything that's happened."

"Don't you think she deserves to know the truth?"

I realized it was Wes Ryder on the balcony with Evan. I could make out their tall figures through the billowing, partially translucent curtains.

"No one *deserves* to know something that awful," Evan said loudly. "Jesus, what if—"

"What?" Wes asked when Evan abruptly cut himself off.

"What if she couldn't take it? What if she harms herself when she hears the news? It'd be my fault. For bringing her to this Godforsaken place. All of it. Do you have any idea what she's gone though, these past few days? Christ, what a nightmare. I love her, and yet *I've* done this to her. I have wronged her in ways I never imagined," I heard him say, even though his voice was muffled.

A tendril of pain wormed its way through the insulation of my denial. It burrowed into my chest at the desperation I heard in Evan's voice.

"It's not as if any of this is her fault. Anna is innocent. She doesn't deserve to suffer," Wes said heavily.

Silently, I backed out of the hotel room and closed the door.

I walked down the hallway to an exit door and stood on the staircase landing. I quickly texted Evan that I'd decided to have breakfast, and that I'd be back in a half hour or so.

Then I waited, with the exit door slightly cracked open.

Ten minutes later, I heard a door open down the hallway. The elevator dinged, and I dared to peek out. I saw Wes Ryder stepping onto the elevator.

We were only on the third floor. I rushed down the stairs. I caught up to him as he walked down the sidewalk next to the parking lot.

"Wes!"

He turned around, looking surprised, and then acutely discomfited to see me running after him.

"Anna."

"Hi," I said, coming to a stop and running my fingers through my mussed hair. I smiled. He blinked and glanced away skittishly. "I thought that was you. Did you come to visit us?"

"I did, yes," he said, his gaze jumping to my face and off it, once again. I understood better now why he was always so uncomfortable around me, why his glances were both hungry and haunted at once. Maybe he hadn't just been in love with Elizabeth once.

Perhaps he still was.

"How are you?" I asked him, recalling that I'd felt angry with him for keeping my resemblance to Elizabeth to himself, upon Evan's request. I needed to make it clear I'd forgiven him, if I were to convince him to give me his news. He waved his hand, as if to say the question had been inconsequential. He seemed embarrassed.

"This has all been one hell of a mess, hasn't it?" I asked softly. "No one would believe it if I tried to tell them the story."

He shook his head and shoved his hands into his pockets. I thought I saw his lips move in a silent curse.

"I don't know what to say, Anna, except I'm sorry."

"You didn't do anything, except keep the fact that I'm Elizabeth and I are doubles. Evan asked you to keep quiet about it, and you have a much longer history of friendship with him than you do me," I reasoned.

He looked unconvinced and uncomfortable. *Very* uncomfortable. He was sweating again, and he looked pale.

"Did you tell Evan the results? Of the genetic test?"

He swallowed thickly and looked back at the hotel. I had the impression of a trapped animal. Somehow, I knew that he was about to say that he'd prefer that Evan give me the news.

"I'm stronger than Evan thinks I am," I said before he could utter a syllable. "It was my cells that were tested. Noah took them from me against my will. He drugged me to do it. I could make a big deal about the fact that Noah, Evan, and you decided to have the testing done without my consent. But *I* want to know the results, too. So I'm not going to complain. I *deserve* those results, above anyone else. Surely you know that, Wes," I said more gently, persuasion thick in my tone.

"Yes," he replied thickly. Abruptly, his reluctance annoyed me.

"Come on, Wes. If I can accept the truth, surely you can," I said, unable to keep the impatience out of my tone. "I am whatever I am, no matter who my biological parents are. You don't have to act like I'm a monster."

He started, meeting my gaze for the first time. He looked stunned.

"I don't think that, Anna. I'm just... this is difficult to say."

"It'll be more difficult to hear," I countered grimly. "But I'm ready, Wes."

He frowned, and then sighed. "I'm not sure how much Evan told you," he said hoarsely. "But we decided to have both your paternity and maternity determined."

"Wouldn't you have to have my father's genetic material to do that?"

"Yes," he said, his gaze flickering around.

"Wes?" I demanded. "Trust me, whatever you say isn't going to come as a surprise to me. I found out from my parents yesterday that I was adopted. I've already suspected and agonized over the possible truths. I've braced myself to hear it."

He met my stare uneasily. "Anna... I'm sorry to have to tell you this, but the genetic testing has proven with an extremely high level of certainty that your biological mother was Elizabeth Madaster."

I just nodded, ignoring the roaring that started up in my ears.

"And my father?"

Someone else said those words, someone that sounded calm and strong.

Wes grimaced. He looked sick.

"The genetic testing shows that your father is Evan. God, I'm sorry, Anna."

Chapter Twenty-Nine

I NEVER RETURNED TO THE HOTEL SUITE.

My mind was blank for the next forty minutes or so. I functioned, because I successfully maneuvered on the lakeside road to reach Les Jumeaux. But I was a machine, performing all the necessary motor movements, while I—Anna—was blessedly absent.

Who was Anna Solas, anyway? Anna Halifax? Anna Madaster? She was nothing. I was no one, just the organic robot that drove the steep, twisting road with much more expertise than the previous, self-conscious Anna would have done. Did I believe Wes? Or Noah? Or Evan?

I don't know what or whom I believed. I existed in a fixed state of doubt, right on the edge of complete and utter despair.

The first time I experienced any sense of emotion was when I pulled up to the shadowed, stone gatehouse to Les Jumeaux. I remembered vividly first arriving there, how I'd felt like I'd entered a dream—a fairy tale—as I stared up at the towering pine forest while sitting next to my handsome, perfect husband. I remembered Evan's small, special smile when I'd handed him back the card key, and how the gate had swung open.

(The gate opened for you because Les Jumeaux is yours. It's your birthright. Your heritage.)

"No," I said out loud emphatically.

Yes, I was now talking to her out loud now. The ghost. The ancestor. Elizabeth.

My mother.

"This place is no fairy tale. It's a nightmare. It's hell," I grated out, gripping the steering wheel tightly.

A silent pause.

(Let's finish the nightmare, then.)

I lowered my window and pressed the card key to the pad. The wrought iron gate to Les Jumeaux slowly swung open.

I used the garage entrance to access the house. In the kitchen, I came to a halt. Sunlight streamed through the terrace windows. Outside, the cerulean blue lake flashed and winked at me. The aspens were beginning to turn in the cooler weather. A breeze gusted through the trees. The leaves rustled and glinted like thousands of fluttering gold coins against the backdrop of the blue lake and dark green pines.

Inside the house, that soft, watchful silence cloaked everything.

(Les Jumeaux isn't a hell. It's your home, Anna. We carry the hell inside us.)

I walked farther into the room. In the sink, I saw Evan's and my coffee cups. It was like finding artifacts that had survived a catastrophe... like the perfectly preserved loaf of bread I'd seen once at a museum exhibition of excavated objects that had survived the volcanic disaster of Pompeii.

It hit me then. The grief. I braced my hands on the sink and wept.

But I'd set some kind of internal limit on my pain. I had a lifetime to cry.

And only hours to exact revenge.

The truth had come to me gradually, in snippets. It hadn't really coalesced entirely in my head until I stood in front of the bathroom mirror in Evan's and my old bedroom, gripping a pair of sharp scissors in my hand.

Maybe the truth had formed incompletely at first because of my denial of it: my refusal to face the ugly truth, my determined rejection of Elizabeth's nightmare message or her voice in my head.

Somehow, I knew that I would never be able to be rid of her, nor would I ever accept her, if I didn't do this thing.

I wore a dive suit without the hood, my long, blonde hair spilling around the black neoprene. My face looked pale, but calm in the mirror as I grabbed a handful of hair. I lopped it off at my shoulder.

When the last long strands fell to the floor and I'd donned a dive hood, I examined myself closely in the mirror.

I looked at the result of centuries of interbreeding. No wonder Elizabeth and I looked so much alike. For a split second, my smooth, flesh and blood face disappeared, only to be replaced by a skull in a dive hood. I started in shock, and my own face resolved over the bones and bleached white teeth.

Somehow, I knew I'd seen an exact replica of her skull. Not only that, I'd seen through my own flesh, like an X-ray. It would be how I appeared one day, when my body lay moldering in the ground. I'd seen her skeleton, the very foundation of the living, breathing, vibrant, flesh and blood woman she'd once been.

(Light from my darkness.

Swim deep, darling.)

Tears filled my eyes. She'd been so alone in that cold, wet world for so long.

"It'll be over soon, Elizabeth," I whispered.

It had all settled in my head now.

I had realized, at some point in my dazed consciousness in the past few days, that Madaster had said something revealing in that tortured, bewildering conversation we'd held in his tower retreat. He'd asked me if Evan knew about the tunnel between the Twins.

Tunnel. Not hallway. Not corridor, as Evan had called it.

He'd seemed smug when I said that Evan had mentioned sealing the corridor between the two mansions. He'd been satisfied to hear that Evan didn't know about the *other* passageway that joined the Twins.

Because now I understood, there had been not one, but *two* passages between the houses.

I was very careful to remain hidden on my trek across the beach to the boathouse. I didn't want Noah to spy me from his tower, so I stayed behind the giant granite boulders along the beach until I reached the dock.

Noah might have spotted me as I hurried down the dock a moment later, hauling my dive equipment. But I was exposed for only half a minute. And I couldn't be anxious about that now. Not when I'd decided what needed to be done.

Besides, given his condition, Noah no longer could visit the scene of his worst crimes. I realized how it must have been a festering thorn in his side for the past few years, the knowledge of that deep, secret place beneath Les Jumeaux, and his inability to access it.

Excellent job, Lorraine.

Grandmother. Cousin. Ancestor.

It's dangerous to dive alone, especially for someone of my limited expertise. But it's *crazy* to cavern dive alone. Some people might have said I was acting suicidal. I was positive I wasn't, though. I knew, because I'd thought about ending it all in the past few days, when I'd looked into Evan's eyes, and wondered what I would do if I found out I'd married my own biological father.

Slept with him.

But *this* wasn't *that*.

I remembered Evan saying that he'd become bent on serving Madaster justice. Now, I'd become the bent and twisted one. I thought of only one thing as I stowed my equipment on the speedboat and started up the motor: Revenge. The word pulsed in my veins.

It was my true birthright.

I anchored a little farther to the south of where Manny had secured the cruiser that day when Valeria and I dived. There was an outcropping of stone here that I believed would obscure Madaster's view of the boat from the tower.

I back flopped into the cold water alone. I recognized the whitish-gray, bleached sand below me, and the skeletal stone outcroppings. When I reached the drastic drop-off of the Great Wall, I turned on my dive light. I swam along the cliff's ledge toward the north, trying to approximate where Valeria and I had dropped over the wall. I feared that I wouldn't find the wide, deep cavern we'd previously entered.

Thinking I'd swum far enough, I kicked over the cliff. More than a thousand feet of water yawned below. Coldness and that dreadful thrill passed through me. I descended over the massive stone wall.

I was insignificant and alone, and I couldn't trust myself.

Terror seized me. Large clouds of bubbles burst from my regulator. I couldn't catch my breath.

(You're not alone, darling.)

(Follow your instinct.)

Stay with me, Elizabeth.

It was the first time I'd ever addressed her by name in my head. Whether it was crazy of me or not, I don't know. I acted purely on survival now. Maybe being a little mad would keep me alive.

Just when I was thinking of surfacing and reorienting myself, I spotted the large hole in the wall below me. I entered the wide cavern, my dive light reflecting off the pale walls. A reassuring feeling of familiarity went through me.

You dived here often, didn't you, Elizabeth?

(Yes. Both into the cave and out of it. The spring has been there since the tunnel was first built. They built around it. You'll see. Follow the light in the darkness, darling.)

A jolt of adrenaline went through me. Like that first time with Valeria, I swam with a confidence I shouldn't have felt. I realized now I'd been—and was now— experiencing Elizabeth's certainty. These were *her* waters.

I got to the place where the tunnel of gray boulders and smooth rock faces narrowed. I looked up, but saw only a stone ceiling. Had I gone too far? Where was that tiny, flickering light that had made no sense to me?

No sooner had I started to worry when I glided out of the horizontal tunnel into a vertical one. The stone floor and roof disappeared. I shined my light upward. I looked up a stone tube. It was like a natural well, approximately ten feet in circumference. I tilted the flashlight down, and realized I was suspended in deep water. My light couldn't find the bottom, it went down so far.

I turned out my light, abandoning myself to the cold, black water and trying to ignore the anxiety tightening my chest.

There it was. The tiny light far above me. It shimmered slightly, as though it reflected upon a circular pool of water. The spring. Stark relief, combined with a sad sense of inevitability, swept through me.

I swam up the vertical tunnel, already knowing what I was about to face. I'd already seen it in the mirror in Les Jumeaux.

I used my flashlight to scan the rock walls as I ascended the vertical tunnel. Twenty to thirty feet below the surface of the pool above me, my light illuminated something that made me start. I almost dropped my light into the unknown depth of water below me.

I hung in the water, my flashlight beam trained on her.

Madaster had intended to dispose of Elizabeth's lifeless body into the void of the vertical drop. But she'd been caught on a suspended rock outcropping. She'd landed in a C-shaped indentation very close to the ledge, one leg bent awkwardly behind her, her torso slumped against the curving stone.

Willing my breathing to even, I slowly approached her.

On the night Elizabeth had disappeared, she'd come here. To see her father. To confront him here, in their secret place. To tell him she planned to cut him out, like a cancer, from her life.

(*Daddy didn't take it well, when I told him that I understood the truth now. Or at least I understood better. Evan, the doctors, the counselors, and other patients had really started to get through to me. I understood better than I ever had before, how horrible my own father had been to me for my whole life. We weren't gifted because we were Madasters. We were sick. Interbred. Emotional cancers twisted and pierced every cell in our body. But Evan had finally started to convince me I could get better... that maybe, just maybe, the Madaster poison could be eradicated.*

When I called Daddy and said I wanted to speak to him, he insisted on meeting here. In our secret place. I think he suspected that I was going to say I never would see him again. That was a truth he couldn't bear. I think he knew he could hide the truth, in this place only we knew about.)

I saw it now, as if it was my own memory, not hers.

Much like I just had, Elizabeth had left Les Jumeaux on her boat and anchored off the coast, near the drop off and the cavern. She'd made the same dive many times in the past, the adventure of arriving through the mysterious depths beneath Les Jumeaux spiking the excitement of her illicit meetings with her father.

It seemed impossible that her lifeless body had landed in this little shallow indentation and stayed here for seven years without tipping over the ledge. Even in death, Elizabeth exerted her will. She'd stuck tenaciously, when she should have drifted into oblivion. Forgetfulness. Her lifeless body was her story.

And Elizabeth Madaster wanted that story told.

She still wore her dive suit and hood. I could see the shape of her slender, voluptuous body. She was remarkably well preserved, due to the tight suit and the cold, low-bacteria content of the Tahoe depths. I'd read about it once before, how divers lost in Tahoe could be remarkably preserved for more than a decade, due to the purity of the water and the protection of the suit.

Only her skull had fully decomposed.

I remained suspended in the black waters for I don't know how long, looking into my mother's face.

Chapter Thirty

*FINALLY, I LEFT HER BEHIND—WE'LL BE BACK FOR YOU, ELIZABETH.
You held on. Your long sleep in the dark, cold water will be over soon.*

I rose to the shimmering pool above me and surfaced. I removed my mouthpiece and dive mask and looked around. It was a round, circular spring inside a granite tunnel.

The spring was natural, but the tunnel wasn't. Surely the Cornish miners who had labored a century ago to build Les Jumeaux and the grounds had cut through the stone here, as well, with dynamite and pick axes. Some Madaster ancestor had paid the miners to keep the tunnel secret. He'd passed on the knowledge of the deep subterranean passage between the houses only to a child or two from the next generation, and that Madaster did the same to his child, and so on.

Madasters thrived on family secrets.

Family secrets like me.

Elizabeth had learned the power of secrets from the cradle, no doubt. She and I were both embodiments of the skeleton in the closet.

I pulled myself out of the water and removed my equipment. The tunnel was lit by a single bulb. This was the source of the inexplicable light I'd seen when I'd swum deep into the cavern. The LED bulb must have been burning constantly for over two years, to some time before Lorraine had pushed Madaster down the stairs and made her husband wheelchair-bound. He couldn't afford to have an elevator built down to this level. It would entail letting strangers view his secret place. It would mean possibly exposing his crimes.

Instinctively, I knew that it ate at Noah, burned in him, his inability to access this tunnel, so prized by generations of Madasters for undertaking illicit activities. After Noah had murdered his rebellious daughter, he'd sacrificed her body to that vertical drop beneath the spring. He hadn't realized that Elizabeth's body had caught on the rock ledge just feet below the spring's surface.

I imagined Madaster felt the closest to her when he visited this place, not realizing that she was literally nearby.

I used my dive light to help with illumination and made my way down the tunnel, the granite feeling like ice beneath my wet, bare feet. To the right of me, there was an indentation carved into the wall. It was a stone room, I realized, the shadows hanging thick where the LED light couldn't reach. I shone my dive light around. I saw a bed with restraints at the four bedposts. It was an antique, wooden bed. How many generations of Madasters had used it?

There was a sensor cap and attached wires lying on the rumpled sheets.

Nausea struck me. But then a cold, hard anger chased it away. I shone the light into a corner. On a table, I saw bottles of pills and liquid, and syringes for IV drug use. At what age did Madaster start drugging his own daughter for the supposed purpose of his "research"?

(I was too young to remember the first time.)

Behind the table, someone had hung a long mirror with a wooden frame. The bed was in the reflection, a mirror for Madaster to witness his own depravity. I stepped up to the mirror and blocked the reflection. I removed my hood and studied my face. My damp hair fell in curls. Acting on some instinct, I shut off my dive light.

The image in the dim reflection was eerily familiar. My hair had always curled when it was shorter, but straightened out to waves when it was long. Now that I'd cut it, it sprang into ringlets, even damp. The tendrils just brushed my shoulders. I looked like my own nightmare standing there, my black wetsuit gleaming, my hair coiling into wet curls that my terror-filled, dreaming brain had interpreted as Medusa-like.

I knew that I looked exactly like Elizabeth at that moment. I recalled Madaster staring at me with hungry glee.

"So alike. And to think... you never even knew her. It's all a matter of genes. Those amazing, perfect genes."

I clicked on my dive light, and my image resolved into that of a young woman whose eyes looked bug-like in her pale face. Of course I was terrified. But it took my own image to hit it home.

What if I, too, had committed incest?

What if Madaster had been right? What if that depravity had been coiled into my genes somehow, a secret biological explosive waiting to detonate?

But... *no*. That's not how life worked. That was Noah Madaster's delusion. I was innocent. Evan and I had been ignorant. I may have the genes of the Madaster family, but I had the life of a Solas. I had the love, security, and respect of a family, something Elizabeth had never known.

(*Yes. You are the light from darkness.*)

In the way of dreams, or my activated unconscious mind, Elizabeth hadn't just been telling me where to find her body. She was also telling me what I'd meant to her. I was the clean part of her, sent away to thrive in the light.

I wasn't my biological mother, no matter how much I looked like her. Evan had been right when he'd said I might as well have been from another planet; I was so essentially different from her. I wasn't responsible for the cancerous corruption that Noah Madaster had passed on to his daughter, and which—I believed—had probably been passed on to Noah by some other Madaster ancestor, and that Madaster by a previous Madaster, and so on and so on, back through the centuries... through all the spidery tendrils of that elaborate, malignant family lineage I'd found in the North Twin library.

I had a vivid image flash into my brain of all those Madasters, and the complicated flourishes of various colors beneath their names. I recalled that Elizabeth's was, perhaps, the most complex of all, the scroll done almost exclusively in scarlet.

Why did I suddenly have the suspicion that Theodore Madaster's choice of colors and the design of the embellishment somehow were associated with the supposed "purity" of the entrant's genes? Had the nearly exclusive use of scarlet ink on Elizabeth's entry somehow been associated with how many Madasters had participating in her ultimate creation?

My scroll might have been even more scarlet, had it ever been drawn. But it wouldn't. This ugly cycle was about to end.

I left the room and headed in the direction that I believed led to the South Twin.

I walked perhaps a hundred feet down the stone tunnel, my light bouncing off the pale gray walls. I finally arrived at a mundane looking wooden door. Anxiously, I tried the knob. What if the entrance was locked? I wanted the element of surprise in confronting Madaster. But also, I eventually, I wanted to show police the tunnel. I wanted to show them Elizabeth.

I heard a distinct click, and swung the door inward. Relieved, I walked into what appeared to be a large subterranean room with some boxes, an ancient sawhorse, two old pickaxes, a bunch of folded tarps, and an ancient looking lantern. The walls were made of stacked, interspersed slate stones of various sizes. I turned my flashlight behind me, and was shocked to see that the door on this side was also made of the same slate, pieces of stone protruding irregularly at the edge like jagged teeth.

A thought struck me, and I shut the door into the wall. It was like sliding two perfectly matched puzzle pieces together. I heard the click of the latch.

The door had disappeared. I stared at a seamless slate stone wall. Noah had hid his secret well. Did a similar room and door exist in the North Twin? I'd never seen one. But this room had to be farther underground then the beach-level floor that I had always considered the lowest level of the North Twin.

I needed to find stairs.

I found them easily enough with my dive light. I ascended up not one, but two steep flights of rough wooden stairs. At the top of these was another door. I entered a room filled with natural light. I realized it was a changing room, with benches and hooks for clothing. Sure enough, when I looked out the window, I saw the beach. I was inside the South Twin proper now. When I pulled the door shut, it blended into the white, wood paneled wall of the changing room.

Not a half a minute later, I strode through the shadowed, musty-smelling great room toward the steep staircase, and Madaster's tower.

Chapter Thirty-One

I NEITHER HEARD NOR SAW ANY ONE AS I MADE MY WAY DOWN THE nearly pitch-black hallway on the second floor. Hopefully, Lorraine was on one of her walks.

I recalled that the small elevator motor had been quite noisy. The mechanical hum would surely give away my presence to Noah or his nurse. Moving stealthily, I opened door after door along the hallway, shining my dive light inside one unused room after another.

Finally, I found the back stairs that hopefully led to Noah's tower.

When I reached the top, there was another door. It opened when I tried it. I peeked inside and looked around, anxious that someone might be in it. It was empty. I was in a bedroom, furnished simply with a double bed, nightstand, and chest of drawers. On the wall was an old-fashioned pewter bell contraption—a maid's bell, I realized. Someone could ring from a distance in order to request service. A pair of tennis shoes with Velcro straps was tucked just beneath the bed.

Ima's room.

I left the nurse's room and padded silently in my bare feet down a carpeted hallway. Just as I reached the entrance to a small kitchen on my right, I heard a voice in the distance.

"That will be all. Go," I heard Noah Madaster say curtly.

"I have some laundry to do. If you should need me—"

"I won't need you. Leave us be, " Noah cut off Ima impatiently.

Us? Who else was in the tower room with Noah besides his nurse?

I stood in the middle of the short hallway, panicked for a moment. Was Ima about to walk through the wooden swinging door ahead of me?

I swiftly moved into the kitchen and hurried to the shadowed depths. A second later, I heard the slight squeak of the hinges on the swinging door. I held my breath, sure Ima was about to switch on the kitchen light and reveal me standing there stupidly.

Instead, I watched from the shadows as she walked past, her face set in that severe expression I recalled too well.

I heard a door shutting at the other end of the hallway. Cautiously, I left the kitchen and went to the swinging wood door. Standing an inch away from it, I put my ear to the crack.

"So you told them both. Separately? As I told you?" It was Madaster's rasping voice. He sounded eager.

"I saw Anna walking in the distance when I pulled up in the car."

I started slightly, recognizing Wes Ryder's voice. Had he come here to give the results of the genetic testing to Madaster? "Evan said she'd gone for a walk, and he was worried about her."

"So you told Evan first?"

"Yes."

"Tell me," Madaster ordered, and I realized he didn't sound just eager. He was greedy. He relished this moment. "Evan first. How did he take it? Give me every detail."

"He was devastated, of course," Wes said. "It was just like you said. He was consumed with worry for Anna, frantic about how she would take the news."

"The fool is in love with her. Maybe even more than she's in love with him. He thought he could manipulate her for his plan, all while keeping her at a safe distance from me. Maybe Evan even thought he could keep Anna at a distance from himself while he carried out his revenge. But he couldn't. She caught him, good and hard. And he never guessed the truth. He thinks of himself as a protector and savior of his wife, but he ended up being the one to plunge the knife into her."

I realized I was fisting my hands so hard, I was digging my nails into my skin. I forced myself to unclench them.

"It was the same with when he was married to Elizabeth," Madaster continued. "Always the knight in shining armor. He looks down his nose at me, he judges me, but *he's* the one. It's *his* interfering self-righteousness that is harming his wives. And now he knows it. Now, he'll have to live with the fact that he's hurt Anna—maybe irreparably—for his entire worthless life."

I placed my hand on the door and started to push, but then Madaster said, "Now Anna." He sounded like a kid fingering his Christmas gifts beneath the tree, savoring that first hedonistic rip of the paper. "How did she take the news that you gave her?"

"How do you think she took it?" Wes sounded angry now. I didn't understand the part he was playing in all this.

"Just answer the question, you weak, useless addict. I don't keep your secrets—or keep you supplied with morphine, or cover your gambling debts—in order to hear your worthless *opinions*." He used the same tone as when he spoke so dismissively—so cruelly—to Ima. There was a pregnant pause, and I wondered if, unlike his nurse, Wes would stand up to Madaster.

"Please tell me you didn't take one look at her and go as spineless and moony-eyed as you used to do with Elizabeth," Madaster said.

"I told her. You son of a bitch."

Madaster laughed. "She's gotten under your skin, hasn't she? Just like Elizabeth? Well, she's a Madaster. Many times over." I heard the pride in his tone, and felt the ripples of revulsion just beneath my skin.

"You sicken me," Wes said.

"The feeling is mutual," Madaster boomed, sounding almost jovial. "But where would we be, without each other?"

"Cell mates?"

"We'll both end up in our graves before that ever happens, me from this damn broken body, and you because your heart has stopped from a self-inflicted overdose of morphine. That or a bullet from my gun. Now stop your sniveling and tell me how Anna reacted when she heard the news."

"I'm sorry to disappoint you, but she didn't say much at all."

"She had to say *something*... react *somehow*, to news like that."

"She thanked me for having the testing done and delivering the news."

"That's it? After you told her that her biological father was her husband? That *is* what you told her, isn't it?"

"Yes, damn it. She seemed to be expecting it. Dreading it, but expecting it," Wes said, under his breath. "I don't understand how you knew."

"How I knew?"

"That she'd leave. I thought your idea was stupid, because surely Evan and Anna would talk once they were together. Surely they'd realize I'd told them two different stories."

"So she *did* leave? In a car? By herself?"

"Right after I told her," Wes said uneasily. "I acted like I was going to my car, but I watched her, from behind some trees. She got into Evan's car and drove away."

My hand curled into a fist on the door. I stood there in the silence that followed, unable to breathe until I heard Madaster's next words.

"It couldn't have turned out better. I'll bet that she left him for good," Madaster said. "She may have Elizabeth's looks, and maybe her strength, but she's not like us—Elizabeth and me. Anna led a sheltered, boring little life. Naiveté practically drips off her. You say she had no reaction when you told her that Evan was her father? Impossible. She must have been horrified to the bone. Put into a state of shock. She got into that car and drove away for good, trust me."

"But how did you know she would leave? What if she'd gone up to their hotel suite and realized I'd told them two separate results?"

"It didn't matter, you fool! Can you imagine what must have gone through her mind when she heard she was married to her father? I would have been happy with even two *seconds* of the purest, sheerest horror on her part. To have hours... days... years... a lifetime of that shame, those are all icing on the cake."

"But *why?*" Wes asked. He may have entered into an alliance with Madaster to torment Evan and me, but he'd clearly done so unwillingly. It couldn't be clearer that he both feared and despised Madaster.

"*Why?*" Madaster asked scornfully, as if he thought Wes had just asked him why a heavy object fell when dropped.

"Why do you want to hurt her, like you did Elizabeth?"

"Because she's *mine,*" Madaster roared.

In the silence that followed, my skin prickled painfully beneath my wetsuit.

"She's just like Elizabeth," Madaster continued after a charged pause. "I could see the disgust and scorn on her face when she looked at me. Evan has corrupted her into believing I'm the devil, and she's swallowed it all whole. They both believe I'm some powerless idiot, sitting here in this damned chair, in this tower, looking down helplessly at that girl. But they are wrong. I'm still capable of exerting my will. I've punished them both, haven't I? Evan has lost what he loves. How will Anna ever stay with him, knowing how he married her to get back at me, manipulated her for his own gain, and that it all came to *this*? You said earlier that he told you he feels her slipping away from him, cringing from his touch. How that must be killing him. He tried to bring me down with a lie. But I fought him with the truth."

"You didn't tell Anna the truth," Wes said.

"It doesn't matter," Madaster replied. "Are you high right now? Did you shoot up before you came up here? Can't you *grasp* this, you trembling addict? What matters is that they suffer... that they pay for what they've done."

"But surely Evan will tell Anna eventually. He'll tell her, and she'll know that I lied to her. Evan will show her the paperwork I gave him from the lab. She'll *know* that Evan isn't her biological father. She'll see firsthand that you are, Noah."

Not Evan's, Noah's. Not Evan's, Noah's.

The words beat in time to the drum of the heartbeat in my ears.

Not Evan's, Noah's. Not Evan's, Noah's.

No. Neither, I thought. *My father is Dick Solas, from Oak Park, Illinois. To me, Noah Madaster was a pedophile, rapist, abuser, sadist, and murderer: a man to be stopped at all costs. Evan had been right about that.*

And that was all Noah Madaster was to me.

"What matters," Madaster was saying, "is that Evan recognizes that he's the source of Anna's misery. Lord, I'd love to see it: her looking at him with complete revulsion. Even if he had to experience that for thirty seconds before she discovered the truth, it would be sweet beyond belief. It would be a worse punishment than death for Evan. And it's not as if Anna is going to be *happy* when she eventually finds out who her real father is. She'll be horrified, just in a different way. She thinks I'm the devil. Well... She'll have to live with the idea of being my spawn."

It may have surprised Madaster—it might have surprised most people—but I actually *was* relieved. Profoundly so. My knees weakened and my hand dropped off the door, inert and useless.

Evan and I hadn't sinned, even unknowingly.

"You're sick beyond belief, Noah," Wes said. His tone struck me as exhausted. Defeated.

"You knew what I was ever since you helped me move Elizabeth's boat that night. Just like I've known what you were ever since I caught you shooting up at your office that day, years ago."

"Does it make you feel better to despise me? As long as you have me, or Ima, or Lorraine, to kick around, you don't have to look into the pit of your own black soul, do you? You don't have to face what you did to your own daughter."

"You're defending Elizabeth again, are you?" Madaster asked, sounding still amused by an old, hackneyed joke.

"You always act like you knew her better than anyone in the world. But Elizabeth was different, when you weren't around. When you weren't influencing her."

I realized that Wes was close to tears. *Wes, Wes. You should have never tangled with the Madasters. Now you're caught in the web.*

"You always acted like you loved her more than anything else in the world, and yet look what you did to her. Look what you've done to Anna, all for revenge against Evan."

"I've barely touched the girl," Madaster said dismissively.

"Evan is worried she might become suicidal, after all the poison you've fed her."

"Elizabeth and Anna are mine," Madaster said, his tone so cold, I felt my spine tingle and stiffen. "*You're* mine, to do with as I want, as well. I never wanted you, particularly, but the dregs have been forced on me, at this point in my life. I need your legs, hands and eyes, to go, do, and see where I can't now. Get out of here, Ryder. Looking at you makes me ill. Call Evan this afternoon. Time for you to be his solicitous friend again. Tell him that you saw Anna drive away after you told her the 'truth.' I'll want a good description of how he's reacting to Anna's disappearance, and—"

I put my hand on the door and pushed it open with force.

Madaster glanced up and saw me. He froze in midsentence, his mouth gaping open. I walked across the Oriental carpet in my bare feet and came to stand several feet in front of him.

I won't say here that Noah Madaster's superiority, cruelty, and narcissism were an act. He was all that, and more. But at that moment, his arrogant façade seemed to melt away.

I realized what had caused his transformation. Fear. But something else, as well. Disbelief?

Hope?

He clutched at his chest, his eyes bulging wide. I saw movement in my periphery and realized Wes had stood and moved behind his chair.

Madaster gave a shaky breath, still holding my stare warily, as if he thought I'd run at him at any moment. Or disappear, like a ghost.

"Can you see her?" Madaster rasped.

I realized he wasn't speaking to me, but Wes. I glanced at Wes, who looked bewildered.

"Elizabeth?" Madaster whimpered in a tiny, childlike voice.

"Is that what you think?" Although I'd expected this reaction, his self-centeredness infuriated me. "You think that your precious Elizabeth has come to pay you a visit? You actually believe she'd seek you out in the afterlife, after what you did to her?"

"Anna, what—"

I put up my hand, halting Wes's question. I stepped toward Madaster, holding his stare. He appeared unaware that Wes had spoken. He seemed utterly transfixed, gazing at me. I knew what he saw. What he *thought* he saw. He saw a woman who looked exactly like Elizabeth Madaster on the night he'd murdered her—Elizabeth's face, the shoulder-length hair, the identical wetsuit. He imagined his daughter had finally come back to him, in the way of his Madaster ancestors.

"You smug son of a bitch. You thought I was Evan's tool. You thought you'd made me yours. But I'm doing this for *us*. Elizabeth and me. She guided me here. Do you know, I think she might have somehow maneuvered this whole scenario? She wouldn't let Evan forget her. She wouldn't let Evan forget *you*. We both know how persuasive, how powerful, Elizabeth could be. Who's to say she'd stop being who she was, even after you murdered her? Who's to say she didn't somehow manipulate all the events that led me to stand here in front of you right now?"

I saw realization spark in his bulging eyes. His mouth gaped open in his cavernous face. He clutched tighter at his chest with his right hand.

"Anna," he growled.

"I heard you just now," I said, pointing at the swinging door where I'd eavesdropped. "Elizabeth comes to *me*. She'll never appear to you, because she knows how much you'd want it. She knows how much you'd gloat over controlling her, even in death. Hearing her... seeing her, that'd validate all your insane ideas about the superiority of the Madasters, wouldn't it? And Elizabeth is fed up to the end of the earth with giving you what you want. Never again. Even after you die, you can seek her out to the ends of hell, buy she'll never let you look on her face again."

"You little bitch," Madaster muttered, spittle oozing from the corners of his mouth.

"I found her body. Elizabeth led me to the tunnel," I continued, ruthless, even in the face of his vulnerability. "I'm going to show the police. You're going to prison for murdering her, Noah. It's going to be all over the news, how you raped Elizabeth when she was a little girl, how you brainwashed her into a sick, incestuous relationship for most of her life, and how when she finally got the support she needed to leave you for good, you murdered her. All of it is going to come out, and there's nothing you can do to stop it. How does it feel? To know you're trapped? Helpless?" I asked. I'm ashamed to say I heard that familiar gloating in my tone, that eagerness to witness suffering. It was his tone. My father's. My grandfather's. I hated it, but I have to admit.

In that moment, it felt fantastic.

Madaster jerked his stare off me, looking to Wes.

"Stop her. If you let her talk to the police," he said in a thick, clotted voice, "I swear to God I'll tell them everything you've done. That you're a morphine addict. That you helped me the night Elizabeth died—"

"I had nothing to do with Elizabeth's death," Wes defended himself, looking at me with panic in his gaze. "I only helped Noah move her boat that night. She'd anchored just offshore from the South Twin. He told me that he'd have my license to practice medicine revoked if I didn't do it. I had no choice."

"I'll tell the police how you caused that landslide, and locked Anna in the sauna—"

"Again, because you insisted I do it," Wes shouted. He looked at me pleadingly. "I never meant to cause you any real harm. I wouldn't do that, Anna. He said it was all just to scare you, make you feel uncomfortable and unhappy at Les Jumeaux."

"You did those things, Wes?" I asked.

"Noah wanted you scared."

"Was Valeria in on it with you?"

"No. It was just a convenience, that she could... "

"Act as an informant in the North Twin," I stated grimly, not even bothering to tell Wes that Evan had been using him for something similar in the South Twin.

"He wanted you to leave Les Jumeaux... at first, anyway," Wes said. "When he thought you were just some random woman who resembled Elizabeth, recruited by Evan to torture him. But then he spoke to more and more people, researched who you were, and how Evan had met you, and he started to suspect—"

"That Elizabeth had a child that spring twenty-four years ago, after she went away to school at sixteen, in San Francisco," I finished for Wes. I looked at Noah. "Elizabeth was always slim. At Christmas that year, she was able to keep the truth hidden before she went away to school again. She knew she couldn't keep the child."

(Light from my darkness. I sent you away for your own good. But I never forgot you.)

"You don't know everything," Madaster said. He was breathing heavily, his nostrils flaring and pinching tight. "She *did* tell me she was pregnant. She told me that she'd had an abortion. And that afterward, she wasn't able to have children anymore."

"You taught her how to lie even before she could walk. Evan told me that he believed Elizabeth couldn't have children, as well. Maybe she couldn't, after she gave birth to me. Maybe something went wrong. Or perhaps she had a hysterectomy afterward. I don't know. All I know is, she gave me up for adoption because she wanted her child raised somewhere safe. Somewhere *clean*. She couldn't bear the idea of that child being exposed to you."

"That's a lie. Elizabeth loved me," Madaster wheezed.

"She hated you with a white hot passion. You convinced her, with your cursed machine, that feeling was *love*. That's one of your cruelest, sickest sins, Noah. When Evan and the doctors started to help Elizabeth to name her feelings for what they were, she couldn't wait to cut you out of her life. But you couldn't allow that, could you?"

"It was Evan's fault. He turned her against me. She started spouting the foulest things that night, in the tunnel. I had to make her stop... " He faded off, panting. He'd slumped in his wheelchair.

I suddenly saw it in my mind's eye: the things Elizabeth was saying against him, these lies they'd put in her head, the hatred and revulsion he saw in her eyes.

He had to stop it at all costs.

I saw his hands at her throat, choking off this new reality that threatened to snap his narrow, narcissistically driven world.

"You strangled her to death," I said.

"I didn't mean to," Noah panted.

"Anna, I think he's—"

"Maybe you *did* mean to. Maybe you didn't. But you *had* to make her stop talking," I said, cutting off Wes. "You couldn't take it. You were too fragile to hear the truth. It killed you, knowing how much Elizabeth had come to despise you. The blindfold you'd put on her from the day she was born had been removed. She *saw* you, that night down in the tunnel. That's why you had Wes lie to me about my paternity. You wanted me to think I'd slept with my own father. You did it because you relished the idea of me looking at Evan the way Elizabeth looked at you the night you murdered her: with utter revulsion and hatred."

Madaster shouted and lurched forward in his chair, nearly spilling from the seat. Suddenly, Wes was there, pushing him back into a sitting position. I saw Madaster convulse. I watched the scene as if through a long, narrow tunnel.

"Anna, call 911," Wes said, two of his fingers at Noah's throat. "He's having a heart attack."

Chapter Thirty-Two

WES SAT ACROSS FROM ME IN THE WAITING ROOM AT THE HOSPITAL. He'd just given me the news. He'd said that Noah Madaster had died of a massive coronary only minutes after he'd arrived at the emergency room.

I experienced neither remorse nor triumph at the revelation.

It struck me that we both looked like human husks, Wes and I, sitting there in that sterile, unfeeling room.

"Anna, I want you to know... I never knew all the details about what Noah had done to Elizabeth. I only knew that he murdered her," he said after a long, numb pause.

"Because you helped him move her boat away from the vicinity of Les Jumeaux?"

"Yes."

I swallowed and sat forward, forcing myself to focus on this shell of a man.

"If you tell the police what you did that night, how you helped Madaster, I won't tell them about what else you did. The landslide. The sauna."

His anxious gaze bounced off me.

"How did you do it? How did you keep me in that room?" I asked, unable to suppress my curiosity despite my zombie state. "Wes?" I prompted when he didn't immediately reply.

"Noah owns a traveler's door lock. It's a portable lock that will hold a door fast."

"You almost killed me, you know."

He met my gaze reluctantly. "I'm sorry, Anna. At that point, he was desperate to make you leave Les Jumeaux."

I exhaled, feeling exhausted. "Well? Will you tell the police? About how Noah asked you to help him move her boat that night? You owe it to her, Wes. You owe it to Elizabeth."

"Yes," he said, sounding shaky. "I'll tell them."

"And about what he confessed, when the three of us were in the tower together? About strangling her?"

He hesitated, but I held his stare. *This is your chance, Wes. This is your chance to make your life something other than a lie. Take it.*

Finally, he nodded. I'd already called the police, just after we'd arrived at the hospital. Wes wouldn't have long to wait, before his confession. Not long, to have doubt and his addiction steal up on him, and convince him to change his mind about admitting the truth.

"I won't tell them about what Noah said about your being addicted to morphine," I said. "But if you don't check into rehab, and soon—like tomorrow—I'll feel obligated to tell the authorities. You realize that, don't you? I'm thinking of your patients. Like Lorraine. They deserve better."

His chin trembled at that. We just sat there for a minute or two, both of us caught up in our miserable thoughts, no doubt.

"What about Evan?" Wes asked. "Does he know? That you went to confront Noah?"

I shook my head. "But I'm going to tell him," I said, flinching slightly at the idea of having to tell him the details of what had happened.

"Anna? Is it true?" Wes asked me uneasily after a pause.

"What?"

"That stuff you and Noah were talking about in the tower, about how you see Elizabeth. About how she talks to you, and that's how you found her body."

I sighed and leaned back in the uncomfortable chair.

"No," I lied gruffly. "I just said those things to get Noah to confess to murder. I knew he was obsessed with the idea that his relatives could communicate to living Madasters. You must realize he was mad."

"As a hatter," Wes said, no hesitation in his voice now. "Does Evan know? About your idea to tell Noah that Elizabeth spoke to you?"

"No. But I plan to tell him," I said, not lying this time. "Wes?"

"Yeah?"

"Would you mind calling Evan?" I was the one who sounded shaky now. My need for Evan was a weakness that was difficult to put on display. "Would you... would you ask him to come here, to the hospital?"

Wes nodded, already digging for his cell phone in his pocket as he stood.

Two Weeks Later

I asked to have the genetic testing redone, so that I could be completely confident of the results. I now knew, without a shadow of a doubt, that I was *not* Evan Halifax's child. I was indeed the product of Elizabeth and Noah Madaster's incestuous relationship.

It was cold comfort, but a profound relief, nonetheless.

Evan and I were the last two people to remain graveside after the small service. I'd asked Evan two days ago what Elizabeth's favorite flowers were, and he'd told me white ranunculus. I'd clutched them for the entire ceremony, even after Lorraine, guided by her new caregiver, and Evan had paid their individual tributes.

"Goodbye, Elizabeth," I said before I unclenched my fist and finally released the flowers. Several white petals sprayed across the polished mahogany of the coffin. That coffin held her body... the proof she'd so wanted found. It was the tangible proof of her hard life, and cruel death.

"She liked them because they seemed pure. Innocent," I murmured, staring at the flowers.

I felt Evan's hand at the small of my back.

"She would have loved you."

"I believe she would have," I replied, wiping away a tear. "And I also think I would have struggled, at times, to love her back. She was beyond complicated, wasn't she? Sometimes, I'm glad I never knew her. I'm sure I would have altered my whole world to give her what she needed. Just like you tried to do. Problem is, Elizabeth never knew what she needed."

"It's a basic human right that Noah had stolen from her," Evan said quietly.

"She believed she was tainted. Cancerous. I was the light from her darkness. I think she thought of me that way, a light somehow safely distant from her. Something to wish on, like that game you and she used to play when you were kids, when you used to wish on the stars. I was that part of her that she sent away, clean and innocent. I was able to see the world the way it was meant to be seen."

His hand moved on my back, soothing me in that way I'd always loved. Ever since Noah Madaster had died thirteen days ago, and Wes Ryder had confessed to the police about assisting Noah on the night of Elizabeth's murder, I'd occasionally let Evan comfort me in small ways like that. He was my weakness. I suspected he always would be.

We'd returned to Les Jumeaux for some uncertain period of time. I'd told the police about the location of Elizabeth's body and Noah's confession of killing her. Wes had held firm in his promise to me, and corroborated my story about Noah's confession of murder before he'd died. He'd been charged with being an accessory to the crime, but Evan was fairly confident that his lawyer could get him a minimal sentence.

Evan and I had been operating on automatic pilot since then, ticking off some imaginary checklist: the recovery of Elizabeth's body, caring for Lorraine Madaster, waiting for the results from the forensic coroner following his examination of Elizabeth's remains.

Ima, Madaster's nurse, had fled Les Jumeaux some time after Noah had been declared dead. The police had so far been unsuccessful in locating her for questioning.

Evan and I had moved Lorraine into the North Twin with us. Much to my relief, she came willingly, allowing me to help her pack up the sadly meager belongings she had squirreled away in a small, first floor bedroom at the South Twin.

I'd insisted that Lorraine get a full checkup at the doctor, as I was no longer convinced that Wes Ryder had been giving her quality care. I was certain Madaster and Ima had been neglecting her. I was relieved to hear from the physician that aside from some dehydration, and the fact that she was very thin and malnourished, Lorraine was surprisingly healthy. She did receive a diagnosis of dementia. But the specialists had hesitated in specifying Alzheimer's type dementia. I began to suspect that Evan had been right in saying that Lorraine's madness had been more a result of living with Noah Madaster, her guilt over her inability to care for her daughter, and her grief over losing Elizabeth. It had led her down a spiraling, inward path of fantasy and delusion. With Noah gone, some of that external pressure for escape seemed to dissipate a little. I increasingly witnessed periods of lucidity and recognition on her part.

Given her relative good health, Evan suggested that it might help Lorraine if we hired a non-traditional health care provider for her, someone with a mental health background versus a strictly medical one. I agreed. But until someone qualified could be found, I said I would see to her, try to assess her strengths and vulnerabilities, get a better idea of how to care for her... of how to make her happy. Of course at the heart of things, I simply wanted to spend time with Lorraine. She was my grandmother, after all.

I suppose there was another reason I found it comforting to spend those difficult days with Lorraine after Noah died. She was a quiet, undemanding companion. And although Evan and I spoke and planned together regularly, I struggled at being with him in any intimate sense... with relating to him like a wife would a husband.

Evan had been a rock since he'd been informed of Noah's heart attack. He'd arrived in record time at the hospital. I'd told him everything on the drive back to the North Twin. I was honest with him about the voices, about believing I'd seen Elizabeth on more than one occasion. He never judged me, although I sensed he didn't entirely believe me, either. I knew he wanted to be whatever I needed of him.

But I didn't know what I needed. Everything had become scrambled up inside me. I functioned on a day by day, hour by hour basis. In trying to regain my bearings, Lorraine had been my unlikely strength. Maybe I understood on some level that we were co-conspirators, after all. Lorraine and I shared the same mission: to destroy Noah Madaster. And the two of us together had succeeded.

I was to learn that Lorraine was a creature of nature, rising with the first glint of sunlight behind the mountains and burrowing under her bedclothes after her evening meal. In following her cycles, I somehow seemed to find my own rhythm again. I had no appetite during that time, but I was forced to partake in meals regularly. Given Lorraine's malnourishment, I had to set a healthy example and share three square meals a day with her.

Lorraine barely tolerated the breakfasts that I pushed on her, anxious as she was to be outside on the beach and in the forest. I followed her on her rambling walks, usually panting behind her, freshly amazed by her stamina. We ate the lunches I stored in my backpack while perched on the high rocks overlooking the lake. These meals she ate like a ravenous wolf, so I learned to pack double the amount. I found myself getting hungry for those lunches, too, if not with as much single-minded greed as Lorraine, at least with a healthy appetite.

She went with me to the overlook several times while I painted. Or while I attempted to paint, I should add. Although she never showed any particular interest in my painting, she seemed content enough during our excursions, foraging for the leaves that were falling from the aspens and maples, her manner endearingly somber and deliberate. She'd acquired quite a collection.

Eventually, I put away my paints and tried to help her. But when I tried to add my leaves to her pile, she frowned fiercely and pushed my hands away.

"What's wrong?" I wondered.

She merely pointed at her leaves. I dropped the ones I'd collected, and knelt on the ground. For the first time, I carefully collected her pile. I picked up a golden, still soft aspen leaf. It was perfectly shaped, with no mottling. All the others were just as lovely. I understood. She hadn't wanted me to contaminate her carefully chosen leaves with my random ones. So I joined her on a more meticulous search.

If anyone had seen us, they would have thought we were both mad. Lorraine and I knew differently. I found a strange measure of peace in our mutual, silent search up there on the overlook.

There was no one else to arrange funeral services for Noah Madaster, so the task had fallen to Evan and me. Lorraine had refused to attend her husband's memorial service at a local church. Evan had wondered out loud if Lorraine had really understood that Noah was dead, let alone the details of his burial. But I had disagreed with him. I was beginning to recognize the stubborn tilt of Lorraine's chin, even when her gaze appeared vacant and unfocused. I remembered the moment when I'd known for a fact that she'd pushed Noah Madaster down the stairs.

I would never underestimate Lorraine again.

The only reason I would have gone to Noah's service was to take Lorraine, if she'd desired it. Since she refused, he had no mourners. For all the power and control Noah had claimed during his lifetime, he'd been buried without a soul in attendance.

Evan and I slept separately. A gulf had opened between us. I sensed he knew that, as we stared down together at Elizabeth's casket that day. He worried he had no way of crossing that chasm. And I certainly didn't know how.

"Anna," Evan said presently as we stood side by side at Elizabeth's grave. "Do you still... does Elizabeth still... "

"Does she still speak to me?" I asked him bluntly.

He nodded.

"No," I said, looking at the submerged coffin. "I don't think she ever will again. Not in that way. She's where she wanted to be. She's resting, now. It's all right, that she'll never speak to me again. I think she'll always be with me."

I studied his somber profile through the dark sunglasses I wore.

"It's all right, Evan. I know you don't believe me about it all... about hearing her voice. Seeing her, even. You think it was all part of some nervous breakdown, an overload of stress, with everything that happened. Part of me doesn't want to believe it, either. One, because I know how crazy it sounds, and two, because it seems to validate all of Madaster's sick claims about communication with the ancestors."

"I never said I didn't believe you."

I smiled. "You didn't have to. You were very patient and kind about listening to my stories. But I saw the look in your eyes."

"You're wrong."

I glanced up at him in surprise, and read the earnestness on his face. "I am?"

"I'm not at all confident in saying that it's impossible, to get messages from... What? I don't know, the other side? On the day that you saw Elizabeth's photo at the library... Afterwards, when you left during the storm... "

"Yes?" I asked when he faded off.

"I thought... no, I *know* that something told me to follow you. Something told me that you were in danger," he said, his gaze fixed on Elizabeth's coffin.

"What told you?" I asked, watching him like a hawk. "Who? Evan? Was it Elizabeth?"

"I'm not sure. It was a voice in my head, but not like you said it was for you, when Elizabeth actually spoke. It was more of a feeling. I don't know. All I knew that it was like my body and my brain got charged. I just *knew* you needed help."

"It was probably her. You and Elizabeth were always close. She told me once that you were a good man."

His head came around.

"She did?"

I smiled in the face of his strained surprise, but tears welled up in my eyes. "She said that she never deserved you. But that I did."

I sensed his stare boring into me from behind the sunglasses he wore. Strands of his dark hair flickered in the autumn breeze. His hand opened at my back, his fingers digging gently into my flesh. I felt that familiar ache at my core, and the inevitable rising panic that always accompanied that feeling these days.

"I feel like the last man on earth who deserves you. Anna—"

"I think that backhoe is meant for here. We should go," I said thickly, interrupting him. I nodded at the yellow backhoe that had paused in the distance, probably upon the driver noticing family still stood at the grave.

I wasn't ready to talk about us. About our future.

I wasn't prepared yet to look into his eyes, and say goodbye.

Chapter Thirty-Three

WHEN EVAN AND I RETURNED TO LES JUMEAUX AFTER ELIZABETH'S funeral, the house was empty. I knew that Lorraine was likely leading her new caregiver, Sasha, on a wild, steep gallop up the mountainside. I gave a quick thanks to God that Sasha was young and in shape.

Evan and I walked up the grand staircase together, both of us preoccupied. Maybe I understood why we were so grave, aside from the obvious. Elizabeth's funeral had been the final step in this tragedy. The years of planning for revenge on Evan's part, the impetus that had brought Evan and me together, Noah Madaster's reign of sadistic power: All of it was over now.

Now I was left with nothing to do but stare the glaring question. *What next?*

Evan paused when we reached the door of the bedroom I'd been using. Our stares met, and held. For a second, my heart jumped.

Then he gave me a small, sad smile. He leaned down and kissed me on the temple. He turned to continue down the hallway. Sharp pain pinched at my lungs and heart. I opened my mouth to say something—but *what*? No matter his deep regret. No matter my desire for him. He'd still dragged me into this ugly scenario for his own selfish reasons.

He was still one of the people responsible for shoving me into that dark, bottomless hole where I'd panicked for days... hours. What did it matter how long it had been? That memory of terror would stay with me for a lifetime.

Noah Madaster had been right. Even *minutes*, believing that I'd slept with my biological father, that I'd fallen in love with him more passionately than I could put into words, would have been enough hell for several lifetimes.

I walked into my bedroom, feeling hollow and bereft. Hopeless.

I shouted in surprise.

"What is it?" I heard Evan ask from behind me a second later, sounding alarmed.

I pointed wordlessly at my bed. A three-by-three-foot mélange of red maple and golden alder and aspen leaves had been placed on the mattress into a tall heap. On one pillow sat a large, perfectly formed pinecone.

"Oh my God. Lorraine?" Evan asked after a moment, clearly bewildered.

I burst into laughter.

"She meant it as a gift," I said.

"How do you know?" Evan asked, turning toward me. He still looked amazed, but humor had started to tilt his mouth.

"I just know. She's been collecting them ever since Noah died. I'd started to help her," I said, reaching down into the pile and rustling the dry leaves. Each one was, of course, perfectly formed. Even though there was no logic to Lorraine's gift, it made perfect sense to me.

I glanced over at Evan, who still looked bemused. I grabbed a handful of dry leaves and threw them at him.

"It doesn't have to make sense, Evan," I said, my laughter fading.

He just stood there for a few seconds, a crimson maple leaf clinging on the lapel of his funeral black suit jacket. His gaze narrowed on me. I felt a rush of heat through my body.

Then it was happening. I stepped into his arms, and his mouth was on mine, his kiss as possessive and wild as it had ever been. More so. And my response was even more passionate. I gave myself up to it, knowing only the full blast of my need for him could evaporate my doubts.

We fell onto the bed of leaves, all the guilt, anger, and uncertainty incinerated to dust. Evan gruffly declared his love for me between kisses and hungry bites on my neck. I declared my love in return, my tone as desperate as my clawing hands. He slid my dress to my waist. I groaned, ecstasy and agony combined.

Our situation was impossibly complex and fraught with emotional entanglement. No one would believe our story, if I tried to explain.

But *this*?

This was simple.

It was then that I realized, in a sex-hazed sense, that Lorraine had fashioned a kind of primitive altar on that bed, a bower of honesty. She really had given us a gift.

But even as I submitted to the power of the moment, something whispered inside of me that it wouldn't be enough.

Later, we showered together in the suite Evan had been using, and lay down on the soft, cool bed. I couldn't stop touching him, my anxious fingertips scouting the planes and hollows of his body, as if I believed I could store up enough memories to last a lifetime. He, on the other hand, held me steady and fast against him, his strength the hallmark of his embrace.

"Evan?" I asked, my cheek against his solid chest.

"Hmmm?"

"Let's say it was true, that Elizabeth came to me from... wherever she was," I said, hesitating at voicing the clichés: the other side, heaven, purgatory, hell. "Do you think she could have been controlling me into doing what I did with Noah?"

"What do you think?"

I lifted my head to peer at his face. He watched me with solemn gravity.

"I think she influenced me, because she knew she could form a connection with me. I'm her daughter. Her sister," I said the last experimentally, seeing how it felt on my tongue. It wasn't as horrible as I'd imagined it would be. "She reached out to me because she *could*. Maybe it was the similarity of our genes, like Noah believed. Maybe it was karma. I don't know for sure. I do know this. *I* did what I did because I chose to. I wanted to make Noah pay for what he'd done to her. To Lorraine. To you. Us."

He merely nodded once in the pregnant pause that followed.

"I killed him," I said to him for the first time. "You know that, don't you?"

His hand moved, cupping my face tenderly. "No. I *don't* know that. You were merely there to witness his lifetime of sins catching up to him."

"I was the embodiment of his sins," I said. "And I knew that when I went into that tunnel, Evan. He was the foulest thing I could ever imagine. But he was a human being. And I wanted him to suffer. I wanted him to pay. I pushed him until his heart gave out on him. And I'm going to have to live with that for the rest of my life."

"*Don't,* honey. Don't make a choice to suffer. Choose *not* to carry this around for your whole life." His thumb moved on my cheek. "You were innocent in all this, Anna."

"I *was* innocent," I said, my gaze touring his face. I had never loved him more than I did in that moment, when I knew for certain I'd lost him.

"Until I wasn't anymore," I whispered softly.

The next morning, I saw him enter the garage just as I was placing my suitcase in the car. I looked away from his face and slammed the trunk shut. I thought I'd seen hollow grief in his expression many times before, but that had been just a trace of what I saw now.

"I thought we decided you wouldn't watch me drive away," I said, avoiding his eyes at all costs.

"I know I agreed I wouldn't try to stop you, no matter what you decided. I lied, I guess. I can't stand it, Anna."

"You have to. *I* have to. Us staying together, it just doesn't make sense."

His fingers slid gently beneath my chin. At his urging, I met his stare reluctantly.

"It doesn't matter what brought us together. The only thing that matters is now. This moment. We were meant to be together."

"It *does* matter, what brought us together. It's like you said before: Noah Madaster—all of the Madasters that came before me: They taint everyone. Everything. That includes us, Evan."

"I know what this is about. You can't forgive me. Can you?"

I shut my eyes. I couldn't bear this. Grief suffocated me.

"Maybe I could. In time. I don't know. But it's not just that." I opened my eyes, entreating him to understand with my gaze. "I love you. I'll always love you. But it's all become so twisted. No matter what we do, no matter how much time passes, Elizabeth came first. She'll always have come first. *We* were only *us* because of Elizabeth. And she's gone now, Evan."

He looked like death in my blurry vision.

"You're still my wife," he said. "You'll always be my wife, Anna. You'll never want for anything. Just tell me what you need, and you'll have it."

I stifled a whimper, and turned away. I jerked open the car door and sat behind the wheel. Using every last ounce of my will, I slammed shut the door, separating us with a final bang.

Evan was wrong.

I would be left wanting for the rest of my life.

Epilogue

One Year Later

I WAITED ON THE OTHER SIDE OF THE ENTRYWAY WHILE A DOZEN chattering tween art students passed by, each hauling a sketchpad and collapsible stool. My gaze lingered on their faces: this one full of laughter, this one reserved, this one sparkling with excitement, all of them beautiful and fresh. Innocent. I remembered my own art class at age twelve, and the thrill of going to the Art Institute in Chicago to view and copy the masters there.

It seemed like forever ago.

I was in San Francisco for a showing at Tommy Higoshi's gallery. Six months ago, on a trip to the city to visit Lorraine's new doctor, I'd reconnected with Tommy. We'd gone out to dinner. Over a bottle of Lafitte Rothschild, he'd confessed how Noah Madaster had gotten to him last year. He explained that Noah had called him and insisted Tommy tell him every detail he knew about me, and about Evan's courtship of me. Tommy had refused at first.

But then, Noah's trademark manipulations began.

Tommy had explained to me that Noah had somehow gained knowledge that years ago, Tommy had paid off a Federal Drug Administration official to push his medical technology through the long and difficult testing process... to put Tommy's product at the front of the line for approval. That knowledge, and the threat of exposure of it, had been Noah's means of blackmail to get the information he'd wanted about Evan and me.

Tommy had been apologetic and distressed by what he'd done, especially when I told him—while avoiding the dirtier details—that Evan and I had split. I'd taken pains to alleviate Tommy of his guilt. No one knew better than I did Noah's methods. I was only glad that Tommy and his wife, Ellen, had been harmed only minimally by Noah's poisonous touch.

Our friendship had resumed. Soon after that, Tommy asked me to do another exhibition at Yume. He'd seen my Tahoe paintings and was eager to show them. I, however, had been dragging my feet about finishing the series.

The collection had been on the verge of completion when the shit had hit the fan at Les Jumeaux. Since then, I'd been hesitant to return to that beautiful, haunted landscape, even in my mind. At some point, I realized why it was so hard for me to finish the series. It made me homesick, thinking of that beautiful place.

Thinking of Evan.

I knew that Evan had left Les Jumeaux and had been working out of both San Francisco and New York. I hated thinking of the Twins standing empty, of their windows looking out at the massive pines, the mountains, and the blue lake with blind, empty eyes.

Tommy's enthusiasm about a showing had been contagious, though.

Over the past few months, I'd found that I could travel in my mind's eye to the overlook. It'd helped me, to transfer those stunning images from inside me to the canvas. It'd been a catharsis of sorts.

Tommy had insisted that the last paintings were even better than the earlier ones. He'd called my exhibition "Tahoe: Light and Time." The showing had taken place yesterday, and by all accounts, had been a huge success.

Now, I was here at the SFMOMA for a quick visit before returning to Lorraine's and my new home in Half Moon Bay.

With the art students gone, the small portrait gallery I entered was silent and empty. I saw movement to my right. My feet froze midstride.

The room wasn't empty, after all.

I approached him slowly. He stood in front of my favorite painting by the Nigerian artist of the young girl. He looked rugged and handsome, wearing jeans and a dark gray shirt that made his light eyes seem to glow by contrast. His stare never wavered off my face as I stopped a few feet away from him.

"I thought they'd never leave," Evan said, nodding in the direction where the kids had just exited. "Or that you'd never come," he added after a pause.

"You were waiting for me?"

"I thought maybe you'd come today and see her before you went back to Half Moon Bay. I took a chance," he said, nodding in the direction of the painting of the girl.

Neither of us spoke for a moment. I had the sudden uncomfortable and yet poignant feeling that Evan knew why I'd come to see the painting before I left. I missed what the girl in the portrait represented.

I missed that innocent part of myself.

"I thought maybe you'd come to my showing," I said, my voice sounding brittle. Seeing him standing there had been a kick to the gut. I knew that Tommy had been in contact with Evan. I had no doubt that he'd told Evan about my exhibition. I'd been jumpy at the showing the entire time, half-convinced that I'd turn and see Evan's tall form, his steady, all-seeing stare on me. When it became clear he wasn't coming, I'd resigned myself to a disappointed calm.

Now he stood just feet away, and my calm had disappeared.

"Tommy let me see the showing the night before," Evan said. He saw my expression and put up a hand in a halting gesture. "Don't be mad at him. I talked him into it. I wanted to see it. Very much. I wanted to see you, too. More so than the paintings. A lot more," he added with a small smile. "But I figured a crowded showing wouldn't be an ideal meeting. I thought you'd be nervous enough.

"Your paintings were incredible," he said after a pause in which I was acutely aware of his searching gaze on my face. "The last ones, especially. They weren't just made of paint. I felt you in them, Anna."

"Thanks," I said, glancing around the gallery and seeing nothing. His presence pulled at all my senses. I couldn't resist looking at him, despite my disquietude. He glanced over at the painting of the girl.

"You may have lost something, Anna. But those last two paintings you did of Tahoe tell me you've gained something, too."

"But at what cost?" I countered quickly. I immediately regretted my outburst. "So... how long will you be in San Francisco?"

"It depends. A couple days. A couple weeks." He shrugged. "How is Half Moon Bay? Are you enjoying the new house?"

325

He referred to the small, comfortable ranch style home I'd recently purchased for Lorraine and me. Evan's and my divorce had gone through a few months ago. It would have gone through sooner, but we'd argued over the settlement. Or our lawyers had.

I hadn't spoken at any great length to Evan since that last morning at Les Jumeaux, when I'd left. I had finally prevailed on the settlement, agreeing only to an amount of money that would allow Lorraine and me to live comfortably, if not luxuriously, and sufficient funds for Lorraine's health and daily care. Evan had wanted to provide more, of course. A lot more. But I couldn't stand it, living off his guilt.

In the end, he'd conceded to my wishes. But I suspected part of his acquiescence was his knowledge that Lorraine had become a very wealthy woman following Noah's death. Lorraine had named me as the executor and beneficiary of her estate. I would never take a penny of it, although I didn't tell Lorraine that. It was Noah's money, and therefore tainted in my mind. But because of the circumstances, Evan knew that Lorraine and I weren't without resources. I thought that's why he'd finally agreed to my terms for the divorce.

"We like the new house a lot. I think Lorraine misses Les Jumeaux though," I admitted, self-conscious that he'd see the truth. *I* missed it, as much as my grandmother. "But she seems happy in the new house. The gardens and yard are large... big enough to give her a little wandering space, anyway."

"How is she?" Evan asked.

I knew that he'd grown closer to Lorraine after I'd left the North Twin. Lorraine had stayed there with him, and her caregiver, for a month or so until I'd found a place to live and sent for her.

"You wouldn't recognize her," I said honestly. "It's amazing what regular attention and care can do. Her doctor actually said she was blooming. Given her mental state, and how she was neglected at Les Jumeaux, it was hard to believe she was barely into her sixties. She looks her age now. Younger. She's got a lot of good years ahead of her."

I reached into my purse and extricated my phone. I showed him a photo of Lorraine and me standing on the sunny terrace of our new house. She'd put on a good ten pounds, and I'd started taking her regularly to a hairdresser. But it was her smile that told the story.

"Amazing," Evan murmured, staring at the photo. His gaze flickered over me. "But I'm not surprised. I know what it's like." I raised my eyebrows, confused by his statement. "To be loved by you. It brought me back to life, too. Once."

He handed me back the phone. I accepted it as a dull roar started up in my ears.

"I've missed you, Anna."

"I've missed you too."

"Have you?"

I looked up at him. "Of course I have."

"You never wanted to talk. During the divorce."

"It was hard enough to get through it as it was; seeing you and hearing you would have only made it harder."

"I suppose I should be glad that it was hard. At least that means you still care. But I'm not glad. I hate that I've contributed to your unhappiness. It stays with me, you know. What I've done to you. Every minute of every day."

"Please don't say you're sorry again," I said in a rush. I didn't want his apologies anymore. I didn't want to feel the burden of his guilt. "I don't want you to be unhappy, Evan. I'm responsible for my own happiness now. I always was, really. I guess we all are, in the end."

I saw him glance over to one of the entrances into the gallery. A woman had wandered into the room.

"Can we sit down here for a few minutes? There's something I need to ask you," Evan said quietly, nodding in the direction of a circular bench at the center of the room.

I suppose he saw my hesitation.

"I won't take up much of your time, Anna. I promise."

I wanted to tell him it wasn't my time I was concerned about. It was my heart. But something made me nod in agreement. We sat side by side on the bench and stared at the Romare Bearden portrait in front of us. The young woman finally left the gallery, and we were alone again.

"I've had a lot of time to think in the past year," Evan began. "To wonder what would have happened if I'd done things differently. To ruminate, I suppose."

I wanted to tell him that I wished he wouldn't, that he would let it all go. Move on. But I would have been a hypocrite to do that. I'd done my share of ruminating, too.

"I know it's selfish of me, but I can't help but wonder if time... if being apart... has changed your mind, even a little. About us," he said.

"Evan, I don't want to rehash all this."

"I keep thinking of what you said when you said goodbye at Les Jumeaux. You said that in time, you might be able to forgive me. It was Elizabeth that seemed to be the main stopping point. You said that Elizabeth would always be first, no matter what. It's true, in a way. Because ultimately, it was her that brought us together. But she wasn't the first for me, Anna. I want you to know that. I did love her, in a very complex and indelible way. But I didn't realize until I married you that I wasn't *in* love with her. *You* were my first. You will always be my first."

"She was your wife, Evan. And she's my mother."

He took my hand in his. His touch felt so good, it hurt.

"No. She was a very sad, tortured woman who will always be a part of our lives. Our pasts. But Amanda Solas is your mother, Anna."

I felt his lips brush lightly against my temple, and choked back a surge of emotion.

"I know you're not ready to forgive me. Maybe it'll take years. Maybe it'll take a lifetime. But I wanted to see you today, to tell you that I'm here. I'll wait, for as long as it takes—"

"Evan, I can't talk about a future with you. It's too much. It's too... *big*," I blurted out. Something wilted inside of me when I saw the shadow cross his face.

"Of course. I understand," he said stiffly.

I touched his arm when he started to stand. He glanced back at me.

"You didn't let me finish. I can't envision a future with you right now." He started to speak—undoubtedly to repeat his words of sad acceptance. I held up my hand to stop him.

"But I didn't tell you what I *can* do," I said.

He sat back down heavily next to me, his gaze glued to my face. "What *can* you do?"

I laughed and shook my head. A tear fell across my cheek. "I don't know. We never did have much of a courtship, did we? So... dinner, maybe? Yeah. I think dinner would be nice."

I saw something flicker in his eyes. Cautious hope, but hope none-theless. His hand covered mine. I didn't know if his hope was warranted or not, but I squeezed his hand back, nevertheless. It was okay, my uncertainty.

Maybe this was a second start. And who of us ever really knows how things will end up when we're still at the beginning?

Printed in Poland
by Amazon Fulfillment
Poland Sp. z o.o., Wrocław